CW01457416

Narman's Pyke

An Eamon Tauk Space Odyssey - Book 1

J.E. Park

Copyright © 2022 by J.E. Park

All rights reserved.

No portion of this book may be reproduced in any form without written permission from the publisher or author, except as permitted by U.S. copyright law.

Newsletter and New Release Info:

http//:jeparkbooks.wpcomstaging.com

Follow me on Facebook at:

https://www.facebook.com/JEParkAuthor

Twitter handle:

@JEPark94519501

Email:

jeparkauthor@gmail.com

Tik Tok:

jeparkguerillalit

Contents

CHAPTER 1

The crack in the voice of *Wasp-Two's* pilot made it sound like he had much more to live for than the rest of us. "Good God! Am I the only one seeing this?"

He wasn't. Having been assigned as Dr. Jella Duverii's bodyguard, I was seated in *Wasp-Three's* cockpit with the command staff instead of in the egress bay with the rest of the troops. I had a clear view out of the forward window. To be honest, the sight of Kanaris-6 unnerved me, too.

Most planets looked serene and peaceful from space, no matter what kind of pandemonium was unfolding upon the surface. Kanaris looked pissed. There was a massive cyclone covering nearly the entire continent where we were supposed to land. It was so violent that we could see the storm rotate even though we were still quite some distance from entry. I was no meteorologist, but I suspected that the clouds were being slung about at speeds registering in the *hundreds* of kilometers an hour. I could not believe we were seriously contemplating landing in something like that.

"My instruments say that thing's blowing at seven hundred and forty-eight knots!" *Wasp-Two* blurted out again. "We can't possibly be going through with this!"

"*Wasp-Two*," our pilot calmly responded. Chief Warrant Officer Je'Sikka Albarn was a seasoned veteran. "Those readings are from near the eye of the storm. Our landing zone is at the edge of the event. Local wind speeds are well under the three-hundred-kilometer-an-hour threshold these vessels are designed to withstand. Just keep the ship on auto-pilot and be ready to grab the controls if something goes wrong."

"But...but..."

1

"Warrant Officer Sirrah," Albarn interrupted. "Just let the dropship's pro-gramming do its job. The ride's going to be bumpy. It's going to wreak havoc on the Marines' stomachs. When it's all over, though, the worst that's going to happen is you'll end up cleaning far more of your staging bay than you probably imagined you would when you launched from the mothership."

I had heard *Wasp-Three's* crew talking about CWO1 Grazny Sirrah before we detached from the *Nebulan Phoenix*. He was another fast-tracked Samaari gaining promotion based more upon his family's wealth than on his merits as a pilot. Typically, a candidate would need to assist on at least fifty combat drops before the squadron even considered them for a slot in the captain's chair. Sirrah had zero. The powers-that-be decided that, at least in his case, Sirrah's training record and ferry sorties were enough.

"Wouldn't it just make more sense to delay this landing until the storm blows over?" the green pilot pleaded.

"We're not delaying the goddamn mission!" The voice cutting into the commlink was Colonel Traegus, the task force's commander aboard *Wasp-One*. "We just got a positive sign of life out of that place along with a mayday signal indicating that we still have an asset on the ground at Narman's Pyke and they are under threat! We ARE going to land where and when we were ordered to! Do you copy that?!?"

The biggest problem with junior officers pulled from the elite ranks of Samaari society was that they were not used to taking orders. They grew up bossing their servants around, so they tended to bristle when others told them what to do. They also rarely suffered consequences for their actions. This is the only reason I can fathom that *Wasp-Two's* pilot would have felt he could argue with a brigade commander. "But, sir! How much good do you think we'll be down there if we make landfall in fifteen billion charred little pieces?!?"

"Warrant Officer Sirrah," Je'Sikka Albarn chimed in once more. "Keep your vessel on auto-pilot like I told you to and you'll be fine. Trust me. I've landed in conditions like these a million times."

Wasp-Three's co-pilot turned towards her. Switching off his microphone so his trembling voice would not be heard outside the cockpit, he asked, "Really?"

Albarn laughed without humor and then shot her executive officer a look that suggested he had lost his mind. "No," she confessed.

The pilot's trepidation caught the attention of our guide, who was seated at my left elbow. "Why can't we wait a few more hours for the danger to pass?" Jella asked me. "These storms are as short as they are devastating. Narman Pyke's elevation is so high that even the biggest cyclones seldom last more than six or seven hours."

The battalion's sergeant-major, Konig Maddahor, was sitting to my right. Overhearing the doctor's questions, he leaned over me to answer her. "Somebody at Narman's Pyke sent off a rocket beacon as we entered the system," Maddahor said. Kanaris-6 was full of Harnillium crystals, which played havoc with magnetic and electrical fields. Radio range was, at best, four kilometers on the ground, so transmitters had to be launched into space to communicate with anyone in orbit.

"Now that we know someone's alive down there," the sergeant continued. "We need to get to them before whatever they're facing does."

"How many people are we expecting to find down there?" Jella asked.

"We've only confirmed one so far."

"One?!?" she gasped. "We're risking three dropships, containing what? Two thousand people apiece? To rescue one person?!? That's insane!"

Maddahor shrugged. "Well, we suspect that that one person may be an important intelligence asset, not to mention related to a League senator."

Jella's jaw dropped open. "A senator's relative is worth the lives of six thousand Marines and billions of credits' worth of spacecraft and equipment?!?"

The sergeant grinned. "It is if you're an admiral looking to make a lucrative move into politics after you hang up your epaulets."

I looked back up at the window as Jella Duverii shook her head in disgust. We were coming at Kanaris fast now, and the cyclone took up our entire view. Our pilot grabbed the intercom and reminded the troops to double-check their restraints. "I expect this to be one of the rougher landings you'll ever experience. Make sure you're all buckled in as tight as you can be."

I leaned over to ensure the doctor was properly fastened against her seat. "Eamon," she said to me. "I've got a bad feeling about this."

Nodding at her sympathetically, I told her, "So do I. Whatever happens is out of our hands, though. There's nothing we can do about it. If it's any consolation, I've seen our pilot in her dress blues. She's got a chest full of ribbons. We're in some of the best hands that the fleet has to offer, unlike those poor bastards sitting in *Wasp-Two* right now."

As if to prove my point, CWO Sirrah's voice broke over the commlink again. "Look, this is madness! We need to abort this landing!"

"Goddammit, *Wasp-Two*!" bellowed Colonel Traegus from the command transport. "You stay the fucking course!"

"We can't, sir! This is suicide!" Sirrah was hysterical.

"*Wasp-Two* co-pilot!" Traegus shouted. "Your commander is relieved! Take the goddamn con!"

"No!" Sirrah protested. Then the line went silent.

Traegus allowed the formation's starboard dropship a couple of moments to sort itself out before trying to raise them again. "*Wasp-Two? Wasp-Two? Wasp-Two*, do you copy?"

There was no response. I glanced at the window and saw we had nearly reached Kanaris's exosphere. I could now feel the gravitational pull of the planet. Right in my gut.

"*Wasp-Two? Wasp-Two!* Someone pick up the goddamn mic right n...!"

"This is *Wasp-Two*." It was Sirrah's voice again, panting as if he was trying to catch his breath. In the background was a lot of commotion.

Traegus was not amused. "Put your fucking co-pilot on!"

"He's dead, sir," Sirrah confessed, oddly calm for a man who had just committed a capital offense. "He was trying to usurp my command, so I had to..."

"YOU DID WHAT?!?" Traegus screamed. "DO YOU HAVE ANY IDEA WHAT YOU'VE DONE?!?"

"It was an attempted mutiny, sir," Sirrah said, clutching at straws in a wild attempt to justify his actions. "He was going to..."

"I'M GOING TO HAVE YOU FUCKING SHOT!"

"Do you have any idea who my father is, Colonel Traegus?" Sirrah asked. He sounded entirely confident that his family's resources could keep him well beyond the reach of military justice. "They'll have *you* shot before me."

"YOU GODDAMN SON-OF-A...!"

"Sir, this landing is currently too hazardous to attempt. It's my duty, in order to preserve the lives of my crew and my ship, to abort this..."

"Sirrah!" our pilot shouted into her mic. "No! It's too late for that! You're too low! If you pull up now, you'll bounce off the atmosphere like a skipping stone! Don't do it! DON'T...!"

"Piss off!" Sirrah spat back. "I know what I'm doing!"

As far as I can tell, those were the last words Grazny Sirrah ever uttered.

●●◄●► ● ◄●► ●●

CHAPTER 2

Wasp-Two did exactly what Je'Sikka Albarn warned it would. When Sir-rah lifted the nose of his vessel, the aft end struck Kanaris's atmos-phere at a catastrophic angle and ricocheted. The entire assault ship spun into a cartwheel, hurtling stern over bow right into *Wasp-One*. Both vessels disintegrated upon impact, burning up in a spectacular explosion during an uncontrolled reentry. In an instant, the lives of four thousand Space Marines were snuffed out forever while the massive debris field left in their wake was perfectly positioned to extinguish two thousand more.

All embarked personnel in the cockpit of *Wasp-Three* fell instantly silent, reeling in equal measures of shock and horror. The crew, on the other hand, burst into a flurry of manic activity. "BANK! BANK! BANK!" screamed the dropship's navigator. "WE'RE GOING TO HIT THE..."

"NO, WE'RE NOT!" Albarn screamed in return, wrenching back on the ship's yoke as hard as she could. *Wasp-Three* careened sharply onto its port side and lurched downward at full power. Hundreds of people in the egress bay screamed in terror, loud enough to be heard through the blast doors separating us. Albarn then swerved to avoid several large hull pieces, a massive elevator gate, and a ruptured fuel cell. Despite her best efforts, an entire thrust engine grazed us on the starboard side somewhere in back. The impact set off what seemed like every alarm within earshot and sent the vessel into a ferocious clockwise spin that left me struggling to keep conscious under all the extra Gs that we started to pull.

"I'm deploying the wings!" yelled the dropship's co-pilot, reaching over to Albarn's side of the command console.

"DON'T YOU FUCKING DARE!" the pilot screamed at him. "We can't deploy the wings until we're clear of the wreckage! If one gets knocked off, we're finished!"

The co-pilot's head darted around the cockpit in panic. "Then what do you want me to do?!?"

"Shut up and stay out of my way until I tell you otherwise!"

I looked to my left and saw that Jella Duverii had passed out. Her helmeted head pinballed between the two bars of her drop-down restraint while her arms and legs flailed limply as far as they could stretch. On my right, Sergeant Major Maddahor was seemingly in prayer, continuously chanting what I called the Space Corps Rosary: "motherfuckermotherfuckermotherfuckermother-fuckermother..."

On the other side of the cockpit, I caught sight of a Navy ensign buckled into his restraints against the opposite bulkhead. He was staring at me with his terror plainly etched upon his face. I suspected he had heard who I was. He was checking to see if I was scared, as if I was some barometer of how grave our situation was.

The truth was that I was just as petrified as the ensign, but I took solace in the realization that if *Wasp-Three* went down, I would be reunited with Misha, Juergen, and Helmut again, wherever they may be. To put his mind at ease, I forced myself to grin and wink at the young officer. I then turned my gaze back upon the chaos around me.

One of the petty officers manning the engineering console screamed out, "Thruster Eight is damaged! I don't know if we're going to be able to stabilize!" How he could read that with all the flashing lights, sirens, and jerking around we were doing, I will never know.

"RRRRRAAAAAAHHHHHH!!!!" Albarn screamed in response, clenching her teeth and fighting like hell to slow down the spinning. From my vantage point, it looked like the yoke was trying to rip her arms off at the shoulders. "TURN EVERYTHING YOU HAVE AGAINST THE DIRECTION OF THE SPIN AND FIRE IT UP SLOWLY! IF WE HIT SIX Gs, PEOPLE ARE GOING TO START DYING!"

"I'm trying, Skipper! I'm trying! I just can't..." In frustration, the engineer beat the console with his fists, trying to batter the controls into submitting to his will.

One of the quartermasters broke down into tears while another, presumably her lover, loosened his restraints to reach over and take her hand, letting her know she was not alone. Through all the mayhem, it was a tender moment. I was touched to witness it.

I caught Maddahor watching the couple, too. He bore an expression that suggested regret rather than fear. It was as if he realized that he was at the end of his life and, having spent nearly all of it at war, he had left no one behind to mourn him. Unable to think of any other way to ease his discontent, I batted my eyelashes his way and offered him my hand in a feeble attempt at humor. To my surprise, the old bastard seized it.

Suddenly, the port-side thrusters came to life, their roar gradually increasing in volume as our revolutions began to decrease in speed. The engineer allowed himself a quick cheer and then furiously went back to work

When the spinning got under control enough for Albarn to figure out which way was up, she turned to her co-pilot and shouted, "Now, Trevor! Now! Deploy the wings!"

There was no answer. *Wasp-Three's* Number Two was slumped in his seat, having passed out from the Gs. Letting out another scream to gather the energy she needed to control the wheel with only one hand, Albarn reached over and pulled the lever herself.

The effect was immediate. *Wasp-Three's* deceleration was so abrupt that, at first, I thought we had crashed. The sudden jolt seemed to force Dr. Duverii awake beside me. "Unh," I heard her groan. "Unnnnnh...uh...*gasp*...unnnn-hhh..."

At the academy, I had been through many high-G training evolutions. To increase our tolerance to such conditions, our instructors subjected us to enough gravitational forces to knock us out more times than I could count. I knew what came next for Dr. Duverii. Reaching to my left with my free hand, I took Jella by the chin and gently guided her head toward the other direction. I was just in time. Our guide grunted twice more in an attempt to keep everything down but eventually erupted, projectile vomiting all over the battalion's XO instead of me. Like *Wasp-Three's* co-pilot, Major Venis was still unconscious so I figured he could return the favor when he woke up.

The dropship's spinning ended with the deployment of the wings, but with the damaged thruster, we all now felt like we were trapped in a giant, space-racing martini shaker. It was still a brutal ride, but at least things lightened up enough for Maddahor to release his grip on my fingers. As he did so, he shot me a look that perfectly conveyed what he would do to me if I ever told anyone we had held hands during the drop.

Albarn did what she could to stabilize the ship but soon realized that things were about as good as they were going to get. "Lieutenant Colonel Bahkmin!" she called out through clenched teeth. "Are you online?"

"Y-y-y-y-yeah," Bahkmin answered, struggling to get his words out while his brain was getting rattled about inside of his skull. "I-I-I-I'm here!"

"I can't make a vertical landing at Narman's Pyke, sir," Albarn told him. "Not in these conditions. I'm going to need a runway."

"There are n-n-no runways on K-K-Kanaris."

"I know. I'm going to have to try to come up with the closest...ah...ah...AH, SHIT!"

The dropship almost got away from her. Albarn broke off her conversation with the battalion commander to focus on steadying the yoke. Then, using her teeth, she ripped off her gloves, exposing the henna tattoos barely visible through the dark skin on the top of her hands. She needed to feel every little vibration coming through the wheel to keep *Wasp-Three* aloft as long as she could.

When she returned to the mic, Albarn was much more to the point. "Sir! We'll be passing over Narman's Pike in seventeen minutes! That will be the closest we're getting to it. I suggest we launch the Psyxies as we fly by."

'Psyxies' were our airborne Marines. Equipped with personal jet-packs, they were commonly known as Psycho Pixies in civilian circles. The term was shortened to Psyxies in military jargon. Our contingent was led by Captain Biers, who did not like Albarn's suggestion at all. "Are you insane, *Wasp-Three*?!?" Biers shouted across the network. "You want to launch us into a two-hundred-kilometer-an-hour hurricane?!?"

"I don't want to, Captain," Albarn retorted. "It's the only way I can see us getting boots on the ground at our objective!"

"You're going to kill us!"

Grinding her teeth into the mic, Albarn confessed, "To be blunt, Captain, your odds of surviving out there are probably a lot better than ours are in here."

"Oh god," Jella groaned beside me after she heard what the pilot said. "Oh god!" She looked like she was getting ready to vomit again.

The commlink was silent as the realization sank into Biers' head that Albarn had a point. "Okay," he moaned into his microphone. "Launch us over the objective. Shit!"

The co-pilot returned to his senses just in time to hear the decision. "I got this," he said as he leaned forward to initiate the conveyors to position the Psyxies for ejection.

"Good," Albarn said. "Welcome back, Princess Aurora."

•●◄●►●◄●►●●

Over official channels, the word "ejection" was the correct term to describe the launch of airborne Marines. The Psyxies themselves preferred "ejaculation." Considering that they were shot out of a tube near the aft end of the vessel, it was easy to see the connection. It was an age-old joke and the Psyxies never got tired of playing it up. I tuned into the jump network to listen to the countdown and see if the harsh conditions they were leaping into would dampen the typical pre-deployment banter. It didn't.

"Prepare for launch!" the jumpmaster called out into the commlink. By now, there were three hundred and fifty troops suspended from the overhead of the egress bay, stretched out horizontal to the deck, queued up to be fired out over Narman's Pyke. "Jump will commence in ten...nine...eight..."

"Oh man, faster! Faster! That feels so good...!"

"...seven...six..."

"Mmmmmm," cooed a female voice. "Use your tongue a little bit more."

"...five...four..."

"Yeah, that's it! Nibble on the tip a little!"

"...three...two..."

"Oh, God! Oh, God! I think I'm cumming!"

"...one!"

"Oh shit! Oh shit!"

"Launch!"

"AAAAAAAUUUUGGGHHHHH!"

All the psyxies screamed that last one as the conveyer bolted into motion and hurled the entire platoon along the ceiling, through the deployment tube, and finally out into the Kanarisian sky. It was a brutal way to go, but the only way *Wasp-Three* could manage the deployment with all the shaking it was doing.

With the Harnillium interference, the Psyxies were out of radio range within seconds of leaving the craft. Wanting to confirm whether his troops made it to their objective or not, Lieutenant Colonel Bahkmin jumped onto the commlink and asked, "*W-W-W-Wasp-Three*, can we m-m-m-make another pass to confirm whether or n-n-n-not the Psyxies landed?"

Bahkmin was in the command module back in the bay, so he could not see the physical exertion Albarn was subjecting herself to in order to keep us all alive. "That's a negative, sir," she responded. "We're on borrowed time already. I need to find the safest place I can to crash."

"C-c-c-crash?!?" gasped Bahkmin, only now comprehending the gravity of our situation. "What do you m-m-m-mean crash?!?"

"Just what I said," Albarn responded. "We're going down…"

"Can't you at least g-g-g-get us back up to the *Phoenix*?"

"No, sir. That would require us to go up. Like I said before, we're going down. At this point, we're gravity's bitch."

"But, b-b-b-but…"

"Aaaaauuuughhh!" Albarn screamed, trying to make the yoke behave. She was tiring. "We gotta get this thing down! I'm making a run for the coast! Our best shot at getting out of this is a water landing!"

That decision breathed new life into Dr. Duverii. She got very excited. "NO! NO! We can NOT land in the ocean! We can't land anywhere *near* the ocean!"

"I think you're overestimating the options I have here, doctor! We either land in the ocean, or we barrel ourselves into the side of a mountain somewhere!"

"I'll take the mountain!" Jella exclaimed. "Look! You don't know what's lurking underneath those waves, captain! I do! We will NOT survive a water landing!"

"AAAAAUUUUGHHH! SHIT!" Our pilot was at her breaking point. "Okay! I'll split the difference with you! I'm going to aim for the beach!"

"NO! YOU CAN'T! YOU…"

Jella paused, realizing that we had no options. Screaming at Albarn to tell her what she could *not* do was not being constructive. "Okay! Wait a second! Let me think! Can you make a pass before we land?"

Grimacing, Albarn gasped, "I don't think so!"

"You have to try! Bomb the shoreline about fifty meters from the ocean's edge. Then try to land. The blast should scare whatever's nearby into deeper water long enough for us to try to run to the jungle."

Albarn did Dr. Duverii one better. "Find me the flattest patch of sand you can along the coast!" she shouted at her navigator. "Then get the coordinates to the gunner and have him drop our entire bomb bay payload per Duverii's instructions during our first pass! When we're twenty clicks from touchdown on our final approach, have him hit the same area with every missile we got! I don't want to crash with any ordnance on board!" Tilting her head back to address Jella, Albarn asked, "That good enough for you, doctor?"

Jella shook her head. "No, but I know that's the best I'm going to get."

We were long gone before the bombs dropped during the first run hit the ground. I could not see anything, but I heard it, even above the din of the storm outside and through the hull of the starship. Showing freakish endurance, Je'Sikka Albarn circled around one last time while descending closer to the planet's surface. At nearly the very moment our improvised landing zone came into view, our pilot screamed, "FIRE!!!"

The cockpit windows instantly lit up with the exhaust of hundreds of missiles launched from batteries just below our feet. An instant later, the horizon erupted into a wall of flame so hot that it made the ocean boil. It was beautiful, the culmination of thousands of years of military development and a force so powerful that, even if only for an instant, it could thwart the fury of nature itself.

As a massive conflagration consumed the distant shores, Albarn reached deep inside herself and stomped her feet down on the thruster brakes with her last reserves of strength. Our momentum pushed us against the bars of our drop restraints as *Wasp-Three* dove into a rapid descent. Then the shockwave from the missiles hit us like a ton of bricks, trying to drive the nose of the dropship into the beach. Albarn attempted to pull the yoke back to climb, but there was nothing left in her. She screamed out as she fought the wheel in futility, tears streaming down her face. What she had done for us was nothing short of miraculous, superhuman even. We were so close to surviving it, too. So close.

The nose of our craft eventually caught the sand and, much like *Wasp-Two* did off of the atmosphere, the immense transport ship spun over itself, cartwheeling over the beach, breaking off the wings and hurtling us more than a kilometer before we rolled to a stop. We landed with a deafening roar and one more thunderous explosion.

Then everything went quiet.

And dark.

CHAPTER 3

"**G**ET UP!" the woman shrieked. I could barely hear her over the wind rushing through the cockpit's shattered bay window. "YOU CAN'T LEAVE ME LIKE THIS! NOT HERE!"

At first, I thought it was Misha. Then I opened my eyes and found that I had not been blown into the Great Beyond. I was still in the cockpit of *Wasp-Three*. The screaming was coming from one of the hand-holders, half of the couple I saw comforting each other while we were still spinning through Kanaris's atmosphere. She had gotten out of her restraints. It appeared as if her beau would forever be entombed in his, however.

As the quartermaster melted down, I glanced to my right to check on Sergeant Major Maddahor. The ship's hull had buckled right behind him, causing the bars of his drop restraint to twist more than sixty degrees with his melon caught between them. His head was wrenched in a very unnatural position, his neck snapped at the base of his skull. Maddahor's lifeless eyes stared into the shadows while his tongue hung limply from his teeth.

"GODDAMMIT PAUL!" the quartermaster screamed in between sobs. "AN-SWER ME!"

"He's dead," I tried to tell her. "Pull yourself together and help someone that can actually benefit from..."

"PAUL!"

"Shit," I cursed, realizing she was not listening to me. Turning the other way, I tried to assess how Jella Duverii was doing. She was out cold, but I could not find any other signs of trauma on her. I could not say the same for Major Venis, the battalion XO seated on the other side of her. It looked as if he and the three crew members to his left were taken out by an overhead control console that broke free after we hit the beach. They were reduced to greasy stains upon the bulkhead. The only other movement I saw inside was the co-pilot, who was writhing around on the deck, looking for his legs, grunting in shock and agony while he bled out.

After hitting the release lever on my restraints, I pushed the bars up over my helmet, groaning as the pain in my shoulders radiated down my arms. Luckily, my discomfort seemed to only be in my muscles. I was able to flex my limbs without feeling like I had broken anything. The shock-absorption mechanisms in our seating restraints were amazing. None of us should have survived such a devastating impact, yet, having been lucky enough to avoid getting hit by flying debris, I had escaped with little more than bruises.

For the moment, I let Jella be, going to the distraught quartermaster to see if anything could be done about the screaming woman's boyfriend. That turned out to be a hopeless cause. He sealed his fate when he loosened his restraints to hold his girl's hand. Inertia had driven him beneath the drop bar before it got throttled backward by some large piece of flying wreckage. He was suffocated by his restraints. Grabbing the dead man's lover by the shoulders, I told her, "He's gone! You have to get out of here!"

"I can't," she bawled back. "I can't leave him!"

"Unless you want to end up just like him, you need to go!"

"NOOOOOO!"

Not having time to argue with her, I moved on. Finding the navigator and the weapons officer still alive, I broke them out of their seats and led them to the window. Glancing outside, I could see dozens of troops combat crawling across the waterlogged sand, doing their best to keep from being taken by the wind. "Get the hell out of here and follow them!" I yelled at the men.

We were only about four meters from the ground, so the navigator looked ready to jump to the beach. I stopped him right before he leapt. "Are you crazy?!?" I shouted at him, trying to be heard over the cyclone. "You'll get blown away!"

Reaching forward, I grabbed the navigator's hand and activated the magnetic strips on the underside of his forearm armor. "Climb down the ship's hull! Don't detach until you're on the ground, then crawl! Keep your profile low and head for the tree line!"

As the two Navy men slipped out of the ruined cockpit, I felt the ship shudder as a massive wave struck it from behind. I cursed, then tried to raise a comrade on the commlink. "Corporal Merik! Corporal Merik! Do you copy?"

After a moment of Harnilium interference squawking through my earpiece, Harlund picked up. "I'm here! I'm here! That you, Eamon?"

"It's me, Corporal," I told him. Most of the troops in my platoon were fodder. They were skin suits just trying to get through their time. Merik was a beast, though. A veteran. Corps analysis of Marine Personal Combat Recorders (PCRs) showed that ninety percent of enemy casualties were inflicted by only ten percent of our troops. Harlund Merik's PCR data showed that he was comfortably within that coveted ten-percent clique. The man was a killer.

Harlund was the only junior NCO in my platoon that I genuinely respected. He had proven himself invaluable to me time and time again. The academy spent twenty years training me on how things should work in the Space Corps. Harlund Merik spent the previous six weeks teaching me how they *actually* worked. He had kept me out of trouble on numerous occasions. "We made it," I told him. "What's your twenty?"

"I'm still in the staging bay."

"You alright?" I asked.

"For the moment," Harlund said. "We're queued up to squeeze through a small breach in the hull. There's a bit of a backup, but I'm near the front of the line."

"You got casualties back there?"

"Oh yeah," the corporal answered. "We got a few hundred killed, at least. Probably twice that too injured to move. The bay's filling up with water every time a wave strikes us, and there're these things in it, some sort of sea beetles bigger than my fucking hand! They're feeding on the bodies. We got wounded drowning in the aft end and...and...it's a real horror show back here. I can't wait to get the fuck out of this thing."

Just then, a gunshot went off in the cockpit, causing me to jump. "What was that?" Harlund asked.

"Our co-pilot," I told him, looking down on the deck. "It looks like he put himself out of his misery."

"Yeah, that's been going on back here, too. What's your situation?

"I got the survivors out of the cockpit..."

"GODDAMMIT, PAUL! WAKE UP!" the distraught quartermaster screamed again.

"...well, at least the ones that want to leave, anyway. Our guide is still alive, so I'm getting her to the tree line as soon as possible."

"You need help?"

"It wouldn't hurt. If you get up by the cockpit, wait for me on the leeward side."

"Aye aye, Eamon. I'm out."

Relieved that Harlund Merik was alive, I made my way back up to the hole in the front of the cockpit to get another look outside. The wind had not let up much, and the rain was still pouring through the shattered window. I had to lower my face shield to protect my eyes from it. The stream of Marines crawling toward the jungle remained steady, if sparse. It was good to see that troops were making it out. As I turned to walk back to Jella Duverii, someone grabbed me by the wrist. "Help me," Je'Sikka Albarn moaned. "Help me."

I reached down and took her hand. "Are you hurt?"

Albarn nodded. "I can't feel my legs."

Looking down, I was relieved to see that, unlike her co-pilot, CWO Albarn's legs were at least attached to the rest of her. Still, if she could not use them, trying to rescue her would be problematic.

"Oh man," I said, squeezing her hand a little tighter. In the Space Corps, the objective was always paramount. Mission Before Marine. Paralyzed, CWO Albarn would not be an asset in achieving our goals. She would be a liability, a drain on our resources.

Per doctrine, the humane thing to do would have been to put the pilot out of her misery and move on. Having witnessed what she did to save us, though, Albarn had earned her rescue. She was what the Citadel would have called "Born of the Red Caste." She was an expert, a hero, one of us—someone who had proven themselves far too valuable to be discarded. I was honor-bound to save our pilot, but it would have to wait.

"I'm going to help you," I told her. "But I'm going to have to leave you here for a little while. I *will* be back. You understand? For right now, rest. You're going to need your energy."

"My crew..."

"A couple of them got out," I reassured her.

"Trevor? My co-pilot?"

Without thinking, I turned my head to look at the body on the deck, only to see one of those sea beetle things next to him, feeding on the brains he had blown out of his skull. Cursing, I pulled my dagger from my boot and stabbed the bug through the head. As I slid it off my knife, I heard Dr. Duverii call out from behind me, "That's a kryptid! Save it!"

"Save it?!?" I shouted back. "What for?!?"

"I'll show you later!"

"Are they dangerous?"

Jella shrugged. "Only if you're wounded, and they've run out of carrion! If you can move, they're easy enough to deal with!"

15

I was slipping the creature into a cargo pocket on my thigh when the surviving quartermaster let out another scream. She spotted a pair of kryptids crawling up her boyfriend's leg and was finally convinced there was nothing more to be gained by standing over a corpse. Hysterical, she ran to the bay window and crawled up the control console to leap out.

"No!" I yelled, running after her. "Don't! Use your...!"

I was too late. She jumped before I could grab her and was blown right down the beach like a human tumbleweed, never to be seen again.

•●<●> ● <●>●•

CHAPTER 4

By the time I got Jella out of her seat, kryptids were beginning to find their way into the cockpit in significant numbers. The little bastards were dropping in from the top of the fuselage through the broken bay window. Others squeezed in through a gap in one of the aft blast doors. To protect *Wasp-Three's* pilot from the little savages, I lifted her feet off the deck and crossed her legs in the captain's chair. "Hang tight," I told her. "I'll be back soon."

"Don't forget me," she mumbled.

"I won't. On the honor of the Corps."

Albarn closed her eyes and seemed to fall asleep in her seat. Jella and I tethered ourselves together at the waist, then began working our way down the hull. Though she had no training in magnetic rappelling, I struggled to keep up with her during our descent. "You need to slow down, Doctor! You'll slip up and make a mistake if you don't!"

Jella shook her head furiously. "I'm not slowing down this close to the surf!" she shouted into her mic. "We need to get the hell out of here!"

As soon as Jella's boots hit the sand, Corporal Merik rushed out from the lee-ward side of the wreckage and grabbed her. The doctor was startled, jumping back and shouting, "Who the hell are you?"

"A friend of Cadet Tauk's," Harlund said as he attached a lanyard to her belt opposite where I had clipped to her, tethering the three of us together. "You ready to make a break for the tree line?"

"Trust me, Corporal," Jella answered. "I'm readier than you are. I've seen the kind of shit that crawls out of the ocean here! You're going to be struggling to keep up with me!"

When I hit the ground, I turned to Jella and gave out some final instructions. "We need to stay low! Belly on the ground! Follow the rest of the troops to our rendezvous point! You understand?"

Jella gave me a quick nod and took off, dragging us two Marines behind her. Propelled by terror, Dr. Jella Duverii was right. Harlund and I struggled to keep up.

It was a grueling crawl toward the jungle. At least it was for Harlund and me. Jella was petite, weighing no more than fifty kilos. Merik and I tipped the scales at more than double that, plus carried half our body weight in gear. While Jella scampered inland atop the surface of the silt, we sank into it. Not only did we have to propel ourselves forward, we had to pull our limbs out of the muck as we went.

There are few people in the galaxy as fit as an Academy Marine. We did not enlist. We were literally born into The Corps, the offspring of the strongest, smartest, and bravest fighting men and women the military could produce. We were raised, and trained, for twenty years on a planet whose gravity registered thirty percent above baseline with an oxygen saturation fifteen percent below it. By the time we graduated from the Academy and were blooded, we would have been considered superhuman had we returned to the world that spawned mankind.

Despite all that, getting across that beach was taking everything I had. It was killing others. I got close enough to somebody for me to hear an NCO yell to one of his subordinates over the proximity circuit. "Bajur! Are you still behind me?"

"Yeah," the Marine panted, obviously struggling and out of breath.

"I think Kilpikonna is stuck somewhere between us! Find him and see if you can help."

"Sorry, Sarge," Bajur replied. I could tell by his accent that he was from Samderis. "I can't!"

"What?!? What do you mean you can't?!?" the sergeant yelled. "If you don't help him, he's going to die!"

"If I try to help him, we're both going to die!" Bajur barked back. "I'm not drowning in this shit on account of some Samaari wannabee who thinks he's better than the rest of us. Fuck him. If he thinks he's so superior, let him drag his own ass out of this crap."

Putting the planetary rivalry aside, Bajur had a point. Stopping meant dying, and our path to the trees was dotted with those who stayed in one spot too long, their graves marked by their battle packs. Attached to the back of every Marine, it was the only thing still sticking out of the silt once they expired.

"Hey!" screamed a Navy crewman as we crawled past. He had lost his helmet, and the proximity communications circuit with it. We could barely hear him over the wind. "Can you give me a hand? I'm stuck!"

He certainly was. His arms and legs were completely buried in the muck, as was half of his torso. He had to crane his head back as far as he could to breathe. The harder he tried to pull his limbs out of the morass below him, the deeper he sank into it. There was no way we could help him. Not unless we wanted to end up in the same predicament. "Please!" he screamed as we passed. "Don't leave me here!"

Harlund paused to look back at the doomed man. "Keep going!" I snapped at him.

"I'm not sure I can," the corporal replied, his voice betraying the surprise he felt at struggling so hard to keep up. He was used to leading the charge, not being dragged along for the ride.

"You have to!" Jella yelled. Nodding in the direction of the unfortunate crewman, she added, "That is not the way you want to go!"

The Navy man agreed. "Please!" he screamed at us. "If you're not going to help me, kill me! Don't let me die like this! Shoot me in the head or something! I'd do it myself if I had a sidearm! Please! KILL ME!"

We ignored him. Pausing long enough to do even that could have been deadly. All we could do was keep crawling, staying on the surface of the sand as best we could. We barely heard the crewman the next time he tried to call out. He had sunken enough for the muck to begin suffocating him, pouring in through his mouth and nose.

"Doctor!" Merik called out. "Unhook me! I'm not going to make it!" Harlund's voice was full of frustration. He could not fathom that, after all he had been through, it was mud that would be the end of him.

"No!" Jella yelled back, yanking the tether to keep him moving. "You're not giving up!"

I knew Harlund better than our guide did. He was not giving up. He was just giving a realistic assessment of his situation. For whatever reason, the corporal was sinking faster than the doctor and me. Unable to keep up, he was a drag on both of us. If he kept us from keeping pace, it could kill us all.

Merik had a chest full of medals from nearly every consequential combat campaign of the last seven years. I could not let him drown in the mud like an animal. Squinting forward, I spotted a gargantuan tree trunk lying in the sand ahead of us, apparently blown there by the storm. "You see that up there?!?" I screamed at the corporal, pointing at the fallen log.

"Yeah!"

"Just make it that far, man! It's not sinking! When we get up there, we'll climb on top of that thing and rest for as long as we can! Can you do that, Killer?!?"

"I'll try!" Harlund screamed. I knew he would. He would give it everything he had. I only hoped that was enough.

Doing whatever I could to pull Merik along, I picked up my pace, powering through the wind, the rain, and the occasional chunk of debris that blew past us. I was motivated by the realization that the further away from the ship we got, the more bodies I saw lying face down in the muck. We were not trained, equipped, or prepared for anything like this.

Jella reached the log first and crawled around in circles while we caught up. Once she got a little slack in her line, she pulled herself up the obstacle, carefully maintaining a low profile.

I arrived next, lifting myself out of the mire and placing my hands on the fallen tree. It was spongy to the touch, tough, but soft and pliable. "This feels awfully weird for a palm," I observed.

"It's not a plant," Jella informed me.

"Then what is it?"

Our guide pointed down behind her. Pulling myself out of the muck, I bent over the doctor's perch and looked at the far side. It was covered with rows and rows of fist-sized suckers. It was not a tree. It was a tentacle. It had likely been blasted all the way there when we bombed the waterline. "Holy shit!"

"Now you know why I don't like the water," Jella told me.

After I had situated myself, I turned around to locate Harlund. He had stopped a few meters behind us. "You've got to keep moving!"

"I can't," Merik replied. "I'm stuck!" He was gassed, too. Harlund was in amazing shape, but I suspected he loaded extra ammo into his pack. He had to work twice as hard as I did to wrench his limbs back out of the muck, and it was sucking the energy out of him. I was barely making it myself.

"Don't pull that shit now, Harlund!" I yelled at him as my heart sank. "You're almost there! Move it!"

"I can't, Eamon! My arms and feet won't budge! The more I struggle, the deeper I sink! Fuck it, man! I'm all used up! Just put a bullet in my head! Don't let me drown in this shit like those other guys!"

"No!" I grabbed the line that attached him to Jella and started to pull. Without hesitation, the doctor began helping me.

"Look, you two," the corporal begged. "Don't drag this out! It's no use! Just cut me off and end this! Catch up with the rest before you end up stuck here too!"

"Stop being an asshole! You've got no more than three meters to go before you're safe! You ain't giving up now!"

I let myself fall over the far side of the tentacle and used my feet to push off it, yanking as hard as I could on the line. That seemed to do the trick. It broke the suction and Harlund began to rise out of the muck. But then he stopped cold.

The corporal's eyes got as big as dinner plates as he gasped, "Something's got me!"

"What?!?" I shouted in return.

"Something's got my foot! Oh shit! SOMETHING'S GOT ME! PULL, GOD-DAMMIT! PULL! GET ME THE FUCK OUT OF HERE!"

For a man who, mere seconds before, was so exhausted that he was begging us to kill him, the prospect of being eaten by some unseen muck monster breathed new life into Harlund Merik. He started thrashing about in the silt, screaming bloody murder and trying to claw his way to the tentacle we were perched upon. For our part, Jella and I began wrenching on the tether with a renewed sense of urgency. Not only did we want to save the corporal's life, we wanted to keep ourselves from being pulled beneath the surface with him.

Though Jella and I were also exhausted, we found the energy to get Harlund high enough so that three of his four limbs were out of the ground. We stalled after that, though, unable to extract his trapped foot. "We have to synchronize!" I shouted. "We gotta pull at the same time!"

"Okay!" Duverii shouted back, struggling to hold on.

"On my count! One! Two! Three! Pull! Pull! Pull! Pull! Pull!"

The strategy seemed to work. Little by little, Harlund's leg began to emerge from the quicksand. It was progress, but excruciatingly painful for Harlund. It felt like we were trying to split the poor man in two. Still, he kept screaming at us to yank even harder.

Eventually, we got to see what had him. His foot emerged from the mud, stuck in the end of some gelatinous creature that looked like a cross between an immense garden slug and a giant earthworm. When Harlund saw it, he screamed out in terror, pulled the sidearm off his hip, and fired three rounds into the beast's head.

Wounded, the organism released Harland from its mouth and retreated beneath the surface but retained its hold on the corporal's leg with a long, black, serpentine tongue. Once again concealed, the worm fought even harder to pull its prey down with it.

"AUUUUUGGGHHH!!" Harlund screamed as his knee popped. He then took aim with his pistol once more and tried to shoot the tongue. That was a much smaller target that proved impossible to hit while being jerked back and forth by both friend and foe. "PULL, EAMON! GODDAMMIT! PULL!"

"I'm pulling as hard as I can!" I shouted back. "Kick it or something!"

"Use your dagger!" Jella cried out. "Try to cut through it!"

Heeding Jella's advice, Harlund dropped his pistol and drew his blade from the sheath on his left thigh. Hunching over, he then sliced at the appendage wrapped around his foot. A geyser of purple blood burst from the wound that Merik inflicted upon the creature, and it finally let go.

The sudden slack caused Jella and me to hurtle backward off the tentacle. I landed on my shoulders in the muck while our guide fell on top of me. Now aware of the horrors lurking within the morass, we both somehow sprung out of the mud to retake our seats on the severed tentacle. Harlund was already up there waiting for us.

Merik was no coward, but he trembled in terror as we retook our positions and tried to catch our breaths. "W-w-w-what the h-h-hell was that thing?" he asked Jella.

Looking back at the ground that the Marine had just escaped from, Jella shook her head. "I have no idea. When I was here before, I only visited the ocean once, in an air explorer, hovering above the surface. We saw enough to know that landing here would not end well for us. We don't know shit about the creatures below the first atmospheric layer, the 'Hot Zone' as we call it. Only that they're bad. Very bad."

"You know," Harlund gasped. "I faced the Ghuldari army head-on on Sivma-11. I was deployed to evacuate Terris Mor after a supervolcano threatened to wipe out its entire population. I had to defend a settlement on Hirapish-2 from a swarm of dechenegs, these fucking bugs the size of horses that looked like a cross between a tarantula and a scorpion. I helped put down two uprisings, hunted Halesian terrorists, and survived being shelled by our own forces on Serra Vai. Right hand to God, I would rather go through all that stuff one more time than crawl across this shit again."

I nodded in agreement and looked toward the jungle we were headed for. "Well, brother," I panted, patting him on the shoulder. "I suggest you drop your gear here to lighten the load before our next leg. We need to haul ass and stay on the surface of this junk like the doctor is. We can't stop and allow ourselves to sink. We can't stay here, and we're only about halfway to where we need to be."

••◄●►◄●►◄●►•••

CHAPTER 5

S eared into the psyche of every Space Marine, from the very first moment they entered basic training, was the mantra that an infantryman's gear was his life. Everything we needed to survive was in that case fitted to the back of our exo-armor. Leaving it behind would deprive us of the supplies we needed to complete our mission. Letting it fall into enemy hands could give our adversaries what they required to deny us. There was no reason for a Marine to *ever* abandon their pack.

Unless it was the pack itself that was trying to kill us.

We discovered that the difference between life and death upon the Kanarisian mud flats was about forty kilograms, the weight of a standard combat pack. The only fully equipped Marines I saw gathered at the tree line, besides myself and maybe four other men, were all females who had the advantage of being about a third lighter than their male counterparts. The rest ditched their shit.

As far as I could tell, there were about two hundred survivors of *Wasp-Three* at the edge of the jungle when we arrived. They were seeking shelter from the wind by crouching down next to a fallen palm that, even while lying on its side, was nearly two stories high. While Jella and Harlund collapsed among the throng, I untethered myself from them and scoured the crowd for troops that looked rested. After collecting a half dozen candidates, I led them to our guide.

"Do you have any idea what's waiting for us in that forest?" I screamed at the Marines while pointing at the trees. Every one of them shook their heads. Redirecting my finger toward Jella Duverii, I told them, "Well, she does! She's the only one we got who knows what we're facing and how to survive it! She's our guide!"

I paused to let that sink in, looking each grunt in the eye. "If anything happens to her, we're fucked! You need to form a perimeter around that woman and be prepared to move heaven and Earth to make sure she stays safe! Got it?!?"

After the Marines voiced their assent, I took off my pack and handed it to Harlund. "Corporal Merik is in charge until I get back." Technically, Harlund and I were the same rank. It could be said that with all the experience he had under his belt, he was actually senior to me. I was a Citadel Cadet, though. I was blooded, meaning that I had taken lives to earn my stripes. That made even the sergeants reluctant to argue with me.

Corporal Merik was no sergeant, however. He argued with me all the time. "What the hell are you doing?!?" he asked as I handed him my pack.

"I'm going back to the ship," I told him.

"What?!?" he exclaimed. "We barely made it over that shit once! You're going to try to cross it two more times?!?"

"I've got something there that I still gotta do." I left it at that and bolted for the beach before Merik could say anything else. I spotted Gunnery Sergeant Malcolm among the survivors, and I wanted to be well out of radio range before he got word that I had returned to *Wasp-Three*.

I didn't make it. I was halfway to the severed tentacle when Malcolm's voice pierced my ears from inside my helmet. "Cadet Tauk! What the *fuck* do you think you're doing?!?"

"Going back to the ship, Gunny!"

"The *fuck* you are! You turn your ass around and get back here on the double!"

Unable to help myself, I grimaced before I answered. "I can't do that, Gunny."

"What the *fuck* do you mean you can't do that!?! You got a goddamn mission to complete, son! From my viewpoint, you just abandoned your post! That's a court-martial offense, Tauk!"

I was in serious trouble. I needed to think quickly to avoid landing before a firing squad after all the dust had settled. "I *am* performing my mission, Gunny! My ability to protect Dr. Duverii depends upon me getting back to *Wasp-Three*!"

"How the *fuck* do you figure that?!?"

"Gunny, by the looks of all the bodies I saw on the way to the tree line, we're losing half our men in the muck because they're trying to cross it fully loaded! It's taking them too long to figure out they need to drop their dead weight! If we lose too many Marines, we'll never make it to Narman's Pyke! We'll be combat ineffective, Doctor Duverii will be dead, and my mission will have failed!"

Though Gunny Malcolm took a moment to contemplate my argument, he remained unswayed. "I'll send someone else back to the dropship! You get your ass back here!"

I picked up my pace, hoping to lose contact with Malcolm before he cornered me with a direct order. To buy time, I told him to repeat himself. "I can't hear you!"

"Bullshit!" Gunny bellowed. "I wasn't born yesterday, Cadet! Get back here and guard our goddamn guide before I put your ass up in front of the colonel!"

"You're breaking up, Gunny!"

"Goddammit, Tauk! Do you know what the punishment is for insubordination?!?"

I swallowed hard and shuddered. "Yes, Gunny."

"And do you think what you're doing's worth that?"

The League's elite had always been drawn to the pilot corps. Most of the Navy's spacecraft were flown by pampered rich kids seeking personal glory. They were not in it for The Cause. They were in it for themselves and adverse to the concept of sacrifice that the Citadel had instilled in me since birth. In other words, the fleet contained far too many pilots like Grazny Sirrah and not enough like Je'Sikka Albarn. The Navy could not afford to leave someone like her in a wrecked dropship waiting to be devoured alive by alien sea bugs.

I thought about Albarn sitting alone in *Wasp-Three's* broken cockpit, paralyzed and listening to kryptids feasting upon the bodies of her crew. I also thought about what would be done to me if I disobeyed Gunny's orders to return to my post. They would hurt me for sure, but I would recover. If I left Albarn in the wreckage of *Wasp-Three*, she would not. Future pilots would be deprived of her leadership and the example she set. Her death would weaken the Corps.

If I go through with this, they'll whip the hide right off my back. Oh well. Those were scars I could wear with pride.

"Cadet Tauk!" Malcolm shouted through my earpiece. "Answer me! Is what you're doing worth the consequences you'll receive for doing it?"

"Yes, Gunny," I told him. "It is. No question."

My earpiece registered Malcolm letting loose a loud sigh of exasperation and a few more choice curse words. "All right, then. You do what you have to do. Just know that when this shit's all over, I intend to bring the full weight of military justice down upon your sorry ass. Do you understand me?"

I nodded my head even though Malcolm could not see it. "Yes, Gunny."

"Okay, then. Godspeed. You be fucking careful out there!"

The men I crossed on the first half of my trip back to *Wasp-Three* already figured it out. I did not have to start screaming at people until a hundred meters past the mid-point. If they wanted to survive the trek across the muck, the Marines had to let go of their packs.

"Abandon your gear!" I yelled. "You won't make it to the tree line unless you drop your shit and keep moving! Weapons only! If you stop, you'll sink in the mud and die!"

Getting the word out was easy enough for most of the way back to the drop-ship. There was only a single breach in the hull above the interior waterline, and the Marines had to squeeze through it, trickling out of the craft one at a time. I heard later that there was a much larger hole in the stern. That one was flooding the staging bay with every wave that smashed against it. With the water came a legion of kryptids to feast upon the dead. There was also a type of alien eel sneaking into the wreckage that was perfectly comfortable biting chunks out of the living. Between the rising sea, the kryptids, the darkness, and the eels, the holding bay became an absolute hell hole.

Realizing that the evacuation was not outpacing the rising water, a pair of surviving combat engineers decided to blow a bigger breach in the side of *Wasp-Three*. The explosion went off when I was still a couple hundred meters away, and before the smoke even cleared, hundreds of Marines poured out of the crippled vessel, stampeding toward the tree line.

"NO!" I screamed out. "NO! DROP YOUR PACKS! DROP YOUR PACKS! WEAPONS ONLY! WEAPONS...!" It was no use. Their ears were still ringing from the blast, and my screams were drowned out by battle cries as the horde rushed past me to escape the horrors of the alien ocean. The only thing I could do was scamper out of their way to keep from getting trampled.

To make matters worse, the wind died down enough for the troops to run upright. Without crawling, even the women got bogged down once they reached the mud field. After several of them got trapped in the muck, the Marines started figuring things out on their own.

It was getting dark when I reached the ship, and I was exhausted. I had to dig real deep to find the energy to climb to the cockpit. I still did it but collapsed into the co-pilot seat beside Albarn once I was inside. The warrant officer looked surprised to see me. "You came back."

Nodding my head, I gasped, "Yeah, I made it. Barely." In the silence that followed, I could hear the kryptids, possibly hundreds of them by now, tearing flesh from the bones of the cockpit casualties.

"Is that sound what I think it is?" I asked Albarn.

Our pilot nodded and showed me the pistol in her hand. "Yes. It's those fucking beetles. I was just coming to grips with the fact that I was going to have to blow my brains out before they turned their attention to me."

I let out a long sigh. I was exhausted and needed rest before I tried dragging Albarn over the muck. We could not stay in the cockpit with the bugs, though. I had to get her outside.

Je'Sikka Albarn could not feel anything below her waist, but that did not mean she was not in a great deal of agony. She screamed so loud when I tried to pull her out of the chair that I had to stop and give her one of my morphine shots. By the time I got her strapped around the armpits to lower her to the beach, she was begging for another.

Navy personnel were equipped differently than combat troops. They did not carry personalized morphine vials on them. Like Jella Duverii, Je'Sikka Albarn was petite. She weighed half what I did, so she essentially got a double dose already. "I don't know if you can take another one, ma'am."

Albarn grabbed me by the collar and cried, "I don't know if I can take *not* getting another one, Cadet! I'm begging you! You're hurting me even more!"

I grabbed the pilot's forearm and checked the vitals on her system monitor. Albarn's heart was racing, and her blood pressure was dangerously high from the adrenaline overwhelming her system in response to the pain. The odds of that killing her were about the same as dying from another hit of morphine. At least with the narcotics, she would be pleasantly stoned if her ticker quit. I ended up giving her the second injection, and she fell unconscious just as I started lowering her out of the window.

By the time we hit the beach, the wind and rain had died down considerably. I could now see differences in the consistency of the sand in front of us. Before me were what appeared to be two vast fields of smoother, shinier beach dotted with the packs of Marines who had perished in the muck. A winding trail of coarser-looking earth was between them, similar to where I was standing. The absence of dead bodies on the rougher path suggested this was the safer way to the tree line, and the troops adjusted their evacuation route accordingly.

I was set to throw Albarn over my shoulder and follow them when I spotted a Self-Propelled Stretcher among the crowd. The SPS was a versatile device, able to navigate a wide array of different terrains. On relatively flat land, such as the beach on Kanaris, it could deploy skids to distribute its weight over the soft surface and propel itself forward on tracked wheels. Over rocky paths, it used a set of eight alloy legs to walk like a giant steel spider over the hazards while keeping the patient level.

"Hey!" I called out to a passing sergeant guiding an injured rifleman out on an SPS. "Where did you get that?"

The sergeant pointed back at the wreckage. "In the egress bay!" We still had to scream at one another to be heard over the wind.

"Are there any more left?" I asked.

The sergeant nodded. "Yeah! But there's a lot more injured than there are SPSs! If you want one, you'll have to fight for it!"

That, I was willing to do. The problem was I could not even get to the hull breach because of the swarm of Marines evacuating the dropship. By the time I got inside, the stretchers would be gone.

While trying to push through the crowd, I watched several SPSs pass by. One bore a Navy ensign. Another, a master chief. Then there was a succession of stretchers carrying Marines. Hope for Albarn arrived shortly after that, in the form of an SPS transporting a man with a large, olive "0" stenciled upon the shoulder of his armor where our rank was typically displayed.

Grabbing the medic walking alongside the vehicle, I pulled him from the crowd and dragged him to where Albarn was lying. The SPS followed. Pointing to our pilot, I said, "Doc, I need to put her on that stretcher!"

Sergeant Gruber scoffed. "It's already occupied! Go get yourself another one!"

I could not believe what I had just heard. To my ears, not only was the medic's resistance to giving up the SPS insubordinate, it was an affront to The Cause. Gruber's patient was a Zero. A criminal dredged from the lowest strata of human villainy. He and Albarn were not equals. Claiming he had as much right to an SPS as a Space Corps pilot bordered on treason. Motioning toward the patient, I pointed out the obvious. "That's a convict laborer! This woman is an officer of the fleet!"

The sergeant looked at the trio of red hash marks on my left shoulder and realized I was a blooded academy cadet. He then swallowed uncomfortably. "Are you the guy who killed..."

"Yeah, I am," I interrupted. I knew what he was going to say. His was a question people constantly asked me. I hated answering it, but this time, I did not mind if it would expedite the process of getting me what I needed.

29

Being face-to-face with me rattled Gruber's nerves a little, but the medic stood his ground. "That man saved my life! He waded through the water to free me from my restraints while those little eels got between his armor plates and started ripping him up! Convict or not, he carried me to safety so those fuckers didn't do the same thing to me!"

Good for him, I thought. *He got to atone for his crimes before he expired. Most Zeros died as pathetically as they lived.*

I peeled back the blanket covering the prisoner's legs. The eels had done a number on the man. They stripped the skin off him from the knees down and shredded his muscles right to the bone. Shaking my head, I told the medic, "I'm sorry, but this guy's a lost cause! He's all used up! I need the SPS!"

"No!" Gruber screamed back. "He saved my life!"

"So did she!" I countered, pointing at Albarn. "She was our pilot! She pulled off a miracle, landing that ship in this shit! She's going back so she can teach others to do the same! This guy's a criminal that..."

The medic shook his head. "Don't dehumanize him like that! He's a man! A living, breathing human being!"

I peered down at the wounded convict. He appeared dainty and fragile, not like someone capable of committing a crime heinous enough to earn a life sentence of forced labor. Despite the horrific nature of his injuries, the prisoner's eyes were wide open. He had something of an angelic, delicate face that bore a smile stretching from ear to ear. He was doped up to the gills, looking like he was having the time of his life. I wondered how much morphine the sergeant wasted on the man.

"We can't just leave him here!" the corpsman pled.

That was enough. Arguing with a medic over a Zero was a ridiculous waste of time that none of us had. Whipping out my sidearm, I shoved the sergeant out of the way and took aim at the patient's head. Gruber tried to stop me. "Don't! Please! Don't do it! He's a human...!"

I pulled the trigger, sending a bullet through the condemned man's temples as the medic shrieked in anguish.

A couple of troops turned toward the sound of the shot and looked ready to intervene. They reconsidered after realizing it was only a prisoner being executed.

"WHY?!?" screamed the corpsman, convulsing into hysterics. "YOU SICK FUCK! WHY WOULD YOU DO THAT?!? I WOULD HAVE CARRIED HIM!"

"Then you should have," I told the man, implying that the patient's death was more the medic's fault than mine. The rage on Gruber's face suggested he did not believe that.

I was not sure I did either. When I placed my sidearm back into its holster, I had to maintain my grip on it for a moment to keep my hand from shaking. I could not allow the troops around us to see me display such an obvious sign of weakness. I had killed men before but this one was different. The others posed a threat to me. They would have killed me had I not killed them first. This was more like an execution. Actually, it felt like murder.

Something was wrong. I was conditioned to kill without hesitation or remorse, especially when it came to our inferiors. Ghuldarians. Terrorists. Class Zero convicts. I was supposed to be able to take their lives with no more regret than if I were swatting a fly. This one made the acid rise from the pit of my stomach and burn the back of my throat. I nearly vomited.

Struck dumb with shock, Gruber fell to his knees and buried his face in his hands. As he mourned, I unbuckled the Zero's body and nonchalantly kicked it off the side of the stretcher, struggling to avoid treating it with even the slightest hint of dignity. I had to keep up my façade. The medic remained seated in the mud, rocking himself back and forth, sobbing while I wiped the gore off the stretcher.

While I was strapping Albarn into the SPS, the sergeant snapped out of his reverie and charged me from behind. Thanks to my training, I was able to deflect the attack and flip the medic onto his back before he realized what had happened. When Gruber lifted his head, he was met by the sight of my pistol pointing at the space between his eyes.

"You want to join that prisoner?" I asked him.

Full of panic, the medic stuttered a few times before rolling over with a whimper. He then crawled to the corpse I left in the mud, cradling the man's head in his arms while he bawled. That was how we left him.

Albarn and I were halfway to the tree line before I could bring myself to look back at *Wasp-Three* again. Gruber and, who I now assumed to be his dead lover, had not moved.

●●◄●►◄●●

CHAPTER 6

I did not prevent many of us from disappearing under the muck. At most, I warned no more than a few dozen troops to drop their packs before they drowned.

Likely fueled by my status as a minor celebrity, word still spread that the guy who killed the Butcher of Deraghun kept hundreds of Marines from drowning in the mud pits of Kanaris. This was a gross exaggeration, and it made me feel like even more of a fraud than I already was. This time, however, the bogus narrative did more than just earn me accolades I did not deserve. It may have helped save my ass.

After getting Albarn settled into the medical camp, I tried to make my way back to Jella Duverii, only to be intercepted by Gunny Malcolm. He was flanked on either side by my platoon leader, Lieutenant Thyster, and my company commander, Captain Mardona.

All three were displeased with me, but none more so than Malcolm. He grabbed me by the throat and, quite literally, tried to wring my neck. I could have broken his arms and freed myself, but that would only have added to the trouble I was already in.

"What did I tell you about going out there?!?" Gunny screamed at me. "Do you realize what fuckin' orders are, Cadet?!?"

"I was trying to save lives," I croaked, struggling to speak with my platoon sergeant's hand tightening around my windpipe.

"So was I!" Malcolm barked, bouncing my head off the side of the palm tree behind me. "I was trying to save yours! Do you know how much it costs to raise a Corps baby? Train it from the time it can walk until it can fight a condemned man to the death to earn its blood stripes? You do NOT send that kind of investment across a field of quicksand to deliver fucking advice!"

Enraged, the gunnery sergeant let go of me to grab a conscripted convict by the hair. Wrenching him to his feet, Malcolm shouted, "That's the kind of shit you send someone like this to do!"

I looked at the "1" stenciled across the prisoner's shoulder. That meant he had been convicted of lesser crimes than the man I had just shot. His sins were along the lines of assault, grand larceny, or being involved in organized crime. Class Ones were just marginally more reliable than Zeros.

"Those may be the kind of men I'd send on a suicide mission," I told Gunny while rubbing my throat. "But I'm not sure I would put the lives of hundreds of Marines in their hands."

Malcolm dropped the conscript and smacked me hard enough to knock me off-balance. "Keep your advice to yourself and follow orders when they're given to you! When you run out there doing what you please, you jeopardize the mission and the lives of everyone around you!"

I thought about how Sirrah disobeyed orders and obliterated four thousand troops in the blink of an eye. Gunny Malcolm was right. I did not regret my decision to return to the dropship, but it was a blatant act of insubordination. It could not go unpunished.

Malcolm glared into my eyes for a couple of uncomfortable moments before saying, "Just so there are no surprises, you will be disciplined for what you did today. No matter how honorable your intentions were, letting you get away with this would set a bad precedent."

"Aye aye, Gunny."

"Good," Malcolm spat. "Now, find Duverii and get back to your mission. And get some rest. You're going to need it."

"Not so fast!" Lieutenant Thyster barked. "You left our guide, one of the most important people on this expedition, alone when you returned to that wreck! She could have been killed! That's a gross dereliction of duty!"

"Sir, I left her in the hands of one of the most experienced combat veterans in the battalion." I then repeated to my platoon leader the line of reasoning I laid on Malcolm. "I can't complete my mission by myself. I need Marines. I had to make sure they survived the trek to the tree line. If someone didn't tell them to drop their packs, many more could've died."

Thyster looked ready to lay into me again, but Mardona preempted him. The captain was not pleased with me either, but he bought my line of reasoning. He also believed what the troops were saying about me, even if I did not. "You did save lives, Tauk. Many of them. Thank you for that."

My company commander's praise was misplaced, but I did not correct him. I needed positive press. "Thank you, sir."

"Cadet," Mardona continued. "I was informed that you executed a Zero out there. Is that true?"

I nodded. "While back at the wreckage, I discovered our pilot was still alive. I needed his stretcher to get her to safety. The medic refused to remove the convict from the SPS to free up the vehicle."

Thyster's jaw dropped open. He looked even more upset. "You shot a wounded man to steal his ride?"

"Would you rather I killed the warrant officer?" I asked. "We have more prisoners than we know what to do with. Pilots of Albarn's caliber are in far shorter supply."

"What the hell is the matter with you?" Thyster asked me. "Shooting unarmed convicts doesn't make you a killer, Tauk! It makes you a psychopath. And probably a felon!"

I was treading dangerous waters. If I was not on solid ground morally, I needed to convince Thyster that I certainly was legally. "Sir," I told him. "Squad leaders are expected to execute Class Zero convicts for being unwilling, or unable, to carry out their duties."

"You're not a squad leader!" Thyster shouted at me. "You're an *assistant* squad leader!"

"Actually, sir," Malcolm chimed in. My platoon sergeant wanted to see me punished for insubordination, not manslaughter. He pointed at the collection of battle packs marking the muddy graves of our drowned Marines. "Sergeant Fulton's dead. Cadet Tauk is, and was, a squad leader."

Thyster growled at the technicality. Stepping forward to get into my face, he asked, "Do you get off on shit like this, Tauk? You think murder is the solution to things that inconvenience you?"

"Sir," I answered. "I didn't enjoy it, if that's what you mean. Warrant Officer Albarn is an extraordinary pilot. She's the reason we're all here. Getting her out of that wreckage, and fixing her spine, will allow her to return and keep doing what she did. That convict? Yeah, we can give him new feet, but is the Corps really going to make that kind of investment in a Zero just so he can come back and carry stuff around?"

Mardona lifted his forearm and began tapping on his system monitor, pulling up information on the man I shot. "The Zero was Vernor Blyte," the captain told us, making me realize that the last thing I wanted to know was that my victim had a name. "He was a prostitute and a low-level drug supplier on Beru Sukka.

He was convicted of administering a hot dose of Helia X to the nephew of a League legislator, killing the boy."

My company commander sighed and lowered his arm. "Nobody up the chain's going to care about what happened to that man. According to the senior corpsman, though, Blyte was popular among the medics where he was assigned. He'd earned their respect and often said he was happier as a Corps convict than he was back on Beru Sukka. Chief Kumar told me Blyte was particularly close to the medic taking care of him."

I let out a long sigh. "It looked like they were lovers, sir. I didn't know that when I shot him."

"Would you have done things differently if you had?" snapped Thyster.

I stood silently, staring at my platoon leader as I thought about his question. After due deliberation, I answered, "No. I concede that my superiors have valid concerns about the judgment calls I made today, but I stand by the results. Jella Duverii has not been harmed, I saved the pilot of our dropship, and I helped keep Marines from drowning in the mud. I freely admit I broke some rules. I'm not looking to avoid accountability for that."

That turned out to be the right thing to say. Mardona nodded at me, indicating he saw my point. "Cadet, you made a lot of rash decisions that could have gone poorly. Luckily, they didn't. You will be disciplined, but I'm going to consider what you accomplished in light of your infractions. Rest assured, though, I'm not going to tolerate any more rogue behavior out of you. Listen to Gunny Malcolm. You disobey him again and I promise I will make you suffer. Am I clear?"

I nodded and rendered the captain a swift salute. "Crystal, sir."

●● ◄●► ● ◄●► ●●

When I was finally released by my chain of command, I stumbled over to where I last saw Jella Duverii and collapsed in the sand between her and Merik.

"My God," Harlund gasped. "I didn't think you were going to make it back."

I nodded. "Yeah, there were times when I didn't think I was, either."

"You look like you could use a treat," Jella said.

"Yeah, I wouldn't mind a nice warm meal and a full night's sleep."

Harlund laughed. "There's no such thing as a full night's sleep in the Corps."

"I think I can help you with that meal, though," Jella told me. "You still have that kryptid I told you to save?"

I had forgotten about that. I felt my cargo pocket. "Yeah, I got it."

"Good. Give it to me." Dr. Duverii pulled her flashlight from her belt. Depending upon the setting, a Space Corps hand lantern could generate heat as well as light. If you concentrated the beam enough, you could use it to cut through sheets of steel. Jella turned hers up just enough to make the bug's shell smoke.

After thirty seconds under the torch, the creature exploded. It went off like a gunshot and sprayed steam upon everyone within a two-meter radius. When the cloud dispersed, Jella was left holding what looked like a giant kernel of moist popcorn. "Try it."

Popped kryptid looked disgusting, but it smelled delicious. I tore off a piece of flesh and cautiously put it in my mouth. The bug had an incredibly rich flavor, tasting like buttered lobster tail. It was as amazing as it was filling. I could barely wolf down half before passing what remained to Corporal Merik. Harlund was not as famished as I was, so after sampling a couple of bites, he nodded his approval and rationed it off to nearby comrades.

The alien bug became an instant delicacy. As I carved out a place in the wet sand to catch a couple hours of shut-eye, I heard several Marines suggest returning to the crash to harvest as many kryptids as they could. As delicious as they were, I am not sure it was the flavor that tempted the troops to risk their lives to feast upon them, though.

It was revenge. The thought of doing to those bugs what they had done to our comrades was a big part of what made them so insanely succulent that night. It was also why I heard a few of the grunts wondering out loud about how those "fucking eels" might taste.

•● ◄●► ◉ ◄●► ●•

There's no such thing as a full night's sleep in the Corps.

Harlund Merik was right. The ghost of Vernor Blyte invaded my dreams that first night on Kanaris. His feet were fine, but his face was twisted and mangled by the bullet I had blasted through it. "Your life is just beginning," Blyte told me in a voice far too familiar to me to be his. That went for the words he used, too. "You're not too far gone yet. You can escape this. There's more to life than just..."

Before Blyte could finish channeling Gori Dravidas, I shot up from the mud, eyes wide open and skin covered in sweat.

Jella Duverii was still awake, sitting a meter to my left. "You know," she said to me, thinking there was a different explanation for all my perspiration.

"The highest temperature recorded on Earth before the human race started to abandon it was sixty degrees Celsius. It's sixty-four here right now."

I could barely breathe, it was so hot. "How does anything live in this shit?"

Our guide shrugged. "They got used to it. They evolved and adapted. As humans, we don't have that luxury."

Jella tapped on her exo-armor. "Without the refrigerants in our shells, we'll die out here if there's no rain. That storm sucked all the moisture out of the air when it passed through. It's going to get positively miserable until the heat evaporates enough ocean to supersaturate the sky again. Give it about eight hours. It'll start raining, and once it starts, it won't stop. On the bright side, the constant cycle of precipitation and evaporation will drop the temperature by about twenty-five degrees. Hey, you notice that you can't hear the ocean anymore?"

I had not. "Huh. Where'd it go?"

"Away," Jella told me, waving her hand toward the horizon. "Between the low-pressure system leaving the area and the big moon being on the other side of the planet, the tide has gone out. The ocean is now miles away." Jella handed me her optical amplifiers. "Check it out. That is one big ass beach."

I put the viewer up to my eyes and trained it out past the wreckage. There was no sign of water, but when I zoomed in to get a closer look at our fallen dropship, I saw thousands of kryptids pouring out of it. Most were crawling toward the retreating sea. Others were headed for the jungle. Some were coming right for us. "Are you sure we don't have to worry about those sea bugs?"

Dr. Duverii shook her head. "The kryptids? No. And they're not necessarily sea bugs. They're really versatile creatures that can live almost anywhere. You find them in oceans, lakes, the forests, up on the mountains, and even in the desert. They're pretty much everywhere here. That's not necessarily a bad thing. They're plentiful and easy to catch, so the one way people don't die on this planet is starvation. Do you notice anything different about the route the kryptids are taking back to the jungle?"

I did. The bugs were following the same path I had. "They're avoiding the grub pits."

"Yep," Jella agreed. "The pits are easier to see now that the sand is drying out. Those creatures that grabbed your buddy seem to be territorial. There are distinct borders between the mud traps where the ground is firm. I'm mapping it out and uploading it to the battle network so we can see the danger zones on our face shield displays. I'm betting once it starts raining again, we're not going to be able to pick them out so easily."

I nodded at the doctor. "That's a good idea." Standing up to stretch, I caught sight of Kanaris's ringed moon through the trees. It looked enormous. "I thought you said the big moon was on the other side of the planet."

"It is. That's Gaiomedi. The smaller one."

"It looks pretty big to me."

Jella shrugged. "That's atmospheric magnification."

As I stared at Gaiomedi, a creature ventured out onto a branch of one of the trees high above us, perfectly silhouetting itself before the moon. It looked nearly as tall as I was and was shaped like a hairless orangutan. It had a large, round body from which sprung four sinewy limbs, each ending in a large, taloned hand. When it turned sideways, I could see that its head hung suspended upon a short, thick neck. It was dropped so far below the beast's shoulders that, from the wrong angle, it looked as if it was protruding from the animal's chest. When it opened its mouth, it showed off an impressive array of pointed teeth that could easily wreak havoc upon a human body.

I dropped Jella's set of night eyes and slowly raised my weapon. "What the hell is that thing?" I whispered to our guide.

Seeing what I was aiming at, Jella leapt to her feet and placed her hand atop my rifle, gently pushing the barrel back toward the ground. "That's a quarakai."

"A what?"

"A quarakai. A sub-species of one, anyway."

"What are they?"

"They're fascinating." Jella paused to pick up the set of optical amplifiers I had dropped. Focusing on the creature, I could hear her snapping pictures. She then pulled out her tablet to log the animal into the zoological database. All Marines were encouraged to document any Kanarisian wildlife they discovered. The program's software even let them name their findings as encouragement to do so. Identifying new life forms was not just Jella's job, though. As an alien zoologist, it was her obsession.

"This is a variant we haven't seen before," Duverii told me. "Ecologically speaking, quarakai fill the niche on Kanaris that great apes would in a replicant environment that we're more familiar with. From an intelligence standpoint, they fall between *Australopithecus* and *Homo Neanderthalensis*. They're capable of making fairly complex tools, they speak a simple language, and they perform funeral rites for their dead. The group closest to Narman's Pyke also uses fire, but we think they learned that from watching us. They pop kryptids with it."

"Are they dangerous?"

Jella shrugged. "They can be. You certainly don't want to get on their bad side. They seem to know they're no match for our technology, so they don't act particularly aggressive towards us. Among each other, though, they can be positively barbaric, especially if they cross paths with a different sub-species."

I looked back up at the quarakai. "You say they use language? Can we communicate with them?"

"Kind of," Jella answered. "Our vocal organs are completely different from each other, so we humans can't articulate quarakai noises, nor can they imitate ours. They can recognize some of our words, though, and we can understand them a little if we're around them enough. One thing we do have in common is four fingers and an opposable thumb on each hand. Our lead biologist was making impressive strides teaching the local creatures sign language."

I paused to wipe a handful of sweat out of my eyes. "No shit? You can teach these things to sign?"

Jella smiled. "Yes. I worked with Dr. Briiz for a little while. I saw it with my own eyes."

To test Jella's account, I waved at the quarakai above us. Once I had the creature's attention, I stuck my other hand up and extended my middle finger at it.

The quarakai quizzically tilted its head to the side and stared at me for a short while. Before it sauntered off further up into the treetops, however, it stuck its arm out and returned the sentiment.

●●<●>●<●>●●

CHAPTER 7

The Harnilium veins that ran throughout the crust of Kanaris reduced the Corps to communicating via the space-age equivalent of smoke signals. We had to fire rockets into orbit to send a message to our mothership, then wait for them to digest our information before they could launch a reply. It was a slow process made even slower by the fact that it was sunrise before the survivors of *Wasp Three* figured out who was in charge.

Lieutenant Colonel Bahkmin was killed in the crash, as were two of our company commanders. That meant we still had three reasonably competent O-3s that could have assumed command. Unfortunately, none of them were senior to our intelligence officer. Captain Nico Briggund was another pompous Samaari who never made enough of a positive impression upon his superiors to be considered for promotion to major.

My platoon leader always kept his views about command decisions well hidden from his subordinates. Still, he grimaced at the news of Briggund's promotion. Captain Mardona caught Thyster's reaction and asked, "Do you have something to say, Lieutenant?"

Shaking his head, Thyster replied, "No, sir."

"Good," Mardona continued. "Now, along with Captain Briggund's appointment to battalion CO, General Kroaht also told us the Expeditionary Force is not launching any more missions to the surface of Kanaris. Not until we figure out what shot our Wasps out of the sky."

"Sir," I said, raising my hand. "Our dropships were not downed by hostile fire. They collided during reentry."

"Really?" Mardona asked, his voice dripping with skepticism. "And how would you know that?"

"I was in the cockpit, sir."

My company commander squinted at me in disbelief. "You were in the cockpit? How the hell did you rate that?"

Gunny Malcolm mockingly answered for me. "The benefits of celebrity, Captain. Colonel Bahkmin decided that no person was better qualified to guard our guide than the cadet who earned his blood stripes killing the Butcher of Deraghun."

Mardona's eyes narrowed at me. "So that's why you rescued the pilot. You had a front-row seat to observe what she did."

"I returned to save Marines," I responded, sticking to my story. "But yes, sir, after seeing what she'd done, I wasn't going to leave her on the bridge."

"Okay," Mardona continued. "You were there. So tell me, Cadet, how did two dropships manage to collide? That's virtually impossible to do on autopilot."

"*Wasp Two* kicked off his autopilot and tried to pull up at the last minute."

Mardona winced. That sounded far too stupid to be true. Had I not seen it with my own eyes, I might not have believed it either. "Why the hell would he do that?"

"He chickened out, sir."

Mardona stared at me for a moment. "*Wasp Two's* pilot was Grazny Sirrah. Do you know who that is?"

I shrugged. "Judging by how he talked back to Colonel Traegus, I'm assuming he thought he was someone important."

The captain sighed. "His grandfather is the head of the Tahnabaht Conglomerate, which holds the mining rights of several different star systems. The Prosperity Party of the Samaari Guild was founded by one of Sirrah's ancestors. The family still runs it to this day. The jurisdictions that party controls are the largest source of the League's tax revenue and, unofficially, it has the largest number of elected parliamentarians on its payroll. Sirrah's family has money, influence, and connections throughout every aspect of League administration, including in the Space Marines. Cadet Tauk, for your own safety, I would avoid spreading the word that a scion of the Tahnabaht Conglomerate lost his nerve during a combat drop."

"But, sir, we're at less than a third of our strength now," I argued. "We're going to need reinforcements. Vehicles. Supplies. Air support. We're not going to get that without other drop missions. The expeditionary commander needs to know we didn't lose those ships to hostile fire. They were casualties of an inept pilot."

Mardona shot me a look of impatience. "Your word alone is not going to suffice, Tauk."

"Then pull up my network video. I had my helmet on and recording."

Captain Mardona lifted his arm and tapped a few commands onto his exo-armor monitor. After several moments of trying, he shook his head. "Tauk, your recording loop doesn't start until this morning. It's gone."

I dropped my visor over my eyes and tried to play it back myself. I quickly found that Mardona was right. "What the hell?!? Try our guide's video. She was there, too."

Our company commander did and got the same result. "Nothing."

I was going to urge Mardona to search the video feed of the two surviving Navy crewmen, but remembered they were equipped differently. Their video and communications recordings would be on *Wasp-Three's* black box. "Talk to the pilot. She'll tell you. We also have the weapons officer and the navigator. They were there, too. We all saw and heard what happened."

My captain looked concerned. Deleted video was an obvious sign that someone wanted to keep the details behind the Wasp disaster from getting out. Depending upon how powerful that someone was, human testimony itself would probably not be enough to change the command's decisions. Still, Mardona was willing to check it out. "Where are they?"

"The ship's crew?" I asked. "I assume they'd be wherever the Navy personnel are mustering."

Mardona gave me a nod. "I'll look into it, but I don't know if it will do much good. Thanks to the Harnillium interference, no one in orbit knows what happened during the drop. They suspect the Wasps were blasted out of the sky. Therefore, there will be no rescue party. The powers above have decided that we're to remain on the surface of Kanaris and, since we're what's left of the reconnaissance battalion, they're insisting we do some recon stuff."

The captain clasped his hands behind his back before continuing. "Our objectives are, one, to determine what happened to Narman's Pyke. Two, identify what threats remain there and advise what will be needed on the ground to overcome them. Three, locate enemy anti-aircraft armament..."

THERE IS NO ANTI-AIRCRAFT ARMAMENT! I screamed in my head.

"...and destroy it. Four, reoccupy Narman's Pyke, if feasible with existing resources. Five, recover a Section 615 intelligence asset believed to still be alive near or in the colony."

"Who is that?" asked Gunny Welpox from Fourth Platoon.

Our company commander shrugged. "I have no idea. It's classified."

"Then how are we supposed to find them?" Lieutenant Snyke, Welpox's superior, asked.

"We're not," our captain answered. "We're expected to secure Narman's Pyke and create a situation conducive to the spook finding us."

Our company commander grinned in spite of himself. He knew that was as stupid as it sounded. Mission objectives like that were why the term "military intelligence" had been considered an oxymoron for centuries.

Mardona let out a long sigh before continuing. "*Wasp- Three* is one hundred percent disabled. There's no power and no way to extract our vehicles from it. As you all know, the Harnillium interference drives artificial intelligence haywire, so our sentient droids are stuck on the *Phoenix*. They can't be landed to help. The Marines are going primitive. We're going to return to the crash site and retrieve whatever supplies we can carry. Then we're going to hoof them all the way to Narman's Pyke."

"How far is that?" asked Gunny Borkhat from First Platoon.

"On the map, one hundred and seventy kilometers," Mardona told him. "That's a straight line that doesn't consider a zig-zagging trail, rising and falling elevations, cliff faces, or obstacles. Our actual hiking distance could be triple that."

After letting that sink in for a moment, our captain said, "We'll march until we're about five clicks from our objective, then reorganize based upon our troop strength before we try to assault the colony."

"Are we anticipating high casualty rates during the march?" asked Lieutenant Griffs, the leader of Second Platoon.

Gunny Malcolm answered for our company commander. "We lost sixty-four troops just crossing from the dropship to the tree line. We're about to hike hundreds of kilometers, in sixty-seven-degree heat, through an eco-system that, if it's anything like any other Near-Earth Environment jungle I've ever walked through, is a place where human beings are likely *not* at the top of the food chain. It's safe to assume that we're going to be arriving at our objective significantly lighter in manpower than what we leave here with."

Dr. Duverii looked at Mardona. "Captain, I was attached to the battalion staff when we disembarked from the *Nebulan Phoenix*. Should I transfer to Briggund's team?"

Our company commander shook his head. "Captain Briggund was our intelligence officer. As such, he feels he's been sufficiently apprised of the threats facing us upon Kanaris."

Thirty officers and NCOs stared impassively at Captain Mardona. No one batted an eye, no one gasped, and no one gave any indication that they were concerned by that. Yet, every single one of us had the same thought on our minds. *What kind of moron chooses speculative assessments over the first-person experience of someone who spent years on this planet? Oh. Yeah. A Samaari.*

Jella Duverii was not a Marine. She did not even try to act like there was nothing wrong with Briggund's decision. "Seriously? He doesn't want my help? What the hell am I doing here then, Captain? You think I survived a dropship crash and a speed crawl through giant grub-infested quicksand just to go on a long walk with the Marines?"

Mardona shrugged. "I consider this a rather positive development. It means that Delta Company gets you all to ourselves. If I can get us back to our full contingent after replacing the troops we lost, I'll have three hundred and fifty Marines I need to get to Narman's Pyke. I want you at my side advising me of what I need to do to keep my people alive."

"That'd be my pleasure," Duverii told him, happy to have a reason to be on Kanaris once again.

"Good," Mardona said. "You can start now. What are we facing on that mountain we're marching up?"

Jella sighed. "To be honest, we don't know much about Kanaris below the first thermal layer. This's what we call 'The Hot Zone.' All I can tell you are things you've already figured out. It's really warm down here. If your exo-armor coolers fail, you're a goner. Especially if it stops raining. Even lying in the shade, you're likely to die of hyperthermia. My advice is to travel at night when the temperatures are cooler."

"Briggund's already ordered us to move during daylight."

Jella sighed again. "Alright. The other thing I have to say is that Kanaris is a wet planet, and the Hot Zone is the wettest part of it. It gets a little better once you get above the first cloud line, but down here, rain is constant. Between the precipitation, the humidity, and our sweat, we're always soaked. Dry is a relative term on this rock. It only means 'less wet.' It's a major annoyance in Narman's Pyke, but down here, it's dangerous. It'll rot your clothes, your equipment, your body, and your mind. We need to push ourselves to get out of the Hot Zone as fast as we can, and we need to take advantage of every break in the rain to dry our clothes and equipment out."

"Noted," Mardona said, genuinely appreciative of the tip. "I'll pass that strategy up the chain. What else do you know about things down here? What about the life forms?"

Jella shook her head. "Of those we know next to nothing. Everything looks terrifying down here, but make sure no one panics and shoots something unless it's actively attacking you. Remember, on Kanaris, *we're* the aliens. A lot of the animals we'll come across have never seen anything like us before. They're going to be curious.

"We don't want to make enemies of things we don't understand. Some creatures, such as the quarakai, live in large groups numbering in the hundreds. Generally speaking, only one of them will approach to see if we're friend or foe. If we hurt them, they'll attack in force. They're no match for our weaponry, but they're big, brawny, and hard to put down. We'll take unnecessary casualties fighting them off."

Our captain nodded in agreement. "We're too undermanned to afford *any* casualties, let alone ones inflicted by poor trigger discipline. I'll make sure that the other companies get the word on this. Anything else?"

"Yeah," Jella answered. "Kanarisian predators are masters at camouflage. Pay attention to the creatures you see, but the ones you don't are the biggest danger.

"Also, remember that photosynthesis requires sunlight. At these lower altitudes, rays of light have to penetrate three layers of clouds to reach us. That's why it appears so dim around here. Beware of green vegetation on the ground. Plants living in darkness do not feed by the usual means. They sting, and their venom kills almost instantly so your decaying body can provide nutrients to their system of shallow roots."

"Holy shit," Mardona gasped.

"Yeah," our guide mused. "What little we know about the stuff down here is pretty nasty. I'm willing to wager that the shit we don't know about is probably even worse."

•• ◄◦► ● ◄◦► ••

CHAPTER 8

J ella Duverii caught me typing furiously onto my tablet after leaving our
briefing with Captain Mardona. "What are you doing now?" she asked.

"Trying to find a surviving armorer," I told her. The primary job of a Space
Corps armorer was to maintain and repair our complex exo-systems. They
were intellectual commandos with a highly technical skillset. The only Marine
more expensive to train was a Citadel cadet. By the time they reached the
fleet, armorers were not only proficient in repairing our shells, they were
technological warfare experts as well.

Unfortunately, what our armorers possessed in raw mental horsepower, they
often lacked in physical prowess. Every one of them that tried to crawl over
the mud pits died. Many others ended up as eel food, never breaking out of
Wasp-Three. Those that had were a prized commodity.

My tablet pinged the location of Sergeant Dimitri Naktada and led us a
quarter kilometer down the tree line, where we found the man alone, staring
into the jungle. "Why aren't you with your squad?" I asked him after introducing
myself.

With a pained look on his face, Naktada answered, "They're gone. Our
compartment flooded quick after we crashed. Most of my platoon tried to swim
to safety, not realizing what was in the water. Three of us climbed across the
ceiling supports to get out. One of the guys lost his grip and fell to his death.
The wind got the other as soon as she stepped outside and blew her down the
beach. I'm all that's left."

"I'm sorry to hear that," I said as sympathetically as I could. Inside, I was
jumping for joy. I had found an orphaned armorer in the wild. "I sure could use
you if you need a new home."

Naktada looked at the insignia on my chest. "You an academy Marine?"

I nodded.

"You the guy that snuffed out Gori Dravidas?"

I nodded again. As much as I loathed being reminded of that, I appreciated the leverage it sometimes gave me.

The armorer looked impressed. "Well, if you were tough enough to kill that son-of-a-bitch and survive that crash, I figure my odds are better with you than with most."

Grinning, I reached out and shook Naktada's hand. "Then welcome aboard. I already have an urgent job for you. Can you recover personal recorder data?"

Naktada shrugged. "Depends what happened to it. You accidentally delete it?"

"No."

"You sure?" Naktada asked. "People do it all the time."

I pointed at Jella. "Mine and hers disappeared at the same time. I doubt both of us screwed up."

The armorer nodded in agreement. "Yeah, that'd be kind of a stretch." Reaching behind his back, Naktada detached a small diagnostic module from the side of his pack. He then pulled a length of cable from the device and plugged it into a port near my neck. Using his thumbs, Naktada started navigating through the analytic programs on his equipment. As he ran his diagnostics, he glanced over my armor. "Nice shell. You customized it."

I nodded. "Yeah, it was an academy project."

Naktada reached down and lifted my hands. "Your gloves are attached and wired to your forearm guards. Why?"

"To keep them from flying off."

Turning my mitt over to inspect the inside of my glove, the armorer noted the metal ring stitched below the palm. "What's that?"

I blushed a little. "A magnet."

"For what?"

I snapped my wrist to turn the device on, then pointed the ring at the sidearm hanging off my hip. In an instant, the weapon burst out of its holster and flew into my hand.

Naktada laughed. "Neat trick."

"Yeah, that's about the only practical purpose I could come up with for it," I admitted. "It took a lot of practice, not to mention a few broken fingers, to learn how to do that. I don't show it to too many people because it hurts like hell. Not to mention, when I turn my hand upside down, the magnetic polarity reverses and will eject the damned thing like it was fired from a cannon. I accidentally launched my pistol a quarter kilometer once."

Despite lacking any appreciable purpose, my modification seemed to impress my new armorer. "I'm sure you'll eventually figure out what to do with it." Changing topics back to the task at hand, he asked, "What data are you looking for here?"

"The video read during the crash." A few seconds after I said that, an alarm went off on Naktada's diagnostic. He squinted at his monitor in surprise, then unplugged it from me.

Before I could ask what happened, the sergeant was already hooking up to Jella's breastplate. Almost instantly, he got the same result. "That was easy," he said with a shrug. "The video's gone. Completely. And your storage disk has been physically damaged. There's no mystery here. It's been erased using a wiping program we usually don't see outside the intel community. This is spook stuff."

"Can you recover it?" I asked.

Naktada looked at me with a hint of curiosity on his face. "You know, most people would be surprised if someone with Section 615 connections took a personal interest in their data cache. You look like you were expecting it."

"I was," I assured him. "Again, can you recover it?"

Shaking his head, Naktada said, "There's nothing to recover. The partition this stuff was stored behind has been erased and physically burned. The wiping protocol then followed the path of that data to track down where else it was stored and burned that, too. Your video no longer exists. What did you two see?"

"What happened to *Wasp-One* and *Wasp-Two*," I said.

"How did you see that from the staging bay?"

"We weren't in the staging bay," Jella told him. "We were in the cockpit."

Naktada let that sink in. "Do I want to know what happened to those dropships?"

"Probably not," I told him. "Is there any other place that video could have gone where it could be pulled and sent to the Expeditionary Commander on the *Nebulan Phoenix*?"

The armorer sighed nervously. "The better question is, if there was, do I want to get it? If I somehow managed that, would I have a 615 agent sneaking up behind me somewhere to punch a knife through the base of my skull?"

"That'd be a better fate than if you can't get it," I said.

Naktada scoffed. "How do you figure?"

"The general staff thinks our dropships were shot down. We know they weren't. Because the command doesn't want to risk any more Wasps, they've ordered us to march all the way to Narman's Pyke without vehicles, air support, medevac, or resupply."

Naktada looked dauntingly at the jungle. "How far away is Narman's Pyke?"

"More than two hundred kilometers," Jella told him.

The armorer whistled and nodded his head solemnly. He then pulled out a pair of optics and passed them to me. Pointing at the trees, he said, "See that opening in the foliage up there about thirty meters off the ground? Look through that and focus further into the canopy, maybe ten meters. Tell me what you see."

It took me a while to find it, but I eventually came across what looked to be three large, writhing silk cocoons suspended off of a high branch. "The white things? Is that what you're talking about?"

"Yep," Naktada answered. "Those were Marines last night. Now they're larvae meat. If you watch long enough, you'll see a giant maggot, about the size of your forearm, fall out of one of them after it's had its fill. One of the Marines was still moving when I got here. That shit was eating her alive."

Jella grabbed the optical amplifiers to see for herself. "Holy fuck," she gasped.

"Exactly," Naktada agreed. "I'm not hiking two hundred clicks through that shit without support. I'll shoot myself before I end up like those bastards."

The armorer drew in a deep breath of air. "Now, whoever set that wiping program off probably has a copy of whatever video they destroyed on their personal system drive."

"Is that part of the wiping program?" I asked.

Naktada shook his head. "No. It's human nature. If someone erased your video, it's because they're trying to protect someone. They'll want to show it to whoever they're protecting to say, 'Hey, look what I saved you from.' The only exception to that rule is if the person who erased the video is protecting themselves."

"So, if you know who erased it, you'll know how to get it?" I was getting hopeful. I had a pretty good idea who was behind our missing data.

"Yes and no," the armorer told me. "The person who activated this software is in intelligence. Hacking into an intelligence asset is a capital crime. Whether I'm right or wrong, I'll be executed for it. I'm not going there."

Judging by the tone of Naktada's voice, I suspected that there were other options. "Is there somewhere you *can* go?"

The armorer nodded. "What you saw, you saw from the cockpit, right?"

"Yes," Jella and I both said simultaneously.

"Then there are recordings of what happened there. Those are backed up in several areas of the ship."

Naktada turned and waved his hand at the wreckage on the beach. "The spook that erased your video has probably done the same thing to the black box in the command center. If the dropship were whole, that'd be plenty good enough. *Wasp-Three* is broken up pretty bad, though. I can guarantee most of the remote servers have been physically severed from the cockpit. That means they're sitting there without power or any network connections to the black box. If I can get one of them connected to a power source, I should be able to find and pull the cockpit video."

I grinned. We were getting somewhere. "How long is that going to take you?"

Naktada shrugged. "I honestly don't know. It depends on whether I find a mainframe in good shape and how easily I can get a power source to it. And if I can avoid getting killed by some alien carnivore lurking in one of the voids. It could take days. Weeks. Months."

I shook my head. "That's not going to work. You need to think in terms of minutes. Hours at best."

The tech wizard scoffed. "That's impossible."

"No, it's improbable," I countered. "It's only impossible if you don't try."

Naktada chuckled nervously. "You going to be able to give me a hand in there?"

"No," I told him. "Your best backup in that place is anonymity."

Naktada frowned. "Cadet, there's stuff I'll need to do in there that I can't do myself. I'm going to need some cavalry to call when I run into a show-stopper."

I nodded and made up a new communications circuit on my forearm console. "If you need me, try to get close enough to punch through this Harnillium whine and ring me up."

Almost immediately, Naktada deleted the channel I created and started forming another. "There are dozens of fully equipped Marine corpses sticking out of the mud all the way from our camp to the dropship. There's enough juice in their batteries to last weeks. I'm configuring them as signal relay stations. That way, I should be able to reach you as long as you're less than four clicks deep into the jungle. I'm also separating it from your PCR recorders. That'll keep our conversations out of any archive storage loop. Whatever we say will evaporate into the ether the instant we say it."

"You can manipulate the feed like that?" I asked.

The armorer smirked. "I can pretty much make the system do anything I want. Nobody gets any information that an armorer doesn't want them to have."

I made a mental note of that. It was a good thing to know.

Naktada pulled out his diagnostic module again and plugged it into my exo-armor. "What're you doing now?" I asked him.

"Pumping your system with the same wiping program that deleted your video to erase any evidence the three of us ever met."

Unable to help myself, I smiled. "So you're going to do this?"

Naktada grinned back. "Or die trying."

The armorer turned his head and looked apprehensively at the trees behind us. "And I mean that quite literally. I am NOT hiking through that jungle all the way to Narman's Pyke. The fuckers are going to have to kill me right here before I step a hundred meters into that shit."

•• ‹•› ● ‹•› ••

CHAPTER 9

When all was said and done, we discovered my platoon had suffered greatly. Second Squad had completely perished in the crash. Of Third Squad, Harlund Merik and the M2117 Machine Gunner, Lance Corporal Maiq Reino, were the only two combat Marines left. The others were laborers. Harlund found himself in charge of two Class Zero prisoners and a pair of Class Ones. The Zeros could not carry weapons under any circumstances. The Ones could be armed only as a last resort. Merik no longer led an infantry unit. He was in charge of a working party.

First Squad fared the best, losing only their sniper and a single rifleman. Fourth, the squad I was attached to, was about half-strength. The entire battalion was in similar disarray, so our first order of business was to reorganize. We pulled Marines from units without officers and used them to fill empty slots on our roster.

Despite the disciplinary action hanging over my head for returning to *Wasp-Three* against Gunny Malcolm's orders, he put me in charge of Third Squad with Harlund Merik as my assistant.

"With the corporal's combat experience," I said to Gunny after learning of my assignment. "Don't you think it would make more sense to promote Merik to sergeant and put him in charge of me?"

Malcolm sighed in annoyance. It was not just me getting on his nerves. His shaking hands suggested withdrawal played a part in shortening his temper as well. I wondered if he brought anything with him to take the edge off his nightmares while we were deployed.

"No doubt, you could learn a lot from Merik," the gunnery sergeant snarled while driving his finger into my chest. "Like how to do whatever the fuck I tell you to. Merik's a man of action, though. He's a killer. He always needs to be in the thick of the fighting. He's unparalleled in executing orders, but not so much in giving them."

"You can groom him."

Gunny Malcolm nodded. "I could. But as a blooded Academy grad, the Corps insists I groom you instead. You know, as part of that, I need to open your eyes a little bit about the situation we're in right now. Captain Briggund is in charge of our battalion. You realize that, right?"

I nodded.

"And you realize that he's a Samaari? From a well-heeled family? His people aren't quite as high and mighty as that fuck you claim crashed *Wasp-Two*, but they're high enough to get him an officer's commission in the Corps."

"Yeah, Gunny. I gathered that."

"Okay," Malcolm said as he stretched to get a kink out of his shoulder. He had a few pieces of Ghuldari steel in there that regularly tormented him. "Let me tell you something about these Sammy fuckers. I've been doing this shit for about as long as you've been alive. I've seen what makes these bastards tick. People like this Sirrah family run their planets like a cult. They try to portray themselves as almost god-like to their people back home. They're all rich. They're all heroic. They're all geniuses. They're infallible. Anyone with the nerve to say otherwise is treasonous, jealous, brainwashed, or just plain evil."

Gunny pointed his finger at his temple. "It's something the Sammy elite have done for so long that they actually believe their own bullshit. They honestly think they're incapable of fucking up, despite being notoriously unreliable on the battlefield. They see themselves as humanity's saviors, the only ones capable of protecting the League from the Ghuldari menace."

Malcolm paused to look me in the eye. "To people like Captain Briggund, reporting that a Sammy highborn did something like chicken out of a landing drop just will not compute. It's inconceivable. In their minds, there is no way that fuckstick died a coward. He *has* to be the hero. Even if Briggund saw this punk destroy four-thousand Marines and two dropships with his own eyes and reported it precisely the way it happened, no one back on the Guild planets would ever believe him. He'd be ostracized, branded a traitor, and the full might of the Sirrah family's wealth, power, and influence would be brought to bear against Briggund's people. It would ruin him. If Briggund plays ball, though, and builds their pansy shitstain up, *he'll* be the hero. Not to mention rewarded handsomely."

"That's insane," I told Gunny. "I'm not Samaari, though. I don't have any loyalties to the Guilds. My allegiance is to the League."

"Thanks to the money they pump into it," Malcolm interrupted. "The League *is* the Guild now. Look, Tauk, what I'm trying to tell you is that we've got a Sammy at the helm. It doesn't matter what you saw or heard in that cockpit. Briggund will never admit that a Sirrah man caused us to lose two dropships all by himself. That's simply not a narrative he can kick up the chain. Because of that, we're going to walk up that hill come hell or high water without any support. Forcing the issue's going to do us more harm than good."

"So what am I supposed to do? Sit on this?"

"For now, yes," Malcolm advised. "If you run afoul of the Sammy machine, they'll crush you. If you thought Gori Dravidas was deadly, well, at least he'd come at you head-on. Face-to-face. Like a man. Those cowardly fucks on high? They ain't got the balls to look you in the eye when they murder your ass. You'll never know they were there until you pull the blade from your back."

Gunny let out a sigh and placed his trembling hand on my shoulder. I got the feeling he did that more to camouflage his shakes than as an attempt to keep me focused. "Keep this shit about Sirrah to yourself until we have an opportunity to tell it to someone who can give it legs. Mardona's a good man. He'll force it when it'll not be a colossal waste of effort. Until then, focus on keeping our guide alive and getting your Marines to Narman's Pyke. Start by going to what's left of Beta Company and filling those open slots of yours."

"Aye aye, Gunny." Believing our conversation was over, I turned away and started walking to where I last saw the battalion's orphans marshaling.

"You better pick up your pace!" Malcolm called out after me. "If you don't hurry, you'll get stuck with all the goddamn rejects!"

●●◄●►◉◄●►●●

I was not fast enough. By the time I got to where our leaderless survivors had mustered, the other units had already acquired the Marines that were worth anything. The acting company sergeant was working hard to inflict the leftovers upon the rest of us.

Among them was an immense private from Gorsu Qat named Akkam Lumuk. Lumuk's single stripe was outlined in orange, indicating he was what the Corps classified as an ECREC (INVOL). He was an Economic Recruit (Involuntary). That meant the Marine was a conscript, pressed into the military from the most impoverished rungs of League society.

Among our poorer planets, like Gorsu Qat, there was little for the masses to do but toil, sweat, starve, and reproduce. Consequently, the destitute needed to be periodically culled, so the Marines would collect as many as they could and kill them off fighting on far-flung alien planets. That sounded cold, and it was, but it beat leaving them to fester at home until they outgrew their planet's resources and ended up slaughtered while trying to bite the only hand willing to feed them on a shit hole like Gorsu Qat.

I understood why the government would want a man like Akkam Lumuk out of their jurisdiction. At nearly two meters in height, I was considered tall for a Marine. I did not even come up to Lumuk's chin. The man was a giant, and though he was not obscenely musclebound, he might have been the strongest Marine of the entire Expeditionary Force. He was a fearsome-looking specimen.

With skin as black as night and a bald head full of battle scars, I figured Lumuk to be a hardened veteran of the incessant gang fighting for which his home planet was famous. The man had to have been a killer. I grabbed the guy the moment I laid eyes on him.

One of the bruin's comrades shook his head in disgust as I turned to walk away with my prize. "Seriously?" the Marine spat. "You think that goon's a better Marine than me?"

The rifleman questioning my judgment was the Yin to Lumuk's Yang. He was short, fair-skinned, and while my new bruiser appeared to be a man of few words, the PFC looked like someone who did not know when to shut up. His accent dripped with the lazy vowels of Samaar Ghun, and his rank was trimmed in white. He was a CITREC, a Citizen Recruit. A patriot. He signed up for the Corps driven by ideology and a sense of duty.

"I don't know how good of a Marine Private Lumuk is," I told the pint-sized rifleman. "But he looks like he could lift an ox."

"I'll wager ten credits he can't spell it, though."

I glanced up at Lumuk, expecting him to respond to the insult, but he did no such thing. He just stood there, staring impassively at the little loudmouth. Suspecting the private might be hesitant to get into a fight seconds after meeting his new squad leader, I spoke up for him. "If I were you, I'd watch my tongue before I turn this monster loose on your midget ass."

The tiny man grinned. "Go ahead. I dare you."

I was on the verge of accepting the infantryman's challenge when I noticed Lumuk quaking in his boots. He seemed terrified of the PFC, which certainly surprised me. "Sergeant!" I called out to the NCO facilitating the reassignments. "What's the major malfunction on these two clowns?"

The staff sergeant, an unusually abrasive man named Kyker, laughed. "You ain't heard about Lumuk?"

I shook my head. "No, I got here just before we deployed."

"Well," the sergeant told me. "He might be the biggest man on the *Nebulan Phoenix*, but he's about as simple and scared as they come."

Looking up at my new soldier, I asked, "I think that man's calling you a coward, Lumuk. You afraid to fight?"

The giant did not deny it. In a low, lumbering voice, he answered, "I don't wanna hurt nobody, sir."

I dropped my face into my hand and shook my head. "I'm not an officer yet, Marine. Don't call me, 'sir.' Call me 'Cadet Tauk.' And what do you mean you don't want to hurt anybody? That's what we trained you to do! It's your job!"

"I didn't want to be..."

"What about the little guy?" I asked, interrupting the pathetic giant. "What's his story?"

"Ah!" Kyker said. "That's PFC Mazada Duum. He's a Sammy. The biggest thing about him is the chip on his shoulder. I will admit that he's freakishly accurate in throwing daggers, though. It's a cool trick but would be more useful in a circus than it is in combat."

Looking back at the short Samaari, I noticed he was equipped with two daggers, one sticking out of each boot. Most Marines only carried one.

"He'd probably be a decent warrior," Kyker continued. "If he spent half the time fighting the enemy as he does fighting his comrades."

"Great." Placing my hand upon Lumuk's spine, I nudged the big fellow back toward the sergeant. "I'll be returning this one."

The sergeant held up his tablet and showed it to me. "Too late. He's your problem now. So's the little guy. Congratulations."

"Wait! What? No! Look! Right now, my squad is a corporal, a machine gunner, and four IRREC laborers. I don't need someone else's problem children right now!"

"Then you should've gotten here earlier."

"I got here as soon as I..."

"Golgho! Stiid! Zeld!"

"Yes, Sergeant!" several troops called out from the crowd behind Kyker. Not a single one of them appeared combat proficient.

"Front and center! You now belong to Cadet Tauk! You're going to Delta Company!"

"Hey!" I protested as the summoned Marines broke formation to join me. "I need technical troops! Proven Ten-Percenters! Killers! I need a grenadier! I need a sniper and spotter team! A combat engineer...!"

"Don't we all? Naidoa! Faarhut! Gai! Loat!"

"You're not listening to me! I need a medic!"

"I got a medic. PFC Kalawezi! You're going with the cadet! Hurran! Briima! Reyn!"

I reached out and grabbed the sergeant by the collar. "Would you stop it?!? I told you I need..."

Kyker batted my arm away. "You need a lot of stuff that we just ain't got. You understand? There were supposed to be more than five thousand Marines landing at Narman's Pyke, Cadet Tauk. Three whole battalions equipped with light armor, artillery, stores, drones, fighter craft, and anti-air armament. We're left with less than a third of the personnel we were planning on for this mission and none of the heavy equipment. We're going up against whoever took that colony with whatever we can carry on our backs! Nobody's climbing up that mountain with what they want, Cadet. We're climbing it with what we got. Is that clear?"

After a long sigh of exasperation, I said, "Yeah, I guess so."

"Good. You're out of the Citadel, aren't you? An Academy Marine?"

I answered the sergeant with a single nod.

"Then you're already an expert grenadier, sniper, spotter, and sapper. You're a goddamn killing machine. Take what you know and use it to train your Marines. If anyone can mold this group into a bunch of killers, it's you."

"I don't have the time."

The sergeant shrugged. "Neither do I. Weir!"

"Yes, Sergeant!" another future corpse called out.

"You're with the cadet, too!" Turning back to me, the sergeant looked at the red hash marks on my shoulder. "The Citadel, huh?"

Letting out another sigh, I nodded my head. "Yeah." I had a pretty good idea what the sergeant's next question would be.

"You wouldn't happen to be the guy who killed Gori Dravidas, are you?"

Breaking eye contact to look at the ground, I answered, "Yeah. That's me."

The sergeant glanced at his tablet once more. "You're still short a convict laborer, aren't you?"

"Yeah, I believe so."

The sergeant grinned. "Well, then! Have I got something for you! Xi!"

Startled, a young woman stepped forward from the ranks. She was of medium height and shapely, which was unusual for a Class Zero convict. Zeros were slaves in all but name and were worked mercilessly. Even though they were on the same rations as the rest of us, their brutal working conditions tended to emaciate them. Even with her raven hair cropped close to her scalp and the dead look behind her eyes, Ritza Xi was an attractive woman. I suspected that the work she did for the Corps had little to do with manual labor.

"I was going to keep this one for myself," the sergeant confessed. "But considering what you did to that Dravidas monster, I'll let you keep her. You know, as long as I can visit every once in a while..."

Xi looked like she was in a daze. Her body was on Kanaris, but her mind seemed to be someplace light-years away. Having a pretty good idea of what she would have been subjected to back at the barracks, I could not help but feel sorry for her. "What'd she do?" I asked the sergeant.

"Bludgeoned her two daughters to death, then slit her husband's throat from ear-to-ear. The crime scene photos are in her file. They're pretty gruesome."

I grabbed my tablet and scanned the bar code on the convict's breastplate, downloading her records from the microchip embedded in her exo-armor. Kyker was not lying. What that woman did to her children was beyond comprehension. They had been beaten to a consistency approaching that of ground meat. Xi's husband, a huge, hulking man she could not have physically overpowered, got off easy. It looked as if she had murdered him in his sleep.

"Why?" I asked the little woman after closing her file. She did not answer. She just kept staring out into space with that deadpan, soulless expression on her face.

"Does it matter?" Kyker asked in return. "They're dead. There ain't no reason that could justify shit like that."

I nodded in agreement. "I guess you're right." Whatever sympathy I had for Xi evaporated the moment I saw those pictures. As far as I was concerned, the woman had not suffered enough.

Grabbing Xi by the collar, I tossed her in with the rest of my squad. She was no longer going to glide through her sentence on her back. She was going to pay for what she had done to her little girls.

●●‹●›‹●›‹●›●●

CHAPTER 10

"They're the best I could do," I told Corporal Merik after marching our new squad members back to our marshaling area. I was frustrated. Though I had yet to experience it in the real world, I was comfortable with the concept of combat. The Corps spent two decades making me a master of that. It was the administrative minutiae of leadership that gave me my very first pangs of inadequacy. I needed Marines capable of completing complex objectives. What I got were replacement troops that probably would not even survive the march to Narman's Pyke.

"There was no one to pick from," I complained. "The billeting sergeant was just throwing names at me." I paused to let out a long sigh. "I couldn't even force the issue as everyone I saw there looked just as pathetic as these people. I don't think there's a killer among them."

Harlund shrugged. "Well, Eamon, I hate to break it to you, but the galaxy isn't exactly teeming with all those black-haired, blue-eyed, fair-skinned, chiseled-jaw, master race types you grew up with in the Citadel." Waving his hand over the troops of our new squad standing at parade rest in the Kanarisian rain, he told me, "This is what we mere mortals look like. You didn't exactly hold your old squad in very high esteem, either."

"Compared to this group," I said. "My old squad looked like Section Kommandos." Section 615 was rumored to have the most elite Special Action Forces in the quadrant. I dreamed about joining them back when I wanted nothing more than to become the deadliest man in the galaxy. After my encounter with the Butcher of Deraghun, however, I was not even sure I wanted to be a Marine anymore.

I shook my head to get Gori Dravidas out of my mind. "You think they're going to make it up that mountain?" I asked Merik.

My corporal strolled closer to our new troops and nodded his head. "Maybe. To be honest, these Marines don't look all that different than the troops I fought alongside on Sivma-11."

"You fought the Ghuldari?" asked Daino Faarhut, one of our new men.

"Was I talking to you, Lance Corporal?" Merik snapped. "Huh? Did I address you?"

"No, Corporal."

"Then keep your goddamn trap closed until I tell you otherwise!"

Stepping closer to Private Lumuk, Harlund looked up and said, "Holy shit! You're a big fucker, ain't ya?"

"He's a big pussy," giggled Mazada Duum, who was standing beside the giant.

In one fluid motion, Harlund turned around and struck Duum so hard across the side of his head that his helmet flew off and landed at my feet. Duum himself spun into the mud. When he came to a stop, Harlund then launched his boot into the Marine's kidney, knocking the wind out of him. Though still gasping for air, Duum leapt back onto his feet with his fists up, ready to fend off Harlund's next attack.

"You raising your hands to me, Marine?" Merik barked.

Realizing that his stance could be construed as threatening a non-commissioned officer, Duum dropped his guard and stiffened to the position of attention. "No, Corporal."

"Do you want to raise your hands to me?"

Duum looked Merik right in the eye. "Boy, do I ever."

Harlund grinned and stepped into Duum's personal space. "Then why don't you?"

"I don't want to go to the brig."

Merik busted out into laughter. "Brig? Brig? You see any fucking brig around here? We ain't got no brig, little man. If you wanna go toe-to-toe with me, I won't be putting you in no stockade. I'll put your midget ass into the fuckin' ground!"

Grabbing Duum by the collar, he dragged him to the formation and practically threw him back into the ranks. "To answer your question, Faarhut, yes. I fought the Ghuldari. I've been in direct combat, unconventional actions, surgical strikes, and a couple of different alien bug hunts. I'm nowhere near the toughest corporal in the Space Corps, but I'm confident I'm more than a match for any of you candy asses." For added effect, Harlund back-handed Duum across the jaw. "Especially you, Shorty."

The corporal kept his eyes locked on Duum while addressing the squad. "You Marines are going to be facing a lot of obstacles in your immediate future. You're going up against extreme heat. You're going up against constant rain. Judging by the look of this jungle, you're going to have to survive creatures you couldn't even begin to imagine yet! And, if you live through all that, you'll still have to face whatever destroyed that colony at Narman's Pyke. Hell, you even have to survive myself, Cadet Tauk, and Gunny Malcolm if you want to get off this rock alive."

Harlund paused for a moment and softened his voice. "Look, you've already got more enemies than you can handle right now. Don't waste your energy making more amongst yourselves. Duum, I suggest you take this opportunity to apologize to Private Lumuk before I tell him to tear you apart."

"I'd prefer to take my chances with the ape," Duum snarled.

My corporal flinched. He looked up at Lumuk, towering above him, then back down at the insolent Samaari. "You serious? You asking me to call a smoker between you and this guy?"

Duum grinned at Merik's suggestion. Smokers were a time-honored tradition in the Corps. The Marines figured that sixty seconds of hand-to-hand combat could work wonders to clear up whatever bad blood two adversaries might have shared between themselves. "Yeah. I'll take him," Duum said.

Tima Kalawezi, our new medic, broke formation. "Knock it off, Maz! Leave Akkam alone! He didn't do anything to you!"

Merik let her outburst go unpunished, turning his attention to Private Lumuk. "You want to have a go at this little shit, big guy?"

Lumuk turned a pained expression toward the corporal. "I don't want to hurt nobody."

"What?" Harlund asked, not quite able to believe his ears. He then turned around to look at me as, technically, I was the man in charge of the squad. "You got anything to say about this?"

I shrugged. "I'm kind of curious to see what these guys're made of. Let 'em have at it."

Lumuk shook his head. "I don't want to fight, Corporal! I don't wanna fight anybody!"

"Then what are you doing in my Corps?"

"They made me come here!" Lumuk bellowed as Duum began removing his armor. "I was workin' my farm with my mama on Gorsu Qat! The police grabbed me and told me since I ain't got no regular job, I hafta come into the Marines! But I had a job! I was working with my mama! I don't know how she

61

gonna..." Tears were welling up in Lumuk's eyes, threatening to stream down his face.

"Drop your armor, Private," Harlund said sympathetically.

"But I don't wanna fight nobody! I just want people to leave me alone!"

Merik lowered his voice and put his hand on Lumuk's bicep. The giant was too tall for the corporal to reach his shoulder. "The best way to do that is to teach this son-of-a-bitch a lesson. Show that Sammy you're not someone to be messed with. Hurt him, Marine. Knock his dick into the dirt. I'm rooting for you."

Lumuk inhaled deeply and held it, trying to collect himself. Then, nodding his head in resignation, he started removing his gear.

"Come on, man," Harlund prodded him. "You land one punch on that little shit, and you're going to knock him into next week. You got this."

"Yeah, Akkam!" shouted Borman Loat. "Knock that Sammy prick's block off."

"You can do this!" Talia Golgho added. "Kick his ass, Killer!"

Seeing his entire squad side with Lumuk enraged Duum. "You ungrateful little bitches," he seethed. "If it weren't for the Samaari Guild, you'd all be slaves of the Ghuldarians by now. Without our cash, you wouldn't be equipped with all that armor. You wouldn't have that state-of-the-art weaponry. You wouldn't be..."

"At war all the fucking time," spat Hektur Naidoa.

"We end up at war because those weak ass shitholes you all are from can't take care of themselves," Duum shot back. "Your own leaders call in the Marines because they can't even fight off a few bands of bandits."

"Those aren't 'our' leaders you're bailing out," argued Daiq Briima, a man with teeth dyed black as night for some unknown reason. His chevron was outlined in yellow. He was a REDREC, a Redeemable Recruit, most likely sentenced to the Corps for political re-education. "They're yours. They're all bought and paid for by the Guild to keep things running the way the Samaaris want them to. You want us to be grateful for that? Fuck you. We'll be grateful when you Sammy pricks start minding your own business."

"Zip it, Briima," Harlund warned. "Talk like that's probably what earned you your yellow."

I noted the exchange. It was no secret that no one liked Samaaris much. Still, I was shocked at how deep the animosity ran. It was not healthy. I needed my Marines united. We had to direct our hatred at our adversaries, not each other.

That said, Mazada Duum was going to make achieving unity very difficult. He embodied every stereotype the non-Guild planets had against the Samaaris.

He was chock full of arrogance and carried himself with an insufferable sense of superiority.

Being an enlisted man, Duum was a rarity in the Corps. Most Samaaris joined as officers. They were practically forced into service by the Guild to keep a finger on the pulse of the military.

Samaaris without the means to earn an officer's commission usually signed on to the Guild Militia, the Blueshirts. They provided industrial security, breaking up strikes and seeking retribution against their employees when productivity lagged. Men who joined the Blueshirts did not typically have the stomach for fighting people who shot back.

That did not apply to Mazada Duum, though. He was a raging asshole, but the man had heart. He was the only one of the new troops that left an impression on me. I hoped Lumuk did not hurt him too badly. I just needed him knocked off his high horse.

When Merik dismissed the squad from formation, they formed a ring around the two combatants. The commotion attracted the rest of the platoon's attention, and they walked over to see what was happening. Gunny Malcolm joined them.

"A smoker?!?" Malcolm snapped at me. "Now? In this heat? We got other shit to do here, Tauk!"

Gunny's words officially registered his disproval. His tone of voice hinted he was as game to see a good fight as the rest of us were. When Malcolm caught the size disparity between the two combatants, he whistled. "You trying to get the little one killed?"

"Killed?" I replied. "No. Just looking to change his attitude. The big guy could benefit from a little confidence boost, too."

"You better be ready to stop it if it gets out of hand," Gunny warned me. "We can't afford any more casualties."

"Aye aye."

"You two men ready?" Corporal Merik asked as our bare-knuckled gladiators put up their dukes.

"Yeah!" shouted Duum as he bounced up and down upon the balls of his feet. "Let's get it on!"

Lumuk said nothing. He just stared at the Samaari and shook. He reminded me of one of those ancient storybook elephants terrified into paralysis by the sight of mice.

Merik glanced over at our machine gunner. "Maiq! Keep time! On your mark! Get set! Go!"

"One thousand one!" shouted Lance Corporal Reino. "One thousand two! One thousand three!"

At first, Duum took a moment to see if Lumuk would advance. When he did not, the smaller fighter faked a jab at the behemoth. In response, Lumuk flinched and stumbled backward, nearly tripping over his own feet. After laughing at the big man's cowardice, Duum charged.

Lumuk tried to strike as his tormentor stepped within range but broadcast his intentions by pulling his elbow too far back to wind up the blow. Before the giant's arm was cocked, Duum swooped in and hit him twice in the gut. I doubted either of the Samaari's punches hurt the farmer from Gorsu Qat, but Lumuk cried out with each one anyway.

Knowing what was coming, Duum jumped back out of Lumuk's reach before our bruin swung. Predictably, the farmer caught nothing but air. The missed punch threw him off balance, allowing his opponent to take advantage of his instability. Duum ducked inside and jammed his boot behind Lumuk's right knee, causing the joint to buckle. Our homegrown Goliath fell crashing into the mud, and before Lumuk could react, Duum savagely kicked him twice in the ear.

"Ouch!" Gunny Malcolm blurted out.

I had a similar reaction. "The little guy's better than I thought."

"Not necessarily," Gunny said. "It's more like the big guy's just awful."

"One thousand twenty! One thousand twenty-one!"

Lumuk reached out to grab his assailant, but Duum was way out of his reach. Failing that, the giant rolled over to lift himself up and get back in the fight. As soon as the Samaari saw all four of the big man's limbs anchored to the ground, however, he struck again. Planting a devastating kick to Lumuk's mouth, Duum split the dirt farmer's lips wide open. He then landed several blows to the back of Lumuk's head that probably hurt the little Marine's hands more than they did his adversary's skull.

Screaming out in fear and frustration, Lumuk lifted his arm and scooped Duum's legs out from beneath him. The little man nearly spun a full hundred and eighty degrees and landed on his head damn near hard enough to break his neck.

"One thousand thirty-eight! One thousand thirty-nine!"

Duum was stunned and disoriented. Hoping to take advantage of the shift in momentum, Lumuk clasped his hands together, lifted his arms over his head, and swung them down on a trajectory aiming to crush the little man's testicles.

With strength born of nothing but pure panic, Duum sent his right leg kicking blindly upward, smashing Lumuk's nose. I heard it break.

The giant bellowed out in agony, clutching his face with both hands while blood streamed out from between his fingers. Duum followed up by leaping to his feet and launching his fist into Lumuk's throat, knocking his opponent onto his back again, struggling to breathe. Knowing the giant was helpless now, the Samaari jumped onto the farmer's chest to throttle him repeatedly about the face with everything he had.

Reino stopped counting as the crowd fell silent. Merik ran in to break up the fight, grabbing Duum by the scruff of the neck and dragging him off his victim. The Samaari, buoyed by his victory, jumped up and down, cheering. No one else joined him.

"What?" Duum asked, glaring at his squadmates. "I won! That bastard was three times my size, and I still beat his ass! I don't get a 'Good job?' No, 'Congratulations,' either? You people are fucking pathetic! Do you all seriously hate me that much just because I'm from a Guild planet? Huh? You can't stand me because the place I grew up in wasn't as miserable as yours? Is that it?"

Frustrated, Duum kicked the ground, spraying mud toward his comrades. "I've got news for you! I didn't grow up with no silver spoon in my mouth either! I ain't no spoiled rich kid! I had to work and fight for everything I got, just like you did! I'm here for the same reasons you are!"

"No, you're not," Hektur Naidoa said as he craned his head to count all the white-lined chevrons around him. "Of the twenty-two of us in this squad, only four volunteered for this shit. You chose to be here, Maz. We didn't."

Dismissively waving Naidoa off, Duum sidestepped toward Abel Weir, another voluntary enlistee. "What's *your* problem? Huh? What do you have against me?"

Weir shrugged. He then pointed his chin at Lumuk, who was still on the ground being attended to by our medic. "I don't know. What'd you have against that guy? What'd he do to you to deserve that?"

Duum stammered for an answer. Unable to come up with one to contradict the fact that he was just a dick, he threw his chest out toward Weir and said, "Maybe I should have challenged you."

Weir started to unbuckle his armor. "Yeah. Maybe you should have. If you want to prove you're such a tough guy, try pulling your shit on someone who knows how to fight back."

My squad's new problem child planted both of his palms into Weir's chest and shoved him backward. Weir responded with a right hook that landed just beneath Duum's eye. Before the two men could really start pummeling each other, the rest of the squad rushed in to pull them apart.

"Hey!" I yelled as I stepped between the two Marines. "Stop it! The smoker's over! You two walk it off and..."

"What the hell's going on here?!?" shouted Lieutenant Thyster as he ripped his way through the commotion. When he saw Lumuk lying in the mud and Duum out of uniform, he quickly figured it out. Catching Malcolm among the spectators enraged him even more. "Are you kidding me, Gunny? A smoker?!? NOW?!? Have you lost your mind?!?"

"He came here to break it up, sir," I said. Technically that was the truth, though we all knew Malcolm's heart was not really into it. "This was me. These two needed to clear the air between them."

Thyster grabbed me by the collar and dragged me away from the rest of the troops. I was not an officer yet, but I would be soon. That afforded me the luxury of not being screamed at in front of the enlisted Marines.

"The Citadel may be without parallel in training killers," the lieutenant snarled at me. "But they've got a lot to learn about making leaders! Do you think you didn't get into enough trouble yesterday disobeying Gunny and abandoning our guide?"

I got the impression that my platoon leader did not really want an answer to that question, so I stayed quiet.

"We got shit to do! We need every Marine we got to do it! EVERY Marine! We can't let them go about fucking each other up for your entertainment! Get your squad under control and into platoon formation! I mean it! We're marching them back to *Wasp Three* to load up what we can, then starting our hike to Narman's Pyke! You got that?!?"

"Aye aye, sir!"

"Good! Now get the hell out of my sight!" Looking past me, Thyster saw his platoon sergeant trying to sneak away. "Gunny! Get over here!" I could tell by the lieutenant's face that Malcolm would catch far more hell about the smoker than I did.

"Sorry, Gunny," I said to him as we passed each other. "I tried to take the heat."

Malcolm shrugged. "No biggie. I've got too much rank to be flogged. He's just going to yell at me."

"You going to be alright?"

Gunny scoffed. "Of course, I'll be alright. I've been getting yelled at by officers for more than twenty years!"

As the sergeant wandered off, I wondered if I would be lucky enough to get away with disobeying Gunny's order with a simple tongue lashing. I highly doubted it.

Approaching my squad, I ordered my troops back into formation. "Party's over, Marines! Grab your shit and line up with the rest of the platoon! Move it!"

While my squad collected their equipment and sauntered off in the same direction our lieutenant went, Harlund Merik stood up to face me.

"Is Lumuk going to be alright?" I asked him.

My corporal nodded. "Yeah, the medic put his nose back in place and stitched his lip. He was a mouth-breather already, so he'll be fine. I'm going to work on toughening him up. The next time those two face off, I'm going to make sure..."

"Hey, Harlund," I interrupted. "I wouldn't get too attached to that one. We got a very dangerous walk ahead of us. I honestly don't think he's going to make it."

Merik grinned and threw his thumb over his shoulder at Mazada Duum. He was sitting by himself in the mud, putting his armor back on without any help from his squad. "I'll wager you ten credits that Lumuk lasts longer than the Sammy does. That guy's probably hated more by his allies than he is by the enemy."

I let out a sigh. "You know, growing up in the Citadel, I've been somewhat isolated from the real world. This shit between the Samaaris and everyone else, is it this bad in the civilian sector?"

Harlund laughed. "Actually, it's even worse. You know, Eamon, I don't envy the position you're in right now."

"Why's that?"

"Well, my man, you've got, what? Twenty or thirty years left in the Marines? If you survive whatever it is we're up against here and make it through your rotation as a platoon leader, you're going to have to make a choice one day whether you're going to kill people like that prick Mazada Duum over there, or people like me."

Shaking my head, I said, "I can't pick sides in an internal conflict, Harlund. My loyalties lie with the League, not with any of the individual planetary systems it's composed of."

Harlund bunched up his fist and pushed it against my chest, giving me a little nudge. "Eamon, the Samaari Guild practically created the League to rubber-stamp its economic initiatives. And mark my words; they're going to be the ones that end up destroying it. It's coming, man. Sooner, rather than later."

"You think we're headed for civil war? Seriously? What'll *you* do if that happens?"

Merik shrugged. "Avoid it. My hitch is up. This is my last deployment. When this shit's all over, I'm going to find some world on the edge of the quadrant and live out the rest of my days in peace. I've been killing things for more than five years now. I think I've more than earned the right to be left alone for a little while."

•●‹●›●‹●›●•

CHAPTER 11

I t took a day to get what was left of the battalion reorganized into an effective fighting force. By the time we figured out who was going where, we were nearly out of daylight. To avoid setting out in the dark, the decision was made to rest for one more night and begin our march to Narman's Pyke the following day.

Once everyone was settled in, I roamed out of earshot and checked the link to my new armorer. "Hey, Naktada," I softly said into my mouthpiece. "You read me?"

After a few seconds of Harnillium whine, I heard him respond, "I'm here."

"How's it going?" I asked.

"Just like I said it would," Naktada told me. "I can't even find a fucking power source. Passageways are blocked. Many of the storerooms are underwater, and there're scavenger parties patrolling all over the place looking for supplies to haul back to camp. It's a bitch trying to avoid them. There's also still alien shit in here. The critters may be small, but they sure sound hungry."

I sighed and dropped my head. "Naktada, I need a no-bullshit assessment. We're heading out in the morning. Can you pull this off by then?"

"Not a chance," Naktada said. "I need a power generator to turn on a directory module to track down the servers. I haven't even accomplished that yet."

My shoulders slumped. "Fine. Get out of there and rejoin us."

"Nope. Can't do that," Naktada told me.

"What?"

"I'm not going anywhere." I could hear the stress in my armorer's voice. "There's shit crawling around all over this ship, and it's getting active now that the sun's gone down. I'm in a safe place now. A place that doesn't smell like rotting corpses and impending doom. I'm staying right fucking here."

69

I clenched my teeth. "Are you okay? Do you need me to come get you?"

"No," Naktada said.

"Are you sure?"

There was a pause before my armorer came on line again. "Yeah, I'm sure."

I sighed into my mouthpiece. "Hey, Naktada. I'm sorry, man. I didn't mean to strand you out there."

"Don't sweat it," my armorer reassured me. "I'm surrounded by four steel walls. I'm probably safer than you are right now. And even if I'm not, it's no big deal. Like I told you before, I ain't going into that jungle. I'm too lazy to walk two hundred kilometers to die. If this planet's going to kill me, it'll have to do me in right fucking here."

●●◄●► ● ◄●► ●●

As soon as we woke up the following day, Jella and I stepped away from the camp to raise Naktada again. He would not answer, but he keyed his microphone so I could hear what was happening around him. It sounded like he was surrounded by Marines scouring the wreckage for supplies.

"Okay," I said softly, keeping my voice low to avoid giving his position away. "Sergeant, you need to get out of there. We're leaving soon. If you don't catch up, you're going to be left behind. If you understand that, click your transmitter once for 'yes' and twice for 'no.'"

I heard Naktada click the transmitter one time. Right after he did so, I saw a Self-Propelled Stretcher amble past, loaded with crates instead of people.

"Are you coming out?"

There were a few moments of Harnillium whine in my earpiece before I heard my armorer click twice.

"Shit," I sighed. "Naktada, are you in danger?" While waiting for his response, I saw another SPS pass us by carrying equipment. Craning my head to look further down the trail towards the beach, I saw three more. None were bearing patients.

Finally, I heard Naktada click the transmitter once. The background noise no longer carried human voices, though. It broadcast my armorer's heavy breathing. "Are you in danger because of the Marines?"

Naktada clicked twice for "no."

"From something else?"

"Click."

Jella grabbed my forearm and pulled up Naktada's vital signs. "Eamon, his heart's racing at a hundred and forty beats a minute. He's terrified."

I cursed. "Hold tight, Naktada. I'm coming for you."

"Click-click!" That was "no."

"We gotta get him," Duverii begged me. "We can't just leave him there!"

"You're not going anywhere," I told her. "But you're right." I patched over to my squad network. "Merik! Merik! This is Tauk! Do you copy?"

"No!" Naktada broke in. He was out of breath and sounded like he was running. "I was hiding from the Marines! When they left, I tried to sneak out behind them! I stumbled into...stumbled into..."

The line went quiet for a moment, just long enough for me to glance at my system display and note that my new armorer's heart rate was now up to one sixty. His blood pressure was dangerously elevated as well. *The man's going to have a stroke.*

"Stumbled onto what?!?" I shouted.

"I don't know what the fuck it is! I just...!"

"Merik here," Harlund answered, cutting Naktada off. "Go ahead, Tauk."

"Stand by, Merik!" I snapped before muting the squad network. Turning back to my armorer, I yelled, "From what, Sergeant? From what?!?"

There was no answer.

"Sergeant! Naktada!" I tried once more. "Do you copy?!?"

Jella grabbed my forearm and checked the monitor. Naktada's heart had flatlined. His blood pressure was zero. "He's gone," she told me.

"Shit!" I exclaimed, taking a few urgent steps toward the beach. Staring at the wreckage of *Wasp-Three*, I felt a lump in my throat. *What the fuck was I thinking?!?*

The mission to recover the cockpit video had virtually no chance of success. Still, I wasted a resource on it that we could hardly afford to lose. I sent a man to his death for nothing.

"Are you okay?" Jella asked, sensing my distress.

"No," I growled. "My squad had an armorer. He showed every indication of being a good one, too! Now we're going up that mountain short a critical resource! Fuck!"

"That's what's bothering you?" Jella asked. "That you lost your armorer? Not that you lost a man? That seems very Samaari of you."

I sighed. "It's one and the same, Jella. I lost a man, yes. That's a tragedy. Because he was an armorer, I will probably lose even more. What happens if the cooler on Merik's exo-armor fails? Huh? Who's going to fix it to keep

71

him alive? What happens if we run into a Ghuldari ambush and Lumuk takes a few direct hits to the chest? Who'll get his shell back together so he survives a fourth?"

"Look, Jella," I tried to explain. "The truth is, on a personal level, I didn't know the sergeant very well. Of course, I'm sad about what happened to him, but in the same way I'm sad about the four thousand other people that died on the way down here."

"I see," the doctor said, though her tone indicated that she probably did not. "Are you going to get into trouble over this?"

I shook my head. "I doubt it. I never got around to scanning the chip in Naktada's shell to add him to my roster. He was never officially attached to me. And thanks to how he rigged the data protocols, there's no evidence that we ever even spoke."

I turned to glance over at *Wasp-Three* once more. "As far as the Corps is concerned, he'll probably be classified the same way as those three Marines in the cocoons we saw hanging from the treetops yesterday. He'll be MIA."

●●◄●►●◄●►●●

CHΛPTER 12

When I pulled Je'Sikka Albarn out of *Wasp-Three*, a sergeant told me there were not nearly enough motorized stretchers to accommodate all the casualties. Yet, while I stood on the trail trying to raise my armorer on the commlink, I noticed all the SPSs crawling past me that morning were loaded with cargo, not patients. Apparently searching for a new fight to take my mind off what I had done to Naktada, I started stomping toward our medical encampment.

"Where are you going?" asked Jella Duverii when she saw me marching toward the beach.

"To the medical camp."

"What for?"

"I think we're abandoning our wounded."

"What?!?" Jella gasped.

Knowing we were probably headed for a confrontation, our guide tapped her mic. "Corporal Merik! We're going to the medical staging area. You may want to join us."

It was not that Duverii felt threatened. It was just that my team's mission was now the same as mine. Jella did not want our officers showing up and wondering where her security detail was.

The medical encampment had been set up where the tree line met the beach. It was a basic shelter, consisting only of a few tarps staged alongside the fallen palm we cowered beside during the storm. This kept our wounded out of the rain but did little else. It did not even keep them dry since they were all lying on vinyl sheets laid directly atop the mud. Apparently, they did not even rate cots.

Marching past the hospital camp was a convoy of burdened IRREC laborers and SPSs laden with supplies, all fresh from the wreckage of *Wasp-Three*.

The ranking medical officer on station was a mere corporal named Kula Sabian. "What the hell's going on here? Why are the SPSs carrying gear instead of patients?" I asked her.

Sabian looked at my Citadel insignia and read the name stenciled across my chest. Her face instantly contorted into an expression of disgust and loathing. I suspected she recognized me not as the man who had slain Gori Dravidas, but as the cadet who murdered Vernor Blyte.

Suppressing her disdain, Sabian forced out an answer as my squad started showing up. "Commander's orders. They need supplies to secure Narman's Pyke. Not casualties. We're to camp here and await rescue after the colony's back in our hands."

"Narman's Pyke is a hundred and seventy kilometers away," Jella gasped. "It might take us a month to get there."

Sabian looked like she was keenly aware of that. "It's not my call, ma'am. Trust me."

Spotting Je'Sikka Albarn lying amidst the wounded, I walked over to our pilot and knelt beside her. "How are you doing?" I asked.

"I've been better," she slurred. Albarn looked a little feverish but was remarkably well for a woman with a broken back.

"Kalawezi!" I shouted.

"Yes, Cadet!" my medic responded.

"Warrant Officer Albarn here looks like she could use some help. What does she need?"

As my corpsman went to work on our pilot, I returned to Sabian. "It's against Corps regulations to abandon our wounded when not in direct combat, Corporal."

"Captain Briggund's leaving two medics and five riflemen here to guard them." Sabian's body language made it clear that she did not enjoy being so close to me.

"That's not nearly enough," I mused.

"Tell me about it."

"Cadet Tauk!" Kalawezi called out. "Albarn's got a pretty serious infection!"

Sabian craned her neck to look at the patient. She then nodded in agreement with my medic's diagnosis. "I gave her a regimen of G-Level antibiotics."

Jella looked at the medic in disbelief. "That'd be effective if we were still on Horfu. That stuff's worthless against the bugs they got here, though. She needs Paxilmiacin."

"I don't have any," the medic answered.

"What do you mean you don't have any?" Kalawezi barked. "That's the main anti-microbial that we loaded onto the dropships! If we don't have Paxilmiacin, even the blisters these Marines get are going to end up killing them!"

"You have Paxilmiacin, Tima," Sabian answered. "We don't. You're taking all that stuff with you. You're leaving us to make the best of what's left behind. Right now, we have G-Packs."

The train of SPSs crawling past us was nearing an end. Seeing that my last chance of taking Je'Sikka Albarn to Narman's Pyke might pass us by, I stopped one of them and checked its cargo. It was carrying socks, cookware, and flares. I unbuckled the load and kicked it to the side of the path before I redirected the vehicle toward Warrant Officer Albarn.

As I did this, I noticed a half dozen men who apparently missed the last SPS out. They were struggling to drag a large red box along the winding route around the mud traps. A trio of figures followed close behind them.

Pulling out my optics, I zoomed in on the stragglers and saw that two of them were our Battalion Commander, Captain Briggund, and his new Sergeant-Major, Antonin Horad. The third was another one of those rare Samaari enlisted men, Sergeant Raza Bhutaan.

Unlike our pampered Samaari officers, there was nothing dainty about Bhutaan. He had a reputation as a methodical sociopath. When Marines called each other 'killers,' it was usually a term of endearment. When they called Raza Bhutaan that, they were acknowledging his insatiable sadism.

It appeared that our battalion commander had tapped Bhutaan to be one of his praetorian bodyguards. That did not surprise me. The sergeant had a reputation for cruelty and carried out his orders without conscience, blurring the line between soldier and serial killer.

Turning back toward our pilot, I ripped the insignia off my armor and stuck it to Albarn's chest. "What's that?" she asked.

"My Citadel pin," I told her. "It's my official nomination for you to join the ranks of the Red Caste."

Before I could pull away, Albarn grabbed my hand. "The Red Caste? Why?"

"Because if it wasn't for you, we wouldn't be here," I answered. Turning back to Kalawezi, I said, "Get her buckled into that SPS and get her up the trail ASAP. Find her some of that stuff Dr. Duverii was talking about. That Paxa-whatever."

"Paxilmiacin."

"Yeah! That stuff! Go! And get some down here for these people, too!"

Sabian narrowed her eyes at me. "You trying to atone for what you did to Vernor?"

"I'm not trying to atone for anything."

No sooner had I turned my back on Sabian when Lieutenant Thyster's voice filled up my earpiece. "Tauk! Where the hell are you? They just wrapped up the salvage evolution. We're getting ready to move out!"

"Sir! I'm at the medical staging area. Captain Briggund's abandoning our wounded."

"What?!?" Thyster gasped. "He can't do that!"

Abandoning wounded Marines was strictly forbidden. It was a law that needed to be followed in both letter and spirit. Violating it was the way mutinies started, such as the Waimair Insurrection that nearly toppled the League two generations before me. The regulation requiring proper care of casualties was named after it. Briggund could illegally order us to leave our injured behind, but anyone following it would be court-martialed right alongside him.

This was serious business. Not only was Thyster coming to see for himself what was going on, he sent Gunny Malcolm to bring Captain Mardona down as well.

Unfortunately, it was our new sergeant-major who reached us first. "You need to get that Navy woman off that stretcher, Cadet," Horad said to me as he approached. "We need that SPS to transport some mission-critical gear to Narman's Pyke."

"I'm sorry, Sergeant Major," I told him. "We need to get this pilot up to the battalion medics before it's too late."

"Well, Cadet," Horad shot back. "Her mission ended when she drove our dropship into the beach. Ours is just beginning. If we don't get that box up that hill, it could put us all in jeopardy."

"What's in it?" I asked.

"None of your fucking business. Now, clear that SPS and let me get it back to pick up our load."

I pointed at the Citadel pin on the pilot's exo-armor. "Sergeant-Major, she's been nominated to the Red Caste. She's been reborn in blood. We can't leave her here."

Horad scowled at Kalawezi's patient. "Whose pin is that?"

"Mine," I told him.

"You nominated her? So what? You're not an officer yet. You're still a cadet."

I shrugged. "Doesn't matter. I earned the right to nominate someone to the Red Caste the moment they tacked that pin to my chest. Legally, she's to be treated as an awardee unless her confirmation committee declines the nomination."

"Take that pin off of her," Horad snarled.

"No." That may have been disobeying a direct order, but as far as regulations were concerned, this time, I was bulletproof.

The sergeant-major stepped forward to get into my face. "You need to remember your place, son. You're a cadet. I outrank you."

"And I outrank you," my lieutenant said as he approached us. Technically, Thyster was correct, but in practice, it was not advisable for a junior officer to butt heads with a sergeant-major. That was an excellent way to invite the wrath of the battalion CO.

"Maybe you do," Horad shot back. "But I'm carrying out the will of our commanding officer. You think it's a good idea to get in the way of me discharging my duties, Lieutenant?"

"Your duty is to provide counsel and guidance to our CO, Horad." Captain Mardona said as he jogged up to us with Gunny Malcolm in tow. "If you're letting him violate the Waimair Article of the UCMJ, you're derelict in those duties."

The captain looked around the wounded troops lying in the mud and, with an unmistakable look of anger on his face, asked, "Who's in charge here?"

When Corporal Sabian stepped forward, Mardona had her explain the situation. As she spoke, I could see the gears spinning in my company commander's head as he contemplated calling back the SPSs that had already left.

"Is there a problem here?" Captain Briggund asked as he arrived on the scene. Our new battalion commander was tall and very thin. His skin had the pale hue of a man who spent way too much time indoors and a build that suggested he was not overly fond of physical exertion. His features were as delicate as his hands, which appeared soft and highly manicured.

"I think there is, sir," Mardona answered. "Leaving these wounded Marines behind could be construed as violating the Waimair Article. If anything happens to these troops, you could be held accountable."

"I'm not abandoning our Marines, Rod," Briggund said. "I'm leaving a couple of medics and about a half-dozen infantry to care for and protect them."

Mardona shook his head. "There're no fortifications here, sir. Five or six Marines are not going to be enough."

Briggund shrugged. "Compared to what I can spare, I think it's pretty generous."

"Sir, if you end up in front of the inquisitors over this, they'll make an example out of you. These troops won't survive here until we get to Narman's Pyke."

Briggund stepped closer to Mardona and lowered his voice so the patients could not hear him. "Rod, look at these poor people. They're all in bad shape. They're not going to make it very long no matter what I do. Their lives will be even shorter if we take them with us."

"Sir, they didn't even leave Paxilmiacin with these troops," Mardona reported. "We're not even trying to treat them. That in itself is pretty damning."

"So, what would be enough to keep the inquisitors off my back then, Captain Mardona? A couple of boxes of Paxilmiacin? An entire platoon of Marines?"

"You've seen the kind of shit we're dealing with here, Captain. A platoon isn't going to be able to hold back the things that can come out of this jungle. We need to take them with..."

"Then how about a company then? I've got roughly a thousand troops to take and hold Narman's Pyke with, Rod. Should I leave a quarter of them here to watch over our wounded so that I can avoid the gallows if something goes wrong?"

Mardona swallowed hard, knowing the game Briggund was playing. He was not going to allow the wounded to trek to Narman's Pyke with us. Instead, he was forcing our company commander to counsel him on how much we should weaken ourselves to look after our casualties. If Briggund went down for failing to take his objective or letting his wounded die, he was making it clear that he would take Mardona with him. "A platoon should be fine," my captain told him.

"Good," Briggund said with a gleam in his eye to show us how easily he could sacrifice the lives of eighty-eight Marines to make a point. Turning to Sergeant-Major Horad, he then said, "Charlie Company, Third Platoon. Get them down here to provide security for our wounded."

I wondered what that unit had done to piss Briggund off enough for him to condemn them along with our casualties. It would have been easier to pick us.

"Is that all?" Briggund asked Captain Mardona.

"Yes, sir," my company commander answered.

"Actually," Sergeant-Major Horad started. "The cadet here has designated that pilot as a Red Caste candidate and insists we take her with us."

Briggund looked at me and flashed the same devious grin he just used on my company commander. Looking down at Albarn, he said, "Congratulations, Warrant Officer! I appreciate what you did for us up there. Your navigator and weapons officer told me all about it. If anyone deserves to be born into the Red Caste, it's you. You can count on my recommendation when it goes to committee."

"Thank you, sir," Albarn groaned.

"Sir, we need the SPS she's on to get your equipment to Narman's Pyke."

"Really?" Briggund asked. "Surely, there's some other way to get that thing up the mountain without depriving a hero of her stretcher."

The CO turned and took a step closer to me. "I've been told that Citadel Marines are just as resourceful as they are deadly." Looking at my name tag, Briggund asked, "Tauk? Is that your name?"

I nodded, noticing that Raza Bhutaan raised an eyebrow upon learning who I was. "Yes, sir. I'm Eamon Tauk."

"You were the cadet who was in the cockpit during the crash?"

"Yes, sir," I confessed.

"And you didn't see what shot down our Wasps?"

Knowing that Captain Briggund was *not* the man I should be sharing my secrets with, I kept my answer ambiguous. "I did not see anything bringing down our dropships, sir."

Briggund squinted at me. "There's a rumor going around saying those two dropships crashed into each other. As an intelligence officer, that makes me suspect we might've been infiltrated. It looks like someone's trying to lure more of our dropships into a trap by implying one doesn't exist. It reeks of classic Ghuldari misinformation. Doesn't it, Sergeant?"

"It sure does, sir," said Bhutaan.

"Do you know Sergeant Bhutaan, Cadet?" Briggund asked me.

"Not personally," I answered. "I've heard of him, though."

"Good," Briggund said. "I've put him in charge of finding the provocateurs who've been spreading these lies. If you hear any of this garbage talk, can I trust you to bring it to his attention?"

"Of course, sir," I lied.

"Good," the captain said while patting me on the shoulder. "I knew I could count on you. I need to count on you for something else, too. Since you've seen fit to nominate our fearless pilot to the Red Caste, I'm left short an SPS. I need you to find a way to get my box to Narman's Pyke. This gear is essential. Losing it could very well cost us our mission and our lives. Is that clear?"

"Yes, sir."

"The contents of that box are also highly classified. It is not to be tampered with or opened by anyone other than me. Understood?"

"Yes, sir."

"Good," Briggund said as he turned to rejoin the battalion. While our leadership meandered away back toward the tree line, Raza Bhutaan lagged behind to speak with me. "You're the guy who got Gori Dravidas?"

I nodded.

Briggund's bodyguard looked me over, sizing me up. "Congratulations. A lot of people think Gori Dravidas was the toughest man in the Corps."

"He an idol of yours?"

Bhutaan chuckled. "Idol? No. More like an obstacle. He was someone that I'd have had to take on if *I* wanted to be a contender as the toughest man in the Corps. It looks like you're that guy now." The Samaari seemed less than impressed.

"You looking to land yourself behind bars for assaulting a superior officer?" I asked him.

"You're not an officer," Bhutaan answered. "Not yet. And you certainly aren't my superior."

Sergeant-Major Horad spun around when he noticed their praetorian was not keeping up with them. "Hey!" Horad called out. "Bhutaan! You coming or what??"

After giving his boss a quick nod, the sergeant faced me and said, "I'll see you around." He then turned and began marching up the path to catch up to our CO.

I let out a long sigh as the killer walked away. I had the feeling that he would, indeed, be seeing me around, and I was not sure how I felt about that. Six months before, I would have relished the challenge of taking on Raza Bhutaan. But that was before Gori Dravidas showed me I was not nearly as invincible as the Citadel had taught me I was.

And before I started wondering what else they had been lying to me about.

●●◄●►●◄●►●●

CHAPTER 13

C oming up with a solution to transport Briggund's box was not difficult. We lashed two large branches to either side of the crate and turned it into a litter that could be carried by a trio of troops in front and back. It was awkward and cumbersome, especially over rough terrain, but it only added five kilograms of extra load to each person bearing it. To further ease the burden, we rotated our troops in and out of litter duty at regular intervals.

Crossing paths with the platoon sentenced to guard our wounded was far harder. No one on Kanaris felt particularly safe, but there was a certain sense of security to be had from being part of a large cadre of Marines. The troops of Charlie Company's Third Platoon had been robbed of that. By the looks I received as the doomed riflemen filed by, they knew precisely who had gotten them sent there, too.

The first person to glare at me was the platoon leader. Her seething eyes burned right through my armor. She knew her Marines were not sent there to shield our wounded. They were there so Briggund could say he made a good faith effort to keep our casualties alive. Sacrificing five riflemen was not enough. Condemning nearly ninety would show he really cared. Eighty-eight Marines were to waste away on the beach to protect the career of one Samaari officer.

The platoon sergeant spat at my feet as he walked by. A couple of riflemen flipped me off. A squad leader thanked me.

"For what?" I stupidly asked.

"If I'm going to die on this shithole," he said. "At least I don't have to march damn near two hundred clicks to do it."

That hurt. It was the same sentiment expressed by Naktada the day before. "Nothing's pre-ordained, Sergeant," I told him. "Fortify and fight."

"Easy for someone to say who's rejoining the battalion. The silence you leave behind when you all pull out will be like sounding the dinner bell once all the creatures crawling around the bush figure out we're by ourselves. If ten thousand souls could not keep Narman's Pyke despite its walls, what chance do you think a hundred Marines sitting under a tarp have?"

Gunny Malcolm was waiting for me at the jungle's edge. "You want some advice, Tauk?" he asked once I was within earshot.

Nodding, I said, "Sure."

"I know you Citadel guys are trained to take charge of every situation, but you need to lower your profile. Sit back and observe for a while. Concentrate on your squad. Leave all this big picture shit to me and the lieutenant before you get anyone else thrown into a really nasty situation. You savvy?"

I nodded. "I do. Can I ask you a question, Gunny?"

"Sure."

"When do you think I'll have to answer for going back to the dropship after we crashed?" Between the Marines I may have doomed, the prisoner I shot, and the armorer I sent to die, I felt like I deserved the punishment coming my way.

Malcolm shrugged. "Obviously, we have bigger fish to fry for the foreseeable future. I can only say that the time will come way faster than you would like it to, no matter how long it takes."

●●◄●►●◄●►●●

The first day of our trek to Narman's Pyke was arduous and unnerving. Visibility was poor. At sea level, sunlight had to cut through three cloud layers and an almost impenetrable forest canopy. It was so hot that the rain seemed to evaporate as soon as it hit the ground. The steam rising from the surface kept us enveloped in a blanket of suffocating fog that limited our vision to no more than a few meters at best. Without the sensor array on our battle helmets, we would have been marching blind.

There were no natural trails going the way we were. There was just a rocky path where the constant rain washed away the soil. It was essentially a shallow river, and the stones were slick.

Four hours into our ascent, an Alpha Company Marine snapped his ankle when he twisted it between a couple of submerged boulders. His buddy tried to carry the injured man on his back. Before the pair made it another two-hundred meters, the buddy slipped, too. The Samaritan dislocated his shoulder while the patient added a broken wrist to his growing list of maladies.

Briggund's Box got progressively more difficult to move as well, even more so when Sergeant-Major Horad was around. He was there when one of our IRREC porters, Orgo Yisht, lost his footing and fell face-first onto the stones. Orgo took out Xi and Krau in the process, causing the crate to drop onto the rocks.

Horad lost his mind. "What the fuck are you trying to do, you worthless son-of-a-bitch?!?" he screamed as he ran to the litter and pulled Yisht out of the water by the throat. The fall had knocked the convict's helmet off and sliced his forehead open above his right brow, pouring blood into his eye. The porter was barely conscious. "Do you have any idea how important that cargo is?!? DO YOU?!?"

Yisht tried to stammer out an answer, but between the blow to his head and the stress of having Horad in his face, the man could not bring himself to spit out a single intelligible word.

Our sergeant-major drew his sidearm and pointed the barrel at the bridge of the convict's nose. "It's worth far more than you'll ever be! If I see you abusing that piece of equipment again, I'll blow your goddamn brains all over the sunny side of this putrid shit hole! Do you understand me?!?"

"Y-y-y-yes, S-S-S-Sergeant-Major! Yes!"

To make sure Yisht got the point, Horad pistol-whipped him, opening up the skin above the convict's other eye before dropping him back into the water. Once Horad was gone, I ordered Yisht to get up and retake his place on the litter.

"What?" Jella Duverii gasped after she heard my command. "Look at him! He's hurt! Don't you think he should see the medic?"

For an instant, I wanted to apologize to Jella and reverse my order. Doing so might have betrayed the way I was starting to feel about her, however. So, instead, I doubled down. "Kalawezi can look at him after he finishes his shift."

"That's bullshit!" Jella argued. "He's human, Tauk! Not a pack animal!"

"I would hardly consider him human," Harlund Merik said as he snuck up from behind us. "Orgo Yisht belonged to a gang on Clepsis Bohriala. They would kidnap the daughters, wives, or even mothers of people owing them money and force them to work off the debts in one of the brothels they ran. Yisht worked as their pimp."

Jella physically recoiled and turned her attention to my squad's only female convict. I could see her wondering what crimes Ritza Xi could have committed, so I told her.

"She sliced open her husband's throat while he was asleep. I saw the pictures. The bitch nearly decapitated him. Then she bludgeoned her two children to death. By the time she was finished, they were unrecognizable."

Pointing to the third person who dropped the crate, Harlund said, "And that's Loman Krau. Serial rapist. He's the worst of the lot. You don't want to find yourself alone with him under any circumstances." Looking up at me, Merik added, "Neither do you, Eamon. Not with that juicy booty of yours."

Our other two prisoners were off litter rotation. My corporal gestured toward the shorter one. "Maynar Vold was a war profiteer. He stole food from troops under siege on Varnat Vular and sold it at exorbitant prices on the black market. The tall guy next to him is Barone Parsons. He was convicted of terrorism. They caught him plotting to slaughter the police department of an entire city on Apalashu, as well as murder a couple of its judges."

Turning back toward Jella, Merik said, "Parsons, Yisht, and Vold are with the Corps for ten years. If they survive their tour, they can return to society and start over. Xi and Krau are here for life, which is, in practice, a slow-motion death sentence. Zeros seldom last more than a couple of years. The Ones know there's a way out, so they work harder at surviving. The Zeros?"

Merik turned his head to point his chin at Xi. "They know they only leave the Corps in a casket. They eventually give up. It's amazing how quickly death will find someone like her when she's finally lost the will to live. I'm amazed she's made it this long."

●●-◄►-●-◄►-●●

We hiked eleven kilometers that first day. It was an exhausting march for my Marines. It was mentally taxing for me. Except for a few hours of sleep, I had been involved in non-stop activity from the moment *Wasp-Three* crashed into the beach. There was so much going on that I did not have time to think.

That changed once we started marching. The lack of an immediate crisis, combined with the monotony of walking, allowed my mind to drift. I thought mostly of Sergeant Naktada, Vernor Blyte, and the platoon I got abandoned on the beach.

But I also thought of Misha, Helmut, and Juergen. Had they survived their blooding rites, I wondered if they would have been stricken with the same doubts I had. Without them, I had no one to confide in. They were the only family I had, killed on the same dark day by the Butcher of Deraghun.

Six months before, I had charged onto the blooding field at the top of my class, convinced I was among the best the Citadel had ever produced. What Gori Dravidas did to us that day shook my confidence to its core. The consequences of the decisions I had made since were chipping away at what little I had left. I felt like an imposter. Unlike Harlund Merik, a man with a reputation for having unnatural combat instincts, I felt as if I had no idea what I was doing.

As we slogged our way over the trail, we were never more than ten or twelve meters from impenetrable jungle on either side of us. The trees shot straight up into the air, towering over us until they could tangle their branches with those growing from the other side. That kept us in darkness, unable to see the sun, or the creatures in the bush beside us.

Though we could hear, and occasionally see, that the jungle around us was teeming with life, little of it ever appeared on the trail. Jella shrugged when I asked her why.

"There's a lot of us here," Duverii told me. "And we're making a lot of noise. We could be scaring the creatures deeper into the bush. It could also be that the animals don't want to expose themselves in an opening where their camouflage won't work."

About an hour before sundown, we reached an incline that would have been impossible to clear before nightfall. Briggund ordered us to make camp, and I got the convicts busy setting up our bivouac.

The rest of my troops collapsed where they stood, digging into their rations. Harlund Merik took the opportunity to teach Lumuk some fighting moves. Harlund wanted to prepare him for his next confrontation with Mazada Duum, who had tormented our giant mercilessly for nearly the entire march.

Once everyone was settled, I stepped to the bushes to relieve myself. I dropped the pelvic flap of my exo-armor, unzipped my BDU trousers, and started to piss. No sooner had my stream hit the ground when I heard a grunt from behind the vegetation I was draining my bladder into, mere centimeters from me. I then watched as eight long, taloned fingers emerged from the leaves and parted the brush, revealing one of the most terrifying faces I had ever laid eyes upon.

It was a quarakai, the thing I had seen the silhouette of the night we crashed. It had a huge, ovular head dominated by two feline-esque eyes with red irises. Below them was a trio of nostrils followed by a long, broad snout equipped with dozens of dagger-like teeth, between which oozed a thick, brown, almost tar-like saliva. It looked like it could have bitten me right in half.

Around the creature's head grew a crown of thick, quill-like hair that sprouted from scaly, olive skin. Its limbs were thin and spider-like, but at the same time, appeared insanely strong.

This was a beast from which nightmares are made, and my instincts were screaming at me to reach for my sidearm and kill it before I got mauled. But I couldn't. My hands were full. I could not get to my weapon before the quarakai got to my throat.

For a moment, we just stared at one another, each trying to figure out what the other was planning to do. Then the quarakai bowed its head to smell my urine. In disgust, it snorted like a horse, making me realize that the lungs on the thing must have been enormous.

After a few moments, I sensed the creature was more curious than malicious. Confirming my suspicions, it slowly reached out and tapped my helmet with one of its claws, as if it was trying to figure out what it was made of.

"H-h-hello," I stuttered at the creature.

The quarakai pulled its hand back abruptly, surprised by the sound I made. It then responded with a series of guttural, low-pitched clicking noises. When it finished, it cocked its head to the side, a gesture I took as expecting a reply. At least, that is what it would have meant had it been done by a human. I had no idea how to interpret quarakai body language. "I-I-I d-don't u-u-understand..."

The creature snorted again, seemingly in frustration. It then made a fist, stuck its hand out, and flipped me off.

"Holy shit!" I gasped, realizing this was the exact same creature I had seen before. Letting go of my trousers, I lifted my hand and excitedly returned the sentiment, pissing all over myself in the process.

Upon seeing my middle finger, the quarakai smiled, displaying all its teeth and making my heart skip a beat. The creature then turned its back on me and returned to the jungle, moving much like the orangutans we could find in a Replicant Earth Environment.

I was in awe, wondering if those were what may have taken out our colony at Narman's Pyke.

I also wondered what it would take to train them to fight on our side.

●●<●>●<●>●●

CHAPTER 14

I was awakened the next morning by my company commander's voice squawking out of my earpiece from the Delta Company commlink. "Cadet Tauk!" Captain Mardona barked. "Tauk! Do you copy?"

"Aye aye, sir!" I responded as I went from deep REM sleep to jumping to my feet as soon as I heard my name called. That was another trick the Citadel conditioned us to do.

"Good! Get Dr. Duverii to the battalion CP on the double!"

"Roger that. I'll be there in five," I said, trying to remember where the Command Post was.

Despite my mental fog, I arrived at the CP in three. Jella did too, in body if not in spirit. She could barely stand up straight and was comically unsteady on her feet. Luckily, everyone waiting for her knew she was sleep-deprived and not drunk. Stumbling beneath the tarp that covered Briggund and his subordinates from the rain, our guide squinted at the officers, trying to clear her head without the benefit of coffee.

Captain Briggund looked rattled. He was too engrossed in what was being shown on a video monitor to acknowledge Duverii's presence. Mardona did all the talking. "We lost three Marines last night, Doctor. All of them basically vanished into thin air."

Stepping up beside Briggund, Mardona pointed at the screen. "This is the recording from one of the watch's helmet cams."

The video was in infrared, showing the guard's point of view. She was doing what she was supposed to, staring down the sights of her M72, scanning the tree line for threats. When the camera panned left, Mardona paused the feed to point out a Marine lying atop the bank. "That's Private Vostov. Now you see him..."

Mardona hit "play." The sentry slowly turned her head to the right, shifting the scenery no more than six or seven meters. We heard a brief disturbance recorded by the Marine's left helmet microphone. The guard swung her head back to where Vostov had been sleeping, but the rifleman was gone. The only clue to his disappearance was the bouncing branches left in his wake.

"...and now you don't," our captain continued. "It was so quick that the watch didn't even realize Vostov was gone. The troops around that poor kid slept right through it. Would you like to see what was recorded on Private Vostov's helmet cam?" the captain asked.

Jella's eyes were wide open now. She nodded her head.

Incorporated into our exo-armor was a computer capable of storing a month's worth of video and sound from every warrior in their company. We were a marching server network when we were not killing things. Had it not been for all the Harnillium interference on Kanaris, our data would have been uploaded into the mothership and broadcast to the League Archive on a daily basis. Every Marine in the company could watch Vostov's video on their facemask display, and once word got around about what happened, they certainly would be.

Vostov's PCR camera was facing the trail, passively recording everything around him while he slept. Then, there was nothing but a blur as the private went flying through the jungle. The Marine's journey ended with a stop so violent that his helmet popped off. It rolled down what appeared to be a giant tongue until it came to a rest, pointing at Vostov's legs being ground between what seemed to be a massive set of molars.

I glanced down at Jella and saw that the look on her face was a combination of both horror and fascination. She tried to suppress the fact that there was a human dying in that video so she could clinically analyze what was going on. "If it's any consolation," Jella told the officers. "Those Marines didn't suffer. Their deaths were instant."

"Do you know what did this?" Mardona asked. Captain Briggund turned his head toward her for the first time. He looked scared.

Jella nodded at Mardona's question. "I think so. I suspect this is a species of *Anwarkanari Predaris*. We call them 'anwar' for short. Think of a creature the size of an elephant with stumpier, hippo-like legs and a large, oversized head that's all mouth. It's covered in long, coarse, feathered fur that looks like..."

Jella turned to look around the trees that surrounded us. She stopped when she spotted a clump of bushes overtaken by a common Kanarisian moss.

Pointing at it, she said, "...that stuff. It's like they're wearing one of those suits your snipers use."

"A ghillie suit?" I asked.

"Whatever you call it," Jella shot back. "These creatures are covered in nearly perfect camouflage. You could be staring right at one and have no idea what it is."

Our guide took a deep breath. "They hunt like frogs. The one we caught on camera, the only one we've ever seen, actually, launched its tongue more than ten meters to grab a leaf-slinker."

"Leaf-slinker?" Lieutenant Draiphus from Charlie Company asked.

"It's kind of like a large, flat snake with a caterpillar head whose rib tips have grown out of its skin to form centipede legs. They're herbivores, but huge. They probably weigh twice as much as Cadet Tauk here."

"Back to the anwar," Mardona said, trying to keep the conversation from straying off track. "How do we kill them?"

Jella shrugged. "I don't know. The only one we've ever observed is the one we caught on our research cameras. We've seen the tracks, and the regurgitation..."

"What's that? What do you mean 'regurgitation?'" Mardona interrupted.

Dr. Duverii pointed back at the monitor. "See that porous, boney plate at the back of the creature's throat? That's probably a filter, something like the baleen of a whale. It looks like anwar grind their prey into a paste that's largely dissolved by its saliva. That's what's probably sucked into the beast's stomach while the harder stuff, the protective shells of its natural prey, or exo-armor in our case, is spit back out. That's what we've come across around Narman's Pyke anyway."

"Are these things common?" asked Lieutenant Shala Feir. She was also one of Charlie Company's platoon leaders.

Jella shook her head. "I don't think so. We saw anwar tracks for quite some distance around Narman's Pyke, but we could tell by a scar on one of the feet that it was the same creature. We were eighty kilometers from base when we first came across prints made by another animal."

"If these animals are so rare," Captain Briggund said, finally opening his mouth. "How do you explain three of our Marines falling victim to them?"

"They're big animals," Jella answered. "Big animals have big appetites."

"So, how do we deal with this, Doctor?" Briggund asked.

Jella shrugged. "You could try to hunt it, but if you go traipsing about in the jungle, not only are you choosing to take this thing on in an environment where the anwar has all the advantages, you risk running afoul of all the other stuff out there that we don't even know about. Adding to the danger is that, because of the Harnillium, our radio range is really short. Any hunting party you send out there *will* get separated from the battalion. You also have to consider that we don't know where an anwar's soft spots are. We don't know where to shoot it. What you think are kill shots might only piss this thing off."

Our guide let out a long sigh. "Captain, our best bet might be to just outrun this thing. Make a dash to the edge of its territory and hope there ain't another one waiting for us at the finish line. Losing three Marines to an anwar is pretty telling of what we're up against."

"Telling of what?" the battalion commander asked.

"Well, sir," Jella answered. "It tasted human prey for the first time last night and found us tasty enough to keep coming back for more. So until we get away from this thing or figure out a way to hurt it, we'll have to get used to losing a few of us a night."

•●⊲⧫⊳●⊲⧫⊳⊲⧫⊳●●

CHAPTER 15

The anwar attack spooked Captain Briggund. He did not like being hunted by something he could not fight back against. Anxious to outrun whatever took our Marines, our battalion commander marched us harder and longer than even he could stand. Only after a three-day trek with no more casualties did the captain feel comfortable enough to rest his Marines for a ten-hour bivouac.

Most of the troops dropped where they stopped and did not move until reveille was called the following morning. Harlund Merik, on the other hand, displayed a shocking degree of stamina. He and Akkam Lumuk, a farm boy used to laboring ceaselessly from dawn to dusk, used every break to train in martial arts. They were sparring when I went to sleep and woke me up when they started again just before sunrise.

I watched Merik's morning session with morbid curiosity. Lumuk could throw a devastating haymaker that would send any of the battalion's Marines into orbit. Unfortunately, his opponent could jump in, land three blows, and leap out of range before Lumuk could even cock his arm back. His punches may have been insanely powerful, but they were utterly useless if he could not get them to connect. I was amazed that a man so large and strong could be so horribly inept at defending himself.

"You know, that's bullshit," Mazada Duum complained as he groggily tripped over a sleeping bag, rudely awakening Daiq Briima. "It's like you all are training him to kick my ass just because I'm Samaari!"

"That's not true, Duum," I reassured him. "Being a Samaari has nothing to do with it. Merik's preparing him to fuck you up because you're an asshole." That comment made Jella cackle. She was also up early, packing away her gear.

Shooting our giggling guide a sideways glance, Duum countered, "Maybe I'd be less of an asshole if people around here treated me with a little respect."

I sighed. "If there's one stereotype about Sammies...uh...sorry. Excuse me." I tried to avoid using the slang for those hailing from the Guild worlds. Though it was not particularly insulting, it was not exactly a compliment, either. The picture the term conjured up reinforced the image of them being pretentious primadonnas. "I meant to say, 'Samaari.' Anyway, what you tend to consider 'respect' is what the rest of humanity considers 'kissing ass.' You haven't done shit to earn anyone's respect, yet you strut around like you've accomplished something other than being born on Samaar Ghun."

"I haven't accomplished anything?!?" Duum snapped. "I'm a bona fide Ten-Percenter, Tauk! An official killer!"

I winced, surprised that Duum got his seven confirmed kills. I had yet to do that myself.

"On top of that," the Samaari rifleman continued. "I fucking pummelled that gorilla over there, and..."

"That cost you respect, Duum," I interjected. "It didn't gain you any. Lumuk's big, but he's a coward. He's probably one of the most worthless Marines in the battalion. Nobody's impressed with what you did."

"But-but-but..."

"There's no 'but.' Beating up the sorriest man we have just made you look like the second sorriest. You know, one thing I notice about Ten-Percenters is that they never need to prove how bad they are. But you do. Where did you get your seven kills at?"

My question put Duum on the defensive. "None of your business."

I drew my tablet like it was a dueling pistol and shot a beam at the microchip on Duum's breastplate. In an instant, his record popped up on my screen. When his combat proficiency data came up, I laughed. "You racked up seven kills on Terrakand? Putting down food riots?"

The color rushed into Duum's face. "Shit got pretty hairy..."

"Give me a fucking break! You didn't get those kills in combat, you little shit! You got them on safari!"

"Yeah, well," Duum stuttered. "I did what I had to do. At least I didn't shoot any wounded men on stretchers."

I shot a quick glance at Jella, hoping she had not heard that. Luckily, she was talking with someone on her commlink and seemed to have missed Duum's comment. Trying to keep her ignorant of what I had done to Vernor Blyte, I lowered my voice when I answered our Samaari. "Yeah, I did what I had to do, too. The difference is that you don't see me bragging about it like it was some kind of accomplishment."

Shaking my head in disgust, I then said, "If I hear you claim to be a killer again, I'm going to make sure everyone knows how you got your seven. You're pathetic, Duum. Too pathetic to be wasting my time. Go pack your shit up and get ready to move out."

After reveille sounded and the rest of my squad started coming to life, I walked over to Je'Sikka Albarn's SPS to ensure she was cared for and strapped in tight. "The route today's pretty steep," I told her. "It might be something of a white-knuckle climb for you. From what I understand, though, these SPSs are pretty sure-footed. If it strays too close to the tree line, I want you to call out for somebody to get you back to the center of the trail."

"Why?" Albarn whispered. I wondered if she had not been told about the anwar attack or had just forgotten about it. She looked miserable and, between her injuries and the painkillers she was on, could barely stay conscious.

Before leaving, I tracked down a medic and asked how our pilot was doing. "About as good as you would imagine a paraplegic to do on a combat march," he told me. "It's hard on her. And us."

"She going to make it?" I asked.

The medic shrugged. "I'm beginning to doubt if any of us will. It's hardly reasonable to expect her to have better odds of surviving than we do."

I did not leave that conversation in high spirits. I wanted to spend more time with Albarn, but there was too much else to do. I had to return to my squad.

After briefing our Marines on the obstacles ahead, we were on the move again. Just before lunch, we encountered a sheer cliff face that had to be scaled. While our climbers ascended the wall to assemble the rope systems that would get us and our equipment to the top, we set a perimeter aiming the battalion's M2117 rapid-fire rail guns at the forest.

We had just finished eating when I got another panicked call from the CP, ordering Jella Duverii to the opposite edge of the encampment. "We got another anwar attack?" I asked.

"No!" the excited voice on the other end of the line shouted. "I don't know what this is!"

When we arrived, we found a young private lying face-down on the ground, screaming in agony. A trio of medics argued amongst themselves about how best to treat her. A fourth struggled to get her out of her exo-armor. "What happened?" Jella asked.

"She got stung!" the private's platoon leader, Lieutenant Lidia Hayvar, told us.

"By what?"

"We don't know!"

Pushing her way through the medics, Jella began interrogating the victim. "Marine! Marine!"

"Her name's Simbi," one of the medics told her. "PFC Simbi."

Jella nodded. "Simbi! Simbi! You've got to tell me what stung you!"

The woman shrieked in pain and was foaming around the mouth. That was a bad sign. "My back!" the victim sobbed. "My neck! Make it stop! Make it stop!"

"We can't until we know what stung you!"

"I don't know what stung me!" the Marine screamed. "I was leaning back against a tree trying to take a dump when it..." That was all the information we were going to get. Simbi screeched out once more and began convulsing.

When the medic got the Marine's back panel off, I picked it up and inspected it. I could see fresh scratches all over her armor, including one that stopped at a seam between two plates. I glanced back down at Simbi as the medics cut away her shirt and saw she had a line of angry puncture marks that perfectly outlined the gap in her armor.

"Stay here," I told Jella. As Simbi came loudly back to life, I ran off toward the perimeter.

A corporal told me the general direction of where the Marine had gone to use the latrine. My nose took me to the exact spot she was stung. Seeing nothing crawling around the area, I took out my bayonet and pressed its hilt against the tree the private must have been leaning against. The bark was unlike anything I had ever seen before. It had a deep ochre hue and was pliant and rubbery. It felt more like animal hide. The harder I pressed against it, the more it gave, until it revealed dozens of thorns hidden within the pores of the plant's skin.

With Simbi's screaming still dominating the background noise, I pulled out my sidearm and pushed it up against one of the thorns. That made it secrete the milky white substance that was putting so much hurt upon our Marine.

Before I could share what I found with the medics, I heard Simbi's screaming come to an abrupt end.

I was too late to help. Not that we knew how to treat her anyway.

●●‹●›●‹●›●●

It took us the rest of the day to get the battalion up that cliff. In addition to losing PFC Simbi to a tree sting, another Marine died after somehow disengaging from the safety line. He fell four stories and splattered himself upon the rocks right in front of Lumuk, who had an anxiety attack before he even started his ascent.

We had to tie him to the cables and drag him up the mountain like a piece of gear.

Captain Briggund met Jella on the cliff top. "You think that anwar thing could follow us up here, Doctor?"

Panting to catch her breath after the grueling climb, Jella looked over the side and shook her head. "I doubt it. They don't have fingers, so they're not equipped for scaling vertical surfaces. They're also huge and heavy. Animals like that evolved on relatively flat landscapes. There's a reason no one's ever heard of a mountain elephant."

Briggund let out a sigh of relief. "Good. I'll sleep a little better tonight."

"Well, sir," Jella said. "I wouldn't go letting your guard down just yet. I'm sure there're plenty of other things up here fully capable of claiming a couple Marines a day if we're not careful."

I saw one of those potential hazards high up in the trees a few hours later. It was another quarakai, but of a different species than the one I saw closer to the beach. Instead of being shaped like an orangutan, this one was more svelte. Its torso was thin and muscular, but the limbs remained long and sinewy, with freakishly long, taloned fingers.

"Do you see that?" I asked as I pointed the creature out to Jella.

As she looked at the quarakai through her optical amplifiers, I watched her smile. "Oh my god!" she gasped as she handed me the device. "Look at its left wrist!"

Taking Jella's optics, I zoomed in to where she told me. The creature was wearing a simple bracelet made of intertwined plant fibers and decorated with a half-dozen colorful shells. It was jewelry. "Holy shit! Have you ever seen that before?"

Dr. Duverii shook her head. "No! It's amazing, though! We're looking at a 'missing link' sort of creature. They're still basically animals but well on their way to becoming an intelligent life form. This is a huge discovery!"

Humans had been exploring space for centuries. We had discovered hundreds of planets harboring life, but never anything resourceful enough to make objects for purely aesthetic purposes. In space biology terms, it was an amazing find.

A little while later, we came across a clearing and set up camp. Just after sundown, the rain briefly stopped, only to be replaced by swarms of flying bugs. Not long after that, a flotilla of what looked like glowing balloons, sparkling with bioluminescence, drifted out of the trees and floated above us.

"What are those things?" I asked our guide, fascinated by the light show.

"Sky jellies!" Jella squealed. "They're just like jellyfish, but they filter the hydrogen out of the gas they exhale and pump it into this bladder above their bulbs. Since hydrogen is less dense than the atmosphere, they float instead of fly. The bioluminescence attracts insects. Well, not exactly insects, scientifically speaking. The bugs on Kanaris rarely have six legs. Anyway, I digress. The bugs try to fly up to the glowing bulbs but get caught in the tentacles beneath."

"Tentacles? Are they dangerous?"

"They're not fatal if that's what you mean," Duverii answered. "Their sting hurts like hell if it contacts bare skin, though."

No sooner had she said that when we heard someone screaming directly beneath the creatures we had been marveling at. Jella turned to me and asked, "You don't think someone..."

I nodded, strongly suspecting that one of our people was stupid enough to try to touch one. The call requesting me to escort Dr. Duverii to the medical team confirmed it.

●●◅▸●◅▸●●

CHAPTER 16

T he moron that tried to hold a sky jelly like a living alien balloon was one of my people. It was Loman Krau, a man convicted of multiple rapes that earned him a life sentence as a laborer with the Corps. Like the jellyfish of our terraformed worlds, the sky jellies' tentacles were covered in nematocysts. When Krau grabbed them, those specialized stinging cells launched dozens of microscopic, venomous harpoons into his palm. It did not kill him, but it made him wish he were dead.

Jella and I were at Krau's side within two minutes of him being stung. He was easy to find with all the screaming he was doing. By the time we arrived, the man's fingers had already swollen so much we could not see the wrinkles in his knuckles.

"I'm sorry, Cadet Tauk," Krau whimpered as we approached. "I didn't mean to do this!"

"What are you apologizing to me for? You only hurt yourself."

"I let the squad down," the convict sobbed. "I know we need every one of us to get that box to Narman's Pyke. I won't be able to pull my weight now. I'm sorry. I don't want to be a burden."

"You won't be," I assured Krau, laughing at his overly dramatic performance. Convicts were not very mission-oriented. All they cared about was living to see the next day. Krau was among the worst of them. He was narcissistic, lazy, scheming, and sociopathic. He could not have cared less about how his absence would affect the others. After hearing his false regrets, I suspected he grabbed the creature on purpose to avoid work.

"Luckily, you've got two hands," I told my malingerer. "You can still take your place on the litter rotation."

Krau started crying even harder. *That* he was not faking. "You can't do that! I'm hurt! I can't carry that box in this condition! I'm not an animal!"

"Thirty-eight of your victims would beg to differ."

The Zero dropped his head to his knee and ran the fingers of his good hand through his hair, trying to regain his composure. Failing, he began unbuckling his boots. "I can't do it! I can't do it anymore! I can barely get myself up these mountains! I won't make it carrying all this extra weight!"

Ripping his boot off, Krau stuck his hoof up in the air to show me how mangled his foot was. The large blisters he developed had popped. The continued friction rubbed away at his wounds even more, and the open sores saturated his socks with blood and pus. It looked hideous. "I can't go any further!"

"What do you think your alternative is? You think I can just call you an ambulance to take you to a hospital somewhere?"

Tears were streaming down Krau's face. "Please! Put me on one of those stretchers for a while! I'm begging you!"

"The SPSs are for equipment and wounded Marines, Krau."

The convict flung his oozing foot up in front of my face. "I AM FUCKING WOUNDED, TAUK!"

"Yeah, but you're not a Marine."

Krau once again hung his head down below his sagging shoulders. "I can't do this anymore," he sobbed. "It hurts so much. I'm sorry for what I did. I'm sorry for what I am. Please have mercy on me, Tauk. Just this once. Have a little mercy."

I let out a long sigh. "Okay, Krau. I'll lessen your suffering." Reaching for my hip, I drew my sidearm and pointed it at Krau's head. The convict screamed and tried to shield himself with his arms.

Upon seeing my weapon, the medics leapt to their feet, falling over themselves to get out of the way. They pulled Jella out of the line of fire with them. "Tauk!" she screamed at me. "What the hell do you think you're doing?!? Put that gun away!"

The crowd downrange parted as well, revealing my platoon sergeant. "What's going on, Tauk?" Gunny Malcolm asked, casually strolling over to me. I noticed his hands were much steadier now. Either his withdrawals were subsiding, or he had found some contraband hooch to take the edge off them.

"HE'S GOING TO KILL ME!" Krau shrieked. "LIKE HE DID THE MEDIC CONVICT! FOR THE LOVE OF GOD, HELP ME!"

Malcolm looked non-plussed. He did not get nearly as excited about killing convicts as Thyster did. "What'd he do?"

I shrugged. "He's in a lot of pain. He says he can't go on. It wouldn't be right to leave him behind for the animals to maul. The humane thing to do is put him out of his misery first."

Malcolm nodded in agreement. "Yeah, it'd be cruel to leave him here alive. Hey, after you do it, put the body closer to the trees and see if it'll attract some kryptids. Those things are delicious!"

Giving my platoon sergeant a nod, I said, "That's a fine idea, Gunny." I then pulled the hammer back on my weapon.

"STOP!" Krau screamed. "STOP! I'LL WALK! I'll walk! Motherfucker, man! You heartless bastards! I'll walk."

"You sure?" I asked, exaggerating the concern in my voice. "I don't want you to suffer."

"Fuck you people," Krau sobbed. "You're cruel. You're monsters."

Gunny Malcolm grinned. "It takes one to know one, doesn't it, son?" With that, he left us, content to continue whatever it was he was doing before.

As Krau struggled to put his boot back on with only one good hand, a medic pointed at the convict's other paw and asked Jella, "Have you ever seen this before?"

While glaring at me, Dr. Duverii nodded and answered, "Yes. The sting's nasty and painful, but not deadly. His hand's going to swell up really bad, to the point where you might need to lance it to relieve the pressure. I'm not a medical doctor, but..."

Seeing that my sidearm was still pointed at Krau's melon, Jella punched me in the shoulder. "That's enough, Tauk!" she snarled. "Put that thing away! You made your point!"

Not wanting to further agitate our guide, I snapped my weapon back into its holster. While Duverii told the medics how she thought doctors treated sky jelly stings in Narman's Pyke, I watched Loman Krau have an epiphany.

"This is it, isn't it?" the man sniveled. "This is all I have to look forward to? Years and years of work, suffering, and misery? It's never going to end. I'm never getting out of this, am I? Goddammit! I'm going to fucking die here!"

When Jella finished with the medics, she turned her attention to Krau. "You're going to be alright. The pain will wear off soon, and you'll be back to normal before you know it."

"Thank you, Dr. Duverii," Loman Krau told her.

"Don't worry about it, Krau. Just get better."

"Okay, I'll..."

I raised my boot and gave my convict a little kick in the jaw to shut him up. "Hey! Krau! Let's get something straight right now! You don't talk to this woman. You don't even look at her. And if you go completely off the reservation and actually touch her, I will leave you in the bush, alive, and let the kryptids pick your bones clean. Are we clear?"

Jella punched me in the shoulder again. "You don't tell me who I can talk to, Cadet!"

I spun around to face the doctor. "Did you forget what this man did to end up here?"

"I didn't do it!" Krau cried. "I didn't do anything! The fuckers framed me!"

"Shut up!" I snapped as I kicked Krau in the chest, knocking him onto his back. "I saw the evidence in your file!"

"They made it all up! They ..."

I kicked Krau again in the side, only to have Jella push me off balance while I was on one foot. "Hey! I said stop it, Eamon! Let me tell you something, asshole! The League's judicial system is more concerned with looking perfect than it is with actually being perfect!" After Jella said that, she looked around nervously, hoping her statement had not fallen on the wrong ears.

Pointing at Krau, I said, "He's guilty, Jella. They had a massive cache of evidence against him! There were tons of witnesses!"

"Tauk, if they had so much evidence and so many witnesses, how'd he get away with doing it so many times before they caught him?"

I stammered, not able to come up with a good answer. Jella lowered her voice and stepped closer to me so that only I could hear her. "If you ever go to trial for something you didn't do, rest assured that the court will have everything they need to convict you, too."

•• ‹•› ● ‹•› ••

As Jella and I walked away from the medical camp, I heard a familiar voice shout out to me from behind. "You do enjoy tormenting the convicts, don't you, Killer?"

Turning around, I found myself confronted by Sergeant Gruber, the medic whose lover I killed the day we crashed on Kanaris. "'Enjoying' isn't the right word. I do it when it's deserved."

Jella looked at Gruber, then back to where we left our Zero. "What did you do, Eamon?" she asked, remembering what our injured prisoner said a moment before. "What convict was Krau talking about back there?"

"He was talking about the one Tauk shot," Gruber spat. "He put him down like a dog to steal his stretcher." Turning his attention back to me, the sergeant then said, "Vernor didn't deserve what you did to him."

"I disagree," I shot back, ignoring Jella. She was staring at me in horror. I was not supposed to care what civilians thought of me, but I did not like the look of contempt on her face.

Trying to justify my actions, I said, "Vernor was a dead man as soon as he lost his feet. The Corps wasn't going to fix him. He'd be rotting away on the beach until the medics euthanized him and used the guy for kryptid bait. I shortened his suffering."

"The medics would have done everything they could for him. That man pulled several of us out of *Wasp-Three*. He earned our trust, Tauk. He wanted to help people. Vernor was one of us."

"Do you know that man poisoned another guy with the dope he was pushing?"

Gruber shook his head. "Vernor wasn't a pusher. His parents were killed after getting caught in the crossfire during an uprising on Mekulas-13. The orphanage he ended up in sold him to the pleasure palaces of Beru Sukka. You know, where the League elites go to indulge their basest urges with impunity. He endured horrors there that you could not possibly imagine."

I could see the sergeant's eyes welling up as he spoke. "The boy who died was not a client, Tauk. He was a companion, someone that Vernor connected with. Someone who promised to free him from that place. The dope wasn't Vernor's. It was the other boy's. When it killed him, the palace didn't want to take the blame, so they offered up the dead kid's courtesan."

"That's what Vernor told you?" I asked the medic. "Did you ever think that maybe he was lying?"

The sergeant bristled at the suggestion. "Vernor earned our trust many times over. I've yet to meet a Samaari with even a fraction of his integrity."

The medic had me there. I had never met one either. "Look, Sergeant. I'm not glad I killed that man. I did what I had to do to save the life of someone who could still contribute to the Corps. When the choice is between a prisoner and a pilot, the convict is going to lose every time."

Tears began rolling down Gruber's cheeks. "But what you did, you...you...you took his life without even pausing. He did nothing that day but save a half dozen medics and get crippled by a swarm of little alien fish. He didn't even look at you! And you blew his brains out like you were swatting a fly!"

"You're right. I did. Look, Sergeant, I didn't know Vernor," I said, holding my hand out to Gruber. "For what it's worth, though, I'm sorry about what happened. Sincerely."

The medic glared at my hand without taking it. "You're sorry about what happened? Are you sorry about what you did?"

I shook my head. "It was an extreme situation that warranted an extreme reaction." I could feel Jella's disapproving glare boring into the back of my head.

"In other words, you'd do it again, wouldn't you?"

I nodded. "I could lie to you and say I'd put more thought into it next time, but I wouldn't. I can't allow emotions to interfere with what needs to be a tactical decision. If I were in the exact same situation under the exact same circumstances, I'd do the exact same thing."

Gruber responded by spitting into my outstretched hand. "Then pardon me for not appreciating your honesty," he snarled.

As the medic stormed off, I turned to Jella to escort her back to the platoon, only to discover she had already left without me.

•●-◆-◉-◆-●•

CHAPTER 17

About four days later, I began appreciating what Jella had told us about the rain. It was unrelenting, coming down all day and all night. My ears were constantly filled with the sound of it tapping upon my helmet and mixing in with the never-ending whine of the Harnillium interference in my earpiece. The two noises together mercilessly wore upon my nerves.

The precipitation added so much more weight to us, too. It got beneath our armor and soaked us to the skin. It seeped into our packs and pooled in our boots. We were all waterlogged and marching with steadily progressing cases of trench foot that shriveled our skin into painfully wrinkled, bloody leather.

Tempers got short. Even Akkam Lumuk broke into a rage after Mazada Duum caused the oaf to fall on the rocks. Lumuk performed even worse in that confrontation than during the smoker round. Burdened by a full complement of gear and charging at the tiny Samaari over a bed of slick stones, Lumuk lost his footing so much that he beat the snot out of himself. Duum won that round without even laying a finger on the man.

Further up the trail, PFC Briima went off on a tangent about the evils of the League Parliament, only to have Faarhut and a couple of the other white stripes try to pound some patriotism into him. That caused the conscripts to rush into the fray, escalating the confrontation until it threatened to explode into a miniature civil war.

Keenly aware of the simmering tensions between the drafted Marines and the enlistees, I had prepared a speech about the importance of unity in the face of adversity. My troops did not get to hear it that day. I just threatened to shoot the next Marine that got on my nerves. I was not serious, but after what I had done to Blyte and almost did to Loman Krau, my Marines took me at my word and kept their mouths shut.

I was not immune to fraying nerves, either. At one point, marching through what was supposed to be our midday break, I noticed our new Zero, Ritza Xi, carrying a pack half the size of everyone else.

"It's a standard female Marine load," Merik told me when I asked why she was getting special treatment.

"Ritza Xi is not a Marine," I snarled. "She's a child-killing psychopath! A prisoner! Load her up like the rest of the Zeros!"

"Hey, Tauk," Merik started, trying to reason with me. "I understand making her pay for what she did, but it's not our job to torment the prisoners. If we give her a man's load, it'll probably kill her at the pace we're keeping. And if she dies or gets hurt, that burden, plus the rest of what she's carrying, is going to end up on someone else's shoulders. That's not going to help us complete our mission. It's going to slow us down."

I felt myself clenching my teeth. "Don't argue with me, Merik! The next time we stop, redistribute the load to make sure that bitch is carrying her fair share!"

"Mission, Eamon," Merik reminded me. "We don't have new gear to give her. We just..."

"For fuck's sake, Merik!" I snapped. "Just do what I fucking said!"

The corporal stopped and stared at me for a second as I kept marching. "Aye aye, Cadet. Aye aye."

A few hours later, once we started marching again after a late lunch, I passed Ritza Xi with her new pack. She was hunched over and wobbling under the weight of it. It looked like her knees were ready to buckle at any moment. Feeling me staring at her, Xi craned her neck in my direction and lifted the visor on her helmet so that I could see her face.

I noticed that Xi no longer had that deadpan look behind her eyes. There was a fire in them now, fueled by fury and determination. I could see that she was not going to give up and die. Not on that day. She was going to take on the extra weight and bear it just to spite me, robbing me of the satisfaction I would get from erasing her from the cosmos.

In the process, she left me even more miserable than I already was. And wondering if she would slit my throat as I slept like she had done to her husband.

●●-◄-●-►-●●

During our dinner break, I caught my Class One convicts taking some of Xi's load off of her and redistributing it amongst themselves. "Seriously?" I asked them, tempted to double their packs also. "That woman killed her kids! Why the hell are you helping her?"

Orgo Yisht looked me in the eye. "Do you really think she murdered her family, Tauk?"

"You think she's innocent?" I laughed. "Let me guess, you're innocent too. Right? You're all innocent, aren't you?"

Yisht laughed. "Oh, no. I'm guilty as fuck."

I was surprised by how casually Yisht acknowledged his transgressions. "Really? You're admitting you were a sex trafficker?"

The convict nodded. "Yes, I was. I deserve the shit you're doing to me. As far as I'm concerned, I don't think you can punish me enough. What I did was unforgivable."

"Then why did you do it?"

Yisht shrugged. "I got desperate. I had eight starving kids at home. I had to borrow money from some pretty unsavory people to feed them. The bitch is, I had the money to pay the fuckers back, but my house got raided, and my credits were confiscated. I'm pretty sure the cops were tipped off by the bastards I was in debt to."

Merik stepped up beside me. I rarely spoke to the prisoners, so seeing us having a conversation piqued his curiosity.

"Almost as soon as the police were done with us," Yisht continued. "The goons showed up looking for their cash. When I told them the cops had it, they tried to take my wife and a couple of my daughters."

My convict took his gloves off and showed me the scars on his knuckles. "I fucked up all three of those pricks by myself. So the next day, the goons sent six. I broke them, too. I grew up on the streets. I know how to use my hands. After that, the mob sent their gunmen. The shooters didn't try to kill me, though. They offered me a job. They said if I could keep the peace in their whorehouses, they'd pay me well, forgive my debts, and leave my family alone. It was an offer I couldn't refuse."

Yisht let out a long, sad sigh. "I worked for them fuckers for two years. I was glad when the League finally busted us. I hate what I did. I deserve everything you bastards throw at me, Cadet."

Looking over at Maynar Vold, I asked, "What about you? You innocent?"

Vold shook his head. "Nope. I stole food from soldiers. Food they stole from me first. And I sold it to the civilians that needed it."

"At exorbitant prices," Merik added.

"We were under siege," Vold sneered. "All the prices were exorbitant."

Looking around, Merik noticed Loman Krau sitting alone, well separated from the rest of the convicts. "Anybody know the story on him?"

"Yeah," Barone Parsons told us. "The guy's a creep. We have an agreement. He stays away from us, and we stay away from him."

"You think he did all those rapes then?" I asked.

Parsons shrugged. "We've never had any heart-to-hearts, but I've been in the system for seven years. You get a feel for who got shafted and who deserves to be here."

Merik nodded toward Krau. "And?"

The prisoner shrugged. "That cat gives off some really dark vibes."

"What about you?" I asked Parsons. "What's your story?"

He shrugged. "Close to Orgo's, actually. A police officer tried to put the moves on my fourteen-year-old daughter. When I confronted him about it, the son-of-a-bitch had me arrested. My wife filed a complaint and threatened to escalate the situation to the governor's office.

"While I was in jail, my house burned down with my wife and kids inside. Of course, it was ruled an accident, but someone, somewhere, put two and two together. They were disgusted enough to spring me from my cell. Within two days, I was arrested again on terrorism charges for plotting to destroy the police who arrested me and the court who signed the order to keep me confined."

"Were you?" asked Merik. "Plotting against them?"

"You're goddamn right I was," Parsons answered, spitting onto the ground. "But I hadn't had enough time to do anything about it yet. They had every reason to worry about me, but the charges they convicted me on were all trumped up."

Parsons maintained eye contact with me the entire time he told his story. I did not want to believe what he said, but I did. "You've been here seven years?" I asked him.

"Yep."

"You're out in three?"

The convict nodded. "I am."

"What are you going to do then? After your sentence is over?" I wondered if time had tempered the prisoner's desire for revenge.

It had not. Parsons flashed me an evil grin. "I've already done the time, Cadet. When I get out of this shit, you can bet your ass that I'm going to do the fuckin' crime."

When we stopped that night, I collapsed in the mud atop one of the banks. I then set about checking the seals of my armor to make sure there were no openings for the Kanarisian bugs to get into. Feeling a couple of raindrops hit bare skin near my shoulder, I reached up to see what was going on. A piece of uniform fabric effortlessly tore off and disintegrated as I rubbed it between my fingers, leaving only a smear of black mold behind when it was gone.

I cursed at the sky. "Is this ever going to end?"

"Not until we get above that first cloud layer," Jella said, instantly lightening my mood. It was the first civil thing she had said to me since finding out I shot Vernor Blyte. "And then, we'll only get brief respites. Maybe a day or two without rain. Even at Narman's Pyke, it pours about fifty percent of the time."

"At least there we won't have to fight Mother Nature during every waking moment," I said.

"Nope," Merik added. "I'm guessing we'll have other things to fight, though."

After a few moments of silence, our designated sniper, Prishtina Gai, asked, "What do you think we're going up against once we get to Narman's Pyke?"

I let out a long sigh. "I have no idea."

"It's probably the Ghuldarians," Vamir Stiid said in between bites of his field rations. "It's always the fucking Ghouls."

"I don't know," argued Abel Weir. "We're an awful long way from the Ghuldarian Belt. If they wanted to mess with the League, there's plenty of other worlds they could attack without being cut off by light-years of hostile territory."

"Yeah, but are any of those worlds chock full of Harnillium like Kanaris is?" asked Qora Zeld. "I hear this stuff is supposed to revolutionize everything from weaponry to space travel. That might make it worthwhile for the Ghuldari to make the trip."

"Maybe," Daiq Briima chimed in, taking a break from antagonizing the white stripes with his subversive political rants. "But how would they know about this place? It's on the other side of the known galaxy from where they are."

"You think that maybe it could be an alien race?" Nadia Reyn, our assistant machine gunner, asked.

"I doubt it," Lance Corporal Reino answered, rolling his eyes. "That's everybody's fantasy, isn't it? Discover the first alien civilization! Be there when we make first contact!" Reino paused to laugh. "We've been exploring the galaxy for centuries now. The only things we've come across smart enough to work a doorknob have been us. Humans. In all that time, we've never even come close to making contact with equivalent intelligence. I doubt we ever will."

Jella Duverii shrugged. "Don't be so sure, Marine. We might've been exploring space for a long time, but keep in mind that we've not even seen a quarter percent of our own galaxy. You know, here on Kanaris, the quarakai are on the verge of becoming equivalent. They talk to each other, they hold primitive funeral rituals, and they make tools. Tauk and I even saw one the other day wearing simple jewelry. They're progressing. Give it ten thousand years, maybe even less now that they've made contact with us, and they might be erecting pyramids like our ancient ancestors once did."

Building upon the thought I had days before, right after coming face-to-face with a quarakai, I asked, "Do you think they could be trained to fight? You know, to handle weapons?"

Our guide shook her head. "No, I don't. Not yet. These things are smart, but it'd be like building an army of chimpanzees. They're too unruly and undisciplined to fight like soldiers..."

Jella trailed off as a thought occurred to her. "But they can problem solve. And they are intimately a part of the environment of Kanaris in a way that we, as an alien species, could never be. They don't have the fine motor skills to operate a rifle effectively and lack the mental processing power to develop complex military tactics, but if they could meet us on *their* turf, under *their* terms..."

Our guide let out a little whistle while she mulled that possibility. "The military contingent of Narman's Pyke was only a few hundred Marines. The rest of the population were scientists, builders, mining specialists, service staff, and family members. Women. Children. If they ran afoul of a large group of quarakai...well..."

"Well, what?" I asked, impatient for Jella to finish her thought.

"Well, they could do some real damage."

"Enough to wipe out an entire colony?" Merik asked.

Jella shook her head after giving the matter a little more thought. "Maybe...I don't know...Naw, I don't think so. Physically speaking, we're no match for them. They're stronger, faster, and far more agile than we'll ever be. Our advantages in intelligence and technology neutralize all that, though. Even if Narman's Pyke only had a few hundred Marines, they had enough firepower to wipe out legions of quarakai armed with, at best, sharpened sticks."

Our guide relaxed a little. "The quarakai couldn't have taken our colony unless they got one of us to do their thinking for them."

It was my turn to speculate. "Doctor, have you studied all the quarakai that are out there? Is there any chance that somewhere on this planet lurks a sub-species that made that evolutionary leap towards high functioning intelligence? Keep in mind that when mankind first leapt into space, there were still humans living in the stone age on that very same planet. Biologically speaking, they were intellectually capable of developing rockets, but they had only ever been educated to hunt game and gather berries."

"We've never seen any evidence of intelligent quarakai anywhere upon this planet," Jella told me.

"Yeah, well," I retorted. "Up until we crash-landed on the Kanarisian Riviera, you'd never seen any evidence of man-eating mud grubs either, did you?"

•●◦•◦•● ●◦•◦•●•

CHAPTER 18

U nable to sleep that night, I decided to walk around the bivouac, eventually approaching the medical encampment to check on Je'Sikka Albarn. To my surprise, I found Sergeant Raza Bhutaan, Captain Briggund's goon, on his knees beside our pilot's SPS. "What the hell are you doing here?" I asked him.

"Whatever I feel like," Bhutaan answered, grinning at me as only a man drunk with impunity could. "What are *you* doing here? Looking for a little challenge to see who the toughest man in the Corps is?"

"I'm a Citadel cadet, Bhutaan," I told the sergeant. "We don't fight for bragging rights. We fight to kill."

"Funny, that's why I fight, too."

Shaking my head, I told him, "Then save it for the enemy."

"Oh, I can take you and still have plenty left for the Ghuldari," Bhutaan assured me. "You afraid to face me?"

"You afraid to tell me what you're doing to our pilot?"

"I'm not afraid of anything. You know, this rumor that our ships crashed into each other is still circulating around the ranks. I'm trying to figure out who the infiltrator is that's spreading it."

"And you think it's Je'Sikka Albarn?"

Bhutaan cast his gaze down at the pilot. "She's so doped up and delirious that she doesn't know her own name right now, let alone what happened during the descent." The praetorian let out a long sigh. "I hate to break this to you, Tauk, but I don't think she's going to make it to Narman's Pyke. That's a shame. It would be helpful if she could tell everyone the truth about what happened up there."

In other words, corroborate the line of bullshit you Samaaris want to peddle about the disaster.

"Albarn's tough," I assured Bhutaan. "She'll pull through."

"I don't know, man," the praetorian argued. "Fate hasn't been kind to the people who rode the cockpit down here to Kanaris. Did you know that the weapons officer disappeared last night? He probably got taken by one of those anwar things. The navigator's heart gave out a few days ago, too. This pilot's the last of the Navy cockpit crew to survive."

Bhutaan's lips might have just been stating the facts, but his twinkling eyes were confessing to murder. Hell, they were bragging about it. Bhutaan not only killed those two men, but he wanted me to know it. He was trying to impress upon me what would happen to anyone who did not toe the company line about Grazny Sirrah.

Shaking my head, I asked, "Do you care at all about what actually happened on the way down here?"

"Nope," Bhutaan answered with a shrug. "Not one little bit."

"Then you're a fool," I told him.

"No, I'm a patriot." The sergeant smirked. "I'm protecting my leadership. In turn, they protect the League. If it weren't for them, we'd all be overrun by the Ghuldari by now."

"You're seriously sticking your neck out for Captain Briggund because you think he can save us from the Ghouls?!?"

"Oh, fuck Briggund," Bhutaan scoffed. "I don't know how that simpleton keeps from drooling all over himself. I don't do what I do for the captain. I do it for the Sirrah family and the Prosperity Party. They're the ones who made the League what it is today and the only ones who can keep it that way."

"You seriously believe that shit?"

Bhutaan took a big step toward me. "I saw it with my own eyes, Tauk. I grew up on Tyannik-8, a Samaari mining colony..."

"I know what Tyannik-8 is." We had to study it at the Citadel.

"Yeah, well, it was paradise. We had everything we ever needed or wanted there. At least we did until the Ghuldari slipped in and started setting bombs off everywhere, sabotaging the mining equipment, and destroying the schools and hospitals. Then they started a rebellion that forced those pansies running the League to pull out."

That was not the way I learned it. I did my strategy paper on the Tyannik Rebellion. According to the parliamentary transcripts I scoured through, the non-Guild planets of the Kyperion League declared that Samaari abuses basically justified the uprising. There was even a bloc actively advocating League intervention on the side of the rebels. Ultimately, though, Samaari money won over enough ministers for the League to stay out of the conflict. The prevailing attitude was that the Guild made the mess, so the Guild could clean it up on their own.

"After the rebels seized control, the purges started," Bhutaan told me. "They grabbed everyone who had any connection to the League and started killing them on the street corners. The economy ground to a halt. Then the famine took hold. Do you know what hell is, Tauk? Hell is being so hungry that you're forced to sacrifice a younger cousin to keep yourself alive. I lost everything there. My home, my birthright, my entire family."

"I'm sorry to hear that."

"Not half as sorry as I am to have lived it," Bhutaan confessed. "You know, the League refused to intervene. Parliament bickered while we were forced to feed upon one another. Unable to sit back as we died by the thousands, Donaal Sirrah rallied the Prosperity Party and sent in the Blueshirts. It was dirty work, but they saved us."

Raza Bhutaan retreated a half step to give me some room. "I've seen the alternative to the Prosperity Party, Tauk. I'll never allow anyone on this side of the Ghuldarian Belt to ever go through what I did. That means protecting the Sirrah family against all threats, be it against their interests, their well-being, or their reputations."

"How old were you when you were on Tyannik?" I asked Bhutaan.

"I was eleven when the troubles started."

"You had a big house? Servants?" Most Samaaris there did.

Bhutaan spat. "Until the uprising. Our help turned on us. I watched one of our gardeners nearly cut my father in half with a machete. Our maids ransacked our rooms and stole everything of value. Our kitchen staff took all our food. Fucking scum."

"You ever see the accommodations of your house staff?"

The sergeant twisted his face up in disgust. "Why would I want to know where those animals lived?"

"Because if you did, you might have an easier time understanding what led to that uprising. It's easier for you Samaaris to blame Ghuldari agitators than to face the truth that people like your old man probably caused those people to rebel."

"You weren't there," Bhutaan growled. "You didn't know my father. He was a good man."

"You ever see him get violent towards anybody working in your household?"

Bhutaan did not answer. He just stood there staring at me, seething. I could tell by the look in his eye that not only had he seen it happen, but he had probably helped punish the servants himself.

"You know, Bhutaan," I told him. "When you put a population on starvation wages, abuse them, and rob them of all the tools they need to pull themselves out of poverty, they tend to resent you."

"Resent? We brought opportunity to Tyannik-8! We invested in that place! Those ungrateful fucks...!"

"The Conglomerate made forty-eight billion credits a year in straight profits off their Tyannik system operations. Thirty-eight billion went into shareholder profits. Five billion went into infrastructure costs, with the lion's share of that going to fund the Blueshirts charged with keeping the workers in line. Roughly twelve billion filtered into the two and a half million people that lived on that planet. That meant if it was divided equally, every person on Tyannik got about five thousand credits a year there. The poverty line was three grand more than that."

I could see Bhutaan's head spinning with all the numbers I threw at him. He obviously needed a summary, so I gave him one. "Life on Tyannik might have been a paradise for you, but for those who were not Samaari, it was pretty goddamn miserable."

"You saying I deserved to watch my family get butchered by those savages, Tauk?"

Shaking my head, I told him, "No, but there's another side to that tale, Sergeant. In fact, there are several. And of all the ones I read while researching my thesis on Tyannik-8, the only one that blames the Ghuldari is the line of shit put out by the Guilds."

"You implying that Samaaris are liars?" Bhutaan growled.

"I don't have to imply it, Sergeant! You admitted a couple of minutes ago that you don't even care what actually happened to our dropships! All you care about is defending the Sirrah family's reputation! That's seriously your playbook?!? Every time the Samaaris fuck up, you have to blame it on the Ghuldari?!?"

Even in the dark, I could tell the color was rushing into Bhutaan's face. "You in bed with the Ghouls now, Tauk?"

"Of course not!" I snapped, jabbing my finger into Bhutaan's chest. "What I'm telling you is that the goddamn Ghouls are less of a threat to the League as an adversary than the Samaaris are as an ally! Right now, this mission's death toll is fast approaching five thousand troops. As far as I can tell, not a single one of them was killed by the Ghuldari! We're dying because of megalomania!"

Bhutaan was so enraged that he was quaking. Subconsciously, his arms dropped to his sides, putting them in a position where it would be easier to draw his weapon. In response, I sighed and slipped my hands into my pockets.

"Is that what they teach you in the academy, Tauk?" Bhutaan spat in contempt. "To hate the Guilds?"

"No," I answered. "They teach us that ideology and fanaticism get Marines killed. And from what I've seen on this mission so far, they're right."

Taking my left hand out of my pocket, I waved Bhutaan off dismissively. "Go ahead. Keep peddling that fantasy of yours about enemy fire taking down our transports. Without resupply and dropship support, we might make it to our objective, but we're not going to survive there very long."

Bhutaan's eyes narrowed. "Are you the one telling everybody that Grazny Sirrah was a coward who destroyed those landers?"

"I'm not announcing it from the treetops, you simple fuck, but that's what happened. I don't care how your bosses want to spin that, but there ain't no enemy anti-air down here shooting down our ships. We're going through a lot of unnecessary misery, not to mention Marines, to keep that dirty little secret of yours hidden. And mark my words, you miserable twat. If any of those Navy crewmen died by your hand, you will be held accountable. Along with anyone who put you up to it."

Bhutaan's hand casually came to rest on the handle of his pistol. "Maybe we should go for a little walk."

"Fuck that," I said as I pulled my right hand out of my pocket to show him the grenade I was holding, pin pulled, and detonator lever switched to "instant." If I let go of that device, both of us would be incinerated instantaneously.

"If you wanna kill me, do it right here in the open," I told him. "You won't have time to erase the video loop this time. Everyone will know what happened. If these Marines suspect Briggund killed military men to salvage the reputation of a dead coward, he'll have a mutiny on his hands. They'll string him and Horad up by the balls and cheer while the kryptids eat them alive."

"So be it, then," Bhutaan snarled. "I'm not letting you slander the Sirrah family."

"Shooting me would be the quickest way to soil their reputation." I laughed at Bhutaan's stupidity. "Look, Sergeant, I don't give a fuck about the Sirrah family. All I care about is completing my mission. Period. Make that pathetic little puke a saint if you want. I'm not going to interfere. If anything happens to that pilot or our guide, though, I'm going to kill you. I don't give a shit who you work for."

Bhutaan's fingers flexed nervously around his sidearm, itching to pull it. Finally, he growled, "You're lucky we need that guide of yours. If she or you go missing, people are going to have questions."

"I don't have that problem," I countered. "If you disappear, no one will give two shits where you went besides Briggund."

The sergeant nodded slowly. "So, what do we do about this?"

Shrugging, I answered, "I suggest we stay out of each other's way."

"Can you keep your mouth shut, Killer?" Bhutaan did not call me 'killer' as a sign of respect. He spat it out mockingly as if he doubted I had what it took to be a ten-percenter.

Ignoring the insult, I nodded. "As long as nothing happens to the pilot or our guide."

Bhutaan looked down at Albarn and shook his head. "I can't vouch for the pilot. I think she's headed to the hereafter no matter what I do." Assuming we had struck a deal, the sergeant turned his back on me and abruptly walked away.

I made sure Briggund's bodyguard was well out of sight before I tried putting the pin back in the grenade. My fingers were trembling. For the first time in my life, I was scared. Not of Bhutaan, however.

I was afraid of what he could do to Jella.

Academy cadets were not supposed to form attachments to anything that could compete with our commitment to the mission. Until my blooding rites, I did not think it possible to love anything but the Marines.

For me, though, the Marines were Misha Donitz, Juergen Kohl, and Helmut Hoeneker. They were the only family I had. When Gori Dravidas butchered them, it was like there was no longer enough of the Corps left for me to care about. There was just a void, and 'nothing' is a difficult concept to lay down one's life for.

It was not until I met Harlund Merik, Jella Duverii, and Je'Sikka Albarn that the hole started to fill. Harlund was a true warrior with a reputation for inimitable courage under fire. He reminded me of Jurgen Kohl. Jella was insanely intelligent and possessed an extraordinary sense of perseverance. She would never allow her spirit to be broken, just like Misha Donitz. Our pilot was a hero, willing to sacrifice herself to save her comrades, as Helmut Hoeneker had.

Harlund, Jella, and Warrant Officer Albarn were the only people in the galaxy with whom I still felt any connection. They were all I had.

And though I doubted they felt the same way about me, I found the idea of losing them terrifying.

●●‹●›●‹●›●●

CHAPTER 19

It was a racket unlike any I had ever heard. PFC Goran Bevedich was walking point when a giant quarakai dropped from the trees and landed right in front of him. Before Bevedich could raise his weapon, the creature jabbed the sharpened end of a pointed stick at his throat and roared in rage.

In response, hundreds of other quarakai swarmed out of the brush and flooded the trail. Most were armed with primitive spears and voiced their fury at an incredible volume.

The Marines responded instinctively. They raised their weapons, clicked off their safeties, and took aim at the threat. Thankfully, none of them fired. It was not because of trigger discipline, though. It was terror. The troops could sense that killing one quarakai would initiate a bloodbath, and they were probably right.

Not that the Marines were afraid of sharpened sticks. It was the beasts themselves that made our blood run cold. This was an unusually large sub-species challenging us. The one holding Bevedich at bay stood a third taller than I did, and unlike the others I had spotted up to this point, its arms were not thin and sinewy. These quarakai were all muscle. It looked like it might take an entire magazine to stop one of them.

"DON'T SHOOT!" I heard Jella scream over the battalion network. "WHAT-EVER YOU DO, DON'T FIRE!"

"You don't give the orders here!" Captain Briggund yelled back. We all heard the tremor in his voice. He was not projecting a lot of confidence.

"If you shoot," Jella warned him. "A lot of us are going to die!"

"If you got some better idea," Private Bevedich chimed in. "I'm open to it." He sounded afraid, too. Unlike Briggund, though, he had a pretty compelling reason to be.

Our guide stopped and thought for a second, which was not easy to do over the roar of the quarakai. Remembering the notes she once read about the early interactions with the creatures around Narman's Pyke, Jella shouted out, "Kryptids! I need a couple of kryptids!"

Popped kryptid had become a dietary staple of the battalion ever since we crashed. The bugs were a common find along the trail, easy to catch, and as long as they were unpopped, they lasted a long time in a cargo pocket. We were eating more of those than we were combat rations.

Barone Parsons was standing a couple of meters to my left. He pulled one of the giant bugs from his pouch and handed it to our guide. "Here. Take mine."

"Thank you!" Jella snapped, snatching the kryptid from the prisoner and starting to run up to the head of the column. I had to grab her by the back of her exo-armor to stop her.

"What do you think you're doing?!?" I yelled.

Struggling to worm her way out of my grip, she barked, "I'm trying to broker a truce! Let me go!"

"You're not going up there! There's no way!" I snapped back. "You trying to get yourself killed?"

"No! I'm trying to show the quarakai what popped kryptid tastes like!"

I suddenly saw where Jella was going with that. Food was a primal need. It was the way humans had befriended animals since the Stone Age. It was a great way to show the quarakai that we were not there to hurt them. "Give me the bug," I told Jella. Turning my head around, I then shouted, "Harlund! Get up here and watch the doctor!"

"Don't cook it until they can see you," Jella said as she handed me the kryptid and tossed me her torch. "Show the bug to them before you pop it. They have to see the magic. Keep in mind how wet it is here. Even with all the lightning strikes, fire is something these creatures see maybe once in a lifetime."

"I don't need the zoological lesson," I informed her. "Just tell me what you want me to do."

"Get as close as you can without agitating them and…"

"They already sound pretty agitated."

"…without agitating them more. You want them to smell it. After you pop the bug, take a bite, then offer it to the quarakai."

"Then what?"

Jella nervously sucked in a long breath of air. "Well, if we're lucky, they'll like it as much as the quarakai near Narman's Pyke did. And hopefully, they'll be so crazy about it that they'll forget about returning the gesture and offering you something that they like to eat."

"And what would that be?"

Jella shrugged. "I'm praying it won't be a piece of that private up there."

Letting out a long list of colorful adjectives, I turned around and took off. As I rushed toward the quarakai horde, I jumped onto the battalion network so everyone could hear me. "I'm headed up front with instructions from Duverii! Everybody hold their fire! Unless that thing kills me. After that, I don't give a shit what you do."

Enraged that the doctor and I were making decisions over the battalion network independent of the chain of command, Captain Briggund stormed over to intercept me with Sergeant-Major Horad in tow.

"What do you think you're doing, Cadet?!?" the captain screamed at me. "Who do you think's in charge of the battalion?!?"

Stopping in my tracks, I answered, "You are, sir."

"Did I authorize you to approach those animals?"

I knew time was of the essence, and the captain was wasting it. Offering the kryptid to Briggund, I asked, "Do you want to take it up there, sir?"

Briggund craned his head toward the quarakai just in time to hear the alpha, the one with the stick jammed up against the private's throat, let out an ear-splitting roar. The captain recoiled, showing me that he had no desire to get any closer to the creatures than he already was.

"Can someone please pony the fuck up and do something?!?" cried our hostage.

The captain looked at the Marine who was about to be impaled, then back at me. He repeated the sequence three more times as he tried to formulate a decision. He only stopped when Raza Bhutaan leaned over and whispered something into his ear. I assumed that he reminded the battalion commander that I was one of only three surviving witnesses that knew the truth about Grazny Sirrah and the loss of our dropships.

The captain's lips bent into a slight grin that was very much out of place, considering the situation. He then stepped out of my way and waved me past. "By all means. Be my guest."

"That's okay! Take your time!" Bevedich called out sarcastically. "My calendar's pretty clear! It's not like I have to be anywhere today! Or ever!"

"You better get going, Cadet," Briggund told me. "Do your thing before those beasts turn that boy into a screaming popsicle."

With the captain's blessing, I finally ran off toward the front of the column.

The quarakai did not appreciate my intrusion. The alpha began shrieking again, and a trio of its henchman rushed forward to block me. I backed them off with the kryptid, thrusting it toward the creatures like it was some sort of magical talisman. They did not seem to be afraid of it, but the beasts still hesitated, curious about what I was trying to do. While they attempted to interpret my intentions, I turned on my torch and pointed it at the bug's abdomen.

The moisture covering the kryptid's shell instantly sizzled and vaporized, as did every raindrop that passed through the beam. The quarakai fell silent and stared at me, transfixed not so much by my cooking technique but by the light I produced from the device in my hand. Thirty seconds later, the kryptid popped like a gunshot, and the quarakai ducked in unison. I held up the bug in victory, showing them the white meat dangling from its carapace.

With all quarakai eyes now on me, I made a big show of pulling a morsel off the kryptid and putting it in my mouth. I then tore off another piece and offered it to the closest henchman. In response, the creature looked to the alpha and croaked several times. After the alpha answered, the beast stepped forward and sniffed at my gift. As soon as it got a whiff of the meat, the quarakai's eyes opened wide, and its salivary glands went into overdrive. It plucked the snack from my fingertips and shoved it into its mouth. The damned thing then seemed to lose its mind.

As the quarakai fussed about the treat he just had, I turned to Bevedich and asked, "How are you holding up, Killer?"

"I've been better," the captive croaked in response. "I ain't gonna lie."

As I slowly advanced toward the monster threatening our Marine, I felt my knees shake. The closer I got, the more massive the alpha quarakai appeared. It was a monster, and it seemed like half of my body could easily fit in its mouth. When I was within reach, the beast let go of the spear with one of its hands and snatched the bug out of mine. It then tore what was left of the meat out of the carapace and shoved it between its teeth.

The quarakai leader's eyes opened wide in a universal expression of delightful surprise, then it pulled its spear away from Bevedich's throat, releasing its prisoner. I clicked the transmit button on the battalion network and called out, "If anybody's holding kryptids, get them out and start cooking! Bring them up here as quick as you can! We're about to have a barbecue!"

Before I knew it, the sound of popping bugs shot out from all over the column, and scores of troops rushed forward with treats for the quarakai. When we exhausted our supply, the animals tore through the jungle looking for more, returning to us so we could cook them. We started a feeding frenzy.

With our path unbarred, a relief ran up to replace Bevedich. We were on the move again, though progress slowed considerably with all the kryptid popping we had to do.

Those quarakai stayed with us for three days, and we felt safe for the first time since leaving the beach. We were surrounded by hundreds of the most terrifying beings we had ever seen, but they were on our side. As long as we kept pumping their bellies full of kryptid flesh, we had allies. We felt like nothing could touch us while under their protection. Not even the anwar.

At a certain point, the creatures stopped cold and would go no further. They gathered at the sides of the trail, chattering as we filed past. "Is this the end of their territory?" I asked Jella.

Our guide nodded. "Probably."

"It's hard to imagine anything out there big and bad enough to challenge something like these monsters. You'd think that they could go wherever they damned well pleased."

Gunny Malcolm stepped up alongside us and, having heard the conversation, added, "Yeah, well, no matter how big and bad something is, there's always something bigger and badder out there somewhere."

Malcolm took a deep breath and turned his gaze forward, pointing his chin further up the trail. "Let's just hope that whatever it is, we don't run into it before we get to Narman's Pyke."

●●‹●›●‹●›●●

CHAPTER 20

G unny Malcolm had been through a lot during his couple of decades in the Space Corps, and his body showed every bit of it.

Though Malcolm's gray hair was full and thick, he kept it cropped short, revealing a nasty triangular scar on the right side of his scalp that he got from standing too close to an exploding hover tank. He also had a large circular chunk bitten out of his left ear, the result of a bar fight over a hooker, from what I had heard.

Malcolm lost the tip of his right ring finger to frostbite on Bat-Klaandu. He also donated a couple of toes to some unseen river serpent on Rabaat-7. That could have gone much worse, to hear him tell the tale. Apparently, the creature attacked him while he was skinny-dipping.

When Gunny was a squad leader, his grenadier jumped in front of him and loosed a shoulder-fired rocket without checking his six first. The back-blast blew Malcolm's exo-armor away and melted the skin off his torso from his nipples to his navel. That was still difficult to look at.

Our platoon sergeant also lost half an ass cheek to cellulitis on Vishmata-14. His left shin still bore the evidence of the broken bone that popped out of it on New Berisephone when he was a corporal. One of his calves was discolored from some sort of parasitic infection he picked up in the swamps of Bah Somik, and both shoulders had the circular hallmarks of having survived Ghuldari small arms fire.

Get a few drinks into Gunny Malcolm and he could tell you a hilarious story about each of his injuries. He wore his wounds like medals. No matter how disfiguring they were, the damage Malcolm's enemies inflicted on the man never bothered him in the slightest.

The damage he inflicted on his adversaries was a whole different story. Those scars were harder to see, as tattoos covered the track marks on his forearms, but they were far more devastating.

While Malcolm could spend hours spinning yarns about bug hunts on Blue Mycanea or epic battles against the Ghuldari across the Haifauna Rift, he never spoke of hunting Galeesi separatists. Nor did he talk about the part he played in putting down the Portuna Rebellion. Had I not stolen a peek into a hacked copy of Gunny's service record, I never would have known that he helped stamp out an uprising on Gallus-2, either. Hell, I did not even know there had been an uprising on Gallus-2.

While Gunny never spoke about the domestic actions he participated in, I suspected those were the reason he woke me up crying in his sleep.

"No!" Malcolm sobbed on the bank. "I ain't doing it! Not anymore! They're children!"

"Gunny!" I whispered, trying to rouse the man before anyone else heard his cries. Seeing Malcolm in such a vulnerable state could drastically affect the morale of the junior Marines. "Gunny! Wake up!"

"You fucking monsters!"

"Gunny!" I was a little louder that time. "Wake up! You're having a bad dream!"

"How could you?!?" Malcolm was increasing his volume. "HOW?!?"

"Who is that?" I heard our medic groggily call out. "Is everyone okay?"

"No, they're not okay!" Malcolm yelled back. Kalawezi's question had somehow penetrated the platoon sergeant's dreamworld. "You murdered them, you..."

Others were starting to stir. I had to put a stop to the outburst. Rolling to my feet, I stumbled over to Malcolm to shake him awake. As soon as my hands touched his breastplate, though, Gunny drew his dagger and thrust it at my throat.

The adrenaline pumping through Malcolm's system, coupled with his proficiency at taking lives with sharpened steel, made my platoon sergeant one of the quickest draws I had ever seen. Lucky for me, my Citadel training made me just a hair faster. The point of the blade just knicked my larynx before I bent Malcolm's wrist and forced him to drop it. Without missing a beat, Gunny then drew his sidearm, which I barely managed to take away before he could get his finger around the trigger.

After disarming Malcolm twice, I rolled him face down into the mud, then intertwined my arms with his to keep him immobilized. The rain made that exponentially more challenging than it should have been, as both of us were slippery as hell. Now awake, but disoriented and confused, Gunny roared with rage as he tried to break out of my hold.

"Shhhhhhhh," I hissed into his ear. "It's okay, Gunny. You're okay. It's just a dream."

The ferocity of Malcolm's struggle suggested that he was not quite ready to believe that. "Fuck you, Lieutenant! You need to call off those troops right now! CALL 'EM OFF!"

"GUNNEY!" I snapped. "That's enough! Attennnnn-HUT!"

The instinct was involuntary. Malcolm's body went rigid, though his eyes darted wildly from side to side. Things were starting to come together for the man. In his dreams, Gunny Malcolm had been in a desert. Waking up in a torrential downpour was incompatible with my platoon sergeant's nightmare. "This isn't Portuna," he told me.

"No, it most certainly is not," I assured him.

I felt him relax as he started to get his bearings. Hearing several nearby Marines stirring out of their sleep, I figured it was time to get Malcolm out of earshot. I pulled him up to his feet and started to drag him away from the platoon, heading in the direction of the medical camp in case something went wrong. "Get your fuckin' hands off me," Gunny snarled once he started turning back into himself.

"In a sec..."

"NO!" Malcolm screamed. "NOW!"

I could have easily kept Gunny under control, but doing so would have created a disturbance and drawn attention to us. That was what I was trying to avoid, so I let the man go.

Once he had spun himself out of my grip, Gunny turned to face me, trembling with rage, fear, and probably a bit of withdrawal. It was difficult to imagine he had much access to whatever he was using to take the edge off his memories while on patrol.

"If you ever lay your grubby little rat-fink hands on me again," Malcolm sneered at me. "I'm going to add more lashes to what you already got coming!"

"Gunny, I was trying to help..."

Malcolm cut me off with a back-handed slap across the mouth. "EVER!" he yelled. "You understand me?"

Rubbing my jaw, I nodded my head. "Aye aye, Gunny. Look, I understand what just happened to you. There's no shame in..."

Gunny let me have it again. "You don't understand a GOD-damn thing, Cadet! Nada! You think you're a killer? Huh? Do ya?"

"I haven't racked up my seven yet, but I've killed a few..."

"You murdered convicts!" Malcolm snapped back. "You ain't killed anyone able to fight back yet! You ain't shit!"

I wanted to tell Malcolm that Gori Dravidas did indeed fight back, but it was not the time nor place to talk about that.

"Killing convicts and enemy soldiers is easy, Tauk," Gunny snarled at me. "They're just as much scum as we are. Murderers. Terrorists. Those Ghuldari animals. Pirates. Bandits. They deserve what we do to them..."

Malcolm took a step closer to me and lowered his voice. "...but mark my words, Tauk. If you survive this shit here and go on to future missions, you'll eventually find yourself confronting people who maybe don't deserve it so much. And when that happens, after you've carried out your orders, *then* you'll be a proper killer. Not a ten-percenter, but a *killer*. *Then* you'll understand. *Then* your opinion about what goes on in my head will carry some weight. Until you reach that point, though, you can keep your fuckin' suppositions to yourself."

In the Corps, being called a killer was a term of respect. It meant a Marine could be counted upon when things got tough. In that one conversation, though, Gunny Malcolm sucked the honor right out of it.

Despite his flaws, I looked up to Gunny Malcolm. I considered him a true warrior, an older version of Harlund Merik.

As he stormed off into the darkness, however, I realized that Malcolm was not so complimentary in his own self-image. He saw himself more as an older version of Mazada Duum.

●●◄►●◄►●●

"You know," Raza Bhutaan said as he stepped out of the darkness behind me. "Your platoon sergeant isn't the only person talking in his sleep lately."

I was startled. Gunny Malcolm had barely passed from my line of sight when the praetorian let himself be known. I did not like the idea of someone as dangerous as Bhutaan getting the drop on me. "What the fuck," I gasped as I spun around to face the sergeant. "Are you following me?"

The Samaari chuckled. "No. I've just been keeping my eye on your pilot back at the medical camp when I heard your voice. You haven't been coming around her much the past few days."

"I've been around," I countered. "She's just been out cold. They have her doped up pretty hard."

Bhutaan shrugged. "I had them pull back the dosage a few days ago so I could talk to her."

"Talk to her?" I asked as I stepped closer to Briggund's goon. "About what?"

"What she saw in the cockpit. I asked her what her story was about how we lost those two dropships."

"I told you to leave her alone."

Bhutaan grinned. "Relax. Warrant Officer Albarn has been around the fleet a while. She knows how things work. She's a smart girl."

"What did she say, Bhutaan?" I asked again. "What was her story?"

"She said her story was whatever I wanted it to be. She's willing to play ball."

I relaxed a little. "So why are you still bothering her?"

The praetorian sighed. "Well, she's building up resistance to the drugs the medics are giving her. She doesn't really wake up, but she emerges into the twilight every so often. When she does that, she tends to relive some of her recent trauma. The medics heard her crying out for Grazny Sirrah to not pull out of the descent. Like I said, your gunny isn't the only one talking in his sleep."

My heart skipped a beat. "Albarn's doped up, Bhutaan. You can't hold her accountable for that."

"I'm not," the sergeant assured me. "It's not her fault, but the damage she can do with those delirious utterances could prove irreparable."

"If anything happens to her..."

"Look, you need to face reality, Killer. I don't have to do anything to her. She's fading. Her condition deteriorates by the day. That woman's suffering, Tauk. The humane thing to do is let the medics put her out of her misery. The smart thing to do is to make that happen before she says something that could compromise the unity of the League."

"Unity of the League?" I scoffed. "You mean the Sirrah family's dominance over it?"

"Don't be naïve, Tauk. Love or hate the Prosperity Party, they're the ruling force of the moment. Tensions are running high among the League worlds right now, and there's some dangerous rhetoric coming out of the lesser systems. We could be on the brink of civil war. If that happens, do you think the Ghouls will sit idly by and wait for us to sort it all out? No, sir. They'll march right in and take advantage of us while we're divided. You want to live under the Ghuldari yoke, Killer?"

"Whatever direction the League takes," I countered. "The League takes. My country is the Corps, Bhutaan. I don't know shit about parliamentary politics, and I don't care about them. I only care about my mission. What happens to the Prosperity Party is your concern. Not mine. My concern is protecting our guide and getting my Red Caste candidate safely back to the mothership. That's it."

"Your Red Caste candidate is where our concerns intersect," Bhutaan informed me. "She can have a pretty serious impact on League politics if she can't control her tongue."

"Nobody will take her seriously in the shape she's in, Sergeant. Whatever she says is nothing more than the inane rantings of a woman in the throes of a morphine bender."

"You better hope no one listens to her," Bhutaan threatened. "The only reason Briggund's letting her live is the credibility she'll have when she tells the League the truth about our ships getting shot down."

"That isn't the truth."

Bhutaan scoffed. "The truth is whatever we say it is." Growing bored with our conversation, the sergeant then said, "It's too late to give you a reality check, Cadet. I need to get a little shuteye before we head out again. Sweet dreams."

As he turned to leave, the praetorian reconsidered and shifted his body to face me again. "Oh, and tell your gunny I hope he can manage to get a good night's sleep soon. Serving under the Butcher of Deraghun could be hard on a man."

I squinted disbelievingly at Bhutaan. "Gunny wasn't on Deraghun."

"No, he wasn't," Raza agreed. "He served with Dravidas on Portuna. From what I heard, what those Marines did there was even worse than Deraghun. It just didn't make the news."

•◦◦◄◈► ◉ ◄◈► ◦◦•

CHAPTER 21

"He's a nice guy once you get to know him," Jella told me a few days later. We were about a third of the way to Narman's Pyke, approaching the first cloud layer and, beyond that, slightly milder climes.

"I told you not to talk to that son-of-a-bitch." We had been marching in non-stop rain for nineteen days. I had been trying to protect Jella, keep an eye on Raza Bhutaan, and make sure Je'Sikka Albarn did not mysteriously die in her sleep. I was stretched too thin and it was affecting my state of mind. Though I genuinely enjoyed Jella Duverii's company, I was her bodyguard. Having her admit that she was sneaking away to speak with Loman Krau, a convicted serial rapist, rubbed me raw.

I could not protect Jella Duverii if she insisted on fraternizing with a known psychopath. That creep might have convinced her that he was innocent, but I, and the League's penal system, knew what he was capable of. "I gave you an order."

Jella scoffed. "Give me all the orders you want, Tauk. I'm not a Marine. I'm not one of your subordinates."

I stopped marching and turned toward our guide. "Okay. Let's play it your way, then. Harlund!"

"What?" Corporal Merik shouted out.

"You got Jella duty!" As Harlund took his post. I drew my pistol and went looking for Loman Krau.

"Wait!" Jella yelled, chasing after me. "What are you doing?"

"Neutralizing a threat to my primary objective," I told her. "If I can't keep you away from Loman Krau, I guess that means I have to keep Loman Krau away from you."

"What?" Jella gasped. "You're going to kill him?"

"Yep."

"You can't do that!"

"Actually," Merik told her as he jogged to keep up. "He can. Class Zero IRRECs can be summarily executed for disobeying orders. Those convicted of capital crimes who aren't fit for military duty are just put to death anyway. These dirtbags are all on borrowed time."

"Eamon, please," Jella begged, running alongside me. "Don't do this! He didn't do anything! I was the one talking to him! I was only trying to get a feel for what landed him here! I..."

Krau was on litter duty. I yanked him off his position so hard that the rest of the bearers collapsed under the shift in balance. They fell to their knees and dropped Briggund's Box for what must have been the fiftieth time. They then looked around in panic to see if the sergeant-major had witnessed it. "W-w-what?" Krau stammered as I led him to the side of the trail and removed his helmet. "I-I-I didn't do anything, Tauk! What do you think I did?"

As I undid the straps at Krau's shoulders to drop his back and breast plates, I said, "I made it very clear that you were not to interact with Jella Duverii, but you did it anyway."

"I didn't seek her out, Tauk!" Krau pleaded. "She came to me! I just answered her questions, man! Please! I didn't do anything!"

Once I had the convict's pelvic protection off, I kicked him in the crotch hard enough to lift him off his feet and drop him to his knees. I then chambered a round and took aim.

"EAMON!" Jella screamed. "NO! YOU WIN! I'll stay away from him! I'll do whatever you say! Just don't do this! Don't kill that man because of something I did."

"I'm doing it for something he did. He disobeyed my orders."

"Please, Tauk!" Krau begged. "Don't kill me for this! Not for this!"

"Maybe I should kill you just for all those girls you hurt." I snarled.

"NO, EAMON!" Jella yelled. "DON'T! I'm begging you!"

I kept staring at the convict through the sights of my pistol. The truth was that I did not want to kill Lomar Krau at that moment. Lieutenant Thyster would disapprove and, as far as I was concerned, ending Krau's miserable life would be a kindness I did not think he deserved. I could make him suffer more by keeping him alive.

Knowing I had achieved what I wanted, I lowered the hammer of my weapon and put it away. My job was far from finished, though. I clenched my fist and planted it in Krau's face, smashing his nose. "I told you not to even look at her!"

I screamed as I hit him again. "You think that was a suggestion?" That question was punctuated by a hit to the mouth that broke several of the convict's teeth.

Jella was crying now. "Eamon! Please stop!"

I didn't. I kept at him, throttling Krau with blow after blow as the column marched by, too miserable, weary, and wet to show any interest in us. I turned Krau's lips into a bloody mess, shredding them against the jagged edges of his shattered teeth. I then went to work on his right eye, and after that, hit him in the ear hard enough to rupture the drum. That was when he went limp.

Getting off of him, I screamed, "Are my orders clear now, Krau?!?"

When he failed to respond, I kicked him in the kidneys. "Answer me, you fucking prick!"

"Yes!" the convict cried. "They're clear! I won't talk to her! I won't touch her! I won't even look at her! I..."

"Get your armor back on and rejoin the formation, you piece of shit. If you can. If you can't, feel free to just lay there and fucking die."

Jella was crying almost as hard as Krau was, "Loman, I'm sorry! I'm so, so sorry!"

"GET AWAY FROM ME, YOU BITCH!" Krau screamed back. "THIS IS YOUR FAULT! YOU DID THIS TO ME!"

Our guide opened her mouth to plead her case, but looked at me instead and realized the more she talked, the more danger she was putting Krau in. "You son-of-a-bitch," she sobbed at me. "He was right, you know."

"Really?" I asked. "Right about what?"

"You're cruel. You're monsters." Wiping tears out of her eyes, Jella then spat, "You're the same person you think he is. You get off on brutalizing people who can't fight back. You're cut from the same cloth, Tauk."

●● ◄●► ●◄●► ●●

130

CHAPTER 22

We emerged out of the "Hot Zone" seventy-two hours later. It took us twenty-two days to get there, marching continuously from sunrise to sunset. At the beginning of the trek, we lost Marines to misadventure, to things like anwar attacks, venomous trees, and falls from high places. By this point in our journey, however, we were losing people to exhaustion. More than two dozen troops had perished since we left the beach.

Captain Briggund looked to be among the worst of us. He was gaunt and feverish. Having spent most of his career as a desk jockey in Corps Intelligence, he was not as conditioned to trail life as the troops under his command. The man appeared to be on his last legs. He must have felt that way too, for as soon as we stumbled across a large clearing and the rain finally stopped, he called our column to a halt and ordered us to make camp for a three-day rest period. While we were down, the Signal Corps troops fired off a rocket to update the *Nebulan Phoenix* of our situation.

As the battalion set to regaining its strength, I started to audit my squad, trying to assess what kind of condition they were in. Harlund Merik had been at this stuff for half a decade. He was used to roughing it. He was tired and sleep-deprived like everyone else, but he was fine. Akkam Lumuk could barely walk. His feet were chewed up badly and his joints were battered from the spills he had taken on the rocks. That still didn't stop him from sparring with Merik as soon as we got settled.

Lumuk's nemesis, Mazada Duum, was actually in pretty good shape. When we stopped, he relaxed by pulling out his daggers and throwing them at kryptids crawling up the sides of the trees, regularly spiking them from more than forty paces away. I hated to admit it, but Duum displayed real stamina and powered through the march with the best of us. If it were not for his attitude, he would have had the makings of a decent combat Marine.

Even though she was a civilian, Dr. Duverii was also in excellent shape. As a field biologist, she spent a lot of time in the wilderness and was used to life in the bush. The biggest complaint Jella had was having to be so close to me. She had been giving me the silent treatment ever since I nearly beat Loman Krau to death.

Our medic was not holding up as well as our guide. Tima Kalawezi was at the end of her rope, and being from the desert planet of Ghad Ghulan, the constant rain had taken its toll on her. She never complained, though. She just pushed herself to keep everyone else going. Kalawezi deserved a break, but I had to put her to work as soon as we stopped.

"Feet," I told her. "Everyone's feet are in terrible shape. I need you to get them all treated and properly bandaged to at least start the healing process before we get going again."

"Aye aye, Cadet Tauk."

"And do it quick," I told her. "I want you off your own dogs and resting as soon as possible, too. I have to check on a few more people, but I'll be back soon to give you a hand."

Walking away from my squad, I spotted Loman Krau lying in the mud. I was amazed he was still alive. After I beat him, Orgo Yisht had to practically drag the man along the route. Yisht harbored no affection for Krau, but he realized they would have to carry more of the load if the man died. It was better to do the extra work until Krau could get back on his feet instead of doing it forever.

"Hey! Tauk!" called out Sergeant Kyker, the billeting NCO that assigned me my replacements after we crashed on Kanaris. "Where are you headed?"

"Checking on someone I got in medical," I answered.

"The pilot?"

"Yeah." Upon hearing I would see Albarn, Jella Duverii stood up and walked my way. She might not have been talking to me, but she never passed up an opportunity to spend time with the woman who saved us all.

"Hey, Tauk, can I ask you a favor?" Kyker asked me.

"Sure, Sarge. What's up?"

"My boys are pretty much all used up. They could really use a morale boost. Some sport, if you know what I mean. You mind if we borrow Ritza Xi?"

I winced at the request and turned to look at my female Zero. Xi was terrified and craned her head toward Parsons and Yisht, silently pleading with her fellow convicts for help. In turn, they cast their eyes impotently at the ground. The two men knew there was nothing they could do for her.

Quaking in her boots, Xi backed up and tried to hide behind Akkam Lumuk, who paused his martial arts lesson when he heard Kyker's request. Lumuk was no help either, but Xi hoped his size alone might scare the sergeant off.

The images I saw of Xi's murdered babies popped into my mind, and for a moment, I considered letting Kyker take her. Then I remembered something Yisht had asked me a few days prior.

Do you really think she murdered her family, Tauk?

I did. But I also thought Vernor Blythe was just another scumbag Zero when I blew his brains out to steal his SPS. It turned out he was a good man.

What if I was wrong about Ritza Xi, too?

Looking at my convict, I wondered if it was possible she was innocent. I thought of Raza Bhutaan and my suspicions he murdered *Wasp-Three's* navigator and weapons officer. If an entitled Samaari could kill two Navy officers and get away with it, what would stop another from railroading some poor homemaker if the truth embarrasses someone with a little bit of power?

If Xi did kill her family, she deserved what Kyker and his men wanted to do to her.

But what if she didn't?

She did it. She had to. The League would not have sentenced a good woman to such a horrible fate if they knew she was innocent.

Look what they did to Parsons. They sent him here because a cop wanted to have his way with the man's daughter. Then they burned his family to death to keep it from being exposed.

At least that was what Parsons told me. He was a convict, too, though. I was not supposed to trust what he said.

But I did...

And Ritza Xi? Did I believe her?

Believe what? She never told me her side of the story one way or the other. But would I confide in me if I were her?

I caught sight of Jella Duverii staring at me in disbelief. Her mouth was agape, disgusted that I was actually considering letting Kyker and his men have their way with Xi. In her eyes, I was taking entirely too long to come to the right decision. She made me feel very ashamed of myself.

Shaking my head, I turned back to Kyker and said, "No. I need her to carry supplies and can't afford to have you guys returning her to us barely able to walk. Besides, your men need rest right now. Force them to sit back and heal."

"Come on, Tauk. Just let us have her for a little…"

"I said no, Kyker. That's it. Leave her alone."

The sergeant turned and looked at Xi, catching her glaring at him from behind Lumuk, seething with contempt. "What the fuck are you looking at?" Kyker snarled. "Piss me off, and I may have to come back for you after dark anyway."

"Hey!" I barked, spinning around to confront the Marine. "I told you to keep your hands off her! Now, if anything happens to her, anything at all, Kyker, then I'm going to hold you responsible." Pointing to the damage I inflicted on Loman Krau, I added, "I mean it. I'll make you look like that guy."

"My platoon leader will have your ass," the sergeant assured me.

"Your platoon leader's a woman. I don't think she'll be as sympathetic as you think."

Kyker stepped toward me like he was getting ready to pull rank but stopped when he remembered who I had killed to earn my blood stripes. His cheeks flushed red with anger as he spat, "Fuck you, Tauk." He then did an about-face and stormed away.

"Fuck you, too, Sarge," I called back to him before he marched out of earshot.

Emerging from behind Lumuk after Kyker left, Xi stepped up to me, still trembling. "Thank you, Cadet."

"Save it," I snapped back. "I didn't do that for you. I can't count on Kyker's men to fight if they're all dealing with some sort of terminal crotch rot they caught from your nasty ass."

As I tried to put some distance between myself and Xi, I caught sight of Jella looking at me. She was not ready to make nice, but her glare had softened considerably. It was progress.

●●◄●►●◄●►●●

At dusk, Captain Mardona pulled the company leadership in for a briefing. The battalion commander had received a messaging pod from the *Nebulan Pheonix* with some significant developments.

"We lost all communications with the beach," Captain Mardona informed us. "They stopped launching comm rockets four days ago. The *Phoenix* tried to send recon drones to the site to record the scene, but they never returned. The assumption is that Charlie Company's Third Platoon has been lost along with all the wounded we left behind." Upon hearing that news, I had to stop myself from slinking away in guilt.

"Captain Briggund again requested that the Expeditionary Force dispatch dropships to reinforce our numbers and evacuate our wounded," Mardona continued. "But the request was denied. They're still not sending anything else down here until we figure out what shot our Wasps from the sky."

I growled. "Nothing shot the dropships, Captain! Briggund's attempts to warp reality is going to get a lot of Marines killed. What's it going to take to make them see that?"

Mardona frowned at me. "The command's not going to reverse their decision based solely upon the word of a fresh cadet on his first combat mission, Tauk."

"I know what I saw, Captain! And heard! Look, if someone isn't willing to tell the Expeditionary Commander what happened up there so they can send reinforcements, this mission will fail! I understand that the *Wasp-Two* pilot was the son of a prominent Samaari, but for fuck's sake! If the Sirrah family's public persona is so important to them, they need to quit pushing their pussy primadonnas into the fucking Space Corps!"

I almost told Mardona to grow a set of balls and talk to Albarn, but a voice from deep within my subconscious persuaded me not to call attention to her. She was already in Raza Bhutaan's crosshairs.

"The situation is what the situation is, Cadet," Mardona told me. "We're a recon unit, and our mission is to recon, to provide intel to the Expeditionary command. We need to reach our objective, discover what caused the collapse of Narman's Pyke, and assess what threats await our main invasion force. Our missions are among the most dangerous in the Corps, Tauk. You knew that and you volunteered for this shit anyway. Now, do you want to carry on with our mission or whine about it?"

"I want to complete my mission, sir! Successfully! Look, I'm a Citadel Marine. If we have to do things the hard way, we'll do it hard and do it better than anyone else in the Corps. We're trained to work smarter, though! And keeping resources from our Marines so we don't tarnish the reputation of a coward, well, that isn't smart! It's the stupidest shit I've ever heard of, and it's getting our troops killed!"

Lieutenant Thyster scoffed at me. He had been acting like he was over what I did to that convict back at the crash site, but his tone suggested otherwise. "When did the Citadel suddenly get so concerned about expending lives?"

The truth is they were not. Most troops were worth little more than the caskets they would get discharged in. The Citadel also taught us not to let them know that. As many of our enlisted people were within earshot, I declined to answer Thyster's question directly.

"Every Marine killed on this hike to Narman's Pyke," I growled at my platoon leader. "Is one less Marine who can to fight what's facing us up there, sir."

"Then you better put all that academy training to work and get as many people to the top of this hill as possible, Tauk," the captain snapped at me. Mardona then glared my way some more before asking, "Is there anything else?"

I had plenty but realized I was just venting. Mardona was not the bad guy here. Knowing that any further complaining on my part would just be a waste of breath, I said, "No, sir."

"Good," Mardona replied. "We can move on then. Captain Briggund was also informed that our Psycho Pixies did hit the ground at Narman's Pyke. They got a rocket off and reported that all but three of our airborne troops survived the landing. That was three hundred and forty-nine fighting Marines on the ground at our objective."

Before anyone had a chance to clap, Mardona held his hand up to silence us. "But they haven't been heard from since. Again, recon drones were sent down, and none returned with video from the site. We're just as blind now as we were when we left the mothership. They were not able to determine what attacked the colony."

Mardona sighed and began pacing amongst his troops. "Alpha and Delta Companies are nearly at full strength. Charlie is at about sixty percent. Beta Company consists of about a dozen Marines and what's left of the Navy personnel who survived the crash of *Wasp-Three*. The squids are dressed and armed like Marines, but they're not trained like us. They have a very different skill set than we do. I don't expect them to help us much when we get to Narman's Pyke. Overall, our roster stands at nine hundred and ninety-four troops, plus a handful of battalion staff. Factor out the wounded, and we're left with about nine-forty. That's three times what the psyxies went in with, but we're going to be arriving in much worse shape than they did."

"Sir," asked Gunnery Sergeant Welpox, one of the assistant platoon leaders. "Briggund was in intelligence. Does he have any guesses of what we might be up against at Narman's Pyke?"

Mardona shrugged. "Conventional wisdom says that we're facing a Ghuldari force that stumbled upon our settlement. They've been much more aggressive towards the League since we defeated them on Sivma-11 a few years ago. Destroying our colony on Narman's Pyke might have been payback."

Harlund Merik shook his head. "The Ghouls would have to go through an awful lot of established League planets to get to Kanaris. It's in the opposite direction of where they typically expand. If they're going to come into conflict with us, it'd be somewhere around the border systems, like where Sivma-11 is. Besides, massacring civilians *en masse* is not really their style."

"Bullshit!" scoffed Gunny Borkhat from First Platoon. "The Ghouls are fucking savages. They'd kill every one of the League's men, women, and children that they could get their hands on!"

"With all due respect, Gunny," Merik responded. "That's the company line the League puts out to work the droolers into a frenzy. That's all good when you need to boost recruitment into the Corps, but in combat, we need to know the reality of what we're up against. We can't go into battle believing our own fairy tales."

"Fairy tales?!?" Borkhat spat, his face turning red with rage. "That's seditious talk, you treasonous little..."

Gunny Malcolm stepped between First Platoon's gunny and my corporal. "Settle down, Mazen. The corporal could have chosen his words more carefully, but his sentiment is spot on. We can't assume who the enemy is waiting for us at Narman's Pyke."

Malcolm addressed Borkhat directly. "If we go in there expecting to fight the Ghuldari and end up facing something completely different, it could get us all killed. It's dangerous to believe our own bullshit. More than once, I've gone into battle with a platoon of kids convinced they were up against a bunch of pushovers, only to get our asses handed to us. Most of the Marines I sent home in body bags were killed more by their own hubris than by hostile fire."

Borkhat dismissively waved Malcolm off. "You saying the Ghouls are better than us, Konor? They're losers, man! We wiped them clean off of Sivma-11 in less than a month!"

Harlund Merik let out a long sigh. "There were around 30,000 Ghuldari troops on Sivma-11, Gunny. We attacked them with 80,000 League Marines. The Ghouls knew they didn't have a chance but refused to surrender. They fought to the last man. Literally. I saw that guy with my own eyes, firing a heavy machine gun at us as we crawled up that embankment to take him out. He mowed us down by the dozens, and because of the brilliant way he dug himself in, our mortars couldn't reach him. We thought we blew him to shit several times, but he'd open up on us again whenever the smoke cleared. When he ran out of ammo, he lobbed grenades at us. When he ran out of those, he detonated charges they planted in the cliff face behind him that set off a gigantic rock slide."

Merik paused, having been forced to dredge up another memory he would rather have left buried. "That was pretty brilliant. He almost had my number with that one. Giant boulders were rolling all around me, smashing my buddies like bugs under boots. He must have killed a hundred of us. We thought he'd buried himself alive, too, but nope. He stood up from his cover, brandished a dagger, and charged down the hill. Those of us that were left opened fire. We must have shot that maniac thirty times before he collapsed in the dirt. Then, when Sergeant Yelio, our senior medic, ran up to check the guy's vital signs, that Ghuldari son-of-bitch used his last burst of strength to stick his blade in the corpsman's throat. They died together."

Harlund had everyone's attention. Standing up to relieve some of the tension inside of him, he then said, "Eighty thousand of us went to Sivma-11 to kick the Ghouls off. We accomplished our mission, but only fifteen thousand of us lived to tell the tale. They killed more than two of our men for every one of theirs that we got. We achieved our objective, Gunny Borkhat, but it was something of a pyrrhic victory."

"That's a load of shit, Merik!" Borkhat responded. "I read the battle reports and the revised doctrine submissions from that action. I..."

It was rarely wise for a corporal to interrupt a senior NCO, but Merik shut him down anyway. "I'm sorry, Gunny," Harlund said. "But I fought on Sivma-11. I don't remember seeing you there."

●● ◄●► ● ◄●► ●●

CHAPTER 23

I heard that Captain Briggund collapsed into the dirt after reading the messages from the Expeditionary Command and did not move for two days. He seemed surprised, not to mention distraught, that the *Phoenix* was still not offering any support, despite the fact it was the commander's efforts to protect the Sirrah name that put us in our predicament.

Word around the campfire was that Briggund was a broken man. He was not eating, was hardly drinking, and had the medics pumping him full of high-powered painkillers to keep his mind off the dangers still ahead of us. It looked like he had given up. Sergeant-Major Horad had to practically drag him out of bed to review the troops and show them he was still in command.

The show the battalion CO put on for us did not inspire confidence. Briggund looked miserable. He was walking with a severe limp and gave us the impression that all he wanted to do was sit down. He hobbled from company to company, hunched over in pain, asking the usual questions like, "How are you feeling, Marine?" and "Where are you from?" More often than not, he moved on to the next person before anyone could answer him.

The only time Briggund showed genuine interest in his troops was when he got to our platoon. "How are you doing, Marine?" the CO asked as he hobbled over to our unit's only Samaari. It was obvious that he had forgotten the young man's name.

Duum greeted the captain with a sharp salute. "I'm doing fine, sir! Outstanding!"

"How's my box?"

Duum marched over to the red crate and patted the top of it. "It's doing fine, sir! We're getting it up the hill safe and securely."

"What the hell...?" Briggund gasped as he got a closer look at his cargo. Dropping to his knees, he glanced over the bottom of the steel case and let out a long string of profanities. Turning to Horad, he snapped, "Have you seen the condition of this case, Sergeant-Major?!? Did you even bother to take a fucking look?!? It's smashed all to hell! The goddamn corners are dented in!" Looking at it even closer, he yelled, "There's a crack in it! What the hell do you sons-of-bitches think you're doing to my shit?!? Are you deliberately trying to ruin a mission-critical piece of gear?!?"

"Sir," I said, stepping closer to the battalion commander. "We've carried that thing more than a hundred kilometers, virtually every meter of it over slippery stones. Yes, people have fallen. I've spilled over a couple of times myself, and I'm not carrying any extra gear." Pointing at the scuff marks on the captain's knee pads, I added, "It looks to me like you have, too."

"Watch your fucking tongue, Cadet!" Horad snarled at me.

My company commander, Captain Mardona, interjected. "The cadet's not speaking out of turn, Horad. He's just pointing out the obvious. You're not dragging something that big and heavy over terrain this treacherous and getting it all the way to our destination in pristine condition. It's going to collect some scars. Just like we are."

Briggund looked ready to explode. "This box needs extra special care! I mean it! It has to go on an SPS!"

I sighed. "I agree, sir. I'll grab one and replace its load with..."

"Oh, no!" Briggund barked, interrupting me. "Take the one with your girl-friend on it!"

"My what?" I asked.

"Explain to your pet project that you have to take her off her ride because you fucked up my box!"

"Sir," I said, trying to reason with the captain. "I can take a load off an SPS, rig it up like we did your box, and put your crate on the stretcher. It'd be a much lighter load anyway. It'd be easier on the porters."

"I'M NOT TRYING TO MAKE ANYTHING EASIER ON YOUR GODDAMN PORTERS! I'M TEACHING YOU A FUCKING LESSON!"

"No, you're not," Mardona told his superior. "You're not going to murder a warrant officer to prove a point. That's an illegal order. I will not carry it out, nor will anyone else. You can pursue it if you want, but I'll take it all the way to a court-martial and happily state my case. Trust me, Briggund, that's a route you do not want to take."

"Watch yourself, sir," our sergeant-major said. "Captain Briggund knows some pretty powerful people."

Mardona turned to Horad. "You seem to be forgetting that I do too, sergeant. I've been doing this a long time."

"I guarantee you, Rod, my people are a hell of a lot more powerful than yours," Briggund scoffed.

My captain lowered his voice. "Well, sir, your people aren't here. They're not even within radio range. Mine are all around us with decades of combined combat experience. You know what can happen in the field when the troops lose faith in their commander, sir?"

Briggund's face suggested that he did not have a clue. Sergeant-Major Horad took the hint, however. "Okay, gentlemen. Let's take this conversation down a couple of notches before something we say gets taken way out of context."

"Fuck that!" Briggund growled. Samaari pride made it impossible for him to turn away from someone he considered inferior. He had to show everybody that he could do whatever he wanted. Stepping into my personal space, he yelled, "You're going to keep hauling my box up that hill on your fucking backs! And every time you drop it, each Marine gets five lashes!"

Seeking out our squad's Samaari, Briggund then snapped, "You! You! What's your name again?!?"

"Duum, sir."

"PFC Duum! You're going to watch this box at all times! If anybody drops it, you're to get Sergeant-Major Horad and report it immediately! You got that?!?"

Duum looked at the Marines in his squad and swallowed hard. He was already unpopular. He knew getting labeled a rat could be fatal out in the bush. Still, he had to humor the captain. "Aye aye, sir," he said without enthusiasm.

Turning back to me, Briggund stuck his finger in my face. "I don't give a shit what your captain thinks are illegal orders, Cadet! Fuck with me again, and your girl gets left in the mud. Am I clear?!?"

"As diamonds, sir."

Shaking with rage, Briggund spun around to limp away from us.

Captain Mardona was seething, standing next to me, watching the battalion leadership walking back to their campsite. His fingers flexed around the handle of his sidearm. It was as if he was seriously contemplating drawing it and shooting both Briggund and Horad in the back of the head.

"What do you want me to do?" I asked my company commander.

"Nothing," Mardona growled. "This is madness, and I'm going to take care of it right now."

Our captain took off after the battalion CO at a jog. Then he leapt at them. He seemed to jump straight up into the air and fly damn near fifteen meters. It was a superhuman display of athleticism that I had never seen before. He smashed into Briggund and Horad at an unbelievable speed, bowling them both over hard enough to knock the sergeant-major unconscious and send our commander spinning head over heels across a stretch of open field. After that, Mardona bounced off the ground, took out a few enlisted men, then flew off into the jungle. After that, he was gone.

As my brain tried to process what I had just seen, someone nearby screamed, "ANWAR!" Then our entire eastern perimeter opened fire at the tree line. I ran over to Jella Duverii and threw myself on top of her.

"Is it really?" Jella asked me. "Is there another anwar out there?"

Pulling my pistol out as if it would be of any use at all, I nodded and shouted, "Yeah! It just got Captain Mardona!"

Though we could not see what we were shooting at, we poured damn near everything we had at that little patch of jungle. After a full minute of automatic gunfire and grenade explosions, Gunny Malcolm ran behind the line, waving his hand in front of his face, palm outward, screaming, "CEASE FIRE! CEASE FIRE!"

When the shooting stopped, Gunny Borkhat and two riflemen ran into the forest to see if they could find Mardona. Borkhat sprinted back out a few minutes later, screaming as loud as his lungs would allow.

His two riflemen were never seen again.

•●‹◈›●‹◈›●•

CHAPTER 24

All hell broke loose after the attack. Nearly a thousand troops were thrown into a frenzy as they tried to get their gear combat-ready and set the SPSs back on course to resume the climb to Narman's Pyke.

Rumor had it Captain Briggund broke both ankles when Mardona hit him. From now on, he would be riding a motorized stretcher to our fallen colony, surrounded by a wall of troops to keep him from becoming an anwar appetizer. Our sergeant-major had to be carried out as well. He had been concussed so badly that he could not have passed a field sobriety test, let alone kept up with troops half his age during a chaotic withdrawal.

My squad evacuated the clearing so fast that I had to chase them down to pick up Briggund's Box. I then had to run to the medical unit, with Jella Duverii in tow, to ensure no one left CWO Albarn behind. "What happened now?" the pilot asked me. She was conscious for the first time in days, but her eyes could barely open. Despite all the excitement, she was struggling to stay awake.

"Same thing as before, ma'am," I told her. "We got hit by an anwar. It took my company commander away right in front of me."

Albarn nodded weakly. "I heard the gunfire. Did they get it?"

I shook my head. "Nope. We shot the shit out of the opening in the brush that Mardona disappeared through, but according to Gunny Borkhat, the trees took most of the damage. He went in after it with two guys, but his riflemen were also killed."

"Did he see it?"

Jella answered that question. She was the one that had interviewed Borkhat, who was still in a deep state of shock. "He never saw a thing, even when it took his Marines. He said it was like they disappeared into thin air. He heard the creature's tongue hit his guy, but by the time he turned around to see what the noise was, the Marine was gone. After that, the two survivors made a mad dash back to the perimeter, but only one of them made it out."

Albarn shook her head. "This place is a vision of Hell itself, isn't it?"

Jella nodded. "It can be. Sure. One of my colleagues here used to call it Moloch's Garden."

Albarn and I both looked at Jella, wondering if that was supposed to mean something. "Who's Moloch?" I asked.

"It was something out of one of the ancient earthly religions. He was some sort of demon or god that people used to sacrifice their children to."

●●⬦●⬦●●

Now that he was riding a Self Propelled Stretcher, Captain Briggund was no longer tiring on the trail. As a result, he marched us longer, faster, and harder than before. Despite the rest we had, the pace he set was excruciating and our Marines started to fail. Borman Loat, the man we were training to be our assistant grenadier, was the first of our platoon to go. He had been fighting an infection in his feet and had just sat down after a sixteen-hour trek. By the time Kalawezi checked on him, he was gone.

My platoon leader, who was also our company commander now that Mardona was dead, grew increasingly frustrated with the speed with which Briggund was driving us. He and I had little difficulty keeping up, but we were not carrying extra loads. It was killing our troops and we knew that if the captain kept up that pace, we would be combat ineffective by the time we reached our objective.

Thyster met with Briggund and urged him to relax the march, but our battalion commander melted down at the suggestion. Jella and I were both within earshot when it happened and saw that the captain was obviously terrified of being taken by an anwar.

"I'm not going to lay down and let those fucking things snack on us!" Briggund screamed, seated on an SPS encircled by his shield of sacrificial Marines. "If we do that, there isn't going to be any of us left to take the Pyke!"

"Sir," Thyster started, trying to reason with the man. "We've lost eight Marines to anwar attacks since we set out from the beach. We've lost thirteen of our people to exhaustion in the last twenty-four hours alone! Statistically, you're more dangerous to our troops than the anwar are."

Briggund bolted upright on his stretcher. "What did you say to me?"

"You heard me, sir," Thyster responded, standing his ground. "You're killing more of your Marines than the creatures are. If you were walking instead of riding, you'd realize that..."

"I can't walk! My fucking ankles are probably broken!"

"Then maybe your mission's over, sir. Maybe we should leave you on the side of the trail and use that SPS you're on to carry equipment like you suggested we do with the pilot you're so keen on killing."

I cringed upon hearing that. I am sure that Thyster did not mean to do it, but pulling Je'Sikka Albarn into any argument with Briggund did nothing but put her at risk.

"I'm not trying to kill the pilot, Thyster! I'm trying to accomplish a mission here! She shouldn't have been on this march in the first place! She should have been left on the beach with the rest of the wounded! She has no business being here!"

I could tell that Thyster was about to reply that Briggund did not either, but he wisely decided to hold his tongue.

Our commander misinterpreted Thyster's silence as coming around to seeing things his way. "Look, Lieutenant, if I could walk, I'd be setting the same pace we're marching right now." That was bullshit. When I turned my head to see if the man who said it did so with a straight face, I caught a couple of his human shields rolling their eyes.

"The reason we're not being decimated by those damn things," Briggund continued. "Is that we're outrunning them!"

Shaking her head, Jella laughed at the battalion commander's ignorance. "Anwar are ambush predators," she mumbled to herself. "You don't outrun them. You run into them."

•●◄◆►●◆◄◆►●•

Without the constant rain of the Hot Zone, it became much easier to handle Briggund's Box without dropping it every hundred meters or so. We only had one incident within four days, but even there, the porters could control the crate's descent and gently laid it down upon the rocks. Still, Mazada Duum lost his mind whenever the container touched the ground. "What are you trying to do?!? Get yourselves flogged by the sergeant-major?!?" the Samaari screamed at his comrades.

"They didn't drop it," Dino Faarhut growled. "If you report this shit, you're going to regret it, Shorty."

145

Hektur Naidoa agreed. "If you report any of it, you'd better sleep with one eye open. They're just having us carry this damn thing to fuck with us. If this shit was really mission-critical, the commander wouldn't have us hauling it like this. He'd have it on one of those SPSs."

"If the captain said it's important, it's important," Duum snapped. "So shut your fucking mouth, pick that box back up, and get moving."

Naidoa looked at the rank on his shoulder, then at the single stripe on Duum's. "You know, Sammy, the last time I looked, a lance corporal outranks a PFC. How about you get under that box and start hauling it?"

"It's not my turn," Duum retorted. "And Captain Briggund himself put me in charge of transporting the box..."

"Uh, I think you got that a little wrong, Maz," Nadia Reyn interrupted. "I was there. He put you second-in-command, under Cadet Tauk."

"Which means you still ain't shit," Naidoa added. "Now, get your ass under that box, PFC."

Duum turned toward me and shot me a look asking me to intervene, so I did. "You heard the Lance Corporal, Duum. You don't try to boss around someone who outranks you."

"But he's only an E-3!" Duum argued.

I shrugged. "That doesn't change the fact that you're only an E-2. Take your place under that litter and start humping that box."

The entire squad laughed at Duum after I put him in his place, even Lumuk. Seeing the big man getting in a few chuckles at his expense pushed the Samaari over the edge. He ripped off his helmet and swung it at the giant, clocking him across the chin. Lumuk stumbled backward, holding his jaw and howling out in pain.

"That'll teach you to laugh at me," Duum snarled. "You miserable sack of..."

Before Duum could finish his sentence, Harlund Merik came up from behind and pummeled the little man in the back of the head. Once Duum hit the dirt, my corporal was on top of him, savagely back-handing the cretin across the cheeks.

"Be careful with him, Harlund," I warned. "We still need him to march."

Merik nodded. "That's why I'm not using my fists." Pausing to wrap both hands around Duum's neck, Harlund squeezed until the PFC's face turned red.

"You're done tormenting Lumuk, you understand me?" my corporal growled. "You keep your goddamn hands off of him! If he tells me that you so much as sneered his way, I will fuck you up in ways you can't even begin to imagine! Savvy?"

Unable to speak, Duum nodded his chin and Merik let go. Harlund slapped him once more for good measure, then jumped up and yanked the PFC to his feet before shoving him toward Briggund's Box. "You got triple shifts on that thing for the rest of the day. Squad! Thank PFC Duum for lightening your load!"

With smiles on their faces all around, my team did what Harlund told them to. Almost in unison, they sang, "Thank you, PFC Duum."

As our squad got itself slowly moving along the trail again, Jella Duverii walked up to me, shaking her head. "You know," she said, speaking to me for the first time in days. "As brutal as you people are to each other, I can't even begin to wonder how you treat your enemies."

•●◄❀► ● ◄❀► ●•

CHAPTER 25

I t started to rain again the next morning, adding to the misery factor of our long march to Narman's Pyke. Two days later, our trail had been transformed into another knee-deep river, just like the one on which we hiked all the way through the Hot Zone.

"How is this place not completely underwater with all this rain?" I asked Jella after our sixth day of getting continuously pissed on. We had started talking again a couple of nights before and were getting back to normal. Actually, we were getting along a little better than usual.

"It all evaporates once it hits sea level," our guide answered. "It's a constant cycle. Rain pours all over the land, then flows down to the beach, where it vaporizes into the air. The ocean winds push it back inland, where the cooler air at higher elevations condenses it and makes it rain again. It never stops."

I noticed that Jella was on my right side, leaving nothing between her and the tree line. That made me uncomfortable, so, putting my hand on her shoulder, I guided her to my left. Realizing that I was trying to protect her, Jella smiled at me in appreciation. Or maybe it was something else. I somehow got the sense that she enjoyed being touched by me. I also realized that, despite my orders, better judgment, and military conditioning, I enjoyed touching her, too.

"How doesn't the soil wash away then?" I asked, trying to keep the conversation going.

Dr. Duverii pointed at the trees. "The plants here have insane root systems. They go really deep, anchoring them to the bedrock, and they're so dense that they can hold on to all the soil they need to survive. There's also so much life concentrated here that there is a constant rain of organic material such as vegetable matter, dead bugs, animal remains, and droppings falling to the floor to keep nutrients flowing to the root systems."

"How about those huge cyclones? Like the one that was going on when we crashed? How do they survive those?"

"That's fascinating, too!" Jella told me. "You've felt how pliant the trees are, haven't you? Only the young ones are really rigid like what we're used to. The mature trees bend and lay down upon one another, forming an almost impenetrable layer shielding the creatures below. It's crazy, too, because the animals know that the rules change during those storms. They shut down and stop hunting each other. Predator and prey will huddle up together and not go back to the natural order of things until it all gets back to normal."

I grinned at the enthusiasm Jella showed when she spoke about the ecology of Kanaris. Her sharp blue eyes made me smile, too. I wondered when all of this was over, when she was no longer under my protection, if she would mind if I tried to kiss her.

"So, if we get hit by one of those storms while we're out here, we should run into the jungle?"

Jella nodded. "I would."

"Even with the..."

I was struck in the back so hard that it took my breath away. The impact sent me smashing into Duverii, knocking her off her feet and into the water. Then, before I could even curse, I was yanked off the trail and sent flying backward through the air, speeding towards the forest in reverse. I could not see what had me, but I had a terrifyingly accurate idea.

The Corps had possessed me since birth. They spent two decades training me to kill anything I could ever possibly need to kill. They also taught me how to survive virtually every conceivable situation. I could take a life without flinching. I could calmly think my way through any catastrophe, no matter how chaotic it became. The bastards even honed my reflexes to the point where they could react and save my life before I even knew I was in danger.

There was not a single Marine in the entire Space Corps better equipped to survive an anwar attack than I was. Yet, that day, my skills were powerless to keep me from being ground to a pulp between a massive set of molars. The only thing that saved me that day was pure, dumb luck.

When my flight through the air came to an abrupt stop, it was not against the teeth of some alien eating machine. It was against a fork in one of those solid, younger trees that Jella had just finished telling me about. The impact nearly broke my spine against my combat pack. My eyes clenched closed from the pain, but my mind screamed out for me to do something.

Your pack! Your pack! The damned thing's got you by your pack!

My right hand shot up and slammed the load release button in the middle of my chest. I expected to fall to the forest floor, but nothing happened. I was still stuck against the tree sideways, my body hovering parallel to the ground. Forcing my eyes open, I looked down and saw two pink, pointed, fleshy arms wrapped around my waist.

Forked tongue? I tried for a fraction of a second to work out the anatomy of the animal that had me but quickly decided that I needed to put my curiosity on hold. I had to get the creature to let go of me, not figure out how it was built.

Still unable to breathe, stunned by the impact, and disoriented by shock, I lifted my head and looked toward the river trail we were trying to navigate. I saw my entire squad staring back at me with their jaws hanging agape, stunned into momentary paralysis by awe and disbelief. In the distance behind me, I heard the deep snort of a very large animal and the sound of cracking wood as the only thing keeping me off the menu threatened to give way. Lacking the air to scream, the only thing I could do was softly gasp a single word. "*Help?*"

At that, Harlund Merik let out an ear-piercing battle cry and charged into the forest. He could not make out the anwar, so he drew a bead on the "bush" the tongue disappeared into and opened fire. A split second later, he was joined by Maiq Reino with his M2117 and four riflemen doing the same. Lumuk did not fire. That stupid son-of-a-bitch ran to the opposite side of my tree, grabbed hold of the appendage that had a grip on me, and tried to play tug-of-war with the beast using its own tongue.

Even the porters ran in to help. They were not allowed weapons, so Parsons, Xi, Yisht, and Vold each grabbed one of my limbs and pulled as hard as they could, trying to get me down. Dino Faarhut and Kalawezi, our medic, tried to peel the sections of tongue from around my waist.

Our bullets did not appear to be doing anything but pissing off the anwar. It reared back and shook its head furiously from side to side. The tree I was stuck against started swaying violently, too, making me wonder how much longer it was going to hold.

"That limb's going to give!" screamed Gunny Malcolm as he ran toward us, seeing the same thing I did. "Peel that shit off of him!" he shouted at Faarhut and Kalawezi.

"We can't!" the medic yelled back. "It's got suckers on it, like an octopus! It won't let go!"

Malcolm ran around the tree and looked at what had me. "Bloody hell! Is that shit a tongue or a tentacle?"

"Does it fucking matter?!?" I screamed back, finally catching my breath.

Malcolm did not answer. Instead, he pulled four grenades off his web gear and stuck them to the suckers on the bottom of the anwar's tongue. He then yelled at Lumuk. "Let that thing go and get over here!"

The giant did as he was told and ran to our platoon sergeant. Malcolm grabbed the private's hands and threaded his fingers through the firing pin rings. "You hold on to these things no matter what! You understand me, son?!?"

Lumuk nodded enthusiastically. "Yes, Gunny! I got 'em!"

As our riflemen continued firing, Malcolm pulled out his dagger and drove it through the anwar's tongue, just in front of the explosives. The beast went wild, roaring in pain and thrashing its head about even harder. Gunny then grabbed the hilt of his bayonet with both hands and used it to pull himself up until his feet were dangling off the ground, using his weight to twist the knife. The blade cut through half of the muscle. The tension it was under ripped it the rest of the way through, snapping it like a giant rubber band.

Gunny Malcolm fell to the ground, landing on his backside while spewing out an impressive array of creative obscenities. The tree I was pulled against slammed back into its natural position and catapulted me several meters through the air back onto the flooded trail, my body smashing up against the rocks barely submerged beneath the water's surface. Without my armor, that landing would have broken every bone in my body.

The anwar's tongue, finally cut free, whipped itself back into the creature's mouth, knocking Lumuk face-first into the mud and leaving him staring at the four loose pins dangling from his fingertips.

I barely heard the grenades go off over the rapid-fire of the M72s. Merik told me later he never heard them at all. They just saw what they assumed to be the creature's cheeks suddenly inflate underneath its mossy coat and pop. The beast then just laid down and died.

When the porters made it back to me, I was fighting to stay conscious. "Are you okay, Tauk?" Barone Parsons asked me.

"I-I-I..." I stammered, trying to get my wits back about me. "I think so. Fuck! I..." I had hit my head and my vision was blurry and erratic, jumping all over the place. I had to concentrate to recognize the convicts trying to help me.

Barone Parsons was an enemy of the state, yet there he was, keeping my head out of the water. Orgo Yisht, the underworld pimp, knelt beside me, trying to peel the anwar's tongue off my armor. Ritza Xi, the child killer, attempted to do the same thing on my other side. Maynar Vold, the war profiteer, was standing downstream, hunched over as if he was readying to catch me if I started floating away. The only convict missing was Loman Krau.

The serial rapist, Loman Krau.

Sitting up in the stream, I panicked. "W-w-where's Krau?" I stuttered, looking around for my missing prisoner.

Thinking of a far more serious question, I leapt to my feet and yelled, "And where the hell's Doctor Duverii?!?"

•●◄●► ● ◄●► ●•

Jella Duverii, as a protected civilian, had a tracker embedded into her armor. All I had to do was press a button on my forearm to set it off. Immediately, a soft tone started beeping in my left earpiece. When I turned my head in the direction of the noise, a red dot shone through my face shield, an augmented-reality "X marks the spot" beacon that told me right where to find her.

My equilibrium was thrown out of whack, wreaking havoc upon my sense of balance. Still, I pushed the porters out of my way, jumped to my feet, and stumbled toward the opposite bank. I tried to draw my rifle from my pack, but I still had a remnant of anwar tongue holding it firmly in place. I was forced to brandish my pistol instead.

If I had to guess, it could not have been more than a few minutes since the anwar first struck. I did not think Loman Krau could have dragged our guide very far, and I was right. I had barely stepped into the forest when I found them both. Jella was unconscious, laying on the ground with my missing convict kneeling over her, trying to undo her exo-armor.

Krau was quite surprised to see me. The convict knew he would not have much time to do what he wanted with Jella, but Loman probably figured he would have gotten more than I gave him. He had stripped himself naked from the waist down but had not even managed to get Jella's breastplate undone. When he saw me wobbling toward him with my pistol drawn, he collapsed on top of Dr. Duverii.

"Please, Tauk," he sobbed. "Just let me have this! I can't do this shit anymore! I can't take it! I want the pain to stop! I just needed one more good experience, one more moment of pleasure, before I die! All I need is a couple of minutes."

"Get away from her, you sick fuck," I sneered. If I had been myself, I could have run over and kicked the psychopath off of Jella. I was on the verge of passing out, though. It was likely that I would lose consciousness just from the exertion. If that happened, Krau could quickly kill me and drag Jella deeper into the jungle. I needed them to separate so I could try to take a shot at him without hitting her. "Get up, goddammit!" I screamed. "Get up, now!"

"I need more time, Tauk! Just a little more time!" I watched Krau wrap his arm around Jella's neck. "Maybe if I took her with me...maybe I could have her in the next world..."

Krau was insane. I tried to pick up my pace to get to him before he could hurt our guide, but I stumbled to my knees and fell onto my chest. I kept my pistol leveled at the madman but knew that if I tried to shoot him, I would kill them both. "Goddammit, Krau! Leave her alone!"

I heard footsteps from behind, sprinting through the forest and coming up fast. I then saw the flash of Barone Parsons leaping over me and falling upon Loman Krau, dragging him off of Jella and throttling him into the dirt. Almost immediately afterward, Malcolm and Merik arrived, with the corporal running over to check on our guide and Gunny kneeling to my left. "You okay, son?" he asked me.

I tried to answer, but all I managed to do was nod my head once before everything went black.

•●-●>-●-<●-●•

When I came to, I was at the back of the column with the medical team. Je'Sikka Albarn was on the stretcher to my right. Jella Duverii was seated on an SPS to my left, wide awake and staring at me. Harlund Merik was standing watch behind her, his weapon at the ready. It appeared that while I was incapacitated, he would be filling my slot as Jella's primary bodyguard. I could hear screaming in the distance. "Is that who I think it is?" I groaned to Merik.

My corporal nodded. "Yep. That'd be the 'soon-to-be-late' Loman Krau. Gunny Malcolm fed the prick his own nutsack. After that, we staked the fucker to the ground spread-eagle and buck naked. The blood's attracted the kryptids, and they're making a meal out of him as we speak."

Harlund reached into his pocket and pulled out something wrapped in an absorbent towel. "Hey, Eamon, speaking of food, try a bite of this," he said while thrusting a piece of meat in my face.

I waved it off, being in no mood to eat after getting a visual of Malcolm feeding Krau slices of his own scrotum. "I got a little case of bed spins going on here," I told Harlund. "I'll puke if I try that. What is it?"

Merik grinned. "Anwar tongue. It's the shit we peeled off your pack. It's a little tough but has something of a beefy flavor to it. It's not what I would've expected a carnivore to taste like."

Turning my attention to Jella, I asked, "Are you okay?"

Dr. Duverii nodded gently. "The son-of-a-bitch choked me out. Quick, too. Once he wrapped his arm around my neck, everything went dark in a split second. I don't even remember entering the woods."

"That was the technique he perfected," I told her. "It was in the evidence file I read. He had a way of knocking his victims out in nothing flat."

"Well, thanks to you, I'm coming away from it with little more than a sore throat." Jella leaned forward and kissed me softly on the lips. "Once again, thank you."

When Jella returned to her seat, I smiled wide. "Not that I'm complaining about what you just did, but if anybody that matters saw that, I'd be in a lot of trouble. Please don't do it again," I paused as I watched her smile at me. "At least not in public, anyway."

Turning to my right, I noticed that Albarn was awake. I reached out and touched her arm. "How are you doing, ma'am?"

The pilot shook her head softly. "Not good, Cadet. I'm really weak. I don't know if I'm going to make it."

I squeezed Albarn's bicep. "Ma'am, you've got to make it. We're on the final leg to Narman's Pyke. I heard talk that we're two weeks away, tops."

Harlund's voice suddenly registered in my earpiece. He was talking quietly on a restricted channel so only I could hear him. "I spoke to one of the senior corpsmen while you were out, buddy. He told me it's a miracle she made it this far."

My face twisted into a grimace. "I went through a lot to get you here," I reminded the pilot. "You have to make it the rest of the way. You have to pull through."

"I'm doing what I can," Albarn told me. Speaking seemed to exhaust her, and she ended the conversation by drifting back to sleep.

With Albarn out, I waved down a passing corpsman. "Hey, doc," I asked her. "I'm really dizzy. You got anything that can make the world stop spinning?"

The medic shook her head. "No, Marine. Just sleep. You need rest so that your body can repair itself."

"I can't sleep out here," I argued.

The medic whipped a syringe from the pouch around her waist and plunged the needle into my neck before I knew what she was doing. "Then try that. Nighty night, big boy!"

"W-w-what?" I gasped. "What'd you do? Why...?"

"Because I don't have time to argue with you, Cadet," the medic told me. "We have to move out, and you need rest."

I was already fading when Harlund stepped over and put his hand on my shoulder. "Don't fight it, man. I'm watching over you. I'll have Kalawezi walk back here to ensure you get the best care."

By the time Jella Duverii bid me "sweet dreams," I was already asleep.

●●◄●►●◄●►●●

CHAPTER 26

Whatever that medic gave me really did the trick. I did not wake up until just before dawn the following day, roused from my slumber by the sound of an SPS pulling away beside me. I also heard a corpsman nearby speaking with someone over his commlink. "Look, Sarge, I realize that," I heard the man murmur. "I don't know why she's still alive. I didn't think she'd make it three days, let alone three weeks. The bitch's tough. What can I say?"

There was a pause in the conversation while whoever was on the other side of the line spoke. During the silence, I noticed it was Je'Sikka Albarn's stretcher that was moving away from us. Putting two and two together, I tried to shake the cobwebs out of my head and pay close attention to what the corpsman was saying.

"I couldn't do it sooner," the medic continued. "Tauk's people were watching over him all night. They just left, though. If I hurry, I can get this done before reveille while that prick's still knocked out."

When I was confident the medic was far enough away not to overhear me, I pressed the button on my forearm console and rang up Corporal Merik. "Where are you?" I whispered.

"Guarding Dr. Duverii back with the rest of the squad," Harlund said.

"I need you down here at the medical camp. Bring Kalawezi. They're going to kill Albarn."

"What?!? Fuck! On my way," Harlund snapped before waking the rest of the squad.

The medic led Albarn's SPS beyond our lower perimeter, passing through the guards after a brief conversation. They then waded down the trail until it curved around the bend and out of sight.

I was still a little off-balance from my concussion and the drugs I had been given hours before, but I was able to slip past the sentries without either of them noticing in the dark. The rain made it easy. The water flowing down the trail was nearly waist deep at that point, and swift. All I had to do was stay underwater and let the current take me where I wanted to go.

When I finally lifted my head to get a breath of air, I was already passing the medic, the man whose lover I had shot the day we crashed on Kanaris. "What are you doing?" I asked Sergeant Gruber as I emerged from the stream.

My sudden appearance scared the hell out of the corpsman, causing him to nearly drop his needle. "W-w-what the hell are you doing here?"

"I asked you first."

The medic nervously looked at Albarn, then turned his gaze onto me. "Look, Cadet, this woman's in really bad shape. She ain't going to make it. She's suffering and..."

My pack and rifle were back with the squad, as was my pistol. That was protocol after having been administered narcotics. My only weapon was my dagger, and I made a point of resting my hand upon its hilt in full view of the corpsman. "So, you're euthanizing her? Did she ask for that?"

After a couple of false starts, the medic stuttered, "W-w-well, no. She's incapacitated. She can't make her own medical decisions."

"So, who's making them for her?"

The medic swallowed hard. "That's...uh...that's uh...I-I-I don't think I-I can tell you that."

I pulled out my dagger. "Not only *can* you tell me that, Sergeant, you *will* tell me that. Now, you can sing the easy way or the hard way. But you will sing for me."

"Look, Cadet, I'm not a fighter. I'm not a killer, like you..."

"That syringe you're holding begs to differ. Don't kid yourself, Gruber. You're a killer, alright. You're just too much of a pussy to look your victims in the eye while you're putting them away."

"Halt!" we heard one of the sentries call out on the other side of the bend. We also caught the distinct sound of one of them getting pummeled in the face with the butt of an M72. After the remaining guard realized a half dozen other Marines got the drop on him, he let go of his weapon and threw his hands in the air.

While I was listening to my squad take down the guards, the medic keyed his transmitter and said, "Sarge! You might want to get down here! I've got a bit of a situation!"

Dropping into a knife-fighting stance, I started to wade toward the medic.

"Oh fuck! Please, man! Stop! Don't hurt me! I'm just getting someone down here to help straighten this shit out! I'm not going to do anything! Look! I'm setting the syringe down on the patient's chest! That's all I'm doing! Please don't...!"

That was about when Kalawezi and Merik rounded the bend. My corporal put the dot of his laser scope right in the middle of the corpsman's forehead while our medic shone her light in his eyes, purposefully blinding him. "What are you doing, Gruber?" she asked.

"A-A-Article 3 procedure."

Kalawezi looked surprised. "With that?" she asked, nodding toward the syringe full of blue liquid. "That's a B-schedule dose. That's not approved for Article 3 euthanasia."

"We're running low on C-packs, Tima."

"Bullshit," Kalawezi countered. "We've got crates full of that shit. We're expecting to do some fighting at Narman's Pyke, remember? There will probably be a lot of Marines asking to be put down if they get ground up too bad." Nodding her head toward the dose, my girl said, "If we're short on anything, it's that stuff. We're not expecting to delay nerve firings for open-heart surgery in a combat zone. It's not a very efficient way of killing someone, either."

"Then why would he use it?" I asked.

"Because its half-life is so quick that it pretty much disappears minutes after injection. It's untraceable," Kalawezi informed me.

"L-l-look everybody," Gruber pleaded. "I'm just doing what I'm told. That's it. I-I-I..."

"What the hell's going on here!" shouted Raza Bhutaan, storming around the bend. He must have been close. "What the fuck do you people think you're doing?"

"Preventing a murder by the sounds of it," Corporal Merik answered, swinging his rifle around to draw a bead on Briggund's praetorian. Like everyone else in the battalion, Merik was keenly aware of Bhutaan's reputation.

"What murder?" Bhutaan asked indignantly.

I let out a long sigh. It did not take a genius to figure out who was behind the order to kill Albarn. I put my dagger back into its sheath. "I'm tired of playing games, Sergeant," I said as I waded over to Bhutaan. It was time to get everything out into the open, in front of a half-dozen witnesses running Personal Combat Recorders. "Why do you and Briggund want this woman dead so bad?" I knew the answer to the question; I just wanted Bhutaan to say it.

Raza scoffed. He knew that he was on the record now. "You don't know what the fuck you're talking about."

"Don't I? You and the captain have been trying to dump her ever since we left the beach. The captain keeps saying he needs her stretcher to haul up his box. Man, there are so many different solutions to that problem, but the two of you keep insisting that the only way we get out of carrying the captain's shit is to give up Albarn's SPS. I figured it was just the two of you being pricks about the whole thing, throwing your weight around, but you really don't want her alive, do you?"

"Shut your fucking mouth," Bhutaan growled.

I grinned at the sergeant. "Make me, Sammy."

Bhutaan drew his pistol, knowing I was unarmed. As he lifted his weapon, he tried to get a warning out to me on tape before he fired, giving him a credible claim of self-defense. "You stop right...!"

Before Bhutaan could aim, I threw my hand out and snapped my wrist to the right, energizing my glove as I pointed the ring in my palm towards the praetorian's sidearm. Raza's weapon was ripped out of his grip and flew five meters through the air until it smashed home into my mitt hard enough to crack my knuckles.

Raza Bhutaan, like everyone else present, stared at the weapon I was holding, unable to believe what they had just seen. Briggund's goon was the first to come to his senses enough to speak. "Magic?" he asked.

I shook my head. "Nope. Magnet."

With the mystery of what I had done solved, Bhutaan reached for the rifle strapped to his back. As he drew, I turned my hand upside down and reversed the polarity of the magnetic field just as I pointed my glove at the sergeant.

I missed. I was trying to stick the weapon in the center of Bhutaan's chest to knock the wind out of him. Instead, it struck the man on the side of his face, wedging itself between his ear and helmet with the velocity of an incoming artillery round. Even though it was up, the sergeant's face shield exploded, and the impact blew Bhutaan's helmet off into the jungle hard enough to nearly take his head with it.

Bhutaan was lifted right off his feet and spun head over heels, crashing into the bank of the trail face-first and upside down beside our medic. Propelled by instinct, Kalawezi grabbed the sergeant by the collar to see what kind of condition he was in, only to drop him into the water once her eyes took in the damage. The skin had been shaved off the right side of the sergeant's face, exposing his broken skull, and his neck was snapped. Raza Bhutaan was dead.

To a Marine, my squad immediately lowered their weapons, suspecting what they were doing had just crossed a line from rescuing a hero to mutiny against an agent of our commanding officer. They had a good reason to be concerned. Knowing I was running out of time to keep us from the gallows, I ripped PFC Briima's rifle out of his hands and took aim at Sergeant Gruber. "For the last time, you pathetic piece of shit, who gave you the order to kill Chief Warrant Officer Je'Sikka Albarn?"

Trembling and with tears streaming down his cheeks, Gruber did not hesitate to answer that time. He immediately pointed at the body floating downstream.

That was not good enough. I squeezed off a round past the medic's right ear. "Say his fuckin' name before I shoot you in the throat!"

"Sergeant Bhutaan!" the medic screamed.

●●‹●›●‹●›●●

CHAPTER 27

I had never met a man with less honor than Captain Nico Briggund. While still lying prone on his stretcher, he held court and asked Sergeant Gruber why he was taking medical direction from a sergeant instead of the ranking NCO of the battalion's medical detachment. The captain acted as if Bhutaan's motivations were a complete mystery to him. Everyone from the patsy medic and the company commanders, all the way down to the convict porters knew better, though.

Sergeant Bhutaan would not have dared pick his nose without the battalion commander's direction. Without even a hint of shame, Briggund painted the plot to murder Albarn as a conspiracy solely between his bodyguard and Gruber. He was not fooling anyone, and once word spread through the ranks of what those two men tried to do, emotions were on the verge of boiling over. The theater that Briggund staged to convince his troops of his innocence only inflamed tensions more.

"Quit beating around the bush, Sergeant!" Briggund barked at the accused medic. "Why the hell were you taking medical orders from Sergeant Bhutaan?"

The CO's questioning reduced Gruber to a sniveling mess. He knew how screwed he was. "He told me it was an order from you, sir!"

"And you didn't think to check with me?" The captain was a terrible actor. I do not think he really even wanted to convince us that he was innocent. He was just going through the motions like a man who knew he was untouchable as long as he could throw a few crumbs to the plebes.

Our captain underestimated the rank and file, though. He thought they wanted blood from the men who tried to kill the pilot that saved us all. They did, but that was not *all* they wanted. To them, the attempt on Albarn proved that no one shot down our Wasps. The rumors they had been hearing gained a whole new level of legitimacy. They were enraged that they were being forced to march damn near two hundred kilometers through Kanarisian jungle without any support from the Expeditionary Force just to preserve the reputation of a highborn Samaari.

Briggund thought feeding Gruber to his Marines would satiate their blood-lust. He was not intelligent enough to realize it, but that was a gross miscalculation. Everyone knew that Gruber was a pawn. It was Briggund they wanted.

I looked at the group of officers standing to our CO's right. They were not even paying attention to the proceedings. They knew it was all a front. Most of the senior NCOs did not even bother showing up. None of Briggund's reports wanted to play any part in the commander's show.

Harlund Merik noticed it, too. "Twenty credits says somebody tosses a grenade under that motherfucker's stretcher," he tried to bet me.

"That's fucked up, Corporal," PFC Duum said. "Joking or not, that kind of talk's irresponsible and could get someone hurt."

"Zip it, you Sammy shitstain," Loriz Hurran, our grenadier, snapped back at him. "You best keep your trap shut before I toss a bomb under *you.*"

Lumuk laughed at that, causing the blood to rush into Duum's face. The Samaari turned around to say something to the hulking Marine but saw Harlund already glaring his way, daring the little man to step out of line. Not wanting my corporal to make good on an earlier threat, Duum wisely decided to shut up.

"Why didn't you check with me, Sergeant?" Briggund snarled again when Gruber did not answer him fast enough.

Tears flowed freely down the medic's cheeks while his face twisted into a sick expression of regret, shame, humiliation, and terror. He was trying to answer the question, his mouth open and moving, but no sound came out.

"Did Sergeant Bhutaan's orders seem medically sound to you?"

Still unable to talk, Gruber at least nodded that time.

Captain Briggund turned his head toward the senior medical officer in the battalion who, at this point, happened to be a Navy NCO. "Chief, were the orders that Sergeant Bhutaan gave to Sergeant Gruber medically sound?"

The senior corpsman shook his head. "That's irrelevant, sir. Bhutaan's attempt to euthanize Warrant Officer Albarn had nothing to do with the patient's interests. He was obviously working to further the interests of a third party." The expression on the chief's face clearly broadcast that he believed Captain Briggund to be that third party. For a Navy man, he was showing a lot of balls.

"That's not what I asked you, Chief..." Briggund paused as he did not know the man's name.

"Kumar."

"Thank you, Chief Kumar. Again, was the order that Sergeant Bhutaan gave to Sergeant Gruber medically sound? You did examine her just now, didn't you?"

The chief nodded his head. "Yes, I examined her."

"And?"

With his face flushed with rage, Kumar let out a long sigh and said what he did not want to say. "It was sound. Warrant Officer Albarn is in very bad shape. She's unlikely to survive the night. That doesn't mean we should spare Sergeant Gruber the gallows, nor the person who ultimately pushed Bhutaan into ordering her death. In fact," Chief Kumar paused to look Briggund right in the eye. "*When* we discover who that person is, I hereby volunteer my services to act as the hangman."

Briggund was not in the slightest bit worried by Kumar's posturing. "I'll keep that in mind, Chief. What do you recommend we do with this heroic young pilot now?"

Kumar's shoulders slumped as he turned away from Briggund and toward me. "Just what Gruber was trying to do. Initiate an Article 3 protocol to end her suffering."

I stepped forward, shaking my head. "She didn't request that measure, nor did she consent to it!"

The chief nodded sympathetically. "You're right, Cadet. She didn't. It's the right call, though. We have Marines here that will probably die if we don't get them off their feet. We need her stretcher if we're going to save them. We must allocate our resources to where they'll do the most good. An Article 3 is the best choice we have. The alternative is leaving her on the riverbank and letting the bugs eat her alive. Son, if that were me in her shape, that's what I would want you to do to me. Put me out of my misery. It's the right thing to do, Tauk."

Shaking my head, I looked at Briggund and said, "Performing a non-consensual Article 3 is against Space Corps regulations. In the eyes of the law, it's the same as murder. If you order this done, you'll be doing it in front of hundreds of witnesses, and when this is all over, I will push as hard as I can to see that you're held accountable for it, sir."

The Captain grinned. "Fine, Tauk. Have it your way. I'm not going to force an Article 3 on our gallant pilot. I would be derelict in my duty as battalion commander to not allocate our resources properly, however. We can't afford to keep dedicating an SPS to a lost cause. We have no choice but to leave her on the bank and move on."

Chief Kumar was mad enough to spit. "You can't do that, sir! That'd be inhumane!"

Briggund shrugged. "If I let you initiate an Article 3 on Albarn, our Citadel cadet will make sure I'm prosecuted for it. My hands are tied, Chief. I wouldn't give it to her now if Tauk begged me for it."

"But, sir!" Kumar begged.

"But nothing. My decision is made. We need to pull out of here before we start attracting anwar again. Dump the pilot, re-allocate her stretcher to where it will do the most good, and prepare to march."

When nobody budged, Briggund sat straight up and screamed, "NOW!" Normally, that would have been enough to get the entire battalion moving with a frantic mania. This time, though, the captain's troops took their time breaking away from the assembly. The lackadaisical manner with which the Marines sauntered away enraged Briggund.

It concerned Sergeant-Major Horad, on the other hand. He knew that the CO had lost the room. The troops had always possessed little confidence in Briggund's fitness to command. Now they had none. He knew that did not bode well for our battalion's commanding officer. Nor did it bode well for him.

Sensing it was time to cozy up to his fellow senior NCOs, I watched him seek out Gunny Malcolm and place his hand on my platoon sergeant's shoulder. "Hey, Konor," Horad started, using the gunny's first name to remind him that they had once been friends. "Can I have a word with you?"

The gaze that Malcolm turned on the sergeant-major held not even a hint of their previous familiarity. It showed nothing but cold loathing. "It's too late for that," Gunny spat back at him.

"T-t-too late for what?" Horad stammered. "To talk?"

"Yep. You're supposed to be the brakes on a bad CO's baser urges, Sergeant-Major. You're not supposed to facilitate them."

"Hey, Gunny, you got it all wrong..."

"The fuck I do," Malcolm snarled. "You've had your nose up Briggund's ass from the moment we crashed here, feeding his fantasy of Sirrah's competence, allowing him to march us up this mountain to our deaths. Don't even think about coming to your senior NCOs now with your hat in hand. We all know what side you picked. You chose to sacrifice your men for a share of Sammy lucre, didn't you? You've been a Marine long enough to know how dirty that money is."

Horad was sweating. He knew that the troops were turning on Briggund and that he would end up hung right alongside him. "Alright! Konor! Look! It's not what you think, but I know I fucked up. How do I make it right?"

Malcolm laughed. He was not stupid enough to say it aloud in front of dozens of recording PCRs. "You're a sergeant-major now, Horad. You're the senior enlisted man in the battalion. You know what to do. You either fix this thing, or you end up fixed with it. You got the balls for that, Sarge?"

Horad did not answer. He just stood there staring at Malcolm with his mouth open.

"I didn't think so," Gunny said, slapping Horad's hand off his shoulder so he could return to his platoon. Malcolm shook his head in disgust as he walked away. "Trying to kill a hero to save a coward," he muttered. My platoon sergeant's volume suggested he did not care if anyone overheard him. "You really disappointed me."

Malcolm stopped and turned around as a thought occurred to him. "One more thing, Sergeant-Major. If you or Briggund send another killer after the pilot, Tauk, or our guide, I'll be sending all eighty of my killers your way."

"Are you threatening mutiny, Malcolm?"

"No, Horad. I'm promising it. And with all this Harnillium interference impeding our feed to the mothership, no one will even know it ever happened. You'd just be another couple of casualties."

●●◄►●◄►●●

Per the captain's orders, the medics left Warrant Officer Albarn on the bank of the trail before we pulled out. Jella and I sat beside her as her SPS was reprogrammed and sent further up the column. My entire squad, minus Duum and the porters, surrounded us for security and support. Chief Kumar marched up as the stretcher rolled forward, pulling a syringe from his pocket.

"This is a shitty decision to make," he said to me. "No one wants this to happen to Albarn, but leaving her here alone is not the right thing to do. Say the word, and I'll put her out of her misery. No one will ever have to know."

Unlike Bhutaan, who I shot for trying to do the same thing that the doc was suggesting, I knew Kumar's heart was in the right place. I bore him no animosity. Lifting myself to my feet, I shook my head. "No thanks, doc. I'm not going to kill her." Bending over to scoop Je'Sikka up out of the mud, I told him, "I ain't leaving her here, either."

"Don't be ridiculous," Kumar scoffed. "You can't carry that woman all the way to Narman's Pyke!"

Jella shook her head. "The doc's right, Eamon. You're strong, but not that strong. She probably weighs sixty kilos. You'll end up killing the both of you."

Corporal Merik had an even more compelling argument. "Eamon, you can't carry that woman and protect Duverii at the same time."

"He doesn't need to worry about me," Jella protested.

"Yes, he does," Merik snapped. "The mission is always paramount. *You* are his mission. Period. If he's derelict in his duty and something happens to you, he'll be court-martialed and shot." Turning back to me, Harlund drove his point home again, "You can't do this!"

I reminded Merik that he did not give me orders. He responded by pushing me away from Albarn and insisting that he was just trying to talk sense into me. I shoved him back and pointed out that, despite all of his combat experience, the last thing he wanted to do was challenge me to a bare-knuckle brawl. He answered that by tackling me off the bank, sending the two of us tumbling into the stream we used as a trail.

In the Citadel, we trained in martial arts daily. It was a combat style taught only to those born into the Corps. It was called Katana-no-Tai. It was brutally effective, and we were forbidden to divulge its secrets to anyone outside the academy. As tough as he was, Merik had no idea how to defend himself against it, so I had my way with him. My biggest challenge was not killing the guy while imposing my will upon him.

"Hey!" Jella screamed at us from the bank as we rolled around in the water. "Knock it off! Right now!"

We both ignored her and continued our conflict. To his credit, Merik fought like hell, but I was just playing with him. "You ready to give up?" I asked when I felt him starting to tire.

"Fuck you," Harlund gasped when I lifted his head out of the water enough for him to answer me. Still struggling, he forced me to dunk him again.

"Stop it, you assholes!" Jella yelled. "Your problem just worked itself out!"

"Huh?" I wrenched my head around toward where I left our pilot, only to find her gone. Afraid that something or someone got to her, I dropped Merik and pulled my rifle off my back. "Where'd she go?!?"

Harlund stumbled to his feet, coughing to get the water out of his lungs. He then looked around frantically until he spotted something that made him bust out in laughter.

"What's so funny?" I snapped.

My corporal pointed upstream at our squad's giant, ambling off to join the column with, from my vantage point, what appeared to be a child in his arms. "Lumuk's got her!"

He did. The behemoth, raised as a farm boy on the dirt-poor planet of Gorsu Qat, grew up carrying heavy bags of grain for hours on end nearly every day of his civilian life. Je'Sikka Albarn was not even enough of a load to slow him down. We caught up to the column in no time, and before we knew it, we were gaining on Duum and the porters with the rest of Delta Company's Third Platoon.

That was where we learned that, despite what Briggund said during Gruber's interrogation, Albarn's SPS was not being used to help transport wounded Marines.

It was now bearing Briggund's Box.

•●•◄●►•●•

CHAPTER 28

Lumuk carried Albarn in his arms for the rest of the day. When we stopped to bivouac at sunset, the team rigged up a simple stretcher, giving the convicts something to transport her on when we set out the following morning. The prisoners did not complain. They had been bearing Briggund's box for weeks, and Je'Sikka Albarn weighed but a fraction of that.

Whenever our pilot regained consciousness, she would scream in agony, letting us know she was back. Once, when Kalawezi bent down to check on her, Albarn grabbed our medic by the collar. "Can't you do anything about the pain?" the pilot pled through clenched teeth. "I can't do this."

"I don't know if I can," Kalawezi told her while checking the vital sign monitor on her patient's exo-armor console. "You've been so weak that I don't know if you'd survive the..." Our medic stopped herself while she went through the pilot's health history. "My god, you're recovering very fast."

"I knew she would!" Jella squealed. "That woman's full of miracles!"

Kalawezi shook her head. "I don't think I would call it a miracle," she told me. "Her BCM history's been deleted."

"BCM?" I asked. "What's that?"

"Blood Content Monitor. She would've been hooked up to one while under medical care. I'm not surprised they removed it if she was going to be Article Three'd, but her exo-armor should've had a record of what was going on while under care."

I was not sure where Kalawezi was going with that. "What does that mean?"

My medic shrugged. "Considering all the bullshit going on around here, I'm thinking Albarn's deterioration was induced. Gruber probably disabled the BCM to keep anybody from seeing what they were putting into her. That prick was likely giving her small doses of something to make it look like she was fading. I'm betting she's improving now because it's wearing off."

"I don't feel like I'm improving," Albarn groaned.

"I know, ma'am. I know," Kalawezi told her patient as she gently patted the sweat off the pilot's forehead. "You won't feel like you're getting better. Not while you're being carried around like this."

"Should we see about getting her back on an SPS?" Jella asked.

Shaking my head, I said, "No. I don't want Briggund to catch wind that she's doing better. In fact, I think it'd be better if you gave her something to knock her back out. If the captain wants her dead to score points with the Sirrah family, I think he'd feel less threatened if it looked like we were carrying around a breathing corpse."

•●◄●►●◄●►●●

Kanarisian rain is unrelenting. It rarely stopped; it just varied in intensity. For the last few days of our hike to Narman's Pyke, it seemed to fall on us with a new kind of urgency. The closer we got to our destination, the harder it poured.

Oddly enough, no matter how long or hard it rained, the water level flowing over our trail never fluctuated much, hovering between ankle and knee-deep. Only a handful of times did it threaten to rise above our waists, and even then, only for very short distances.

A couple of days from the end of our journey, the clouds really opened up. The rain was coming down so hard that it felt like the gods were pissing on us. We had seen a lot of precipitation since we landed on Kanaris, but never had we seen anything like this.

What struck me odd at that time was that, despite the deluge, the depth of the trail water seemed to be decreasing. "You notice that?" I asked Jella, pointing at the stream.

Our guide nodded. "Yeah, I thought it seemed easier to walk today."

"You have any idea what's going on?"

Jella shook her head. "Not a clue."

I had been trained to exercise caution around things I did not understand. I knew something was wrong, so I called Gunny Malcolm on the platoon commlink and asked if he had noticed the drop. "Yeah," he told me. "Does your girl have any words of wisdom for us?"

"No, but I got a bad feeling about it. If you don't mind, I'm going to have my squad walk the bank."

169

"Suit yourself. You want me to ring a dinner bell for the anwar?"

Malcolm had a point there, but anwar had long tongues. I doubted a few meters would save me if my number came up again.

The torrential rain was nothing but misery. It cut our visibility to nearly nothing and the roar of the downpour drowned out almost everything else. At one point, though, I detected a low-pitched rumble in the ambient noise that made me stop and shout at my squad to quiet down.

At first, I thought I was mistaken, but then it registered in my ears again. "Do you hear that?" I asked Jella.

The guide craned her head. "Hear what?"

I listened once more and noticed the rumble became a little louder. Then I lost it again as the intensity of the rain increased. When that died down, the racket was even more pronounced than before. "That! That low..."

"Grumbling sound?" Jella asked, nodding. "Yeah, I hear it, too. Or is it static?" Jella took off her helmet to see if it was some sort of radio interference. It wasn't. Putting her cover back on, she asked, "What is that?"

A couple of the other Marines also detected it. They stopped and looked further up the path, wondering what it was. I gazed down at the trail and noticed the water was rapidly rising. Then it struck me. "LAHAR!" I screamed. "Get off of the trail and head for higher ground!" I pressed the button on the battalion commlink and repeated the warning.

Captain Briggund was not far from me. Sitting up from his stretcher, he yelled, "What the hell is a lahar?"

By then, the sound of rushing water was quite clear, even above the din of the rain. He did not need me to answer, but I did anyway. "Flash flood!"

The lahar was already upon us. As much as we feared the forest, there was no time to do anything but run straight into it. I saw Briggund, a man allegedly hobbled by broken ankles, leap from his stretcher and bolt up the embankment just seconds before his SPS was washed away. None of our self-propelled stretchers survived the flood. Our extra food, our ammo, our wounded, and Briggund's Box were all consumed by the raging current. Even many of our healthiest troops got swept downstream.

The entire battalion scattered throughout the forest. When confronted with a rampaging wall of water, mud, timber, and stone, half of the Marines made a mad dash to the west bank. The other half fled to the east. Right out of the gate, the flood divided us in two.

As the water rose, we had to rush deeper into the jungle to stay above it. The paths to higher ground were numerous, but narrow. Time after time, we were confronted by life and death decisions that split us into smaller units. It also spread us out. When I finally stopped running from the rising water, I was in a group consisting of Jella, Gunny Malcolm, Vamir Stiid, Maiq Reino, a half dozen troops from First Squad, and a handful of Second Platoon Marines.

Gunny Malcolm had access to the battalion roster on his forearm console. With that, he could pull up the name, location, and vital stats of every Marine making the march to Narman's Pyke. At least, he would have been able to in a perfect world. On Kanaris, we had to contend with Harnilium interference that limited our communication range. "How many troops can you see?" I asked.

Malcolm shook his head. "Seventy-seven."

I gulped. "Is Corporal Merik one of them?"

Gunny shook his head. "Nope."

"How about Lumuk? Or Albarn?"

Gunny scrolled through his mini display. "Nope. I don't see either of them."

"Captain Briggund?" asked one of the women from Second Platoon, for entirely different reasons.

Gunny shook his head and grinned a little. "Not so far." Malcolm let out a little chuckle before dropping his arm into his lap. "You know, Briggund asked me if I was interested in filling the sergeant-major slot a couple of hours ago. I think he's soured on Horad."

I raised an eyebrow. "Really? That's a jump of two pay grades. Are you interested?"

Gunny shook his head. "Not even remotely."

•• ◄■► ● ◄■► ••

We heard the first scream minutes after the sun went down. At first, it was born of terror, but it morphed into cries of shock and pain before long. This was not an anwar attack. Whatever got to that Marine made the poor bastard suffer.

No sooner had that commotion subsided than the next one began. A third victim made himself known before the second one stopped. That outburst was accompanied by an eruption of gunfire, followed by the shrieks of something that was certainly not human. After enough shots were expended, the creature's screeches finally stopped. The human's did not. It was not until we heard a single report from an M88 sidearm that the forest fell quiet again. I wondered if the Marine shot himself or if he was lucky enough to have a buddy put him down.

Gunny Malcolm flipped the safety off on his M72 and aimed into the darkness. "Give me something, Doctor," he told Duverii. "What are we up against here?"

Jella was clutching my arm. "I-I-I don't know. It...it...it could be any n-n-number of things."

As she spoke, I heard something big rustling along the ground in front of us. I had my infrared on but could not see anything at first. Then, clearing a small ridge to my left, was an alien version of a three-meter-long centipede. It was equipped with a pair of mandibles as long and thick as my arms. The giant bug went through the motions of lunging our way to menace us but ultimately kept its distance. "Oh fuck," I gasped. "Is that something I can shoot first?"

"Not yet," Jella answered. "I know this one. Gunny, are you locked and loaded?"

"You bet your ass I am," Malcolm assured her.

"Good," Jella told him. "These are soroquids. Besides being a lot bigger, they're different than the centipedes you're used to. These are social creatures. They hunt in groups. That one in front is distracting us while others sneak up from behind. They can communicate with one another, so if we're going to get them, we have to keep them thinking that the front one has our undivided attention."

"Okay," Gunny groaned. "I can work with this. When I say 'go,' Tauk, you take out that abomination you already have in your sights. Second Platoon! You take aim at our flanks and rear. Kill anything that looks hungrier than you are. Third Squad, aim forward. First Squad, you're aiming up, checking for anything ready to pounce on us from above. Safeties off!"

When the collective clicking of all our weapons going live reached the soroquid's ears, it reared back. It was intelligent enough to know something was up but not enough to know what.

"Three," Gunny whispered. "Two...One...GO!"

I let my M72 rip, pumping enough ammo into the soroquid's head to split it in half. The Second Platoon Marines spun around and caught four more ready to pounce on us from our six. Rattled and terrified, one of my First Squad comrades saw something move in the treetops and squeezed off a round, knocking down what appeared to be a smaller, hairier, distant relative of the quarakai. It hit the ground squealing like an agitated pig as it tried to get away from us. The troop it traveled with called after it in distress.

"Don't shoot those!" Jella screamed. "Those are barbalu! Lesser quarakai! They're harmless!"

"Sorry!" the rattled Marine said, just as something in the woods sunk its teeth into the wounded animal and abruptly cut off its cries. The tone of its family above changed from fright to anger. They did not attack, however. Instead, they threw feces at us.

"Son-of-a-bitch," Gunny Malcolm cursed as he wiped fresh excrement from his face shield. "This is going to be a long night."

●●◄●►●◄●►●●

CHAPTER 29

The nocturnal forest is very active on Kanaris, and we watched all manner of creatures cross in front of us. Most of them were harmless, but anything large and unfamiliar looks terrifying in the dark.

We had a second soroquid encounter, but because of the defensive perimeter Malcolm organized us into, we eliminated it before it got close enough to do us any harm. We also attracted the attention of a humungous, six-legged, lizard-like creature covered in razor-sharp, spiked armor. It kept inching toward our position, but we were unsure if it was driven by curiosity or hunger. Not willing to take any chances, Gunny tossed a flash-bang grenade at the beast and frightened it off.

Not one of us slept a wink. We spent the night scaring off predators and getting poured on by rain and barbalu shit. When morning came, we saw that the water had receded enough to make our way back to the trail. We survived the night without taking any casualties.

As everyone prepared to move out, I walked over to the soroquid I killed to look it over under the light of day. "It's amazing," I told Jella as she stepped beside me. "It's exactly like a centipede from home in every way besides size."

"And eyes," Jella added. "Most centipedes are essentially blind. Not these. They see better than we do. Especially at night."

She was right. I did not notice it the night before, but soroquid eyes were not the black, soul-less orbs you would expect to find on a giant bug. They had irises. And eyelids.

"From an evolutionary standpoint," Jella told me. "The centipede model is a very successful design. We come across them all the time on life-bearing planets. Ants, too. And scorpions. And crabs. We see a lot of variations on the crocodile theme, as well. Our basic human design is not unique either. You see

174

it on the quarakai here on Kanaris and on the willomi on Torvatuana. Head upon a torso, two arms, and two legs. Bipedalism seems to come with brains. Or the other way around."

While hiking back to the trail, a welcome voice came across the squad commlink. "Ah! There you are!" Harlund Merik said. His signal was weak, almost drowned out by the Harnillium interference, so I guessed he was still a couple of kilometers downstream. "I'm glad you made it, Tauk."

"Me too, buddy," I told him. "You by yourself?"

"No," Merik answered. "I'm with Gai and Faarhut. Weir got killed by this fucking centipede thing..."

"They're called 'soroquids.'" I told him. "We ran into those bastards, too."

"We were getting ready to take one out in front of us when more of the bastards took Weir and a couple others from behind. That was a pretty dirty trick. Reyn drowned also. I saw her go under as we were running for higher ground. We also stumbled across Vold's body. Or what was left of it anyway."

It was a deadly night for my squad. I let out a sigh as I shook my head. "What a disaster," I said to Merik. "If the battalion suffered the same attrition rate as we did, we're going to be in rough shape when we finally reach Narman's Pyke. Harlund, gather up whoever you can and lead them to the trail. We'll rendezvous upstream."

Merik suddenly dropped off the squad network and patched through to me privately. "Actually, Eamon, you may want to come to me. I found something you're going to want to see. Bring Gunny with you."

•●◄❰ ● ❱► ●•

"That motherfucker," Gunny growled when he first laid eyes on what Harlund Merik showed us.

Briggund's Box had been swept away by the lahar. It hit a tree hard enough to break the top right off it, but the straps kept the contents largely contained, though waterlogged. Inside, we found four cases of Larillian wine, each bottle costing more than any of us Marines made in a month. There was also a pack of platinum bullion, blocks of vacuum-packed cheeses, Haruvian silk pajamas, several bottles of premium brandy, and scores of other luxury items.

"The captain was planning to throw quite the soiree when we reached Narman's Pyke, wasn't he?" Merik laughed.

I was seething. "He thought this shit was more valuable than Albarn's life. I swear, if that son-of-a-bitch..."

"Shut it," Gunny snapped, preventing me from saying something that could be recorded by my PCR and used against me later.

"So, what are we going to do with all this Sammy shit?" Merik asked.

Gunny chuckled, pulling out his dagger. He reached inside the box and cut open one of the cheeses, passing it to Jella. Malcolm then broke open a crate of wine and popped the cork from one of the bottles. "Right now, we're going to relax and have ourselves a little picnic."

Despite standing in a forest rich in quarakai, massive six-legged lizards, giant centipedes, and the occasional anwar, we feasted for almost an hour. It felt wonderful. It was the first time in weeks that we let our guard down, and we gorged ourselves on cheese and sausage. I passed on the wine as Academy Marines do not drink. I did not object to anyone else having their fill, though. I caught Gunny slipping a couple bottles of brandy into his pack for "evidence." When we finished eating, we all took turns pissing on Briggund's Box before making our way back to the trail, which was ankle-deep once more.

When we returned to our rendezvous point, I was shocked to see Lumuk and Albarn waiting for us. "You made it!" I called out. "I hate to say it, Lumuk, but I didn't have high hopes that you'd survive this, especially with an unconscious pilot in your arms. To have you come out of this alive – and bringing her with you – defies comprehension. I don't think I could have managed both."

Tima Kalawezi gushed over Lumuk. "We'd all be dead if not for Akkam," she told us. "We got attacked by those giant centipedes. One of them made for the pilot, but this big son-of-a-bitch grabbed it by the...the...what do you call those things that come out of the sides of their heads? They're like fangs?"

"Mandibles," Jella answered.

Kalawezi pointed at our guide. "Yeah! Those! Lumuk grabbed both of them and ripped 'em right out of that fucker's head! The thing went screaming back into the forest after that. He did it with his bare hands!"

Merik gave his project a celebratory slap on the shoulder. "Good job! You're quite the hero!"

"I ain't no hero. Corporal," Lumuk replied, his voice cracking. "I ain't never been so scared in my life."

"That's what heroes do, Lumuk," Harlund told him. "They do what they have to even when they're terrified. You think I wasn't shitting myself out there all night?" Merik shook his head. "Lumuk, you ripped the fangs out of a giant centipede. You still think you're going to be scared of a little shit like Duum?"

As luck would have it, my squad's only Samaari walked up just in time to hear Harlund say that. Duum did not seem to care, though. Not this time. I could tell by his eyes he had been deeply affected by what he had lived through the night before. The man had that thousand-yard-stare. His rifle and sidearm were missing, as were the two daggers he kept in his boots. It looked like he had exhausted all his weaponry fighting off the horrors of Moloch's Garden. After what he had survived, he could not have cared less what Merik said about him.

"Hey, Duum," I said, putting my hand on his neck. "Are you okay?"

My Samaari raised his visor as a single tear rolled down his cheek. "No," he answered, staring at me with haunted eyes. As much as I disliked the man, I wished I could have passed him a bottle of Briggund's wine to help soothe his soul.

"I'm glad you're back," I said, patting him on the shoulder. "Really. Scavenge yourself up a rifle and sidearm, then relax as long as you can. It looks like you earned it."

Marines trickled into our rendezvous for hours. As far as my squad went, two of my convict porters, Barone Parsons and Ritza Xi, showed up not long after Duum. One of my riflemen, Talia Golgho, stumbled into camp an hour after them. Another convict, Orgo Yisht, turned up just before dark. Three of my squad were confirmed killed that night. Three others, Hurran, Naidoa, and Briima, went missing and were never seen again.

We all hoped that Captain Nico Briggund had disappeared, but he survived also. He was one of the last Marines to rejoin the battalion.

"That prick's walking pretty well for a man who supposedly had two broken ankles," I overheard Gunny Malcolm tell our platoon leader.

Lieutenant Thyster, who spent the night half-buried in mud and somehow survived alone, dropped his guard and responded with a level of candor that was highly unusual for a Space Corps officer.

"Of all the things we saw last night," Thyster told the gunnery sergeant. "It's going to be that monster who kills the most of us."

●●◄►●◄►●●

Despite having safety in numbers, none of us slept the second night, either. When the sun rose, we set out again. We were walking zombies at that point. There was no conversation, no complaining, and no distractions. The battalion plodded mindlessly through the rain, putting one foot in front of the other, doing whatever we could to survive, one step at a time.

After several hours of climbing, we discovered what had caused the flood. Our trail had been dammed, the rain drainage blocked by roughly stacked lumber, rocks, and mud, held in place by large logs dug vertically into the dirt.

"Did it collapse?" Briggund asked a couple of our surviving combat engineers who were looking over the structure's remains.

An exhausted technical sergeant from Charlie Company shook her head and pointed out the craters in front of the blockage. "No, sir. It was destroyed. Someone blew it."

Jella and I walked over to Harlund Merik, who was inspecting a small segment of the dam that remained intact. Remembering him telling us how an intentional avalanche nearly killed him on Sivma-11, I asked, "You think the Ghuldari could have done this?"

My corporal shrugged. "The tactic is definitely in their playbook, but look at this thing. The logs are just piled on top of each other and filled with dirt and rocks to plug the holes as best they could. It's pretty crude. It must've leaked like a sieve. It's like it was thrown together by a bunch of big beavers or something. If the Ghouls did this, I think they would've done a better job."

Turning to Jella, I asked, "You think this is within the technological capabilities of the quarakai?"

The doctor shook her head. "They could pile a bunch of junk to make a dam, but look at the ends of those logs."

I did. The ends were smooth, as if they had been cut by a power saw, but without the blade marks. They were also scorched and scored. "Holy shit. It's almost as if they were sliced by lasers or something."

"Or something," Merik added. "Look at the larger logs. It took several swipes of whatever they were using to get through them. It's not like you 'swing' laser beams. It doesn't make any sense."

It did not seem that our battalion commander, who used to be an intelligence officer in charge of interpreting this kind of stuff, could figure it out, either. Not that he even tried. Anxious to get to our destination, Briggund ordered us forward after a thirty-minute investigation of the broken dam.

"Sir," Captain Milus Taiga, the CO of Alpha Company, objected. "If this thing was built, and then destroyed, to take us out, we're already in the enemy's crosshairs. We should be proceeding more cautiously."

"Send an advance party to scout the trail ahead, you mean?" Briggund countered. His words were impregnated with fatigue and condescension. "With a four-kilometer radio range? You'd be sending those point Marines to their deaths."

"We could send out platoons at intervals," Taiga argued. "Set ourselves up as radio relays to extend our..."

"And spread ourselves out? Do you not remember what happened to us while we waited out the night in the forest, Milus? We were in small groups then, and we were decimated out there. We lost more than two hundred and fifty Marines! More than a quarter of our force!"

"Most of those Marines were swept away by the flood."

Briggund turned on Taiga. "You don't know that! I heard Marines screaming all fucking night out there! We're safer when we're together and near the trail..."

"But, sir!"

"But nothing, Captain! Who's in charge here? Me or you?"

"You, sir," Taiga grumbled.

"Right! I am! Now, get your Marines back on their feet and start marching their asses toward Narman's Pyke! Now!"

Not long after we left the broken dam, we passed through a second thermal layer, climbing through another cloud forest. Several hours later, we emerged into sunshine, the first we had seen in days. It did nothing to raise our spirits, though. We were too far gone. After our evening meal break, we were hiking through a clearing when Jella looked around and said, "I recognize this place. We're close to Narman's Pyke now. We're almost there!"

Word that we were nearing our destination burned through the ranks like wildfire. We did not know what awaited us at the fallen colony, but we knew our suffering was coming to an end, one way or another. Our pace quickened, and I could feel the return of the battalion's morale. Then we rounded a corner and confronted a sight that stopped us cold.

Strung from the trees, on either side of the trail, hung the naked bodies of three-hundred and forty-nine of our airborne Marines. Those were our Psycho Pixies. They had been tortured, mutilated, and disemboweled before being hoisted into the canopy. Their torsos had been sliced side to side and top to bottom, then peeled back and pinned to their backs, making them look as if they had all been dissected during some morbid science class experiment. Their faces still expressed the agony and pain they had felt as they died.

Jella could barely believe her eyes. "Eamon," she told me. "Things decompose very quickly here. The kryptids haven't even started swarming them yet. Those bodies are fresh. These people were alive just a few hours ago."

Harlund Merik shook his head. "I can tell you right now that the Ghuldari didn't do this."

"Neither did the quarakai," Jella added.

"Who did it isn't really important right now," I told them both. "What matters is that whoever it is, they not only knew that we were coming, but when we'd arrive."

I looked into the treetops with a renewed sense of scrutiny. "They're watching us."

●●◄◈►●◄◈►●●

CHAPTER 30

Captain Briggund was not willing to wait until morning to inspect the perimeter of Narman's Pyke. The moment the sun dropped below the horizon, two reconnaissance teams set out under cover of darkness to sweep along the walls for clues as to what wiped out the colony and murdered our Psycho Pixies.

Leaving Jella under the watchful eye of Gunny Malcolm, my squad was assigned the counter-clockwise patrol. Our battalion commander must have felt that this was one of the last opportunities to get me killed before I could spill my guts about what I saw from *Wasp-Three's* cockpit.

Being barely two days removed from a hellish night spent in the bush, we were apprehensive about patrolling the forest in the dark. This was despite Jella's assurances that, unlike the creatures further downstream, those in the immediate vicinity of Narman's Pyke had been dealing with humans for decades. The predators had learned to fear us and kept their distance from the settlement.

While the prospect of running into an anwar, hostile quarakai, venomous trees, and giant centipedes weighed heavily upon our minds, it was the unknown that truly tormented us.

Ten thousand people lived in Narman's Pyke the last time the League had heard from them. The current population appeared to be zero, and judging by how we found our Psyxies, we assumed our colonists met an equally macabre demise. Something did that to our people, and we had no idea who or what it was. All we knew was that it was still out there.

The outer perimeter of Narman's Pyke offered little insight into what happened. In fact, from our side of the concrete walls, we could not tell anything occurred at all. Everything looked eerily intact. "You seeing this, Jella?" I asked, trying to get our guide's take on the condition of the colony before we got drowned out by the interference.

"I see it," Duverii responded from the command post. "It doesn't look like the perimeter was breached."

"Don't worry about the wall," Gunny Malcolm cut in over the commlink. "Look around it. Check for evidence of combat. And traps! Make sure your point man's got his eyes on the ground."

"You hear that, Duum?" I called out. After catching our Samaari tormenting Lumuk again, Harlund put him at the front of the line. "You keep your eyes on the dirt and make sure you don't step on anything nasty."

"Okay," the private whispered hoarsely. It sounded like all the moisture had been sucked out of his mouth. He had yet to tell anyone what happened to him after the flood, but I knew it must have been especially horrific. He broke down when I informed the squad that we had drawn night patrol duty.

When I glanced at my corporal, I caught Merik looking up at the canopy, shaking his head in disbelief. "You see something?" I asked him.

"The trees are growing right up to the walls," Harlund answered. "Our entire expeditionary force could march to this very spot, all half-million of us, and the people on the other side of those fortifications would never know we were here until we were knocking on their front door."

"I noticed that, too," I told the corporal. "Still, it didn't seem to stop them from keeping tabs on the seven hundred of us coming up the hill."

A few meters to my right, I noticed a couple of my Marines taking a closer look at one of the trees. "You got something, Faarhut?"

The lance corporal nodded. "Bullet holes."

"Ours?"

Faarhut nodded again. "I think so."

I stepped over to the tree and took a look for myself. The cavities were the right size and shape to have been made by a League round. I pulled a probing rod from my web belt and stuck it in the hole to gauge the trajectory and determine if I was missing an ambush point somewhere. It did not appear that I was. The bullets were fired from ground level, in front of the wall.

I took a few steps to my left to inspect the twenty-meter-high concrete cliff looming over us. There was nothing to be seen. "Whatever we were shooting at did not appear to return fire," I reported.

Faarhut breathed a sigh of relief. "It was probably just an animal then. Not the Ghouls."

The woman filling our sniper billet, Prishtina Gai, corrected the ammo bearer. "Or they took out the opposition before they had a chance to shoot back."

I adjusted the optical filter on my face shield video until our exo-armor plates glowed bright yellow. Then I walked over to the tree and picked up a handful of mud, squeezing it through my fingers. Nothing. I did it several more times and got the same result.

When I did the same thing by the wall, I found tiny yellow shards in the earth I grabbed. Watching me through the video feed I was transmitting back to the command post, Gunny Malcolm sighed into my earpiece. "Those are fragments of BalisTek, aren't they?"

"That's affirmative," I answered. BalisTek was the material from which our armor was made.

Harlund Merik shook his head. "Shit."

"What?" asked Akkam Lumuk. The giant never wandered far from Merik's side for fear of crossing Mazada Duum. "What does that mean?"

Merik pointed at the holes in the trees. "It means we missed, Lumuk."

Turning around to point at the fragments of exo-armor I held in my glove, my corporal then added, "And the enemy didn't."

•●-◑-●-◐-●•

It was the middle of the night before we linked up with the clockwise patrol, a squad from Alpha Company. "You guys see anything?" Merik asked his counterpart as we made contact.

Corporal Ditz shook his head. "Nothing besides a few bullet holes here and there." Commenting on how different the weather was at this altitude, he added, "Not even any wind or rain. Man, is it still up here or what?

Merik nodded. "It is. It sure is nice for a change, though, isn't it?" Turning to me, my corporal asked, "So, what now?"

"I guess we go inside," I told him. "One team should scale the wall and open the gate for the rest of us."

"Which squad will be the lucky one to do that?" Ditz asked.

Grinning, Merik made a fist and pounded it into the palm of his hand three times. "You wanna 'rock-paper-scissors' for the honor?" Ditz agreed and, at the count of three, threw out a rock, smashing Harlund's scissors. That meant we were going up.

Wanting to see our situation from a higher vantage point anyway, I told Merik I would lead half the squad up the wall, leaving him in charge of the remaining five on the ground. After picking my team, we loaded grappling hooks into the rappelling harpoons we brought and fired them over the ramparts. Once we were sure our lines were securely anchored, we fed the cords through our belt winches and lifted ourselves to the top of the fortifications.

As I ascended the wall, I glanced down and saw a layer of fog, glowing with a lime hue, rolling in toward the Marines we left behind. "Hey, Harlund," I called out to my assistant squad leader. "You see that stuff coming at you?"

"That fluorescent fog?" Merik asked back. He did not seem very concerned. We were in full battle dress, with our helmets sealed around our throats. Nothing got in or out of our headgear, not even our voices. Even though we could hear each other over the commlink, I could scream at the top of my lungs and a person resting their head on my shoulder would never have known it. If sound could not breach the barrier, neither would some eerie, radiant mist. "It's pretty, isn't it?"

"It is, but I don't trust it," I told Harlund. I then tried to raise Jella to see what the fog was, only to find that we were out of radio range from the CP. It was not that we were that far away; it was just that the concentration of Harnillium around Narman's Pyke was extraordinarily high. In this area, transmissions got drowned out by interference within three kilometers instead of four. Unable to contact our guide, I told all our troops to climb the wall before the fog reached them.

As the rest of our Marines were scaling the fortifications, I looked over the colony. There were no signs of life anywhere. Everything was dark, and there were no overt signs of any past calamity. The buildings were whole and intact, and there was not so much as a broken window to indicate anything had gone awry. Even the glass greenhouses were in pristine condition. "It's like everyone just packed up and left," Talia Golgho said beside me.

An Alpha Company private suffered a winch malfunction and fell three meters back to the forest floor just as the fog reached the wall. When he landed, he was completely enveloped in it. His squad leader, Sergeant Thalese, shouted down to his man with concern. "Gilling! Gilling! You alright?"

I heard the private trying to catch his breath below us. "Yeah," the Marine gasped over the commlink. "I think I'm okay. I just knocked the wind out of myself."

"What about the fog?" Thalese asked.

"What about it? As far as I can tell, it's fog. It's just a little prettier than we're used to seeing."

"Okay. Good. You got any slack left in your line?"

"Yeah," Gilling answered.

"Great. Tie it to your belt. We'll rig it into one of our winches and pull you up."

As Thalese toiled to get his man up the wall, I rappelled down into the deserted colony with my squad and started towards the front gate.

When we reached one of the greenhouses, I let myself inside. I was amazed to see how meticulously it was kept up. There were rows of corn, strawberries, citrus trees, peppers, and all sorts of other fruits and vegetables ready to be harvested. There was not so much as a speck of dust on the floor nor a tool out of place. That meant the power had been on recently to allow the machines to do their jobs. I had a feeling that the energy could be restored to Narman's Pyke by simply flipping the right switch.

"Eamon? Are you there?" I could barely hear Jella's voice through the interference.

"Yeah, I'm here."

"Is everybody okay?"

"So far," I answered. "Hey, Jella, what's up with the glowing mist?"

"Nothing," Dr. Duverii answered. "When the air cools enough to form fog, certain atmospheric gases are concentrated and then agitated by the electromagnetic field given off by the Harnillium. It's harmless. How does the colony look?"

"Brand new."

"No signs of danger?" That was Gunny Malcolm's voice cutting into the conversation.

"Besides the three hundred bodies hanging from trees outside the front gate? No, other than that, everything's fine."

"Smartass," Malcolm growled at me. "Get to the main entrance and let us in."

"Will do, but first we need to find the power plant and…" I was interrupted by the complex's generator firing up in the background. Shortly after it got running, the lights started going on all around us.

"Alpha Company already found it," Malcolm told me, stating the obvious. "Just walk up front and open the door."

"Aye aye, Gunny."

As we hiked toward the main gate, Harlund Merik patted me on the shoulder and pointed at the top of the wall, which was now awash with the glow of floodlights. Perched upon the ramparts was a single quarakai, staring down at us with its feet dangling over the edge. It was one of the smaller sub-species, standing a head shorter than we did. This animal had seen better days. It was missing an eye and a significant amount of lip skin along the left side of its toothy snout.

When it caught me looking at it, the quarakai snorted and made its hands into fists, but with the index and middle fingers pointed out. It then made a big show of banging its wrists together that way. "What the hell is it doing?" Harlund asked.

Remembering what Jella told me weeks before about the colony's lead biologist and his efforts to communicate with the animals, I said, "I think it's signing to us."

"That's sign language?" Merik gasped. "Seriously? That thing's trying to talk to us?"

"I think so."

"Well," my corporal started. "What's it trying to say?"

"I have no idea."

Frustrated, the quarakai tried a different tact. It stuck out its thumb and dragged it across its neck, the universal sign for slitting someone's throat.

Harlund lifted his M72 and drew a bead on the creature. "Is that fucking thing threatening us?" Merik growled.

"No," I said, pushing the corporal's barrel back toward the ground. "I think it's trying to warn us."

●● ◄◆► ● ◄◆► ●●

CHAPTER 31

The gates to Narman's Pyke were thrown open just before sunrise. I spent the next hour watching a ragged column of exhausted Marines file into the deserted colony. Most dropped into the dirt as soon as they were within the perimeter, simply too tired to march another inch.

Captain Briggund barely made it a dozen steps inside before falling to the ground himself. He was not well. Driven well past the limits of his endurance, he was broken both physically and mentally. He was in a great deal of pain from nearly every quarter of his body while the stress of leadership, the horrors he had experienced in the jungle, and the toll of incessant rain had significantly rotted his mind. His grasp on reality was tenuous at best, and his understanding of our situation was abject fantasy.

"Send a rocket up," I heard him tell Sergeant-Major Horad as he tried to motion for a medic's attention. "Let them know that Narman's Pyke is once again in League hands."

"We lost the rockets in the flood," Horad reminded our battalion commander for the twentieth time. "We don't have anything to launch."

"I'm sure there are communication rockets on-site," Briggund countered. "Form a detail to scour the colony for them. Get one off as soon as possible! Also, find Lieutenant Thyster and have his men bring me my box."

"Delta Company doesn't have it anymore, sir," Horad told our delirious captain. "We put it on an SPS, remember? We lost all the SPSs in the flood, too."

Briggund shook his head in disbelief as if it was the first he was hearing of this. "What?!? Sergeant-Major, we need that box! Get a detail together and bring my gear back up here! Right away!"

"But, sir..."

187

Briggund bolted upright as his delirium was replaced with alarm. He was no longer concerned about creature comforts. He was now worried about the consequences of a superior officer discovering he had his Marines hoofing his contraband up the mountain. He needed that evidence removed. "But nothing!" the CO roared at Horad. "I gave you an order! Get me my box!"

Our sergeant-major knew what shape his Marines were in. Going back for Briggund's box was a suicide mission that would cause a lot of discontent within the ranks. Horad wanted to protest but knew reasoning with the captain would be a futile effort. Too exhausted to argue, he turned away to get the unpleasant task over with, unaware that I was close behind him.

I followed Horad to Gunny Malcolm, who was conferring with our platoon leader about the company's plan of the day. I was glad to see Jella Duverii a few meters behind them, helping Kalawezi tend to our paralyzed pilot. Though I knew I had left Jella in good hands, seeing her with my own eyes helped alleviate the separation anxiety I was starting to develop whenever we were apart.

"Hey, Konor," the sergeant-major called out, once again addressing our platoon sergeant with more familiarity than Malcolm was comfortable with. "The captain has a mission for your platoon."

Malcolm sighed. "You've already had one of my squads walking the perimeter all night. You might want to find someone else."

Horad shook his head. "This one's too important, Gunny. We need it done right."

Malcolm sighed again. "What is it, Sergeant-Major?"

"We need you to lead a detail back downstream and retrieve the captain's box."

Our gunnery sergeant laughed right in Horad's face. "Oh, you do, do you?"

Not liking Malcolm's tone, the sergeant-major growled, "Do you think something's funny here? That box contains mission-critical gear."

"Bullshit!" Malcolm barked, stepping forward into Horad's personal space. "I saw your boss's box, Horad. Broken open and spilled all over the forest floor. Booze. Sausages. Bullion. Silk pajamas. That's what was in it. If that Sammy wants his shit so badly, he can walk down there and get it himself."

Horad swallowed hard. There was no way he could return to Briggund and tell him that. Widely regarded as the Samaari officer's toady, the only ally the sergeant-major had anymore was our CO. If he lost the captain's favor, he would be very vulnerable. Backed into a corner, Horad had no choice but to double down on his orders. "I don't believe you. Get your men ready to ship out."

Lieutenant Thyster stood beside his gunnery sergeant. "That's not going to happen, Horad."

"With all due respect, sir..."

"With no respect whatsoever," Thyster shot back. "Go get fucked, Sergeant-Major."

Unable to believe what he had just heard, Horad blinked a couple of times. "What'd you just tell me?"

"TO FUCK OFF!" Thyster shouted, reaching his breaking point with Captain Briggund's reindeer games. In one fluid motion, he ripped off Horad's helmet and slammed it into the sergeant-major's chest. "DO YOU HEAR ME NOW?!? GET THE FUCK OUT OF MY FACE AND AWAY FROM MY MARINES!"

The conversation died down around us as all eyes turned to Thyster and Horad. Realizing he was going nowhere with Delta Company, the sergeant-major retreated, walking over to a group of Marines that did not have an officer present. "Where's your platoon leader?" he asked them.

"In the digestive tract of a giant centipede," an exhausted corporal answered.

"That's unfortunate," Horad responded. "On your feet. I've got a job for you."

The corporal snickered. "What? March downstream to fetch the captain's slippers? I heard you talking to Thyster. Fuck that. Go find yourself another sucker."

The color rushed into Horad's face. "I told you to get on your feet!"

"Sarge, the last thing you want me to do is get on my feet. If I stand up, it'll be to break your goddamn jaw."

Horad went apoplectic, shaking with rage as he drew his sidearm. "Stand up!"

"No, Horad!" Thyster shouted back at the sergeant-major. "You stand down! Put that weapon away, right now!"

The corporal was unfazed as Horad aimed his pistol between the insubordinate Marine's eyes. Going back into the jungle was a death as certain as it would be slow. Getting one's brains blown out involved far less suffering. At this point, it would almost have been a mercy killing.

"Go ahead, Sergeant-Major," laughed the young Marine. "Shoot. I fucking dare you."

Horad pulled the hammer back on his weapon just as several of the corporal's comrades drew their rifles and took aim at the sergeant-major.

"Whoa, whoa, whoa, whoa, whoooooa," Malcolm pleaded as he brought his own rifle up to the firing position, targeting the junior troops. "We all need to settle down. You boys need to lower your weapons before this escalates beyond our control. This is not the way to go about this."

Briggund's sergeant-major looked over the Marines in his vicinity. Half a dozen men were pointing weapons at him, but no one except Malcolm seemed to see the folly in that. Six weeks before, Horad thought slipping into the sergeant-major billet was an opportunity. Being the right-hand man to an important Samaari officer should have been a huge boost to his career. Instead, it had cost him everything: his dignity, his reputation, and the respect of his fellow NCOs.

"Look, boys," Gunny told the rebelling Marines. "I understand your frustration, but what you're doing right now is a huge mistake that you will *never* be able to take back. You need to lower those rifles."

The blood rushed into Horad's face as Gunny pled with the insurgents. He and Malcolm had once been friends, but he knew that it was not his life our platoon sergeant was bargaining for. He was trying to salvage the souls of the men threatening to kill him.

"What're you going to do, Sarge?" asked the insolent corporal. "You going to stare at me all day, or are you going to strap on a set of balls and pull that fucking trigger?"

The corporal's eyes were blazing with hatred towards our sergeant-major, as were those of his cohorts. That did not concern Horad, though. It was what he saw in the eyes of those *not* pointing their rifles his way that convinced him all was lost. It was indifference. There was not a single Marine around him that cared whether he lived or died.

"Do it, Sarge," prodded the corporal. "Shoot me, you pussy! See what they do to your sorry ass after I'm gone!"

"Shut the fuck up!" Malcolm snarled at the young soldier.

"Or what?!?" laughed the corporal. "Or the geezer kills me? Fuck him!"

Horad's hand began to shake. Insubordination was one thing. The disrespect his junior troops were showing him was something altogether different. He deserved a little respect. He had earned it as a veteran of a dozen vicious campaigns. He had friends die in his arms, friends closer to him than he had ever been with his own family. He did not deserve this. He had served the League with courage. With fidelity. With honor.

Until now.

I saw Horad wince with shame. He had been in the Corps for more than thirty years. He had seen ass-kissing senior NCOs put their careers above their Marines more times than he could count. He swore that was something he would never do. Yet there he was, threatening to murder a young man because he would not lay down his life to save an officer's silken skivvies.

Not that it mattered. An order was an order. Horad was a sergeant-major. The highest ranking punk in front of him was a mere corporal. When he told junior Marines to do something, they had to do it, or the whole damn system would break down. Right or wrong, those men were going downstream to get that box.

"For the last time," Horad growled at the corporal. "Get off your ass."

"Horad!" barked Thyster. "You're issuing an illegal order! Put that weapon away right now!"

"You too!" shouted Gunny at the grunts. "Drop your rifles before someone gets hurt!"

"Horad!" our lieutenant shouted. "Are you fucking reading me?!?"

As Thyster and Malcolm screamed over each other to resolve the standoff, the corporal threw more fuel upon an already incendiary situation. Grinning smugly at his aspiring executioner, he told him, "I ain't going after that crate, Sarge. You do it. It's only fitting that Briggund's box be retrieved by Briggund's bitch."

That was the last straw. The sergeant-major screamed out in fury, allowing his target just enough warning to roll out of the way before Horad pulled the trigger. Before the sergeant-major could squeeze off another round, one of the corporal's comrades returned fire and blew Horad's jaw clean off his face.

There was a split second of silence as what had happened began to sink in. We all knew things were about to go very bad very quickly, but no one seemed prepared to make the next move. We just braced for the explosion, staring silently at Horad as he crumpled to his knees with his hands darting furiously about his face, trying to cover what was left of his mouth. No one moved to help him, nor did anyone try to hurt him further. We were too busy figuring out what side we were supposed to be on.

Horad's vital signs started going haywire, so his exo-armor automatically transmitted a distress signal to the command staff. That triggered the alarm among the battalion's praetorians. They rushed away from Captain Briggund to find the sergeant-major, with weapons pointed at anyone who got in their way.

The squad that shot Horad knew who was coming for them, so they fired upon the captain's bodyguards as soon as they came into view. Unable to determine friend from foe among scores of Marines wearing the same uniform, the guards shot at anybody in Horad's vicinity. That included us.

Predictably, the situation deteriorated into instant bedlam. In self-defense, I raised my weapon at the security detail, only to be tackled to the ground by Gunny Malcolm before I could squeeze off a shot. "What do you think you're doing?!"

"I-I-I was..."

"I wasn't looking for an answer!" As Gunny attempted to knock some sense into me, Marines were taking sides in the conflict without really understanding what was going on. The white stripes, the voluntary enlistees, rallied around the chain of command. The conscripts took the side of the mutineers. Delta Company, who had a front-row seat to what happened, sympathized with the rebels, but Thyster kept his troops from committing to a lost cause.

"Right or wrong," our lieutenant screamed into the company commlink. "Those men are not only mutinying against Briggund, but the Corps itself! They may get the CO, but even if they win this battle, it'll end with a few hundred of them up against the half-million Marines still on the mothership! They can't overcome those odds! There are other ways of holding Briggund accountable for this shit show! This is NOT the...!"

Thyster was cut off by a bullet fired by one of the rebels. It ricocheted off the top of Stiid's helmet, bounced up behind the lieutenant's face shield, and barrelled into his skull through his left nostril. Our platoon leader was dead by the time he hit the ground.

Thyster was a popular officer who was highly respected by his Marines. After he was killed, the entirety of Delta Company took aim at the mutineers. The troops no longer equated the conflict with Captain Briggund. It instantly morphed into a fight to avenge our fallen platoon leader.

As I tried to get out from underneath Malcolm to join the fray, he grabbed me by the chin and forced me to look at him. "You stay out of this, Tauk!" he barked. "Focus on your job! Get the guide to safety before she gets caught in the crossfire!"

For a split second, Jella had slipped my mind. After Gunny reminded me of my assignment, I forgot all about the battle at hand. All I could think about was protecting Dr. Duverii. This time, though, getting our guide out of danger was not about my mission.

It was only about her.

CHAPTER 32

Jella Duverii was not a Marine. She was a civilian. She was also extremely intelligent, so I expected her to run for cover once the shooting started. I did not think she would try to become the cover itself. She was lying atop our broken pilot when I found her, using her body to shield Albarn from the bullets whizzing overhead.

Sprinting to our guide, I pulled her to her feet. "We gotta get out of here!"

"What about Albarn?!?" Jella screamed. "We can't leave her here!"

I nodded and turned to our medic. "Kalawezi! Take the pilot's head! I got her waist! Together we'll..."

I was interrupted by Talia Golgho getting struck in the throat right in front of us. She was thrown to her back and started writhing on the ground, unable to call for help as blood began pumping into her lungs. She was a goner, but Kalawezi rushed to her side anyway.

"I can't go!" my medic shouted at me. "I'm needed here!"

Kalawezi was right. She had to stay. Looking for other options, I swung around and spotted Akkam Lumuk. He was on his knees, frantically jerking the muzzle of his weapon in a dozen different directions, trying to figure out who to shoot. Lumuk was worthless in combat, capable only of presenting an unmissable target to the opposition.

"LUMUK!" I shouted as my ears registered the crack of a bullet tearing by my cheek. "Grab the pilot and follow me!"

The giant did not have to be told twice. He slung his rifle over his shoulder and, with speed I did not think him capable of, rushed over to scoop Albarn off the ground. The four of us then took off to find shelter.

"Where are we going?" I yelled as I led the way across fifty meters of open ground. I had no idea what our destination was.

Jella pointed at a set of doors at the base of a nearby building. "There!" she screamed back. "That's the entrance to a storm shelter! Albarn should be safe in there!"

Someone opened up on us just as we reached our objective. Jella and I dove for the dirt and avoided getting shot, but a round hit Lumuk where his shoulder met his neck. The behemoth hollered out in surprise as the impact spun him around and threw him to the ground. Luckily, he landed on his back with our pilot on top of him instead of the other way around.

"Lumuk!" Jella cried. "Are you okay?!?"

The private shrieked in pain and terror. Still, he leapt back to his feet and continued charging. "I'VE BEEN SHOT! I'VE BEEN SHOT!" Fueled by adrenaline, it was he who now led the way.

Our giant abruptly stopped when he reached the bunker's access. His hands were too full of Albarn's limp body to open it. I was there a fraction of a second later, nearly ripping one of the doors off its hinges to get us out of danger. I was immediately met by one of Briggund's praetorians sticking the tip of his rifle in my face. "Where do you think you're going?" barked the sergeant barring our path.

"Getting our wounded under cover so we can..."

"Tell them to get their asses back out there and fight!" Captain Briggund shrieked hysterically from below. "Or shoot 'em! If they're a threat, shoot them!"

"You heard the captain!" the guard told me. "Get out there and..."

Another bullet cracking past my ear convinced me there was no time to argue. I took the butt of my rifle and smashed it into the sergeant's jaw, snapping his head violently to the right. When I stopped my follow-through, I pulled the stock back nearly as hard, driving it into the other side of the Marine's face with enough force to spin him a hundred and eighty degrees at the top of the stairway. I then planted my foot in his back, kicking him off the landing and onto the concrete floor below.

"NO! NO!" Briggund shrieked as he saw me running down the steps. "GET OUT! GET OUT!" Then, turning toward his remaining bodyguard, he screamed, "SHOOT HIM! SHOOT HIM NOW! HE'S GOING TO KILL ME! SHOOT HIM!"

Pressing the barrel of my weapon against the corporal's face shield, I yelled, "You can fight alongside me or against me! Your call!"

"KILL HIM!" Briggund shrieked. "KILL! HIM!"

The Marine turned his back to me, drew his sidearm, and pointed it at our Commanding Officer. "Shut up!" he shouted. "Shut the fuck up! If I hear another peep out of you, so help me, God! I'll fuckin' shoot you myself!"

"NO!" Briggund cried, throwing his hands up to shield his face before falling into a hysterical heap in a far corner of the bunker. "Don't shoot! Don't hurt me! Pleasepleasepleasepleaseplease! Don't hurt me!"

"Jella! Lumuk! Get down here!" I shouted up the stairs. "Pronto!" As Jella descended the steps, I picked up the unconscious Marine's rifle and handed it to her. "Do you know how to use this?"

Our guide shook her head. "No! I've never fired a gun before!"

I turned on the laser sight and pointed at the red speck of light it projected onto the wall. "See that red dot? That's where the bullet is going to go! You put that dot on whatever you want to kill and squeeze the trigger! There's not enough distance in here for you to miss!"

"They're in there!" I heard someone shout on the other side of the hatch. "Briggund went through those doors! I've been watching! No one's come out!"

Upon hearing that, the captain's guard overturned a heavy wooden table for us to take cover behind as we trained our weapons at the opening. I glanced over at the name stenciled on the praetorian's breastplate and asked, "You ready, Tolt?"

The corporal scoffed. "To kill our own Marines? No, not at all."

Nodding in understanding, I added, "I don't think they're going to give us much of a choice."

"I know," Tolt said, shaking his head in disbelief. "You think there'll be enough of us left after this to fight off whoever took the colony?"

I shrugged. "To be honest, I'm not convinced that enough of us survived the drop to do that."

"How many of them are in there?" I heard another mutineer call out beyond the doors.

"I think five shooters!" came the answer. "And a couple of wounded!"

Someone started banging on the door. "Hey! You're outnumbered! Come on out!"

"Not a fucking chance!" shouted the praetorian.

"Look, man," the mutineer pleaded. "We don't want to hurt you guys. We just want the captain! Send the Sammy out, and you all can do whatever the hell you want down there! We don't give a shit!"

"NO!" screamed the captain. "DON'T LET THEM GET ME! KILL THEM, MARINE! KILL 'EM ALL!"

Tolt turned his head to gauge my reaction to the rebels' demands. The look on his face hinted he was open to the offer.

I shook my head. "As much as I'd love to let them have the son-of-a-bitch, those men are doomed. Maybe not today, but eventually. There's no way they can take on the troops back on the mothership."

The corporal nodded in agreement. "Yeah, I guess you're right." He then trained his eye back on his rifle's sights. "Sorry, Charlie!" Tolt screamed at the rebels outside. "I'm not surrendering the captain! Think this through, Marine! You can't possibly win!"

"This isn't about winning or losing, man! It's about right and wrong! We're all dead, Killer! The only question is whether we die like Marines or like eunuch servants of a Sammy overlord!"

Tolt looked at me again. "Fuck. He makes a great point."

I nodded. "That he does. Hell, had those bastards not murdered my platoon leader, I might consider letting them have their way with that little shitstain." Pausing to let out a long sigh, I then told the corporal, "We have a duty, though. You're a white stripe enlistee. I'm an Academy Marine. We both took oaths. We gave the Corps our word. We'll never be able to consider ourselves men of honor if we break that promise."

I could hear Tolt grinding his teeth as he turned to look at Briggund again. "I don't know," he said, shaking his head. "It's not like the Corps is holding up their side of the bargain."

"The Corps never promised you anything besides three squares a day and a steady paycheck," I reminded the corporal.

"What's it going to be, fellas?" the mutineer asked as he pulled the door open. "You sending that pathetic little prick out here or what?"

"I'm afraid we can't do that!" Tolt shouted back.

"Fine," the rebel responded. "Have it your way."

At that, we watched a grenade sail through the open door, take one bounce off the steps, then roll below the unconscious sergeant still lying at the foot of the stairway. From outside, we heard a man cry out, "Fire in the hole!"

Tolt turned to me with eyes as large as dinner plates. I turned toward Jella and Lumuk. "GRENAAAAAAAAAAADE!"

It's amazing what a small group of Marines can accomplish in just three seconds. Before I finished screaming my warning, Lumuk reached over and grabbed Jella by the back collar of her armor. Forgetting his strength, he wrenched her off her feet and threw her into the same corner as Captain

Briggund. He then lifted Je'Sikka Albarn from the table he had laid her out on and turned to join our captain and guide.

As Lumuk bolted for refuge in the farthest corner of the bunker, Tolt and I dove for the ground, hoping the table would shield us from the blast. "Oh fuck!" I heard Tolt gasp, "Gering!"

Assuming that was the sergeant I knocked out, I shouted, "Stay down! There's nothing you can..."

That was as far as I got before the grenade reached the end of its fuse.

●●◄●►●◄●►●●

I came to without a helmet and choking on the smoke. The lights were out. Our only illumination was a single beam of morning sunshine cutting through the haze from a crack in the doorway above. I was gagging on the taste of blood and spent cyclonite, unable to hear anything but the ring of tinnitus. My vision was blurry. I could make out nothing but shadows. To add to my disorientation, the entire world was spinning sickeningly fast around me.

I screamed out Jella's name but could not even hear my own voice, let alone hers. I then reached out to see if Tolt was still there. Feeling his arm, I grabbed it and pulled it towards me, only to discover there was no body attached to it. I tossed the severed limb aside and screamed, "Tolt!"

"It's not mine!" the praetorian shouted beside me. He sounded a million miles away, but at least I heard him. That meant the ringing in my ears was starting to subside. "It's Gering! I think he absorbed most of the blast! There's pieces of him all over the place!"

I nodded and continued feeling around the floor. "I can't find my weapon!"

Tolt broke into a violent coughing fit. "Me neither!"

The doors slowly opened above us, and a pair of Marines stepped through the entrance, their M72s at the ready. Giving up on finding my rifle, I drew my sidearm and tried to take aim. I could not keep my hand level enough to draw a bead on my target, though. Firing would have accomplished nothing besides revealing my position. Tolt was in similar shape. Having a better vantage point than I did, he cried out, "We're fucked! There has to be a dozen of them out there!"

As the Marines took aim at the sound of Tolt's voice, a burst of automatic gunfire erupted from behind me. At first, I thought it was Lumuk finally growing a backbone, but my eyes were able to focus just enough to see the shooter was far too small to be the farmer from Gorsu Qat. It was Jella Duverii, emptying an entire magazine to stop the mutineers from penetrating the bunker. Her shooting methods might have been inefficient and undisciplined, but she got the job done. Both Marines fell screeching down the steps.

When the doors opened again, they revealed what looked to be an entire squad bunched up just outside, ready to rush in. One of them was pulling the pin from another grenade.

Idiots. I was glad to have my adversaries' tactical stupidity on my side. I snapped my wrist to activate my palm magnet and turned my hand over to reverse the polarity. I then aimed the ring in my glove at the Marine getting ready to blow us to Hell again.

The explosive was ripped from the insurgent's hand and sent tumbling into the middle of the mutineers. The anti-magnetic beam also caught the weapons of the troops around him and forced them backward while pushing me across the floor, deeper into the bunker. When one of the rebels tripped over another, it caused a small chain reaction resulting in several mutineers collapsing into a heap, concentrating them around the grenade when it went off.

Two or three of the insurgents were killed outright. The rest were concussed and dazed, leaving them vulnerable as Tolt and I emerged from that very same state. Acting fast to press our advantage, we gathered rifles from the two men Jella had shot and charged up the stairs.

There was no time to take prisoners. We shot the Marines too wounded to flee so they could not hit us from behind when they regained their senses. We then zeroed in on the troops running away in retreat.

Tolt and I were still too disoriented to shoot effectively. We fired more than a dozen times but only hit one mutineer. Frustrated, I grabbed a grenade, pulled the pin, and snapped my wrist again to power on my glove. I then turned my hand over and launched the device from my grip. It was too much. The explosive sailed right over the heads of my targets and hit the colony wall before it exploded.

Briggund's bodyguard stared at me in amazement. "What kind of black magic fuckery is that shit?" he asked.

"An experiment," I answered, pulling another grenade from the web gear of a nearby casualty. "I'm still trying to figure out how to use it."

My second launch had the same result as my first. So did my third. I lowered the trajectory for my fourth and struck one of the rebels square in the back. The impact lifted the Marine clean off her feet and sent her rolling across the ground far enough to escape the blast zone. When the grenade exploded, it killed a pair of her comrades instead. The two remaining survivors were cut down by gunfire as they tried to crawl to cover. With our immediate threat neutralized, Tolt and I retreated back into the bunker and sealed the doors behind us.

Miraculously, Gering was the only fatality of the grenade that detonated in the bunker. The fact that the device went off underneath him was the only reason Tolt and I were still alive. Besides Gering, Lumuk was hit the worst. He was standing during the explosion and the concussion sent him careening into one of the walls.

Jella quickly set to taking care of Lumuk while Briggund sat on the deck in the corner, squeezing his legs tight around his chest, rocking himself back and forth. Je'Sikka Albarn, paralyzed and unconscious, also survived the attack despite being dropped by Lumuk when the grenade exploded.

After we were situated, Tolt and I retook our positions guarding the door. When Jella finished tending to our wounded, she strolled over and sat beside me. Handing me my helmet, she said, "I found this."

"Thanks." I looked over my mangled headgear. The face shield was damaged, so I could not use the Data Center Overlay or see any PCR video from my comrades' cameras. Fortunately, the commlink remained operational, so I could still listen in. I expected a replacement would not be hard to come by. After the fighting was over, there were sure to be plenty of Marine corpses littering Narman's Pyke. They would not be needing their helmets anymore.

Jella tenderly took my hand and squeezed it. "What are we going to do now?" she asked me.

"Nothing," I answered. "We're going to sit tight until the thunder dies outside."

●●◄●►●◄●►●●

CHAPTER 33

T hings eventually quieted down after a couple of hours and a pair of really big explosions. The battle was over, but we did not know who the victors were until I heard Gunny Malcolm's voice in my earpiece. "Tauk? You copy? Are you there?"

"Yeah! I'm here! You okay?"

"I'm fine," Gunny answered. "What's your situation?"

I looked around the storm shelter as if I did not know. "I'm hunkered down with our guide, the pilot, Lumuk, the captain, and one of his guards."

"Briggund's with you?" Malcolm sounded disappointed

"Yeah, we got him,"

"All right. The fighting's over. Come out and rejoin us."

When we emerged from the bunker, we were shocked by the scene before us. The compound was littered with Marine bodies, lying twisted and broken all over the place. Lined up along the wall were over a hundred troops, on their knees with their hands behind their heads. To the prisoners' rear stood their former comrades, pointing rifles at the backs of their heads.

Upon seeing this, Captain Briggund furiously marched toward the defeated mutineers. "SHOOT THEM!" our commander screamed. "SHOOT THEM ALL!"

Lieutenant Hayvar, one of the few officers we had left, stepped forward to intercept our CO. The look on her face suggested that she had had enough. Gunny Malcolm was backing her up. "Sir, you need to shut up right now unless you want the rest of our Marines to turn against you."

"Are you out of your mind?!?" Briggund balked. "I'm not letting this treasonous scum get away with this!"

JE. PARK

Hayvar got right up into the captain's face. "Let's get something straight, goddammit! Look around you! You did this! YOU! This is YOUR fault! You're done here! You're effectively relieved of command! To save your life, I'm allowing you to pretend you're in charge, but make no mistake, Captain. If you interfere with me, I'll put a fucking end to you! Do you understand me?"

Gunny Malcolm looked Briggund right in the eye. "Hayvar's got the remaining officers and the weight of the senior NCOs behind her, Captain. We're going to allow you to save face by claiming you're too incapacitated to command. You'll sit out the rest of this mission in the medical camp."

"But I'm not injured," Briggund whimpered, forgetting that he had been faking maladies to justify riding to Narman's Pyke on an SPS.

That really pissed Gunny Malcolm off. He pulled his sidearm from its holster. "I can fix that, sir."

Briggund hung his head in defeat. Relieved he did not have to shoot a captain in front of witnesses, Malcolm slipped his pistol back where it belonged. "Good. Tauk, get your wounded to the medical camp and take the captain with you."

"Aye aye, Gunny."

We found the medical corps in utter disarray. The corpsmen ignored us, rushing about to save the lives of those more grievously injured. It looked like they were losing that battle. There were too few medics and too many casualties. All around us we heard Marines crying out for help, only there was none to be had. One of those voices caught my attention and hit me like a gut punch.

"Harlund!" I shouted, looking down to find my corporal lying in the dirt, clutching his stomach with both hands as if trying to keep his intestines from running out. He was in a great deal of pain. "You got hit?!?"

Through clenched teeth, Merik groaned, "Yeah! Can you believe this shit?"

"For fuck's sake! After all you've been through, I thought you were invincible!"

Despite his agony, Merik laughed. "I know, right?!? I got through Sivma-11, Halesia, Terris Mor, and Serra Vai with barely a scratch on me! And I get popped in the belly by our own guys on this goddamn shithole?!?" Catching the sight of Captain Briggund behind us, Merik craned his head around to ensure our commander heard him. "I can't believe I'm gonna die on account of that fancy fuck!"

"You're gonna be alright!" I told the corporal. "I'm going to get our medic down here to..."

"I don't need a medic!" Merik gasped as he grabbed my arm. "I need morphine! I gave all mine to Yisht when he got hit."

"A convict?!?" I was taken aback by Merik's lunacy. "You gave your morphine to a convict?!?"

Harlund bit his lip and nodded his head. Then he started breathing as if he was trying to deliver a baby. "Yisht needed it more than I did at the time! Arrrrrrrghhhhhhh! Fuck! This hurts!"

"Just hold on, Harlund! I'll get you some help right away!" Punching up the squad network, I shouted for our medic. "Kalawezi! Kalawezi! Come in! Come in, goddammit!!"

Merik shook my arm to get my attention. "She's gone, Eamon! She ain't coming!"

"What?"

Harlund let out a single sob as the pain became too much. "She's gone, man! They're all fucking gone! Zeld! Faarhut! Stiid! I don't know who else, but there's more! We were at the epicenter of this shit, man. The rebels and the guards both shot the hell out of us! I don't know if there's anybody left! AUUUGH! Come on, Eamon! Just get me some morphine! I can't take this!"

Lumuk reached into his med-pack and pulled out one of his doses. I shook my head. "No way, Private! That shot's measured for you. Harlund's a third your weight. That shit'll kill him."

With tears running down his face, Lumuk nodded. "I know."

Looking at me, Merik nodded also. "So do I, man. Please. It feels like I'm shitting a belly full of broken glass here. The medics already triaged me as a lost cause. I'm going to die. Please don't let me go like this! Please, Eamon! Make it stop."

Letting out a long sigh of resignation, I took the syringe out of Lumuk's hand. After removing the cap from the needle, I jabbed it deep into Merik's thigh and pressed the plunger. The effect was almost immediate. Harlund's entire body seemed to relax, and he smiled at me. "Yeah, maaaaaan. That's what I'm talking about. Niiiiiiiice." I placed my hand on the corporal's chest as he closed his eyes.

"Remember what I told you right after we landed, Eamon?" Merik groggily asked after a couple of seconds.

"About what?"

"Civil war," Harlund answered. "I told you that one day you'd have to make a choice about whether to kill a prick like Mazada Duum or someone like me."

I nodded. "Yeah. I remember that."

"Good," Harlund said. "After this clusterfuck, I'm pretty sure the day you have to make that choice is coming sooner rather than later. When it arrives, choose wisely, Eamon. Pick the correct side, man. You know what's right and what's wrong. Do what's right. Don't do what I did. Don't die with murder on your conscience."

I did not understand. "What do you mean, Harlund? What did you do?"

Merik winced, but not because of physical pain. "I killed my brothers and sisters, Eamon. I probably snuffed out a dozen of them during this fight. They were Charlie Company Marines. I shouldn't have done it, Eamon. I shouldn't have done it."

Harlund was fading fast now. Still, his eyes opened one last time as he struggled to point a bloody finger at our disgraced commander, still lurking a meter or two behind us. "Had I known that I was going to die today, I wouldn't have killed our Marines, Eamon. I'd have iced that Sammy motherfucker over there."

Those were Harlund Merik's final words.

●●◄●► ● ◄●► ●●

CHAPTER 34

W hen we returned to Delta Company's marshaling area, I discovered that Lumuk, Jella, and I made up almost half of my surviving squad. Maiq Reino, my machine gunner, Prishtina Gai, our sniper, Mazada Duum, and one of my convicts, Barone Parsons, were all that remained. Of the twenty-two Marines that had left the beach, only seven of us were left to stand in formation.

Yet, the roster list on my forearm monitor said there was supposed to be eight. I scrolled down the names until I found who was missing. It was one of my convicts, Ritza Xi. Her vital sign readout said she was alive, but in distress.

Looking at my other convict, I asked, "Have you seen Xi?"

Parsons shook his head. "Not lately. We got separated in the crossfire. We tried to stay together, but it didn't work out."

"She didn't join the mutineers, did she?"

My convict scoffed. "I doubt it. She had equal contempt for both sides in that fight. She'd have been happy to watch you all kill each other off." Parsons' tone suggested he would have been, too.

"She's still alive," I informed him.

The look on Parsons' face softened. "Really? Where is she?"

I hit the tracker beacon on my exo-armor monitor and immediately got a ping despite the Harnillium interference. "Not far," I said. "By the looks of it, she's probably in one of those storm bunkers."

Jella stood and picked up a stray rifle. "We have to go get her."

I sighed. Actually, we did not. Ritza Xi was a Zero. The woman forfeited her human rights when she murdered her family. Still, she came to help me when I got attacked by the anwar. I owed it to her to return the favor. After gearing up, I stepped over to our equipment cache and grabbed an orphaned M72. Tossing it to Parsons, I asked, "You know how to use it?"

The convict nodded. "I did five years in the Corps as a white-striped enlistee. I've seen more action than you have."

As far as convicts went, Barone Parsons was unassuming and dull. He never warranted a deeper dive into his personnel file. I had no idea he was a former Marine. "Why didn't you ever tell me that?"

Parsons shrugged. "We're not exactly confidantes, are we?"

I shook my head. "No. I guess we're not."

When we took off to locate our missing convict, I noticed Jella walking with us. I stopped to tell her to stay behind but realized no one was left to guard her—no one I trusted, anyway. Lance Corporal Reino was a good Marine but was battered and exhausted. Lumuk was worthless even in the best of circumstances. Prishtina Gai was an evil shot, but she was not forceful enough to take control if things got hot. Duum was the most capable of them all, but his loyalties were suspect. No matter what Parsons and I were walking into, the doctor was safest with us.

As suspected, Xi's tracking beacon led us to another subterranean shelter a couple of blocks away. It was quiet there, with little indication that anything was awry. That made me suspicious. Even after opening the door to Xi's hiding place, nothing seemed amiss.

"Is anybody in there?" I called into the bunker, getting no response. Only after listening really hard could I make out the labored breathing of a woman in the darkness. "Xi?"

I was answered by a single sob. It was her. With my weapon poised to fire, I descended the steps and threw on the lights, only to be met by a scene of pure carnage. The first dead Marine I found was seated against the wall with his pants around his ankles, clutching his groin. It looked like he had bled out after having his genitals blown off. The second was also half-naked, but had been shot in the head. The third man killed without his pants on took several bullets center mass with a tight enough grouping to pierce his chest plate. He left a long blood trail as he tried to crawl out of the bunker but expired before reaching the steps. The fourth corpse was not shot at all. He had been bludgeoned to death, much like the children I saw in Xi's crime scene photos.

Despite being no detective, it was easy to piece together what had happened. When the mutiny erupted, a group of Marines decided to party instead of fight. They got their hands on Ritza Xi and dragged her where no one would hear her scream. During her assault, Xi got ahold of one of the Marines' sidearms and opened fire upon her attackers, killing three of them.

The fourth Marine appeared to have disarmed her and tried to beat her to death. Xi was a mess. Her face was unrecognizable, deformed by swollen bruises and covered in blood. I could tell by the sounds coming from her lungs that she also had internal injuries.

Still, my convict was in better shape than the man who took her pistol away. He was twice her size, three times stronger, trained in martial arts, and had years of combat experience. None of that was a match for Xi's unbridled rage, however. Had I not turned his body over to see the name on his armor, I would never have known it was Staff Sergeant Kyker, the man who had assigned her to me.

Shaking my head in disbelief, I turned to my convict and asked, "How?"

Xi's disfigured lips parted in a painful grin, revealing her broken teeth. "He...he...tried to restrain me. In...a bear hug. I bit him in the throat. Tore...his...jugular out. Then I made him pay."

I could picture it now, Kyker holding his neck in a futile attempt to keep himself from bleeding to death while Xi had her way with him. The man would have been helpless. Just like he thought she was.

Though I could picture the attack, I still did not believe it. It took a motivated person to fight that hard, someone with something to live for. Ritza Xi hardly fit that bill. She was a lifer. She could only leave the Corps in a body bag.

"Why?" I asked her. "Do you really want to see tomorrow knowing it only holds more misery for you?"

Ritza started to cry. "Yes! And I want to survive the day after that! And the day after that! I want to live as long as it takes until I can talk to my father one last time! I want him to see my eyes when I tell him I did not kill my babies! I want him to know I'm telling the truth!" Xi sobbed hard enough to spit blood out of her mouth. "And now I'll never be able to!"

I glanced over at Jella and caught her wiping the tears from her eyes. She believed the prisoner's story.

Xi took a moment to regain her composure. She then forced her eyes open to take in the carnage she had wrought. Xi, a Class Zero convict, took the lives of four Marines. It did not matter what they had done to her. She was the property of the Corps, to be used in any way a Marine saw fit. For her, there was no such thing as self-defense. Xi committed a capital crime, killing those four men. She knew it was my duty to execute her immediately.

The condemned woman looked up at Jella, resigned to her fate. "If you make it out of here, please tell my father it was Mikkal, my husband, who killed my daughters. He went mad after smoking Eldaan Spice. Let my daddy know that I avenged our girls. He'll know who he needs to kill to avenge me."

Turning to me, Ritza Xi then said, "Do what you have to do, Tauk. I'm going to die with a clear conscience. That's more than I can say for you."

Gunny Malcolm found me sitting against the wall of one of the colony's laboratories with my head resting on my knees. I was spent. Not so much physically, but spiritually. Sensing the state I was in, Malcolm fell to the ground at my left, then passed me a bottle of Beru Sukka brandy, one he had liberated from Captain Briggund's box.

"I don't drink," I reminded him.

"I'm not offering you a drink," Gunny slurred. He was sloppy drunk. "I'm ordering you to!"

"Look, Gunny, I appreciate the gesture, but..."

Gunny Malcolm cut me off by slapping me across the face. "Drink it!"

I reluctantly took the bottle from Gunny's hands and sniffed the liquid inside. It made me want to gag.

"For fuck's sake!" Malcolm growled. "Don't play with it! Drink it! You're the man that defeated the Butcher of Deraghun! You shouldn't be afraid of a little booze!"

Hearing Malcolm invoke Gori Dravidas added to my melancholy. I put the bottle to my lips and turned it up, filling my entire mouth with liquor before swallowing it in a single gulp. It was strong stuff and reminiscent of drinking fire. After it settled in my stomach, I felt like I was exhaling for half a minute.

"You know," I confided to Gunny after I got my breath back. "I didn't defeat Gori Dravidas. He defeated me."

Malcolm snorted. "Bullshit. If Gori defeated you, you wouldn't be sitting here."

Gunny never referred to anyone by their first name. Remembering what Raza Bhutaan told me, I asked, "You knew him, didn't you?"

The old man grabbed the bottle out of my hands and took a long pull from it. "Yeah, I fucking knew him. I spent a quarter of my career serving with that man."

"Was he as bad as they say he was?"

Malcolm spat. "He was worse. Far worse. Not half as bad as the rest of us, though."

The answer made me choke on my own saliva. "What?"

Our platoon sergeant lifted his bottle to take another drink but stopped before the elixir hit his lips. He looked inside it and sighed in disappointment, as if the brandy was not even remotely strong enough. "It's a nasty business we're in, Cadet."

"I know," I told him.

"No, you don't," Malcolm snapped. "This shit here on Kanaris? This's just a walk through the woods. Literally. It ain't no real action. You want a fight? Try facing those fucking Ghuldarians. They're fanatics—every last one of them. Still, the horrors you see fighting soldiers ain't nothing like what happens to you while you're putting down a rebellion.

"Wars between professionals can be savage, but they're clinical. Both sides just have a job to do, and they try to carry out their objectives as expeditiously as possible. Your goal is to kill as many of your adversaries as you can in the shortest amount of time possible. You want to make them die, not suffer. Insurrections are different. Your enemies feel like you've wronged them somehow and want you to pay for it. It's very personal."

Gunny reconsidered and took another drink of brandy. "Rebels and terrorists don't just shoot you. They try to hurt you in the worst ways imaginable. They'll go after your friends and family if they can't get to you. The shit they do is barbaric, driving you to the point where you become even more savage than they are. You get locked into this struggle with these animals where you're trying to outdo each other with wanton cruelty."

Malcolm went to take another sip of brandy but, remembering his manners, passed it to me instead. "One day, a few of our Marines disappeared from camp. They vanished into thin air like they were taken by an anwar, except there ain't anything like that on Portuna. It's a Replicant Earth Environment. Anyway, we found them a few days later, tied to trees just outside this little pissant village in the backwoods of Kusan Plaat. The men had been tortured and mutilated in ways that defied comprehension. The woman, well, you can guess what they did to her."

My platoon sergeant grimaced as the memories of that day came creeping back to him. "All the stuff the guerillas did to our people, they did it in that village. Hell, we found our Marines' blood in the hut the inhabitants used as a slaughterhouse. They knew exactly who did that stuff to our troops, but they wouldn't give anybody up. They saw what the rebels did to our Marines, so they knew what the bastards would do to them if they cooperated with us. So, we had to show them that they needed to fear us more than they needed to fear the rebels. Men, women, children. They all died slow."

Malcolm's hands were shaking. "I gazed into the abyss that day, Tauk. And the abyss gazed right back at me. There was no way I could ever leave the Corps after that. I signed up for this outfit to hunt monsters. By the end of my first hitch, I'd become one. We all did. No one back in the civilian world could comprehend what we did or what drove us to do it. They'd think us hellspawn–demons–if we ever told them what happened in that place, and they'd be right. You have to be a psychopath to win a war like that, and that's what we became."

Shaking his head, Gunny took his bottle back once I had sipped from it. "After that, everybody that dared raise their hands against us became a Portuna. Once your mind gets twisted that bad, you can't ever seem to untangle it. Gori Dravidas tried, though. He saw that what we were doing was creating more monsters than we were putting down. He tried to stop it, tried to bring what we had done into the light. So the League had to discredit him. They showed its citizens the crimes *he* committed. Once the people saw what war was actually like, they were outraged. They wanted Gori's hide, which you culled for them."

"During my blooding ceremony," I started to confess. "Me and my quad, the three cadets I grew up with, were sent into the Crucible to track down and kill four convicts. We made short work of three of them, but Dravidas was tough. He got Helmut Hoeneker first. That was no easy feat. Helmut was a badass. Dravidas decapitated him and left his head on a pike for us.

"Misha was a tracker. She could sneak up on you over a crunchy layer of autumn leaves, and you would never hear her coming. Dravidas somehow got the drop on her and snapped her neck. When I found her, it looked like her head was on backwards. I was with Juergen when we found that fucker and we both charged him at the same time. It didn't matter. He had Misha's dagger, and despite our training, Dravidas plunged that blade into my brother within seconds of making contact. He opened him up from his naval to his Adam's apple in one fluid motion, through Juergen's ribs and everything. He then dropped the knife and went after me with his bare hands."

I swiped the bottle of brandy from Malcolm and took a swig. I was feeling the effects of the alcohol by now, and I enjoyed it. "It was a long fight. I held my own for quite a while, but it never felt like I had control of the situation. Dravidas looked like he was having the time of his life, though. Eventually, I spotted an opening and went for it, realizing too late that he baited me. I gave him hell and made him pay for letting me get that close to him, but ultimately, the man got his arm around my neck and choked me out.

"When I came to, Dravidas was standing over me, holding Misha's dagger. 'They're never going to let me out of here alive,' he told me. 'You fought well. You've got heart. It's a shame you're going to waste it all in the Corps. I hope that, before it's too late, you'll realize one day that there's more to life than killing.'

"After that, he handed me Misha's blade and offered me his neck."

"And you took it?"

I nodded. "I slit his throat in cold blood. I saw what he did to my comrades. They were the only family I had ever known. I wanted him to pay for that."

"And they made you a hero for that shit?" my platoon sergeant spat in disgust.

I scoffed. "Yep. They sure did. I'm no hero, Gunny. In fact, by the looks of things around here, I'm one of the biggest fuck-ups to ever march through the gilded gates of the Citadel."

"How do you figure that?"

Laughing in frustration, I answered, "I left the beach with twenty-two Marines, Gunny. You know how many I have left?"

Malcolm did. He was in charge of the company roster. "You got four killers and two convicts."

"One convict. Ritza Xi is in sickbay, beaten half to death."

Gunny chuckled. "Yeah, I heard you sprung that dirtbag medic who tried to kill your pilot to work on her."

Nodding, I said, "I did. I told Gruber if she lives, I'll put in a good word for him at his court-martial."

"And if she doesn't?" Malcolm asked.

"Then I promised I'd kill him slow before he's tried."

"You know," Malcolm told me. "That woman killed four Marines."

I shrugged. "At worst, she killed four deserters who ran away from combat to have a good time. At best, she killed four mutineers. Either way, she's a killer. I want her fixed, and I want her back."

Gunny nodded in approval. "Okay, then. I'm not going to argue with you. We need all the killers we can get. Not that she'll be enough."

"You think we have a chance?" I asked, pointing my chin out at the trees beyond the walls. "Against whoever's out there?"

Malcolm shook his head. "Naaaah. We're probably down to two hundred Marines and just over a hundred surviving mutineers. We've got fewer killers now than the Psycho Pixies had. Whoever's out there can walk right in and take us pretty much at will."

"Then why haven't they?" I asked.

Gunny Malcolm's voice was laden with resignation. "After what just happened? Hell, if I was them, I'd sit back and wait, too. Why should they risk their lives to take us out when we're saving them the trouble and killing ourselves?"

Malcolm had a point. We were screwed.

"You know, Cadet. Don't be too hard on yourself about the losses you took. You're doing all right."

I scoffed. "How do you figure that?"

"Your job was to get our guide to Narman's Pyke alive, was it not?"

Turning my head to where Jella Duverii lay sleeping on the other side of the street, I nodded slowly.

"Then it looks to me like you did what you were supposed to. Trust me, that wasn't easy. Give yourself some credit, Tauk. Congratulate yourself on the successful completion of your very first mission."

Gunny Malcolm raised his bottle in the air, offering me a toast. "Here's to hoping it doesn't turn out to be your last.

●●◄●► ● ◄●► ●●

CHAPTER 35

"**T**auk!" screamed Lieutenant Hayvar from my earpiece. I was sound asleep, but hearing the anger in her voice forced my eyes to spring open, only to be blinded by the Kanarisian sun. I bolted upright just in time for the world to spin around me like an out-of-control roulette wheel. My ears were ringing, my head was pounding, and, at first, I had no idea where I was.

"TAUK!" Hayvar shrieked again, adding even more agony and confusion to my muddled mind.

"Huh?" I murmured, looking around as I tried to figure out where that voice was coming from.

"TAUK! Can you read me?!?"

"Y-y-y-yeah," I stuttered. "I mean, yes ma'am! I'm here! I'm here!"

"Tauk! Are you alright?"

"Y-yes. I-I-I'm," I paused as my chest tightened up, making me gag. "I think I'm okay...yeah, I...I...I'm fine." There was an uncomfortable pause on the commlink while I waited for Hayvar's reply, which never seemed to come. Unable to bear the silence, I asked, "So...uh...how are you?"

"Tauk," Hayvar said, sounding very annoyed. "Get our guide to the CP on the double! We've got something here I need her to see."

I gagged again. The taste in my mouth had me wondering if, after I helped Gunny Malcolm drink that bottle of brandy, I might have accidentally grabbed a midnight snack out of one of the latrine pits.

"Do you read me, Tauk?!?"

"Yes, ma'am!" I barked, jumping to my feet only to find that my legs were not working. I took two steps and fell to my knees. While I tried to regain my balance, I told the lieutenant I would be there shortly. I then got back on my feet, hunched over, puked, and fell forward, planting my face in a puddle of my own vomit.

•● ◄●► ● ◄●► ●•

"What the hell is the matter with *you?*" Hayvar asked when she first laid eyes on me that morning. I was not sporting a very good look.

"I don't know, ma'am," I answered. "I got some kind of stomach bug or something." I stole a glance at Gunny Malcolm. He drank far more the previous night than I had but looked normal. Better than normal, actually. He did not have any shakes.

A slight breeze wafted in from my back, carrying my acrid aroma to the lieutenant's nostrils. Her face twisted up in an expression of disgust. "Cadet, are you drunk?" she asked me.

Before I could lie to her again, Gunny Malcolm said, "Academy cadets don't drink, ma'am."

Lieutenant Hayvar might have doubted me, but Gunny's word was golden. She dropped her suspicions and moved on to the task at hand. Guiding Jella to a monitor set up in one of the storm bunkers serving as our command post, our CO dialed up a sentry posted up on the north edge of the compound's tallest building. His PCR video was playing on the screen. "PFC Duno, can you hear me?"

"Yes, ma'am."

"Can you show me again what you pointed out before?"

"I'll try," the sentry responded. The video on the screen then zoomed into the treetops of the forest around us. It kept focusing further and further out until it stopped at a point that must have been two kilometers away from the colony, showing a group of quarakai.

"You notice anything weird, Doctor?"

Duverii nodded. "Those are a sub-species of quarakai I've never seen before. They're definitely not of the group that were indigenous to Narman's Pyke when I lived here."

They were certainly unique of the creatures I had seen before. Like the quarakai we fed popped kryptid to, these were big, muscular beasts. They had the long, toothy snouts and reptilian eyes of the familiar groups, but they also had a flap of loose skin that ran from their wrists to their ankles. Aside from their heads, they looked like a cross between a hairless mountain gorilla and a flying squirrel.

Jella noticed that, too. "They're gliders," she told the lieutenant. "They can probably sail right over these walls from the trees outside the perimeter."

"You see anything else concerning?" Hayvar pressed.

"Yep. They're not out there doing quarakai stuff. They're not feeding. They're not grooming each other, building nests, or chattering among themselves. They're just sitting there. Watching us. Waiting."

That was not the answer our CO was expecting. Hayvar stepped up alongside Jella and looked closer at the screen. Unable to see what she was looking for, she called the sentry again. "Duno, can you show us the one from earlier?"

"Sorry, ma'am," the Marine answered. "It disappeared a while back and none of us have seen it since."

The lieutenant cursed. Turning her head toward the screen's microphone, she said, "Computer! Pull up Screenshot Seven."

Instantly, the live video feed was replaced with a still image showing a quarakai wearing a piece of metallic headgear. Jella gasped and zoomed in to get a better view of the device. The picture resolution was perfect, and we could clearly distinguish what appeared to be a camera, a microphone, and a wire traveling from the apparatus to the creature's left ear cavity.

Sergeant Gruman, the battalion's only remaining armorer, expounded upon the contraption. "It looks to have been made from components stripped out of a standard-issue, M8413 Space Corps battle helmet. Those things out there have pretty big heads. The helmet wouldn't fit them, so they tore it apart and improvised it into a high-tech tiara."

Hayvar turned to Dr. Duverii. "Are they capable of doing shit like that?"

Jella shook her head and walked up to the screen, zooming in for a better view of the quarakai's hands. "See how their fingers end in talons beginning at the last knuckle? You know what that means?"

Everybody within earshot shook their heads.

"Like our own nails, those claws are made out of alpha-keratin. That means there're no nerves in them. They have no feeling in their fingertips. Their hands are made for digging into trees, the skin of their prey, and for fighting. They're not designed for precision electronics work. The quarakai didn't do this. That's human technology."

"Ghouls," spat Lieutenant Hayvar. "They've co-opted the fucking wildlife!"

"Don't underestimate the quarakai," Jella warned. "They're significantly more advanced than animals. Quarakai may be primitive, but they're intelligent beings. They communicate with each other using language, just like we do. You can reason with them if you can decipher their lingo. That means they can follow directions. And orders. It looks like our adversaries figured that out before we did. That's big trouble for us. How many do you think are out there?'

Hayvar shrugged. "Based upon our sample survey, we estimate there are seven thousand quarakai within a two-kilometer radius of Narman's Pyke."

Jella inhaled deeply. "And how many of us?"

"Not even remotely enough," Hayvar answered.

It was about that time that the perimeter sentries started reporting movement on the ground. Jella thought that odd. "Are they quarakai? With the skin flaps for gliding?"

"Negative," one of the sergeants reported back. "These look like smaller versions of the ones we saw on the trail."

"Unbelievable," Jella gasped. "Quarakai are territorial. The greater species only tolerate lesser quarakai, like the barbalu. Physically, those aren't any danger to them, and they can even become a potential food source if their usual prey dries up. They consider larger species a threat and will not share territory with them at all. The Ghouls didn't just co-op a troop of quarakai; they united natural enemies into a fucking quarakai fighting force!"

Hayvar had heard enough. "Great. Just what we needed. We get all the way here, lose most of our supplies, decimate ourselves, and now are about to get overrun by a stone-age army."

"Lieutenant Hayvar," I said. "Jella...I mean...Dr. Duverii and I were in the cockpit during the descent. We saw what happened. There are no guns shooting down dropships. Now that Briggund's gone, get word to the *Phoenix* that..."

"Tauk, find me a communications rocket, and I will do exactly that," our CO told me. "For a colony that is surprisingly well equipped, the armory and rocket bay have been emptied. You got any better ideas?"

"No, ma'am," I told her.

"Tragically, neither do I." Turning back to Jella, Hayvar said, "Thank you for your insight, Doctor. If you'll excuse me, I have to plan a battle."

As Jella and I took our leave, Gunny Malcolm stepped toward me and pushed his canteen into my chest. "Drink this."

The thought of consuming more alcohol sparked a rebellion in my stomach. I nearly threw up again. "You're insane, Gunny. I'm not..."

"It's water," Malcolm snapped. "You need to rehydrate. Guzzle it and drink two more. After that, shake the cobwebs out of that skull of yours. I need your 'A' Game. So does Duverii."

•• ‹•› ● ‹•› ••

As we left the Command Post, I turned to Jella and said, "Drop your visor. I've got to show you something." After she lowered her helmet's face shield into the combat position, I rewound my PCR video until I found an image of the mangled quarakai I had seen the day before. Transmitting it to Dr. Duverii, I asked, "Is that the type of quarakai that was here when you were?"

"Oh my god!" Jella gasped when she saw the picture. "I'll do you one better. Not only do I recognize the species, I know that particular quarakai. That's Tukko!"

"You can recognize these things?"

Our guide shrugged. "Like anything else, if you spend enough time with them, you can start telling them apart. It starts by noticing the different patterns on their skin, but it doesn't take long for you to learn their faces. Oh, Tukko! What happened to you?!?"

"I think it was trying to sign to us."

Jella nodded. "Tukko was one of Doctor Briiz's quarakai, so that doesn't surprise me. Man, if we had someone that knew the signs he taught his subjects, we could learn a lot from that creature."

Our guide scoured the walls and the trees beyond. "With thousands of hostile quarakai out there in what used to be his territory, Tukko's in this complex somewhere. He'll remember me! We've got to find him!"

"You think he knows how we can defeat these things?"

Jella scoffed. "Defeat them?!? There's no defeating them! There's thousands of them out there!"

Frantically scouring the walls and rooftops, Duverii flipped up her visor and cupped her hands around her mouth. "Tukko!" she screamed. "Tukko! It's Jella! Tukko!"

"If that thing's half as smart as you say it is, it's probably a long way away from here," I told her. "I highly doubt it's within earshot."

"It takes much more distance for a quarakai to get out of earshot than it does for a human." Jella lowered her visor and set her commlink controls to megaphone mode. "TUKKO!" her exo-armor speakers roared.

"Jella, I'm sorry, but we don't have time for a quarakai reunion right now. We need to..."

"That creature is the key to our survival!" Jella snapped, cutting me off.

"How do you figure? It didn't save the colonists or the Psyxies!"

"Look, Eamon," Jella pleaded. "If Tukko survived whatever got the colony, it wasn't because he beat them or outran them. It was because he knew where to hide from them." Switching back to her megaphone, the guide screeched, "TUKKO!"

I sighed. "Jella, it knew these things were coming. It tried to warn us about them. Your quarakai got a head start and got as far away..."

"TUKKO!"

"...as it could get."

"TUKKO!"

"It's long gone and..."

"Tukko!" That was not broadcast over Jella's megaphone. That was her natural voice, squealing with delight. When I turned to see where she was looking, I caught sight of a quarakai charging at us from one of the deserted streets.

Several other Marines also saw it and raised their weapons. I had to jump into their line of fire and activate my own megaphone. "HOLD YOUR FIRE! HOLD YOUR FIRE! WHATEVER YOU DO, DON'T SHOOT!"

Everyone stood there stunned as the creature knocked our guide to the ground and wrapped its arms around her. Had Jella not been convulsing in laughter, I would have thought she was getting mauled. Turning towards the Marines, I waved them back to put them at ease.

"It's all right," I assured them. "Carry on! This one's on our side."

●●<●>●<●>●●

CHAPTER 36

"How did you find that thing's hiding place so fast?" Gunny Malcolm asked as we gathered on the parade ground to get our marching orders from Lieutenant Hayvar.

"We didn't find anything," I told my platoon sergeant. "The damned thing recognized Jella and practically dragged us there. It was trying to get us to escape with it."

Malcolm bobbed his head up and down, grateful to have a hope of surviving the impending onslaught. "The sewer, huh? I guess that makes sense."

"It's one large, long tunnel running fifteen kilometers beneath the surface, right under the wall. It emerges halfway down the face of a massive cliff, with large rock terraces on either side of it. Jella knows where it is. She used to see it while flying out on exploratory expeditions to the west. She said it's more than a kilometer from the top of the cliff and below it is still something of an abyss. If you tumble off the edge, you'll fall for several clicks before you hit bottom. There's room for a couple hundred people and it's concealed from above by the brush."

"How long could we hold out there?"

"It still rains like hell here, so we'd have plenty of water. Between kryptids and our rations, we might be able to hold on indefinitely."

"I hope you're right," Gunny told me. "A squad from Alpha Company is clearing the pipe now, and right behind them are the medics moving all the wounded that can be saved."

"What about the wounded that can't?" I asked.

Gunny sighed. "There's nothing we can do for them. They're being left under Gruber's care in the medical camp so that when we're overrun, it'll look like they got us all."

I did not like that idea one bit. "That feels like a violation of the Waimair Article to me."

"It probably is," Gunny confessed. "But after listening to Hayvar's plan, there probably ain't going to be anyone left to complain about it." Malcolm paused as he caught sight of our commanding officer approaching the parade ground. "Nor will there be anyone left to prosecute. Alright, you get out of here and rejoin your squad. You know what to do, right?"

"Aye aye," I assured him. "Fight long enough to ensure the mutineers are focused on the enemy, then fall back to the sanitation complex."

Gunny slapped me on the shoulder. "Don't dilly-dally. You get there as quick as you can."

"You don't have to worry about that," I assured him as I ran off to rejoin what was left of my unit.

I had barely taken my place in formation when I heard Malcolm's voice screaming out of my earpiece. "AH! TEEEEEEEEN...HUT!"

Hayvar's loyal Marines were assembled in the rear of the formation, save for those on the rooftops scanning the trees for threats. The rebels were standing in rows before us. Our CO marched up to them first.

"Make no mistake," Lieutenant Hayvar growled at the rebels. "I would like nothing more than to line all of you up against that wall and have you shot!"

Pacing before the prisoners with her hands clasped behind her back, our new commander shook her head in anger. "But I can't. I need you. Every last one of you. Outside those walls are thousands of alien creatures getting ready to leap over our fortifications and tear us apart! They're animals, Marines. Literally. We can't reason with them. We can't negotiate with them. We can't even surrender to them. These are creatures likely trained and conditioned by the Ghouls to enhance their predatory instincts, and they're about to be unleashed upon us. We're their prey."

"They're not animals," I heard Jella say into my earpiece. She was in the sewage pipe below us but still close enough to watch Hayvar through my PCR feed. "They're sentient beings. Primitive, but intelligent. She's underestimating them."

"By my count," Hayvar continued. "We have three-hundred and twenty-eight Marines capable of fighting back against these things. We all need to take up arms and hold this colony against the horde preparing to attack us. That means we're re-arming the mutineers. The Class One convicts are being promoted to combat troops. We're even going to have to issue arms to the Zeros. Everybody able to fight needs to fight."

"I'll be frank," the lieutenant confessed. "The situation is bleak. There're too few of us to beat these things back, and the specter of meeting our end between the jaws of these fiends is horrific. I understand the temptation to take your service weapon and pop a hole into your own forehead to avoid such a fate. I'm asking you not to do that, though. I'm asking you to give these things hell.

"You're probably wondering why you should fight when defeat and death seem all but inevitable. Well, let me give you a reason. Yourselves. There's a secret article in the Uniform Code of Military Justice that allows me to pardon all crimes in return for extraordinary courage under fire. The odds are long, but if we save this colony, I will pardon all of you for your crimes, and you will immediately be released from your sentences, free to leave the military and carry on with your lives as best you can. Conscripts will be eligible for discharge also."

Parsons was just a couple of meters away from me. I turned to look at him and caught him smiling. Raising him on a private channel, I asked, "What are you so happy about?"

"I'm getting the fuck out of here," Parsons answered.

"You think you're going to survive this?"

"I know I am," the convict assured me. "I've still got a purpose to fulfill, Cadet. I'm going to die doing that. Not this bullshit."

I watched Hayvar point her finger at the rows of rebel Marines. "You troops earned yourselves a position tied to a stake in front of a firing squad. I'm allowing you the opportunity to not only redeem yourselves, but to regain your freedom. Is there any among you that wishes to refuse this offer?"

"GO AHEAD!" shouted someone from the trees over the megaphone of a league-issued set of military exo-armor. "REFUSE THE OFFER! YOU WERE RIGHT TO FIGHT BACK AGAINST THE FUCKERS! KILL THEM AND JOIN US!"

Half the Marines still in the command's good graces rose their weapons and pointed them at the trees. The other half took aim at the mutineers, lest they get bad ideas.

As the troops tried to zero in on an enemy, a lone man equipped in Psycho Pixie armor and a jet pack flew out of the forest and landed atop the wall.

"YOU WANT FREEDOM?" the pseudo-Psyxie asked. "WE CAN GIVE IT TO YOU A LOT QUICKER THAN THEY CAN, IF THEY REALLY INTEND TO GIVE IT TO YOU AT ALL."

All weapons shifted to the man addressing us. He seemed unconcerned about that, though. "WE TRIED TO REASON WITH THE AIRBORNE. WE

TRIED TO EXPLAIN TO THEM WHAT HAPPENED HERE, BUT THEY DIDN'T CARE. THEY TRIED TO BETRAY US ANYWAY." Waving his arm out to where our Psycho Pixies were still hanging from the trees, the man said, "LOOK WHERE THAT GOT THEM."

"Don't listen to him!" shouted Hayvar over the network. "You can't trust a word any Ghuldari shitstain tells you!"

The intruder laughed at Hayvar as he removed his helmet. "I'm no Ghoul."

"Oh my God!" gasped Jella over my earpiece.

"What?" I asked back. "Do you know him? Who is that?"

"He's one of ours!" Jella told me. "He was the vice-governor! No one took over Narman's Pyke, Eamon! The colonists took it themselves!"

••◄►●◄►••

"I got him in my sights!" Prishtina Gai called out over the commlink. She was not with us on the parade ground. She was perched upon one of the compound's rooftops with a sniper rifle. "My crosshairs are on the bridge of his nose! Do you want me to take the shot?"

"No!" Gunny yelled before I had the chance to. "He's the person we need to negotiate with! Keep that scope on target, though! Be prepared to take him out if I tell you to!"

"If you're not a Ghuldari provocateur, who the hell are you?" Lieutenant Hayvar asked the intruder.

"I'm Mailes Ghona," the man answered. "I came here as the vice-governor almost a decade ago. Now, I'm in charge."

"What'd you do to the governor?" our CO asked.

Ghona scoffed. "What did *I* do to the governor?!? *I* didn't do a damn thing to Dagmar Wikk, Lieutenant! You did, though. Well, maybe not you personally. Our contingent of Marines, *your* people, tied him to a stake and set him on fire. His wife and kids, too."

"What?!?" gasped Hayvar. "For what?"

"Insubordination," Ghona told her.

"What do you mean 'insubordination?' The governor doesn't report to the military commander! It's the other way around!"

"Not if the officer in charge of the troops is Samaari," Ghona corrected her. "The Sammies have a hard time accepting orders from anybody that isn't from a Guild planet. They're even worse when they have money from the Tahnabaht Conglomerate propping them up."

I heard Gunny curse over the platoon commlink. Lieutenant Hayvar clenched her teeth. Both wished a lot of ill will upon the Samaari nation right about then for creating yet another mess we would have to bail them out of.

Turning to my right, I glanced over at Mazada Duum. His face was twisted in rage while he kept his sights focused on the governor's chest. "Duum," I told him. "Lower your weapon."

"What for?" the Samaari asked. "If we get the order to blow that lyin' sack of shit away, I want to be the one to do it!"

"Yeah, well, I'm not risking you taking a shot at him before we get the order. Drop your muzzle before I drop you."

Duum cursed as he lowered his rifle to his side and gave me some serious stink eye.

"Governor," Hayvar called out. "What happened to the Marines that were supposed to be guarding Narman's Pyke?"

"The same thing that happened to your airborne troops. The same thing that'll happen to you if you don't choose your next course of action very carefully."

Our commanding officer dropped her head toward the ground and shook it in frustration. "You killed the Marines?"

Ghona nodded. "Most of them. A little less than a third switched sides. They're with us and quite okay. That option's open to you, also. Surrender right now and join us. We'll spare you."

"That's not going to happen," Hayvar assured him.

"Then you're going to leave us no choice but to kill you, Lieutenant. Is that what you want?"

Our CO sighed. "Of course, that's not what I want! I don't want to kill you, either. But I will if it comes to that. I'd rather it didn't. What are you looking for, Governor? What do you want?"

"I want you to march back from wherever you came from," Ghona said bluntly. "Go away and leave us alone. After what the Marines did to us here, we have no intention of living under League administration again."

"Governor, you know we can't just leave. That doesn't mean we can't work this out, though. I would love to get to the bottom of what happened here and..."

Ghona cut our commanding officer off. "*You* may want to get to the bottom of this, but the League will stop at nothing short of our total annihilation. Look, I'm not negotiating with the League. That ship has sailed. Right now, I'm negotiating with each of you on a personal basis. If you want to live, join us. Or gather your shit and go back to wherever you walked here from. Now. Anything else is certain death. Look, you can't win this."

"No!" Hayvar countered. "*You* can't win this! At most, you have what? Nine-thousand people and a quarakai army equipped with teeth, talons, and spears? That'll be plenty to wipe what's left of us out, but after we're gone, you'll have to contend with a half-million more Marines orbiting the skies above us! You can't possibly take on that many troops alone!"

Governor Ghona laughed. "Alone? Who says we're alone?"

As if on cue, thousands of quarakai emerged from below the wall and took their place alongside the colony's governor. Duum raised his weapon again and drew a bead on Ghona's chest. This time, I did not stop him.

Once the quarakai had shown their numbers upon the ramparts, Governor Ghona beamed a mischievous smile at our commanding officer. "Last chance, Lieutenant."

•●◄●►●◄●►●•

CHAPTER 37

"**F**ire!" yelled Gunny into the commlink.

A fraction of a second after Malcolm issued the command, Prishtina Gai squeezed the trigger. She was not quick enough. Either Ghona's instincts were unnatural, or wearing League equipment allowed the governor to hear Malcolm's order at the same time Gai did. Regardless, he activated his jet pack and blasted himself off the wall to avoid getting hit. In a flash, he had disappeared back into the trees.

Immediately after Ghona's escape, we learned the colonists had snipers too. While Gai had the governor in her crosshairs, the Narmans had Hayvar in theirs. Unfortunately, our CO was not equipped with a jet pack. Within three steps, an insurgent bullet found the sweet spot between Hayvar's helmet and her exo-armor, severing her spine at the base of her skull. It was an amazing shot.

As the roar of gunfire erupted from within the compound, the quarakai lept from the ramparts, gliding to the ground using the flaps of skin at their sides. The Marines tried to take them out while they were still in the air, but the beasts were quick. Once they landed, we discovered they were damned near bulletproof, also.

One of the creatures came at me as soon as it touched down. I immediately struck it with a three-round burst that hardly phased it. I had to switch my weapon to full auto before I had any effect at all. When the quarakai finally dropped lifelessly onto the pavement, it was close enough to bleed on my feet.

Sensing more coming at me from behind, I turned to find a trio of the monsters running my way. Knowing I had little chance of stopping all three of them with a rifle, I popped loose a grenade, lobbed it halfway between us, then took off in the opposite direction. It went off right as the creatures reached it, killing one and blowing the leg off another. The third caught shrapnel in its eyes and fell writhing into the dirt, clutching its face with both hands while it unleashed a demonic shriek.

With four quarakai down, I was afforded a split second to assess the situation around me. It was pure pandemonium. Many of the mutineers decided to take Ghona up on his offer. They fell to their knees, put their hands up, and were instantly attacked anyway. The quarakai ripped them to pieces where they knelt, sparing no one.

Caught out in the open, the loyalists ran for cover in several different directions, unable to form a line of defense. They fared little better than the rebels. It was not that the Marines weren't killing quarakai. They were. We were mowing them down by the dozens. It was just not enough to turn the tide of the onslaught in any meaningful way. There was no other option but to cut and run. Our resistance crumbled while hundreds of troops made a mad dash toward the sanitation complex.

"What are you doing standing there with your mouth open?!?" screamed Gunny as he sprinted by, dragging me with him as he passed. "Are you trying to get yourself killed?!?"

"No!" I yelled back. "I was trying to figure out how to save...."

"There ain't no saving anybody out here! We gotta get to cover! We gotta hide! The best we can do is sneak out at night and kill 'em in their sleep! Get to the fuckin' pipes!"

Gunny did not have to tell me twice. I pulled out all the stops and booked toward the sanitation complex as fast as I could. Being an academy Marine, I was born and bred for peak physical performance. Malcolm did not have a chance of keeping up with me. I did not think anybody else in Narman's Pyke did, either. Then I saw our former CO, Captain Briggund, blow past me as if I was standing still. Apparently, when it came to speed, terror trumped fitness.

When I craned my neck to check if Gunny Malcolm saw what I had, I discovered there were two hulking quarakai right on his heels, and the space between them was shortening fast. Slamming on my brakes, I swung around and pulled my rifle up to its firing position before loosing an explosive round from the grenade launcher mounted beneath the barrel of my M72. My target had its mouth open when it was hit, and the incendiary shot right down its gullet before it went off, liquifying the creature's insides. I dropped the other quarakai with automatic gunfire and was relieved that it collapsed and died much quicker than the first one I had shot.

Seeing no friendlies to my rear, I pulled another grenade from my web gear and set the detonator to "proximity." I tossed it behind us to explode when the next set of quarakai rounded the corner. I heard it go off no more than five seconds later but did not look back to see what it got. At that point, I had to run. There were still three blocks between me and the sanitation complex, and odds were long that I could beat the quarakai to it.

"RUN!" I heard Maiq Reino yell at me. He had somehow gotten ahead of us. "RUN, GODDAMMIT! THEY'RE GAINING ON YOU!"

I could not answer. I was getting gassed and did not want to waste oxygen replying to my machine gunner. I tried to boost my speed, but I was already giving it everything I had.

"FOR FUCK'S SAKE, TAUK!" Reino screamed. "THEY'RE GOING TO FUCKING GET YOU!"

"Then shoot 'em!" I gasped.

"I CAN'T! YOU'RE IN THE WAY!"

As if fate itself intervened, I tripped. I careened face-first into the pavement, my helmet being the only thing saving me from a disfiguring case of road rash. While I was still rolling down the street, Reino and two other machine gunners opened up on full auto.

M2117s were far more effective at putting down glider quarakai than the M72. There looked to be a couple dozen of the bruins breathing down my back, but Reino and his buddies shredded every last one of them as I combat crawled to the intersection. I did not jump back to my feet until I was safely up range. "Holy shit, am I glad to see you!" I yelled at my gunner.

"Yeah! Yeah! Whatever!" Maiq snapped as he and his buddies continued firing down the street. "You can kiss me later! Get out of here now before we start running out of ammo!"

"Have you seen anyone..."

"GO!" Gunny Malcolm screamed at me as he grabbed the back collar of my armor and threw me toward the sanitation complex. He then turned his attention to the machine gunners. "YOU, TOO! FALL BACK TO THE NEXT INTERSECTION! NOW! GO! GO! GO! GO! GO!"

At the end of the next block, I ran into Barone Parsons. More accurately, he ran into me. We exchanged no niceties; we just regained our balance and returned to our stride. By now, there was a mob of us running for the pipes, and we were trying to break free of the pack. We were too bunched up and tripping over each other.

As we approached the last intersection, a screaming mob of alien malcontents cut us off. They came at us from our flanks, and before we knew it, a group of at least fifty hulking gliders stood between us and our objective. There was no time to issue orders and no time to formulate strategy. All we could do was fight.

The machine gunners swung around and pointed their weapons north, firing over our heads at the beasts towering above us. Most of the Marines reached for grenades and started pitching them where the enemy was most concentrated. The rest used their M72s to cut down those that had survived the explosives.

After exhausting my first magazine, I glanced back at the machine gunners just in time to see them taken from behind. I watched in horror as a quarakai grabbed Reino by the shoulder and effortlessly ripped his left arm clean off his torso. It then clamped its jaws around his neck and tore out his throat, nearly decapitating him.

We were surrounded. The streets in all directions were full of quarakai converging upon our position. The situation looked hopeless. "What do we do now?" I heard one of the Marines ask Gunny Malcolm.

My platoon sergeant looked at the private with crazed eyes and screamed, "We charge!"

"What?!?" the Marine cried. "Are you fucking crazy?!?"

"If we stay here, we die! Our only hope is to break through these fuckers and get to the basement of that building!"

"But...!"

"CHAAAAAARRRRRGGGE!" Pulling a grenade off his belt, Malcolm yanked the pin out and tossed it into the group of quarakai gathered between us and the complex. He stepped into the gap it created when it went off, opened fire, and threw another. Following his lead, the rest of us did the same.

It was a bloodbath. Instead of following every instinct I had and running away from the beasts, I rushed them. Grenades were going off all around me and bullets were flying centimeters from my head. I was certain we were killing as many of each other as we were slaying the enemy.

The instant I stepped into the melee, I was struck upside the helmet by one of the gliders. Had it not been a glancing blow, it might have taken my head off, but luckily, it just knocked me senseless. Another grabbed me by the arm and tried to yank me towards it. At nearly the same moment, a grenade went off and blew me in the opposite direction, with the creature's disembodied hand still clutching my sleeve. Before I could remove it, a bullet ricocheted off the top of my helmet while another struck my battle pack, hurtling me deeper into the carnage.

I was tossed left and right by the quarakai and the explosions, making it impossible to get my bearings. At one point, I caught a glider's attention, and it reached out for me. Unable to raise my rifle, I pulled my sidearm and pointed it at one of the alien's eyes. As I was squeezing the trigger, a blast threw the quarakai out of my line of fire and one of my fellow Marines right into it. Instead of killing the creature, I blew away a comrade.

Before I could comprehend what I had done, another explosion knocked me to the ground. Then another launched me back to my feet. An instant later, a third lifted one of the smaller quarakai off the pavement and sent it careening into my chest, lifting me off the ground and launching me through one of the sanitation complex's shattered windows.

"FUUUUUUUUCK!" I screamed after landing on the deck inside the building. I then remembered what the quarakai did to Reino and screamed out again.

Before I could scream it a third time, Gunny Malcolm pulled me off the floor. He was covered in blood and missing an eye. "Come on, Tauk!" he gasped as he dragged me deeper into the building. "Come on! We made it! We're almost there!"

Malcolm and I were not the first Marines to get into the building. Nor were we the last. A dozen of us had broken through in the confusion and were approaching the finish line. To encourage the others, Malcolm powered up his commlink and yelled, "Keep fighting! Don't give up! Get your asses into the building and get down to the basement!"

The first wave of us got into the sanitation facility largely unnoticed by the enemy. There was too much confusion, too much gunfire, and too many explosions in the street for them to focus on the building behind them. As more Marines stopped shooting and started running, however, that changed. Only five or ten more humans breached the building before the creatures began coming in, too. Before long, the fight inside was raging just as hard as it was outside.

But Gunny and I were ahead of it, running, jumping, and falling down the stairways until we disappeared into the darkness of the bowels below, guided by the beacon Jella activated before she led the wounded into the sewage tunnel.

Had it not been for Gunny Malcolm, I would have been a goner. That last explosion had rung my bell, and I could barely think, let alone walk. Malcolm was practically dragging me along. I was confused and terrified. "Gunny! They got Reino! One of those fiends ripped his goddamn arm off!"

Malcolm smacked me. "Focus, Tauk! They didn't just get Reino! They got damn near everybody! They'll get you too if you don't concentrate on getting to the pipes!"

"Oh shit!" I gasped. "Prishtina! She was on the rooftops! She needs to get down here!" Since Malcolm had my right arm, I had to use my chin to activate the roster on my left. When the list of my active troops popped up on the display, there were only four names on it. Prishtina Gai's was not one of them. She was gone.

Two of my survivors were already in the pipe. Ritza Xi was a medical patient and evacuated with our pilot. Akkam Lumuk was worthless in a fight, so I sent him down to help move our wounded. That left two of my people still out there.

I had just seen my convict. "Parsons!" I shouted over the commlink. "What's your twenty?!?"

"Ahead of you," my Class One prisoner panted back. "I'm hauling ass! You better too!"

"I am!" I yelled back as Malcolm started practically throwing me down the steps. "Duum! Mazada Duum! Where are you?!?"

Hearing no answer, I tapped into his PCR video to glean his situation through his eyes. Unfortunately, things did not look good. He was in the building but thick in the battle above us. The little man was surrounded and hysterical, but fighting like a beast. "DUUM!" I yelled at him. "GET OUT OF THERE AND GET BELOW!"

"I'm trying!" Duum screamed back. He was bawling. "There's too many of them I can't get..."

A tremendous explosion went off, filling the room with debris and smoke. I could see the Samaari get tossed ass over elbows through the air, but he hit the ground running, using the reduced visibility to cover his escape. "I'm coming!" he sobbed into the network. "I'm coming! Don't you leave without me! Do you hear me?!? Don't you fucking leave!"

I wanted to reassure Duum that we would not desert him, but even with my head muddled by the abuse I had been subjected to, I knew he would not benefit from promises that could not be kept. I was blunt. "Your fate depends on you!" I screamed at him. "If the quarakai beat you to the access hatch, we have to seal it! Don't force us to leave you behind!"

Gunny smacked me across the helmet. "If you don't shut up and focus on getting to the pipes, you're the one that's going to get left to the quarakai! Move it, goddammit! Move!"

It was three more flights of stairs until we reached the lowest level. After that, it was a flat-out, hundred-meter foot race toward the discharge pipe's access hatch. Though there was little light down that deep, I could tell by the chatter there were a couple dozen Marines in front of us. It sounded like there were triple that behind our backs. There were even more above, but they were actively engaged with the attacking quarakai.

"COME ON!" I heard a familiar voice screaming in front of me in the darkness. "COME ON! HURRY UP! GET IN HERE BEFORE IT'S TOO LATE! MOVE! MOVE! MOVE!"

It was Lumuk, standing outside the hatch with no weapon or helmet on. He was covered in sweat, frantically gesticulating, trying to motivate Marines into the tunnel that would lead them under the wall. "What are you doing here?!?" I yelled at the giant as I got close enough to see him.

Lumuk seemed too terrified to answer me. The M2117 machine gunner next to him spoke in his stead. "The docking wheel on the access hatch is corroded!" the private answered. "He's the only one strong enough to close it!"

Tired of the effort I was putting into all of my questions, Gunny Malcolm dropped me to the deck. "Go!" he snapped. "Get inside!"

"But Duum..."

Malcolm planted his boot into my backside. "Move it! You're in the way!"

To appease Malcolm, I stumbled through the opening but fell against the wall just inside the doorway. "Lumuk!" I shouted. "Get in here! If you're the only one who can close this hatch, you can't afford to get caught on the wrong side of it!"

Lumuk stopped screaming at the troops and looked at Malcolm as if unsure what to do. "You heard him!" Gunny roared. "All you're doing is playing cheerleader! Do it from the other side of the door!"

No sooner was Lumuk inside when the first quarakai rushed out of the shadows. It zeroed in on a Marine just steps from the door and snatched her away so fast that it snapped her neck.

The machine gunner opened up on the creature, blowing the beast apart before it could grab someone else. He then cut down several more behind it, allowing a late rush of troops to reach safety. Gunny emptied his magazine on another. A few more of our comrades got past the quarakai and darted into our passageway, but it was apparent that time was up.

Malcolm himself backed through the opening as he reloaded his weapon. "Lumuk! Get ready to secure that hatch!"

"But...but...there's people still out there!" Turning away from Malcolm, he stuck his head out of the opening. "HURRY UP! RUN! WE GOTTA SECURE THE DOOR!"

"NOOO!" I heard Duum scream out in the distance. "I'm coming! Hold it open!"

Quarakai were now hitting the ground level in force, skipping the stairs and gliding down into the lower levels. They were landing between the fleeing Marines and the discharge access we were guarding. If they got into the pipes, we would all be goners. "Gunner! Get in here!" Malcolm ordered the M2117 crewman. "We're closing the hatch!"

Akkam Lumuk had every reason to leave PFC Duum outside with the quarakai. Yet, the simpleton seemed prepared to risk us all to get his tormentor to safety. With our machine gunner now inside our escape tunnel, Lumuk stuck his head out of the opening and pleaded with Duum to hurry up and run.

"Close that access!" screamed Gunny as he tried to pull Lumuk back inside.

"DUUM!" the giant bellowed out into the corridor. "RUN!"

Despite his wounds, Malcolm jumped up to slap the farmer across the back of the head. "Did you fucking hear me?!? SHUT THE GODDAMN DOOR!"

"DON'T!" I heard my Samaari rifleman shout from the midst of the chaos outside. "PLEASE! I'M ALMOST THERE!"

My platoon sergeant pulled back and punched Lumuk in the kidneys to force him out of the way. He then slammed the access hatch shut and tried to turn the wheel himself. He could not get it to budge.

"NOOOOOOO!" shrieked Lumuk, distraught about leaving someone he knew behind. Even if that someone was the source of so much misery for him. "WE GOTTA GET DUUM!"

Malcolm pulled his sidearm and pressed it beneath Lumuk's chin. "SECURE THAT HATCH RIGHT NOW!"

The giant let out a scream of anguish so loud it made Malcolm flinch, but he finally started doing what he was told. Bawling uncontrollably, Lumuk wrenched the wheel clockwise to secure the opening, yelling, "I'M SORRY, DUUM! I'M SORRY!"

As Lumuk worked to seal the door, my Samaari reached the entrance and started pounding on the other side. "Open up! Please! Let me in! Don't do this! Don't leave me out here! Let me..."

Duum was interrupted by a tremendous explosion on the other side of the steel. Then there was another. And another. Then gunfire, cursing, and the cries of mortally wounded men and quarakai. Our last stand at Narman's Pyke was approaching its zenith less than a meter away from us on the other side of that access hatch.

It was still raging as Gunny Malcolm whipped out his torch and welded the access wheel closed. He then forced us to march into the dark, leaving scores of Marines to meet their doom just behind our backs.

●● ◄❖► ● ◄❖► ●●

CHAPTER 38

C onsidering the carnage we endured to get to the sewer, the fifteen-kilo-
meter trek beneath the walls was relatively uneventful. Twice, we stumbled upon a hunting pod of the giant centipedes that caused so much grief after
the flood. We knew how to deal with the bastards this time, though. We did not
suffer any further casualties.

The other creatures we encountered did not pay much attention to us. The
ground was covered in slimy, black, worm-like creatures, but they were more
interested in devouring waste remnants than Marines.

At one point, our lead man's helmet lamp lit up a set of huge, bulbous eyes
in the distant darkness. There were six of them, arranged in an arachnid-esque
pattern, yet the moans the creature made as the light burned its retinas sounded
very mammalian. In fact, it was eerily human-like, which added to the tunnel's
creep factor. We were all relieved that the animal scurried away before we
got close enough to see what it looked like. After that, the only other things
we came across were large, eyeless, six-legged salamanders that grazed on the
black worms.

The most significant danger to us in the sewer was rain. When we first set
out beneath the surface of Narman's Pyke, we noticed beams of light cutting
through the darkness and realized the colony's storm drains led directly to our
tunnel. If it started pouring again, which it was sure to do on a place as wet as
Kanaris, we would be in serious trouble. If we did not drown in the pipes, we
could end up washed over the side of the cliff where the tunnel ended.

For once, our luck held. The skies above Narman's Pyke waited until we
started emerging from the tube before they opened up again. I was somewhere
in the middle of the procession, still meters away from the tunnel's exit, when
I heard Jella's voice outside. "Is Cadet Tauk with you?"

"I don't know," answered an exhausted Marine.

We never got around to taking attendance after we sealed the tunnel access. We were too disturbed about the people getting mauled on the other side of the hatch. Besides, when we started walking into the dark, there was probably not a Marine among us who thought we'd survive the journey to the cliff. Getting to know one another just felt like a waste of effort. As chatty as I was fighting through the quarakai, I did not say a dozen words underground.

"Tauk!" I heard Jella yell again. "Has anyone seen Tauk?!?" I caught myself smiling as I detected the panic in her voice.

Barone Parsons heard her, too. He stopped to let me pass him. "It's better if yours is the first familiar face she sees coming out of the tube."

I would have eased Jella's discontent and called her over the commlink, but Gunny had us shut it down before we started walking. Now that we knew the enemy were Narman separatists equipped with the same stuff we had, Malcolm did not want them tracking us by electronic emissions. I could only guess that whoever was in charge of the wounded did the same.

Though I wanted to run out and see Jella again, I had to be careful at the end of the pipe. The ledge in front of the tube was barely wider than the width of my feet, and one misstep would send me tumbling into the clouds below.

There were two ledges, one on either side of the pipe. Jella, along with most everyone else, was on the larger one to the left. The instant my feet were planted safely on stable ground, our guide leapt into my arms, pushed my helmet off my head, and pressed her lips against mine. "You made it!"

"I made it here," I said. "For whatever that's worth. It's only a matter of time before they find us."

Jella turned her head and looked at Tukko, the mangled quarakai that had led us to the pipes. "Those gliders took over his clan's territory and wiped out his entire troop. He's all that's left. That creature has been hiding here since the fall of Narman's Pyke. Look at the canopy above us. That'll keep us concealed from anyone flying over. We've got rations, medicine, kryptids, and, my god, more water than we know what to do with. We can stay here a long time."

I let out a sigh. "Tukko probably didn't get caught going into the pipes, though. We did. It won't be long before they figure out why we were all rushing for the basement of the sanitation complex."

Our guide cast her gaze back at the pipe just as Gunny Malcolm emerged from it. "You think they'll come for us out of there?"

"No," I answered. "Sooner or later, I *know* they will. They have to. Our only hope is that General Kroaht gets off his ass and sends help soon. Considering what he's done so far, I'm not counting on him, though."

Jella smiled. "Well, if they're not going to help us, I'm not going to just sit here waiting to get massacred."

I grinned at our guide. It sounded like she had a plan. Considering we only had, at best, fifty Marines still capable of putting up a fight, I wondered what trick she had up her sleeve to take on the Narmans and thousands of airborne quarakai. "What are you thinking?" I asked her.

Jella kissed me once more and said, "I'm thinking that you carry me over to a dark, secluded corner of this ledge we're on, rip my clothes off, and fuck me senseless until the quarakai start pouring out of that pipe to tear us all to pieces."

That turned out to be a pretty good plan. It was much better than anything I could come up with.

●●◄●►●◄●►●●

The time I spent sitting on that ledge, waiting to die, might have been one of the happiest periods of my young life. A week after we escaped Narman's Pyke, during the next break in the rain, I was lying naked on the ground, with Jella beside me. I was looking beyond the ledge at the mountains rising above the clouds. It was night, and I could make out the glow from that fluorescent green mist I first saw the night we arrived. It was beautiful, especially with Gaiomedi, Kanaris's ringed moon, filling the sky behind the peaks.

In the distance, hovering just above the treetops, were scores of sky jellies, twinkling with bioluminescence as they tried to lure creatures into their tentacles. Flocks of what Jella called "laughing dragons" flew above us. From a distance, they looked just like the mythical beasts of ancient Earth lore. Up close, they looked like hairy, flying serpents. They were filter feeders, ravaging swarms of flying bugs with the baleen ridges just behind their lips. Their calls to each other sounded just like laughing humans, hence the name.

Our perch above the abyss had quite a view. I could have built a house upon it and spent the rest of my days right there, watching over creation with Jella Duverii at my side.

Looking at Jella's body, bathed in the white light of Gaiomedi, I heard the voice of Gori Dravidas speaking to me in my head. "There's more to life than killing."

"What?" Jella groggily asked me, stirring from her dreams.

"Shhh," I told her. "I didn't say anything."

"Yes, you did. You said, 'there's more to life than killing.' I heard you."

"I said that out loud?"

Jella rubbed the sleep out of her eyes. "Yeah. What suddenly gave you that epiphany?"

"It wasn't an epiphany. It was what Gori Dravidas told me. Right before I slit his throat."

"The Butcher of Deraghun told you there's more to life than killing?" Jella laughed. Shaking her head, she added, "If he did say that, he's right, you know."

"Not for an academy Marine."

"Why not?" Duverii asked. "What's stopping you from just walking away from this bullshit, turning your back on all the fighting and hiding somewhere off of the League's radar?"

"My honor. I took an oath..."

"An oath? You mean that promise you made to the same people who tried to kill Je'Sikka Albarn to protect the reputation of a high-born coward? The people who condemned Ritza Xi to slavery so that some minor official did not have to face the embarrassment that his junkie son murdered his grandchildren? I don't see the honor in keeping promises made to monsters, Eamon."

She was right. It made me think of what Merik told me as he was dying.

You know what's right and what's wrong. Always do what's right. Don't do what I did. Don't die with murder on your conscience.

Jella placed her hand on my arm. "If we get out of this, let's run away, Eamon. We'll go beyond the edge of the Kyperion Quadrant, find some distant world out there, and settle it. We'll get away from the League. Away from the Ghouls. Away from everything. There's no purpose in this shit."

"I was supposed to make us safe," I confessed to Jella. "I was supposed to keep us free from Ghuldari conquest.

"All you're doing is making sure no one threatens the League elite, Eamon. You're keeping the Samaaris free to wring credits out of people who don't have credits to spare. My god! Briggund was willing to send people to their deaths just so he would not be deprived of his wine!"

"Captain Briggund is not representative of the League," I said, wondering what fate befell that worthless sack of shit.

"Eamon," Jella pleaded. "It is. It didn't use to be, but that's what it's become. I didn't grow up secluded in the Academy like you did. I was raised in the real world and have seen what these people do. There's no honor in dying for something as corrupt as the League. There's even less honor in killing for it."

"But you're here," I reminded Jella. "You came here to help the Leauge take back Narman's Pyke."

"No," Jella countered. "I came to help figure out what happened to the people I grew up with. I came to help my friends. My family. The League just gave me a ride."

"Now that you know what happened, what do you want to do?"

"I want to go home and leave them alone," Jella told me. "I want them to live as they see fit. I don't want them enslaved under Samaari overlords."

"Would you join them?"

Jella sighed and shook her head. "No. I want to live, Eamon. I have a lot of things I need to do. Even though I may agree with their cause, I have no desire to die for it. I've seen what's waiting for them on the *Nebulan Phoenix*. They don't have a chance." Squeezing my arm, she added, "But we do. Come on, Eamon. Run away with me."

I was going to tell her I would. It was on the tip of my tongue. My mouth was open and I was getting ready to swear a brand new oath when one of the Marines guarding the entrance to the pipe screamed out, "Halt! You stop right there before I blow your fucking head off!"

Thinking that that was the tip of the Narman offensive readying to pour out of the pipe now that the water was low again, every able-bodied Marine, including me, grabbed their weapons and sprinted to the end of the sewer line. "Don't shoot!" We heard a voice echo from somewhere deep inside the tube. "Don't shoot! Please! I'm one of you!"

"Identify yourself!" the sentry yelled.

"I'm Duum!" the Marine yelled. "Private First Class Mazada Duum!"

I saw Gunny Malcolm swing around and look at me with an expression of shock on his face. First, he could not believe that Mazada Duum survived the slaughter. Second, he did not expect to see me prepared to engage the enemy completely in the buff.

"Does anyone know PFC Duum?" the sentry called out.

"Yeah!" I answered. "He's one of mine! Let him through!"

Duum emerged from the sewer with his rifle slung over his back and his hands up in the air. His armor was gone, his uniform was in tatters, and his skin was black with soot, dried blood, and burned flesh. He could barely walk and the look in his eyes was a combination of relief, terror, and loathing.

When I saw Mazada Duum, I was hit with a similar mix of emotions. Chief among them was shame over having deserted the man back at the sanitation complex. As his squad leader, I had to say something to him, but I had no idea what that should be. The only thing that came to mind was, "What happened to your armor?"

"I had to ditch it to squeeze into one of the storm drains," Duum stoically replied as he turned his gaze towards me. Looking over my naked body, he then asked, "What the hell happened to yours?"

•● ◁●▷ ● ◁●▷ ●•

CHAPTER 39

"**Y**ou fuckers left me," Duum spat, close to tears as one of the medics patched him up. "You fucking locked me out to get torn apart!"

The rifleman was right, and I felt horrible about it. Unable to maintain eye contact, I turned my gaze to the SPSs that Je'Sikka Albarn and Ritza Xi were lying upon. The medics kept the patients doped up and unconscious, but they were healing well.

Gunny Malcolm felt none of my shame. "We had to do what we had to do," he told the young Marine. "If those quarakai had gotten past that door, you'd have had no place to run to. All of us would've been killed."

Duum was not buying that. "But...but..."

"Suck it up, Marine," Malcolm growled. "It was simple math. Do we sacrifice six lives to save a hundred, or will we likely condemn a hundred souls on the slight chance of saving a half dozen more? It's a tough choice, but not even in the top ten of the toughest decisions I've ever made. Probably not even in the top fifty."

Malcolm leaned back and laughed. Beaming with pride, he looked over his shoulders at the other NCOs standing behind him. "Check this guy out! Can you believe this shit? This little Sammy got locked out of the pipe with a hundred of those goddamn glider quarakai, and here he is! Sittin' here before us able to tell the tale! Is this kid a fuckin' killer, or what?"

The NCOs laughed with Malcolm. A couple reached over and slapped Duum on the shoulder. "That's good soldiering, kid!" one of them said.

"No shit!" added another. "That's the way you do it. Never give up!"

"How did you make it out of that?" Gunny asked.

You could see Duum's demeanor change. He was not used to being genuinely respected, and he was eating it up. "I don't know, Gunny. Right after you shut that hatch, the grenades started going off, and everything went black. I came to the next day under a pile of quarakai bodies. I crawled out of that and found a hiding place where I stayed damn near two days. I waited for it to get dark, then tried to poke around and see what was what in Narman's Pyke."

"And?" Gunny asked. "What's the situation at the colony?"

Duum shrugged. "It's deserted except for the corpses. They left all the bodies, the human ones, anyway. It looks like the quarakai took some of theirs. The rest are getting picked apart by the kryptids."

"They retreated?" a sergeant asked.

Malcolm nodded. "Yeah, they gotta know that sooner or later, the general's going to attack in force. The Narmans can take on a few hundred of us armed with only light weapons, but they're smart enough to know they'd get obliterated by a full-blown landing. They'd do much better luring us into the jungle, onto their turf, and picking us off in pieces. Their only hope is to wear us down."

Duum let out a sigh and looked up at the clouds. "You think they'll ever come down here and help us?"

"Yeah," Gunny answered. "There's too much Harnillium on Kanaris for them not to."

Joining the Samaari, Malcolm craned his head to look at the heavens with his one good eye and added, "Whether they get here in time to save us is a whole different question, though."

●● ◁► ◉ ◄► ●●

Days later, on another clear Kanarisian night, Jella and I were seated at the cliff's edge, looking at one of the mountains opposite us. It was glowing from the luminescent mist again, and the sky jellies were out in force, putting on a spectacular light show. As I peered through a set of optical amplifiers, I spotted a slight pink glow beneath the trees along one of the distant peaks. Marking the location, I passed my night eyes to Jella and asked, "What do you think that is?"

"I have no idea," she said after finding what I was talking about. "That's kind of the hue of raw Harnillium, so maybe that's just a spot where it's sitting out exposed or something. Hmmm," Jella mused. "It seems to be getting brighter."

It was. By that time, I could pick it out even without my optics. "Wow," I said as I watched the spot glow with even more intensity. "Something's going on over there. That's not..."

Before I could finish my sentence, a giant fireball cut through the dark sky, shooting toward the pink light at several times the speed of sound. A second or two after it passed us, we were hit by a sonic boom that threatened to pierce our eardrums. Then night transformed into day as an enormous mushroom cloud rose from where the distant glow had been an instant before.

"Did they just nuke that fucking mountain?" Jella gasped.

"No, I don't think so," I told her. "I think that's just one of our bunker-buster..."

Another explosion, even bigger than the first, kept me from finishing my sentence. Stunned, all I could do was stand there with my mouth agape, gawking at what I had just witnessed.

Jella jumped up beside me and grabbed my arm. "What the hell was that? Did you see it?"

I nodded. "It was a secondary explosion. There was something there! There was some sort of munitions dump or..."

Another distant mountaintop suddenly went up in flames. Then another. Running closer to the tube, where there was a break in the canopy, I looked deep into the sky behind us. I saw dozens of shooting stars cutting into the atmosphere.

Akkam Lumuk saw them, too. "They're coming!" he screamed, running around the ledge like an excited child. "They're coming! They're going to save us!"

Gunny Malcolm walked up behind me and put his hand on my shoulder. "Yep, it looks like the cavalry is finally coming."

"It's about fucking time," I told him.

A corporal from Charlie Company walked up to us and asked, "You think maybe we should hike back to Narman's Pyke and help them out?"

Malcolm scoffed. "After all they've done for us? Naw, fuck those people. Let someone else do the heavy lifting for a change."

●● ‹●› ● ‹●› ●●

CHAPTER 40

W e were spotted by a passing troop transport the following day and evacuated to Narman's Pyke in three trips. Being one of the few able-bodied
Marines left of *Wasp-Three's* survivors, I was on the last ship out.

When we landed back at the colony, it was teeming with activity. Fresh
troops marched all over the grounds, staging artillery and other heavy equipment into defensive positions. Others had already begun clearing the forest
around the colony to deny the Narmans the cover they needed to launch
another sneak attack.

Upon stepping off my transport, I was shocked to be greeted by Sergeant
Dimitri Naktada, a man I thought I had sent to his death back on the beach.
"What the hell are you doing here?!?" I shouted as I ran forward and embraced
him. "I thought you were dead! Your vital signs flat-lined and..."

Naktada grinned. "I told you. Nobody gets any information that an armorer
doesn't want them to have. I killed my vitals feed and shut down my exo-armor
until you all pulled out."

"You played dead?" Jella asked, as stunned as I was to find Naktada alive and
well. "Why?"

"Like I told you, there was no way I could pull the cockpit video and sensor
data from *Wasp-Three* in a matter of hours. I needed weeks. I also needed
help. After the battalion marched off, I left the wreckage, recruited a couple of
Charlie Company Marines as assistants, then set about pulling the footage of
what happened to the other dropships."

I shook my head in disbelief. "We heard you stopped sending rockets to the
mothership."

The armorer nodded. "That was the one thing we did not have much of.
You guys took almost every damned one of them with you. We only found a

few that had been submerged in salt water. The first couple fired off okay, so we did not know we had an issue. Then they started misfiring and destroying themselves. We opened a couple up and discovered they were all corroded. We had to cannibalize the lot to make a single rocket that had a chance of making it beyond the Harnillium blackout zone. We decided to save it until we had real intel about how our Wasps got destroyed."

"What about the drones they sent to check on you guys?" I asked.

Naktada shrugged. "Never saw them. We wouldn't have, though. They probably wouldn't have seen us, either. After you left, we fortified the wreckage. The grunts cleaned out all the nasties, got the air conditioning working, put together a functional operating room, and salvaged a huge store of rations and medications. When they were done with that, I had everybody working to help me track down and reconnect the backup servers to pull the landing video. It took a while, but we finally figured it out, and..."

"There!" I heard Captain Briggund yell over the crowd as he speed-marched toward us. "That Cadet! His name is Tauk! He's a Ghuldari agent that tried to lure you into an ambush!"

The Samaari officer was flanked by a pair of Section 615 agents in black fatigues without exo-armor. Their only weapons were the sidearms hanging from their hips.

Shaking my head, I asked, "He lived? How the hell did that son-of-a-bitch make it through all that?"

Jella shrugged. "It's natural. No matter how bad the disaster is, the cockroaches always find a way to survive."

"Cadet Tauk," one of the agents said as he approached me. "How are you feeling? Do you need medical attention?"

I shook my head. "No, I'm fine."

"Good," the agent said. "Would you like to answer a few questions?"

"Oh, you're goddamn right he would!" snapped Gunny Malcolm as he marched up to us. "He's got all kinds of shit to say about this clusterfuck! So do I, as a matter of fact."

Stepping toward Captain Briggund, Malcolm invaded his personal space and looked him right in the eye. "Who's in charge of this operation?"

"Colonel Palkrait," one of the agents answered.

"Dalton? Dalton Palkrait?"

"That's right," said the other.

"Awesome," Gunny said. "He's a good man. You got any hover pods down here yet?"

Agent One nodded. "I've seen a few. Both two and five-man rigs."

Malcolm grinned, "That's perfect! I've got something you guys are really going to want to see. Call Palkrait and tell him Gunny Sergeant Konor Malcolm wants a motorized squad to escort us down the mountain a bit. Let him know that it'll be well worth his time. On hover pods, I'm thinking we can be there and back before nightfall."

The agent looked at Malcolm's wounds, paying particular attention to the patch of gauze covering the gunnery sergeant's empty eye socket. "You sure you don't want to get some medical attention first?"

"And let this son-of-a-bitch use his connections to destroy the evidence I want to show you before we can get there? No way. I got all the medical attention I need right now. All I want is a ride and an official witness."

"Do you know who you're fucking with?" Briggund snarled.

"Captain," Malcolm smirked back. "I know it better than you. You don't have a fraction of the pull you think you do. You didn't have it before, and you certainly won't after all this shit."

Backing up, Malcolm told the agents, "You're going to want to put someone on the captain. You don't want him making any contacts with the mothership until we get back."

Malcolm pointed at me and said, "Cadet Tauk will be happy to tell you whatever you need to know. Use your manners during the debrief, though. He's a good kid." With that, Malcolm walked away, dragging one of the agents with him.

As I was led to an interrogation room set up in the civic center, I crossed paths with a group of medics escorting an SPS to the colony's launch pad. In it was CWO Je'Sikka Albarn, in a rare state of consciousness.

"Hey!" I said, spinning around to face my Section 615 escort. "I need a minute. That's the pilot I rescued from *Wasp-Three*. We practically carried her all the way here."

"I can't let you go anywhere alone," the agent said.

"Then come with me."

"We can't. We need to get to..."

Without waiting for the spook to finish his sentence, I bolted away to intercept the stretcher.

"Hey you," I said as I pushed a couple of medics out of the way to grab Albarn's hand. "Where are they taking you?"

"Back to the mothership," the pilot said, smiling after she recognized my face. "They're going to fix my legs."

"That's great! You made it!"

"Thanks to you," Albarn told me.

The Section 615 agent caught up to me just then, grabbing me by the shoulders. "Come on! I didn't give you permission to talk to anybody! Let's go!"

"Why did you do this?" Albarn asked as the agent dragged me away. "Why did you risk so much to save me?"

I laughed. "I don't know! Maybe I just have a weakness for pretty girls in pilot uniforms!"

"That's too bad!" Albarn called out as the SPS started rolling again.

"Why?" I shouted back to her as I tried to wriggle out of the agent's grasp.

Je'Sikka Albarn giggled weakly. "Because so do I!"

•● ◁▻ ● ◁▻ ●•

After hours of answering questions about everything that happened from our approach to Kanaris until our rescue from the ledge, I had had enough. "Look, Agent Kejoliin, that's all I have to say. If I'm under arrest for anything, take me away and lock me up. Otherwise, I'm done talking. I'm telling you the truth. Grazny Sirrah chickened out and crashed into the command ship."

Kejoliin sighed and stopped typing on her tablet. "Okay. Let me show you something. This is video that Naktada recovered from one of *Wasp-Three's* remote servers. It was taken from a camera mounted in the cockpit right above your head."

A beam of light emerged from the agent's tablet and projected video of the disaster on the wall beside us. It was hard to watch, but I studied it intently, looking for something that might cast doubt upon what I had just told the Section 615 investigators. I found nothing. The video showed everything just as I remembered it.

"Is that how you recall the collision happening?"

"Exactly," I answered.

"Do you notice anything on here that you do not see?"

"Huh?" I asked. "I don't understand your question."

Looking back at the projection, Agent Kejoliin said, "Yeah, I guess you wouldn't." She tapped another button on her tablet and the same event appeared on the wall but shot from a slightly different angle. "This is the footage from the undercarriage camera. You notice anything in this view you don't see in the other?"

I shrugged. "Not particularly."

"Look at the storm," Kejoliin suggested as she toggled between the two video clips.

I noticed the black spot in the center of the cyclone on the undercarriage view. It was obscured by *Wasp-Two* in the video taken by the cockpit camera. "The eye," I told the agent. "You can see the eye of the hurricane on the other clip."

"That's right," Kejoliin told me. "Now, keep watching that."

The new angle was not grossly different from the view I saw with my own eyes, but it certainly was not the same. From the standpoint of how the dropships behaved, nothing changed. For a fraction of a second, however, the cyclone's eye disappeared, filled with a flash of pink light. Almost instantaneously, the two Wasp transports collided.

"What was that?" I asked.

"The flash of a weapon powerful enough to bring down a dropship at the edge of Kanaris's atmosphere."

"But there's no missile. There's no..."

"It was energy," Kejoliin told me. "Some sort of plasma burst."

"Plasma burst?" I laughed. "Bullshit. We don't have weapons like that. As far as I know, neither do the Ghouls. Where would the Narmans find that kind of technology?"

"I don't know. That video allowed us to pinpoint exactly where to find it and take it out, though. After we destroyed it, we learned it glows pink as it's charging. That allowed us to locate the others and take them down, too."

I stared at the screen, slack-jawed. "I don't believe this. You're still trying to cover up for that son-of-a-bitch Sirrah, aren't you?"

"I showed you the video," Kejoliin told me.

"So what?" I shrugged. "Video can be doctored. You can make up any video evidence you want to..."

"You told me you saw the secondary explosion yourself."

I did, but that was explainable. If I wanted to recreate something like that, all I had to do was drop a pink space buoy to the surface and activate it to replicate the glow. A secondary explosion could be simulated with a delayed munition attached to the primary. The auxiliary bomb could detonate as long as a minute after the main one. It was something that would not take a terrible amount of sophistication to pull off.

"What I saw on that ledge doesn't matter," I said to the 615 Agent. "I could have just seen what you wanted us to see. It's easier to do than to create some sort of futuristic death ray that can blast ships out of space."

"There have been scientists on this colony for three decades researching the potential of Harnillium," Kejoliin countered. "They must have figured it out."

"I'm not buying it," I let her know. I wanted to speak to Naktada. I trusted him far more than the Section 615 narrative. He would tell me if that was the same video he turned over to the mothership.

"Look, Cadet Tauk," Kejoliin pleaded. "Briggund thinks you tried to lure our dropships into a trap. The undercarriage video tends to support that claim. Having seen the vantage point you had from the cockpit, however, I fully understand how you reached your conclusion. I know you're not a Ghuldari agent, but I need you to realize that you're wrong about what happened to those dropships."

"Whatever," I said dismissively. "What do you want me to do? Sign a statement exonerating Sirrah? Whip it out. I'm tired of this shit. I'll sign whatever you want."

"I don't need a statement from you," Kejoliin told me. "I don't want one either. That video is all we need."

"But you want me to stop talking about it."

Kejoliin nodded. "Of course. We want you to tell the truth."

"I am!"

"No," the agent said, correcting me. "You're saying what you *think* is the truth. That's not what happened, though."

"Fine," I laughed, dropping my head into my hands. "I'll say whatever you want me to. I just want to get this over with."

Kejoliin sighed. "That's not good enough. I need you to believe it."

I waved my hand at the wall she was using as a projection screen. "It's going to take more than doctored video to do that."

The agent nodded. "I guess it will. Fine, I can..."

Kejoliin was interrupted by a ping from her tablet, indicating she had a message. The Section 615 agent read it, then glanced up at me. "It looks like this is going to have to wait. Colonel Palkrait ordered all able-bodied *Wasp-Three* survivors to the parade ground. Immediately."

I sighed. I was exhausted and only wanted to go to bed. "Can I use the latrine first?"

"Nope," Agent Kejoliin told me. "That wouldn't be seeing the colonel immediately, would it?"

●● ◄●► ● ◄●► ●●

CHAPTER 41

Colonel Dalton Palkrait was a severe-looking man. He was tall and exceptionally fit for someone in his forties. His eyes were unforgiving, and his mouth permanently contorted in a way that made him look like he was on the verge of screaming the word "fuck" at any given moment. Palkrait's fatigues were sharp and flawless, his head closely shaven, and his face dominated by a long scar that ran from the top of his head, behind his ear, and to the back of his neck.

Once we were assembled, the colonel ordered us to the position of attention and kept us there as he paced in circles at the front of the formation. Every "able-bodied *Wasp-Three* survivor" turned out to be thirty-eight souls.

"I've been in this fucking Corps for nearly thirty years!" the brigade commander yelled at us, his face turning a concerning shade of red. "And I have never seen a clusterfuck quite like this one! More than a thousand Marines walked off that beach you crashed upon, and this is all that's left?!?"

The colonel shook his head. "I can't believe what went on among you in the weeks since that crash. Murders. Mutinies. A complete breakdown in discipline. Open insubordination and the blatant disregard of regulations up and down the chain of command! That's why you got your fucking asses handed to you by a mob of oversized alien monkeys when you finally got here! What happened in Second Battalion is as unbelievable as it is unforgivable!"

Walking up to a private in front, the colonel balled up his fist and lightly punched the Marine's breastplate. "I don't blame you, though. In fact, I'm standing here in awe that anybody managed to survive that shitshow, let alone damn near forty of you. I promise you, there will be a full investigation of what went on down here, and those at fault for this mess will be held accountable."

After pausing for effect, Palkrait said, "One investigation has already been concluded, however. Marines, if you look to your right, you'll find Lieutenant Jaukin standing next to something he found out in the jungle."

As we craned our heads toward the officer, he ripped the tarp off a crate he had been standing guard over. It was Briggund's box. With a single, swift kick, Jaukin tipped it over, spilling clothing, booze, delicacies, and bullion onto the ground."

"Let me be clear," Colonel Palkrait told us. "There is NO excuse for mutiny. EVER! That said, in this case, I have compelling evidence the responsibility for this insurrection lies just as much in the actions of your commanding officer as it does on the heads of those who took up arms against your battalion's leadership."

As if on cue, Gunny Malcolm and one of Palkrait's master sergeants dragged Captain Briggund out before us. His hands were bound behind his back, and a black hood was thrown over his head. He was not walking under his own power. "You can't do this to me," we heard him whimper when they came to a halt. "I'm an officer! I have rights!"

"If you're an officer," Palkrait snapped back. "Then act like one! Quit sniveling and take responsibility for your actions like a Marine!"

Lieutenant Jaukin marched to the prisoner and ripped the hood from Briggund's head. It was immediately evident that Gunny Malcolm had been allowed to work the captain over. Once Briggund was unmasked, the sergeants let go of him, dropping the captain into the mud.

"Get up!" screamed Colonel Palkrait. "Stand at attention!"

"Please!" Briggund sobbed. "Don't do this! Have mercy on me! I'm sorry!"

"I gave you an order!" The colonel yelled again. "AH-teeeen-HUT!"

Briggund did not move. He was paralyzed with fear.

Spitting on the ground in disgust, Palkrait continued while my former CO writhed in the muck. "Any officer knows he needs his troops to complete a mission. He puts the needs of his Marines before those of his own. Only after he has seen to it that his people are fed does he eat himself. An officer knows that his subordinates are warriors, not servants."

The colonel turned to address the captain directly. "Seeing how you assigned more worth to your unauthorized personal effects than the lives of your Marines, or even that of the pilot that you owed your own life to, you are no longer worthy of the privilege of being a Marine officer." Pulling his dagger out of his hip sheath, Colonel Palkrait walked over to Briggund and, while the sergeants held the prisoner down, cut the captain's bars off the disgraced officer's shoulder plates. Briggund screamed as if his nipples were being sliced off.

When he finished, Palkrait put his dagger away and faced the formation. "Nico Briggund is guilty of a Class Four dereliction of duty resulting in needless loss of life, breakdown in discipline, and the degradation of confidence in the institutions of the Kyperion League Space Corps. This charge was aggravated by corruption, infidelity to the cause, and the possession of contraband. Accordingly, I have revoked his commission to lead and stripped him of all pensions and privileges."

"You can't do this!" Briggund cried. "You can't make me a prisoner! I'm a Samaari!"

"I'm not making you a prisoner, man," Palkrait assured him. "I'm making you an example. Nico Briggund, I sentence you to death by hanging."

"What?!?" Briggund gasped. "I'm a Marine! You can't hang me! Hanging's for civilians!"

"You're no Marine," Palkrait snarled. "You're a disgrace!"

As the sergeants struggled to lift Briggund to his feet, a military policeman emerged from behind us, carrying a length of rope. He threw an end over the arm of a low-hanging light post and then fashioned a crude slipknot out of it.

"Holy shit," gasped the Marine standing next to me. "They're not even going to drop him and break his neck. They're going to strangle him!"

"Yep," I responded to her. "They want him to suffer, don't they?"

While the sergeants forced the rope around Briggund's neck, Palkrait addressed the formation once more. "No one's been wronged by this man more than you were. If you wish, you can all take part in Briggund's execution. Go ahead and take your place on the line. All you have to do is pull once I give the command. There's enough room for all of you."

Thirty-seven Marines broke ranks and jogged over to the lamppost to grab hold of the rope. I was the only one who did not. "You don't want a piece of this?" asked the colonel when he saw me standing fast.

"No, sir," I told him. "I'd rather look him in the eye as he chokes."

Palkrait nodded. "Then, by all means, step up there and get a better view."

Once the captain's former subordinates were in position, Colonel Palkrait asked them, "Are you ready, Marines?"

"Wait!" Briggund cried. "WAIT! Don't I at least get any last words?"

"Yeah," the colonel answered. "Those. PULL!"

At once, Briggund's Marines heaved upon the rope, lifting the condemned man off the ground. His face immediately flushed red and his mouth sprung open, revealing a swelling tongue. His eyes bulged so far from their sockets that, for a moment, I thought they were going to pop right out of his skull. In a pointless struggle for his life, Briggund's legs thrashed wildly into thin air, trying to kick something that would drop him back to the ground.

"Hey!" called out one of the Marines holding the rope. "Maybe we should lower him, let him catch his breath, then hang his Sammy ass again!"

"You'll do no such thing!" the colonel screamed back. "You're getting the justice you deserve! Making fun of this makes you worse than he is! Hold him up there and get this shit over with so we can all get on with our lives! Is that clear?"

"AYE AYE, SIR!" the Marines called out in unison.

Briggund did not last much longer than that. His legs started kicking with less and less vigor. A minute or two later, the captain was still, his body swaying lifelessly in the breeze. Palkrait let him dangle for a while to ensure he was dead before giving the order for the Marines to let go. When they did, Briggund fell to the ground in a lifeless heap.

"You see what you wanted?" Palkrait asked me as Briggund's executioners walked away.

"Yes, sir," I answered, standing in place.

The colonel nodded in understanding. He then looked at the blood stripes on my shoulder. "Academy Marine, huh?"

"Yes, sir."

"You wouldn't happen to be the guy who killed Gori Dravidas, would you?"

●●◄●►●◄●►●●

CHAPTER 42

Jella Duverii was not in the military. Instead of sleeping in tents like most of the fifty thousand Marines now occupying Narman's Pyke, she was housed in an apartment. I was fortunate enough to share it with her since I had no squad assigned to me anymore. Her quarters were spartan, but nice. The only complaint was that a few stray rounds had broken the bedroom window, resulting in some trespassing wildlife.

"So, the bugs on Kanaris have four or eight legs, right?" I asked the doctor, who was curled up in bed beside me.

"Yes," Jella cooed groggily. "You remember that?"

"Of course I do," I answered. "What I don't remember is you telling me that the lizards here all seem to have six." As I said this, I watched a pair of the creatures scurry across the ceiling. They looked like reptiles but moved like insects. They were creepy. "Those things aren't dangerous, are they?"

Jella giggled. "No, they're fine. There are a couple of poisonous species you have to be careful about, but just like in a Replicant Earth Environment, they advertise how dangerous they are. If you see any animal that's brightly colored, it's best to leave it alone."

"Don't you mean 'venomous,'" I asked her.

"I'm a scientist," Jella reminded me. "I know the difference between 'poisonous' and 'venomous.' *Kanaeri vividula* are poisonous, not venomous. They're gorgeous, too. And docile. They mainly eat Peluru beetles, these nasty, stinging bugs. When the Kanaeri lizards digest their food, they separate the toxins from their prey's venom sacs, concentrate it, then secrete it through their skin. If you pet one, you'll notice yourself developing a mild fever a few hours later. Then comes the stomach cramps. Then the explosive diarrhea. After that, the delirium sets in, and you're wracked by hallucinations for a few days.

When that's over, you've either died or recovered. The human mortality rate is about thirty percent without treatment. With treatment, survival is pretty much assured."

"Good," I told her. "That's one less thing I have to worry about."

After a short yawn, Jella asked. "Are you worried about tomorrow?"

"Not really," I answered. "It's just the Disciplinary Review Board. They only confirm the charges. They don't actually dole out punishment. That's the colonel's job."

"You don't think they're going to railroad you? Trump up some stuff so they can lock you away somewhere to keep you from saying anything about Grazny Sirrah?"

"They might," I admitted. "There's nothing I could do about it if they did. As far as I know, the inquiry is mainly about me disobeying Gunny Malcolm and abandoning my post to return to *Wasp-Three*. I also have to justify what I did to Vernor Blyte."

I felt Jella's body shudder beside me. "I hate that you're capable of doing something like that."

With a shrug, I said, "I'm not proud of it, Jella. On the other hand, it was the right decision."

Jella bristled. "No, it wasn't. I talked to Naktada. The Marines we left on that beach turned *Wasp-Three's* wreckage into a palace compared to what we experienced. They had power, air-conditioning, food, ammunition, and medicine. They lost a few of their patients, but only the ones that would not have made it under any circumstances. That man would have survived, Eamon."

I sighed. "No, he wouldn't have. He was a Class Zero convict with no feet. League protocols would have required the medics to euthanize him."

"He was a valued member of the medical team," Jella countered. "They loved him. They respected him. He was one of their own. They wouldn't have put him down."

"Then someone else would have. The League is not going to use its resources to treat a Zero. Not when it has so many others waiting in the wings to take his place. The League will fix a pilot, however. That SPS was best used evacuating Albarn."

I heard Jella grinding her teeth. She knew I was right. "I swear, Eamon, sometimes I hate the fucking League."

"Me, too."

Shocked to hear an academy cadet say that out loud, Jella sat up in bed. "Really?"

I nodded. "This isn't how it was supposed to be. It hit me during the mutiny. The rebels were the ones fighting for a noble cause. Not us. They didn't rise up because they were afraid of dying while securing Narman's Pyke. They did it to keep from getting their lives thrown away just so that a pampered primadonna could go to bed in comfortable pajamas. Harlund Merik died regretting that he fought for the wrong side. I don't want to do that."

Jella looked concerned. "You're going to fight for the Narmans?"

I shook my head. "After they gutted our psyxies and strung them up from the trees like chandeliers? After they promised our mutineers safe haven if they switched sides and then turned the quarakai on them anyway? Look, I'm sure they had their reasons for taking up arms against the military here, but they don't exactly strike me as the good guys, either. I don't want to fight for the Narmans. I don't want to fight for the League. After the time we spent hiding out on that ledge, I realized that the only thing I want to fight for anymore is you."

"Me?" I heard Jella's voice crack.

"Like you said, Gori Dravidas was right about there being more to life than killing. I'm going to find a way to walk away from it, Jella. As long as you're with me."

Jella bent down and kissed me on the lips. "I'm with you."

"What about your people here?" I asked her. "You told me you came here because you wanted to know what happened to your friends and family."

"And now I know," she said. "I've been gone a long time. I wish those I know the best and hope they succeed, but I don't know how they can do that with a half-million Marines preparing to take control of this planet. It's a lost cause. I'm all for fighting for a principle, but I'm not okay with embarking upon a suicidal exercise in futility that'll make no difference whatsoever. Kanaris is a beautiful, dangerous, and fascinating place, but it's not my home anymore. I was happy here, but I've been happy in plenty of other places, too. I'll be happy wherever we go as long as we're together."

"Then it's settled," I told her. "When I go in front of the DRB tomorrow, I'll admit to insubordination and confess that I pilfered some of Briggund's personal effects from that box he had us carrying."

"You stole some of the captain's stuff?"

I shook my head. "Nope. But I'll cop to getting smashed on his brandy and being hungover as hell when the quarakai attacked."

"Are you trying to get yourself locked up?"

"It's my quickest route to a discharge. If I'm lucky, they'll put me in the brig for a couple of months, declare me unfit for duty, then toss my sorry ass out of the Corps."

"And if you're not lucky?" Jella asked.

"I lose my commission and start a standard five-year enlistment as a buck private."

Jella bit her lip. "Is desertion an option?"

Before I could answer, I was interrupted by someone pounding angrily upon Jella's door. "Doctor Duverii! Open up! This is Section 615! You've been ordered to Landing Zone 486 by Colonel Palkrait! Immediately! Open up!"

Jella grabbed the sheets and pulled them up over her bare breasts. I grabbed my underwear and my sidearm. Jogging to the door, I took aim and asked, "It's the middle of the night! What for?"

"Tauk? Is that you?" asked the agent. "We've been searching for your ass, also!"

"I bet you have," I mumbled as I clicked the safety off my pistol. I knew they were there to silence us. There was no routine business ever done at that ungodly hour. I assumed that they had gotten their marching orders from the Sirrah family.

"Tauk! Quit fucking around and open the door!"

That was the last thing I wanted to do. At the same time, there was nothing else I could do but let them in. I needed a plan. I needed time. I needed time to come up with a plan. "J-just a second!" I stammered. "I-I-I...uh...I need to get dressed."

"Let us in, then get dressed!" the agent barked back.

"But Dr. Duverii isn't..."

That was all the negotiating the 615 Squad was willing to do. The door burst open, torn right off its hinges, and I fired through the opening. Unfortunately, no one was there to hit, and my round ricocheted harmlessly off the corridor wall. I saw a single flash from the darkness beyond, then felt four sharpened electrical leads puncture the skin on my bare chest. After that came the electrical current that ripped through my muscles, causing my limbs to thrash out violently in all directions.

Then I fell still, completely unable to move.

•● ‹●› ◉ ‹●› ●•

CHAPTER 43

B y the time I got the use of my muscles back, I was shackled to a seat in a Sitaara Raptor assault fighter that was revving its engines in preparation for liftoff. Colonel Palkrait was enraged, holding my jaw in his hand. "You shot at the 615 agents?!?" he yelled, half out of anger and half to be heard over the Raptor's thrusters.

"They were breaking into our room in the middle of the night," I told him. "I thought they were coming to kill us. You'd have tried to shoot them, too."

It was not a good answer, but it was true. Palkrait nodded in understanding and then let go of my face. Turning toward Agent Takawa, he said, "I didn't tell you to go in hot."

Takawa shrugged. "You didn't tell us not to, either." Section 615 reported to a different command structure, so the agent did not fear Colonel Palkrait. Takawa's people did not have to grant our commander's request to collect Jella and me, but they knew the more they supported the Marine command, the more cooperation they could expect. The way Takawa saw things, he did the colonel a favor and bristled at Palkrait's criticism. "When you want us to bring someone in at three in the morning, we assume it's because you think they're dangerous."

"Or," Palkrait countered. "It's because I'm not ready to let the cat out of the bag about what we saw out there yet and don't want fifty thousand troops wondering why we're paying so much attention to that mountaintop."

The colonel sighed and turned back to me. "Obviously, I didn't send anyone to kill you."

"Then why did you send them?"

"Because I wanted to show you something." The colonel looked me over one last time, trying to ascertain my frame of mind. "If I release you, are you going to give me any trouble?"

I shook my head. "No."

Turning to Jella, he asked, "What about you, Miss?"

Jella shook her head also.

Directing his attention to the guards behind us, Palkrait ordered them to remove our restraints. As the agents went to work, the colonel asked, "You still think Grazny Sirrah collided with *Wasp-One*, Tauk?"

Sighing in exasperation, I snapped, "Does it matter, sir? I already made it clear to 615 that I'll toe the company line."

"It matters, Tauk. Look, son. The League is on the precipice of civil war right now. It's a powder keg, waiting for a spark to set it off. The Samaaris are bound to overreact if they perceive us as slandering one of their prodigal sons. The non-Guild worlds could easily revolt against League conscription if they believe Samaari entitlement cost them six thousand of their sons and daughters."

Leaning back to make himself more comfortable, Palkrait then said, "If that Sirrah kid really did cause that disaster, I wouldn't give two shits what the Samaaris thought. I don't want the League to implode upon itself over a misunderstanding, though. After what I saw on that mountain, I think we're going to need a united front to face the threat before us." After a long sigh, Palkrait added, "Hell, we might even need to bury the hatchet with the Ghouls so we can combine our forces on this one."

As the Raptor's engines got louder, Palkrait leaned closer to me so he could still be heard. "You know, you're right. The video that 615 interrogator showed you could have been manipulated. They're pretty good at that kind of stuff. We're taking you someplace where you can see what shot those dropships out of the sky with your own eyes. That okay with you?"

I nodded and then looked out of the window. The Raptor was rising above the walls, and I could see that we had already made noticeable progress clearing the trees away from the Pyke's fortifications. The Marines were no longer going to let glider quarakai sail down into the perimeter unchallenged. The plan was to clear enough lumber so that they had to fly across a kilometer or two of barren no-man's-land to get to us. That would give our watches, not to mention the radar-guided automated sentry guns on the ramparts, plenty of time to shoot them down before they could do us any harm.

As we got a little higher, I could see more technicians installing anti-missile batteries along some open ground between the domed residential buildings and the west wall. Apparently, Palkrait anticipated being attacked by something more than a quarakai horde wielding sharpened sticks. They had also been up all night installing listening posts, artillery batteries, and battle drones. The colonel was not just occupying Narman's Pyke. He was preparing for a siege.

After we ascended above the treetops, the pilot turned west and gunned the engines, zig-zagging over the canopy to avoid getting shot. When we reached the cliff, the raptor dropped over the side, plummeting below the thermal layer to take cover inside the clouds. I caught a brief glimpse of the ledge we had hidden on for two weeks, waiting to be rescued. I suspected that Tukko was still on it. Jella's quarakai refused to come with the rest of us.

There was not much to see but mist as we flew across the chasm to the western mountains. Colonel Palkrait took the opportunity to make small talk. Turning to Jella, he asked, "Have you ever been to the Malakai Ranges, Doctor?"

"I used to go there all the time," Jella answered. "We did bio surveys there at least once a month."

"So, you're familiar with the area?"

"I was at one time, yes."

"Even Toranad Peak?"

"Sure," Jella told him. "I was staring at it when you blew it up."

Palkrait nodded. "When was the last time you were there?"

Jella shrugged. "I was fifteen or sixteen. Maybe ten years ago?"

"You ever see anything unusual?"

"You're going to have to be more specific, Colonel," Jella said. "This is Kanaris. Everything's unusual, even when you're living here. Nothing ever becomes routine."

Our CO chuckled. "Fair enough."

The Raptor ascended rapidly once we reached the valley's far side, bolting out of the clouds and shooting up the mountain, flying just above the treetops. I saw a laughing dragon collide with the starboard wing and instantly disintegrate into a cloud of pink mist and shredded meat. The pilot overshot the summit by about a kilometer, then hovered in place while the assault ship's sensors scanned the surrounding area for hidden threats.

Only when the lieutenant at the controls was satisfied that our landing zone was safe did she begin her vertical descent. Even then, she opened the bay doors on either side of the craft so that the crew's door gunners could sweep the tree line with their M2117s, prepared to open fire if anything seemed amiss.

The summit of Mount Toranad was significantly higher than Narman's Pyke. It was freezing at that elevation, cold enough so that it snowed up there instead of rained. Since I was dragged out of Jella's apartment in my skivvies, I was dressed only in a pair of loose-fitting coveralls and rubber utility boots. The wind rushing in from the open doors cut through my hide to chill me right to the core.

Jella was dressed a little better than I was, but not much. Through chattering teeth, she asked, "Why do these things always open up before they land?"

"Safety," the colonel answered. "My second assignment in the Space Corps was as an aide to General Haufadu, the military advisor to the governor of Sala-Manau. Sala-Manau was a Guild planet, so it was a safe zone. Things were pretty relaxed there.

"Anyway, some malcontent with a bug up his ass about something the governor did during a previous assignment decided to take him, and those of us unlucky enough to share a Raptor with the guy, out with a shoulder-fired anti-aircraft missile."

Palkrait grinned at the memory. "He aimed at us as we were landing, put his crosshairs center mass, and fired. The missile went right where it was supposed to, intending to hit us mid-ship. Well, that fuckin' thing sailed right in one door and went right out the other. Scared the shit out of us.

"Because the missile was fired so close, our defenses did not have time to engage. They were still trying to figure out what was happening when the rocket turned and went after us for a second time. Knowing his radar had yet to get a lock on the threat, the pilot turned the ship sideways to the weapon's trajectory. Again, the missile flew right through the opening, never hitting a damn thing. It was finally destroyed while turning around to make a third pass."

The colonel giggled a little as he wrapped up his story, apparently finding near-death experiences a lot funnier than I did.

When we touched down, the assault team accompanying us disembarked and fanned out to secure the perimeter. When they signaled that all was clear, the rest of us followed them. I felt naked and vulnerable, being out in the field without my exo-armor or a firearm. I would have asked for something to defend myself with, but it was already made clear that I was there to observe, not fight.

There was plenty to see. We were in the blast area, standing amongst the debris of what had once been an enormous generator of some sort. It was built unlike anything I had ever seen. Energy production was not exactly my forte, but I had been around enough starship power plants to know this was not League technology.

"You ever seen anything like this before, Doctor?" Palkrait asked.

Jella shook her head. "No, sir."

"You ever hear of the Narmans developing weapons like this? Using Harnilium as pulse fuel?"

Shaking her head again, Jella said, "No, but that wasn't my field. I studied alien zoology. If the engineers were developing stuff like this, they wouldn't have told me about it. I wasn't in that clique."

"You think the Ghouls could have done it?" I asked, shivering violently. I would have asked for a jacket, but I wanted to project toughness to the colonel.

Palkrait shrugged. "That's probably the only other explanation. It had to either be the Narmans or the Ghuldari. Or it's aliens."

Looking at the destroyed equipment, I could have believed that last option. The cold did a good job preserving the remains scattered over the blast site, however. Everything was human.

"Colonel," one of the assault team's sergeants called over. "We have a recon team approaching from the east. They got a prisoner."

"A prisoner?" Palkrait asked, arching an eyebrow. "Good. Looks like we'll get some answers about this."

Half an hour later, five Marines emerged from the bush, one with a woman slung over his shoulder. She had a black and white checkered scarf wrapped around her face. At first, I thought it was being used as a blindfold, but as they got closer I could see blood seeping through the fabric. It was a bandage.

Walking up to the colonel, a corporal dropped his prisoner at Palkrait's feet. When the woman hit the ground, the cloth wrapped around her head came undone and a frigid blast of wind carried it off into a nearby bush, revealing the hideous nature of the prisoner's injuries. She had been badly burned and the right side of her face was reduced to a pus-weeping mess of charred flesh.

"That happen when we bombed this place?" Palkrait asked, pointing at the captive's wounds.

"No, sir," the Marine answered. "We did it. She and her cohorts ambushed us. She was wounded in the firefight."

Looking at the girl's injuries without even a hint of sympathy, Colonel Palkrait told her, "That's what you get when you mess with the Space Corps." Turning to the squad leader, our CO asked. "We take any casualties?"

The Marine nodded. "Five killed. Two wounded."

The prisoner laughed. "And that's what the Space Corps gets when it messes with us."

Jella did not recognize the captive's mangled face, but she heard something familiar in the woman's voice. "Deena? Deena Vulk?"

The girl turned her head toward the doctor. "Duverii? Is that you?"

"Yeah, Deena! It's me!" Jella exclaimed, staring at the prisoner with a confused look on her face, as if something was not computing. "What are you doing here?"

"I live on this planet," Deena snapped. "Don't you remember? What are *you* doing here? With these fucking monsters?"

"I came here to save you!"

"You're doing a great job," the prisoner scoffed.

Jella looked gobsmacked. She opened her mouth as if she was going to respond to Deena Vulk but appeared incapable of forming words. Her situation had just gotten exponentially more complicated, and she had no idea how to deal with it. There was obviously a history there. I wanted to ask Jella about it, but not in front of the colony's CO and a couple of 615 agents.

As Jella stood staring at the captive, Colonel Palkrait turned toward the sergeant. "Did you get all the militants that ambushed you?"

The Marine shook his head. "She's the only one I know we got for sure."

"You let them get away?" Palkrait gasped.

"We didn't let them do anything," the corporal retorted. "We took their position. When we got there, though, they were gone. They vanished into thin air! The only one left was her!"

The tension on that mountaintop increased dramatically. The assault team trained their weapons on the tree line and tried to pick out anything that appeared like it might have followed the recon patrol back to the LZ. Though I was without a weapon, I scoured the perimeter with them.

Just beyond the southern edge of the clearing, I found an anomaly. It looked like heat shimmer, something that would have been normal beneath the thermal layer. At our altitude, with temperatures hovering just a few degrees above freezing, it was grossly out of place.

I stepped up to the corporal who had delivered the prisoner and said, "Look to your four o'clock position. You see anything odd?"

The Marine turned his head and scanned the tree line, stopping when he saw what I had. "Got it."

"You might want to take a shot at that."

The corporal looked at the colonel for guidance. After Palkrait nodded his permission to open fire, the Marine turned to me. "Okay, pal," he said. Without my uniform on, the rifleman had no idea what my rank was. "When I count to three, you're going to jump out of my way to the left. You ready?"

I nodded.

"Okay. One...Two..."

"TAKE COVER!" the prisoner screamed. She was not warning us. She was calling out to her nearly invisible comrades quietly encircling the landing zone just behind the tree line.

The corporal lifted his weapon and opened fire. When the bullets reached the edge of the clearing, they did not hit the brush and splinter the wood as I expected. They hit the shimmer and looked like pebbles breaking the surface of a still pond, sending ripples cascading out from their points of impact. Then the "trees" fired back.

I lunged over and tackled Jella into the dirt just as a rain of bullets cut down the corporal. Palkrait rushed back to the assault ship, ordering the crew to light up the forest and prepare for liftoff. When I returned to my feet, a grenade went off not far from where I was standing. I was spared being hit by shrapnel, but without the protection of any exo-armor, the blast's concussion knocked the wind out of me. I was stunned and thrown back down upon the turf, gasping for breath.

"Eamon!" Jella shrieked.

Staying close to the ground, the prisoner rolled over to the fallen corporal and, with her hands still cuffed behind her back, started rifling through his pockets for the keys to her restraints. "I can't believe you're with the fucking League!" Deena Vulk screamed at the doctor.

"I'm not!" Jella screamed back as she tried to crawl to me. "I'm not a Marine! I came here to help the League rescue you!"

"The League is what we needed to be rescued from!" Despite the severity of her injuries, Deena Vulk moved with purpose and speed. The adrenaline pumping through her system must have kept her pain at bay.

"I only wanted to help!" Jella cried.

"If you want to help, join us!" Finding what she was looking for, Deena undid her restraints with the ease of a master escape artist. After she was freed, she turned to her old friend. "Come with me, Jella!"

"No," the doctor whimpered. Her voice was uncharacteristically laden with both fear and confusion. I got the impression she was struggling to make sense of Deena Vulk's presence on that mountain but unable to put the pieces together.

"Well, then," Deena said as her face twisted into a frown. "If you're not with me, I guess that means you're against me." The rebel lifted the pistol out of the corporal's holster, pointed it at the doctor's head, and pulled the trigger, opening Jella's skull and splattering her brains all over the ground.

"NOOOOOOO!" I screamed, suddenly finding my wind and a newfound sense of urgency toward procuring a weapon. Before I could even roll to my side, Deena fired twice more, pumping two rounds into my chest before running off into the forest.

•●◄●►●◄●►●•

CHAPTER 44

I do not remember being dragged aboard the assault ship. I just opened my eyes and found myself face down on the deck, sprawled out at the edge of the egress door as the Raptor lifted off. The body of the slain recon corporal was beside me, having been dragged inside the vessel by Agent Takawa. Jella was still lying on the mountain, her dull blue eyes staring lifelessly at the sky.

There were other bodies out there, too. The majority were ours, but we got a couple of the Narmans despite their advanced camouflage technology. As we retreated, I spotted the enemy emerging from cover. Most were firing at us, trying to bring us down, but others rushed out to remove their dead.

A couple of figures stood out from the rest. They were a little taller than average and instead of wearing Narman field jackets, they wore long, heavy cloaks with hoods pulled up over their heads, obscuring their faces.

"Who the fuck are those guys?" I heard Agent Takawa ask one of the Marines from his seat atop the corporal's corpse.

"Targets!" yelled the door gunner as he opened fire.

The tall men dove to lower their profiles as the ground exploded around them. When one looked to see where the bullets were coming from, I noticed the glow of circular goggles from the darkness behind his shroud. He then turned his head to speak to his partner. And when I say he turned his head, I mean he *turned* his head. To the tune of one hundred and eighty degrees.

"What in the ever-loving fuck!" yelled Takawa. "Did you see that shit!"

"Y-y-y-yeah," stammered the door gunner. "I saw it, man! That ain't no fucking human!"

Before anyone could say anything else, one of the cloaked creatures raised its weapon and fired. Instead of bullets, a bright pink plasma burst, a smaller version of the one that brought down our dropships, shot out of its barrel. The blast instantly ripped a hole through the Raptor's deck and hit the door gunner from below, splitting him open from groin to sternum and filling the staging bay with the stench of burnt pork.

"Whoa! Fuck this!" screamed the pilot's voice over the intercom. She accidentally activated her microphone when she wrenched the Raptor's yoke to the right to send the assault ship lurching violently starboard. "Nope-nope-nope-nope-nope."

The sudden bank sent me sliding across the deck towards the opposite door. With my path straight out of the aircraft lubricated by the blood pouring out of my chest, the only thing that kept me from being ejected from the Raptor was a Marine who was only half strapped into his seat, leaving him an open hand for which to grab me. A truly superhuman effort from Takawa kept the agent from riding the corporal's body out of the vessel as well.

The Raptor took another hit while it was turning toward the colony. That spooked the pilot, who opened up the thrusters and launched off Mount Toranad at full acceleration before the bay doors were fully secured. It was like being locked in an elevator with a raging tornado as Marines, weapons, and loose equipment were blown all over the airship's interior. Somehow, that one rifleman kept me from flying away.

The assault transport stabilized once its bay doors closed and we ducked beneath the clouds again. That allowed a corpsman to unbuckle himself and drag me to a medical station. With the help of another Marine, he lifted me onto a bunk and ripped open my coveralls, looking for the holes that Deena Vulk poked in my chest.

"Son-of-a-bitch," the medic cursed. "Where the hell is your armor? Do you know what your blood type is?"

"A-Negative," I moaned.

"Good. It's one of the rare ones." The corpsman pulled a tube from the wall, attached a big needle to it, then sunk it into my arm. "You're getting synthetic blood. It's better than natural."

I was sleepy. And cold. Those were not good signs. "How bad is it?"

"Well," the medic told me. "It certainly isn't great. You're out of action. Going home for a while. You might even be eligible for a discharge."

Discharge. That would have come in handy before that bitch murdered Jella.

With all the strength I had left, I reached out and grabbed the corpsman by his collar. "Don't let them send me away. Make them fix me. I gotta stay here."

With a look of shock on his face, the Marine medic asked, "What for? What the hell do you expect to do down here on a shithole like this?"

"Did you see those things out there? They were aliens. We made contact!"

The medic nodded with a look of deep apprehension while he grabbed my hand and made me let go of him. "If those were truly aliens," he told me, pushing my arm down against my side. "We didn't make first contact. The Narmans did. That's not good. Did you see their weapons?"

The corpsman hit a couple of buttons on the overhead console, programming the ultrasonic sensors to find out where the bullets in my body were located. "You know what, Killer? We've been imposing our will over every Near-Earth Environment we've discovered for centuries. We've dominated them all because nature is no match for our technology. We may have finally come across something we can't contend with."

"Fix me up, doc," I pleaded. "I'll give them something to contend with."

The medic laughed. "How are you going to do that? By the looks of it, they got weapons that make ours look paleolithic by comparison."

I grunted as fresh bolts of pain ripped through my chest. The doc was correct. The aliens probably did have weaponry far more sophisticated than ours. Still, they used Narmans and quarakai to do most of the fighting so far.

The medic produced a syringe of powerful painkillers and pumped it into a vein in my hand. The drugs went to work almost immediately, and I felt myself fading. I was suddenly too tired to talk but could not stop myself from thinking.

They attacked with quarakai. That means we have numbers. If the aliens were here in force, they would have fought us themselves. They must be few. We can take them. We can kill them.

I remembered what Jella Duverii told me while we were hiding on the ledge. She told me she agreed with what Gori Dravidas said before I slashed his throat.

There's more to life than just killing.

I pictured Jella's body lying below us as we took off from the mountain top, left behind to feed the kryptids after we fled. She did nothing to deserve that.

There's more to life than just killing.

I committed the mangled face of Deena Vulk to memory. She had apparently once been Jella's friend, yet murdered her on the summit of Mount Toranad. Despite Gori Dravidas's words echoing through my head, there had to be a reckoning with that bitch.

There's more to life than just killing.

I thought of Maiq Reino. Of Prishtina Gai. Of Lieutenant Hayvar. Of the Marine I accidentally shot in the face while fighting the quarakai outside the sanitation complex. Of the mutineers slaughtered as they knelt on the ground with their hands up in the air, trying to surrender.

There's more to life than just killing.

The morphine was coming on strong now. I was almost under. I felt warm again. Serene. At peace. I envisioned Jella sitting on the edge of our cliff hideout while watching the sky jellies floating above the clouds. She smiled and looked at me with irises so blue that they practically glowed in the dark.

There's more to life than just killing.

I felt tears welling up in my eyes. I missed her already.

There's more to life than just killing.

I must have muttered that out loud. "That's right," I heard the medic tell me through the fog in my head. "There *is* more to life than just killing."

Hearing my thoughts echoed back to me in someone else's voice sounded ridiculous, yet they hit me with a sense of sudden clarity. I had an epiphany.

No, there isn't more to life than just killing. Not while I still have a score to settle.

The End

Next in Series – Moloch's Garden

Click HERE to pre-order Moloch's Garden now for just $4.99! ($5.99 after 01 Jul 23)

Author's Note –

Did you enjoy this story? If so, I invite you to *please* leave a review on Amazon.com! Good reviews not only raise the visibility of an author's work; they massage our fragile egos. It keeps us from priming our muses with absinthe and psychosis.

Also, be sure to sign up for Guerilla Lit, the J.E. Park newsletter, for news, announcements, and information on how to score the occasional free novella!

The Nest

Want to find out what happened to Mazada Duum in the jungle the night of the flood?

Sign up for Guerilla Lit, the J.E. Park Newsletter at **https://jeparkbooks.com** and get the bonus novella, "The Nest," for free!

Kanaris is a hot, wet planet teeming with inhospitable jungles where human beings are not at the top of the food chain. To survive the long trek to the lost colony of Narman's Pyke, PFC Mazada Duum knew he had to keep up with the battalion, where the Marines had strength in numbers. And under no circumstances should he EVER leave the trail and enter the rainforest.

When one of Kanaris's many calamities forces the Marines off the path and spreads them out across a vast swath of alien bush, every leatherneck will spend the night facing a primitive terror that even their worst nightmares could not conjure up. Mazada Duum's small squad, on the other hand, will face the motherlode.

*For it was they who found **The Nest**.*

Next in Series - Moloch's Garden

There was an extraterrestrial menace on Kanaris with the potential to wipe mankind from the face of the galaxy, yet Eamon Tauk could not have cared less about it. He had his crosshairs on a human, the woman responsible for murdering his beloved. Beneath the specter of alien annihilation, all Tauk really wanted was to get his hands around the throat of Deena Vulk.

He knew getting to Vulk would not be easy. Her alien allies possessed weaponry that made his look paleolithic in comparison. The Narmans she fought alongside were mostly Marine deserters with an intimate knowledge of the League's weaknesses. They were also frighteningly familiar with the Kanarisian landscape and how to use the terrors lurking within it to their advantage.

The deadliest item in the Narman arsenal, though, was not their weaponry. It was a cause with which the conscripts under Tauk's command could sympathize.

Of every menace converging to deny Tauk his vengeance, the greatest threat to his objective, not to mention his life, could be the realization that in this war, Eamon Tauk may not have been fighting for the good guys.

Click HERE to pre-order now for just $4.99! ($5.99 after 01 Jul 23)

Acknowledgments

N o great task is ever undertaken alone, and this was certainly no exception. There were plenty of people who offered me their encouragement and support in getting this, and the subsequent books of this series, written.

The first people I have to thank is my family. This has been a LONG effort, more than three years in the making. There was a lot of time taken away from my wife and children to get this done. So, to Patrina, Regan, Mason, Carson, Fairen, and Linden, I love you and thank you for your patience, your enthusiasm, and support.

I also need to thank the authors of the Grand Blanc Authors Meetup, who have continually read, critiqued, and listened to my work for five years now. Doug Allyn, Kathleen Rollins, Gloria Goldsmith, Brenda Hasse, Richard Drummer, Jeanie Hunt and anyone I may have missed, THANK YOU!

And finally, my beta readers! Beta reading is no easy task. It is a HUGE undertaking and requires a lot of time and effort to do. It also requires commitment. You really have to be dedicated to the project to see it through. There is no such thing as casual beta reading and these people are an author's most valuable asset in cultivating a story. So, Rich Sorgenfrei, Matt Shefke, Deann D'Onofrio, and Tim Geniac, thank you so much for your help and invaluable assistance in helping me get this done.

And, of course, to you, the reader, thank you for taking a chance on an unknown author and reading this work. I hope you enjoyed it enough to continue on with the following books in this series.

ABOUT THE AUTHOR

J.E. Park grew up in a suburb of Detroit, MI, where his efforts in seeking misadventures in the Motor City's punk rock scene and pursuing his vices dashed any aspirations in pursuing a higher education. They certainly did not help further his aspirations for a career in politics, either.

After graduation from high school, J.E. Park joined the US Navy and spent the next six years bar-brawling his way across the Far East, gaining the experiences that formed the foundation for his first novel "Tequila Vikings", a tale of a troubled young man navigating the military politics, violence and wanton hedonism woven into the naval culture of the early 1990s.

J.E. Park was a former contributing writer to the now-defunct comedy website Zug.com where he was best known for penning an article on harnessing the hallucinatory experiences of the smoking cessation aid Chantix for recreational purposes, positing that whether a condition is considered a side effect or an unintentional source of amusement depends largely upon the patient's attitude about the whole thing.

J.E. Park currently lives in a suburb of Flint, Michigan with his family where he has successfully used the region's suspect water quality as an excuse to stop neglecting his drinking.

Also By J.E. Park

The Tequila Vikings Series

Tequila Vikings

Olongapo Earp

Neptune's Martyrs

Novellas

Acid and Ozymandias: Notes from Skid Row

The Nest

Printed in Dunstable, United Kingdom

63477531R00160